SHADOWS

OF THE

FUTURE

* * * * * *

BOOK EIGHT

* * * * * *

D.W. Neuman

ALSO BY D.W. NEUMAN

FICTION

<u>Shadow Series</u>
Shadows of the Mind – Book One
Shadows of the Soul – Book Two
Shadows of the Service – Book Three
Shadows of the Past – Book Four
Shadows of the Heart – Book Five
Shadows of the Sand – Book Six
Shadows of the Serpent – Book Seven
Shadows of the Future – Book Eight

ISBN (978-0-9907247-4-2)

To Connie.
Simple words.
But, alas, those words pale to illustrate
just how much you mean to me.
Still, I never get tired of saying them.
I love you.

Carol.
Your tireless anticipation, as you check your email
for the next chapter, always brings a smile to my face.
A tremendous Thank You to my number one fan!

And to Cress.
In the briefest of moments we were
affected by both your smile and your laughter.
Look after Lou from the Other Place.

Who controls the past
controls the future.
Who controls the present
controls the past.
-George Orwell

Only you can control your future.
-Dr. Seuss

1
The Other Place

Where am I?

What's happening?

Who is that?

Rebecca saw herself lying in the hospital bed. She had a tube coming out of her mouth and there was a nurse currently attending to her.

What's going on? I don't understand. Why is the nurse smiling?

The woman turned and left the room.

At the end of the hallway the elevator doors opened and Rebecca watched as Thomas, Laura, Sam, Gavin and Emily made their way to the nurses station. After a quick discussion that nurse picked up the phone and made a call.

Why are they here? Are they here to see me?

Rebecca looked down at her own hands. *They seem real.* She walked over to the mirror on the wall and was unsure of her own reflection. *It's me, but it's not me.* Rebecca took her right hand and traced the scar down the right side of her face like she had a thousand times before. But this time when her fingers ran down her cheek the scar wasn't there. It was gone.

Rebecca was confused but she began to put the pieces together.

Am I dea...

"What the hell!?"

The door to the room flung open as Dr. Holmes realized Rebecca's machines had been disabled. The family stood outside and watched through the window as he hastily checked Rebecca's vitals. But then his shoulders slumped and eventually he turned around and slowly shook his head from side to side. "She's gone."

"I can save her! I can save her!"

Laura bent down and hugged her son. "It's too late Gav."

It was at that moment that Emily and Gavin finally broke down as the entire day washed over them in one huge torrent of emotion. Rebecca had been shot; they'd been kidnapped by Aleman's men; told they were going to die; escaped and now were too late to save Rebecca. Thomas and Laura took and held their children close as all of then openly, as a family, wept together.

Rebecca pressed her hands against the glass and watched her adoptive family weep for her passing. It was at that moment that the absolute clarity of her situation washed over her.

Don't be sad Gav. I love you and I'll always be with and watch over you.

"Hello Rebecca."

Rebecca turned away from her lifeless body on the hospital bed; away from the people she called family and turned towards the male voice that had pronounced his presence behind her. As she turned to face him Rebecca was surprised to find a man, ordinary in all aspects.

"Who are you?" she asked.

The man smiled playfully at her discomfort. "Not what you were expecting I take it?"

"I…um…well…"

"It's okay. We get that a lot."

Rebecca quickly composed herself. "Who are you?" she asked again.

"Are labels that important to you Rebecca?" the man countered.

"Not necessarily. But right now I'm clearly far out of my depth. Having a name or your occupation, if there is such a thing wherever we are, would be a welcome aid to my comfort."

The man smiled as Rebecca attempted to maintain her calm demeanor.

"Well said Rebecca. Most people I happen across are still very much at odds with their death. You, on the other hand, are handling this initial transition quite well."

"What can I say? In the past five years I've seen more than I can explain; things that used to frighten me. Why should this be any different?"

"Yes, I agree. You have seen many oddities during the time you walked the Earth."

The hospital faded from view as their surroundings rapidly changed. In the blink of an eye the two of them stood in a large flower filled meadow; the tantalizing smells from a variety of different blossoms filled her nose and assaulted her senses. Rebecca looked around before she returned her gaze to the mysterious man.

"Where are we? I want to go back and be with my family."

"All in good time my dear," he said as he chuckled to himself.

"Why do you laugh at me? Who are you?"

"My apologies, I meant no disrespect. I was merely amused at my own play on words. But to answer your burning question, although it's entirely irrelevant, you may call me the Caretaker."

"The Caretaker?"

The man nodded. "Yes, and I'm at your service."

"And what is your role in this place?" Rebecca asked as she swept her arm around to encompass where they stood.

"I am a guide."

"A guide or my guide?" Rebecca probed.

3

The Caretaker smiled again. "You have a thoughtful style about you. You are clearly not an ordinary individual, nor do I sense you would limit yourself to be judged as such."

Rebecca was confused. Every time she asked a question the man deflected. Her brows furrowed as she tried to obtain a fresh foothold on both the Caretaker and her new existence.

She finally responded. "You are correct. I would not limit myself."

"Good. Very good."

Unconsciously she raised her right hand and began to trace her scar. She stopped when she didn't feel it anymore. He gazed at Rebecca.

"Would you like it back?

"My scar?"

The Caretaker nodded.

"I...I don't know. Sometimes when I touched it I would feel grounded."

"And you currently are in need of that assurance?"

"Maybe," she replied hesitantly. "This is a lot to suddenly take in."

"Another truth. So be it."

Beneath her hand Rebecca felt the scar reform, the same scar she received during the attack in Hawaii years before. A sense of relief washed through her as she finished caressing it.

"Better," he asked.

Rebecca nodded. "Yes, strangely enough. Thank you."

He shrugged. "I did nothing. You made the change."

"Me? How?"

"I am but a guide, not an instructor. Everything you ever need to learn is already within you."

More riddles. Rebecca turned and gazed out over the large meadow and took in its beauty. "What do I do now?" she inquired with her back towards him.

"What do you want to do?"

"I want to see my family."

"You can do so at any point."

She turned back to look at him eye to eye. "Strange. Before you said 'all in good time'."

"Did I?" he responded.

"And then you laughed."

"It was more of a chuckle."

She pointed her finger at him. "Ah ha. So why change your wording?"

"As I've said before, you have a particular perception that lingers about you."

"What does that mean?"

"It could mean anything, or it could mean nothing at all. It's all up to you Rebecca."

"You're not going to make this easy, are you Caretaker?"

"I am only a guide."

"Fat lot of good that does for me right now when all you do is talk in riddles."

"Perhaps it's the questions you choose to ask and not the answers themselves that are confusing."

Rebecca stood her ground but kept her mouth shut. *He is a distraction. This whole thing is a distraction. What do I know? I know I'm dead even though I don't feel dead. Is this the afterlife? This is nothing what I expected, and neither is this Caretaker fellow.* She racked her brain. *What do you want to do? That's what he asked me. Does that mean I have options? What's the meaning of this place? Why am I here?*

Rebecca opened her mouth and made a statement. "I am dead."

He nodded in agreement. "Yes, you are."

"What is this place?"

"This place is not for everyone. Some will come and stay for but an instant, while others arrive and wallow for eternity."

"What is to become of me?"

"That is your choice. What do you want to do?"

"I…I don't know."

"There is truth in what you say."

"Caretaker. What is this place?"

"I have answered that question."

"What is this place called?"

"It is only known as the Other Place."

"Alright. How does this Other Place exist?"

"Good, a more appropriate query. The Other Place is made up of the universe's boundless energy. As creatures, such as yourself, pass from one plane of existence to another, that energy is drawn here."

"Why?"

"It is what it is, no more and no less."

"What's its purpose?"

He smiled again. "You will either figure that out for yourself or you will not."

Yet another roadblock. "Fine. Why did you chuckle earlier?"

"Did I?"

She took a different tact. "Why did you chuckle at the use of the word 'time'?"

"Better. The word 'time', and its true definition of the word, have no meaning here."

Rebecca cocked her head ever so slightly to the side. "No meaning?"

"Correct."

"When did I die? Today? Ten minutes ago?"

"Yes and no."

She stepped back and let her brain work on what he'd said as he looked on. *Time has no meaning. Time has no meaning. Time has no meaning.*

"But yet you said that some will wallow for eternity?"

"Yes, I did."

"But how is that possible if time isn't a factor?"

His smile broadened. "Hold on to that very thought Rebecca. That is the key that very few ever discover."

She pondered for a few more seconds before speaking again. "If that's true then, even though I felt like I died ten minutes ago, I should be able to attend my funeral this instant."

The Caretaker nodded enthusiastically. "By all means do so. Perhaps when you return we'll go over the rules. I always seem to forget about that."

"Rules?"

"When you return. As far as you're concerned you have all the 'time' in the world to learn about them."

The Caretaker slowly faded away until Rebecca was all alone in the meadow.

"Well that was a bit frustrating. Course, what do I expect, I just died."

The seriousness of her statement gave her pause.

"I'm dead," she said out loud. "I'm actually dead. Well shit, that sucks. I guess it's 'time' to go see what they're saying about me.

Rebecca concentrated on Gavin's face and the love she had for the boy. She faded from the meadow and reappeared by his side.

Sam spoke first.

"Rebecca was, and has always been, a prime example of humanity. She was a medic in the service and came to us wanting to give more. And she did just that, time and time again as she unselfishly protected all of us. It goes without saying that she touched each of us deep in our hearts. She was family and she will be missed.

"Roberta's deception surprised me, but at the end she realized what she had known all those years with us, that she had become family and we weren't the bad guys we were made out to be. She worked long hours and always went above and beyond what her role required to make sure we were taken care of. I'm saddened by her loss and I'll always remember how she touched and enlightened our lives. Rest in peace."

Sam stepped down from the podium. The rest of the family stood and individually walked by both caskets to say their final goodbyes.

Laura put her hand on Rebecca's casket. "Thank you," she whispered. "You have no idea what you meant to us or how much you'll be missed. We love you."

At Roberta's Laura said, "I hope you finally found the peace you were looking for."

Emily stopped next to Rebecca. "I love you Becca. You were the big sister I never had and I'll always miss you."

When it was Gavin's turn he put his head down on Rebecca's coffin. "You were the best Becca. You looked out for Em and me. I know I'll see you again, and maybe then it can be my turn to look after you. I love you."

Rebecca tried to console Gavin. She knelt down and attempted to place a hand on his shoulder, but instead it passed right through his body. He didn't move a muscle or acknowledge her so she stood back up.

I love you too Gav.

She looked around the room at her adopted family and smiled even though no one else saw or knew she was there.

"Caretaker. I know what I want to do."

"And what is that?" the familiar voice inquired behind her.

She didn't turn around to face him this time. "I choose to look after my family. To protect them."

"An unusual request, but certainly not the first time I've ever heard it uttered. You are free to protect them, but…"

"But?" she countered as she finally turned around.

"But be warned. There are rules. The biggest rule is that you must not directly interfere with their lives. They must never become aware of your presence at any time. Others have done so in the past and have paid the consequences for their actions."

2
Thursday Oct 4, 2001

The Director of Central Intelligence, Robert Duncan, sat behind his desk and poured through the myriad of documents and paperwork that was arranged in front of him. He tried to remain focused on the fact that America was days away from launching a joint attack, along with the United Kingdom, against multiple Taliban and al-Qaeda camps in Afghanistan. The devastating aftermath of 9/11, that had occurred three weeks prior, still weighed heavily on his and every other American's shoulders. War was coming.

But, despite all that, Robert Duncan's thoughts consistently drifted back to the beginning of the week when he'd dropped in on the Clark's and made his proposal to them.

*   *   *

"Hello Thomas. May I come in?"

"I...I guess...sure."

Thomas stepped sideways, the DCI walked in, and Thomas closed the door behind him.

"I hate to be so bold but I don't have a lot of time. I'd like to address everyone at once, if that's alright with you?"

"What's this about?" Thomas asked.

"Your future."

"Is that right? Interesting." Thomas pointed to a chair at the head of the family room. "Please take a seat."

"Thank you."

Sam, Bill, Julie, Kim, Laura, Hobbes and the children slowly gathered from various parts of the house as curiosity spread about

11

who had knocked on the door. All eyes were locked on the mysterious stranger. Thomas spoke up before anyone asked who he was.

"This is Robert Duncan. He's the head of the CIA."

"This is highly unusual, sir," Sam said as he sat down on one of the couches.

"What brings you to our neck of the woods Director?" Bill asked with a slight edge to his voice. "We're drowning in a ton of litigation already so I hope you haven't come to add to the pile."

The DCI smiled and took no offense at Bill's attitude. "Please, everyone take a seat. I need to make this quick before I catch my plane back to Virginia."

"What's this all about?" Laura asked as she and Thomas sat down. Emily and Gavin came over and they put them on their laps.

Bill and Kim also found seats next to each other while their children sat on the floor. Hobbes and Julie were the last ones to settle down before their kids also found a spot.

Robert Duncan spoke up. "The media is having a heyday with your reputations."

"Tell me you didn't come all this way just to tell us the obvious," Bill spat out.

"No, Mr. Nicholson, I did not come to San Francisco on a whim just to rub your face in what is obviously a very painful and unnerving time in your lives." Bill settled down. "However, I did make the trip to hopefully talk you all into a future together."

Laura cut him off. "We haven't had time to discuss it as a family yet."

"Fair enough, but since I'm here I'd like to make an argument for it, if I may."

Laura looked around the room and then finally at Thomas. Surprisingly she wasn't met with any resistance.

"Please continue Mr. Duncan."

"Thank you. Now Laura, before I begin, I need to ask you and Thomas one question."

"Which is?"

"To be vague, is anyone in this room, the children included, not in the know?"

"Proceed Mr. Duncan," Thomas replied as a confirmation.

"Very good. Thank you." The DCI looked around the room at everyone before he continued. "I'll be blunt. You are the future and I want you to work for me."

Sam addressed the DCI. "Are you referring to all of us or just the Clarks?"

"A valid point, Mr. Paige."

"Sam. Call me Sam."

"Very well, Sam. My offer goes out to all of you."

"But before," Thomas said, "when we met you only wanted my family and I."

The DCI nodded. "That's true. But as you're well aware, things have drastically changed in that regard. May I be brutally honest Sam?"

"It's the best policy."

"Very well. SANDBOX is all but a distant memory. Rumor has it that when you are summoned to D.C. next week to face your indictment, you'll ultimately lose your business, your reputation and your money."

"We'll fight it and we'll win," Bill declared adamantly.

"No, Bill, you will lose and lose badly. The American public wants blood and the U.S. government has already decided to make you an example in an effort to elicit confidence in the governing body."

"That's bullshit. We didn't do anything wrong."

"You were complicit, regardless that any wrongdoing was happening under your noses. But let's say, for arguments sake, that you could win. Your reputation has and will forever be stained with that complicity, not to mention the incompetence they won't hesitate to place on your shoulders."

"What's your point then sir?" Sam pressed. "Did you come here today to offer us all a job or something?"

"Indeed. Exactly that; jobs."

"Doing what?"

"I want to create a separate compartmentalized division of the CIA; one that only reports to me. My vision is to reinvent how the CIA conducts its business, from interrogations to information gathering. I call it PsyOps, or Psychological Operations. This family cohesively works very well together and I want that trend to continue."

"I'll ask the same question," Sam said. "Doing what?"

"Laura Bond, now Laura Clark. For years you worked as a psychiatrist running your own business. That changed drastically when you met Thomas and when you discovered your children had special abilities. Based on the quick conversation we had over the phone I'm going to deduce that perhaps you can tell when someone is lying or not."

Laura didn't reply and maintained her blank poker face

"And since that's not a no you would be perfect as the PsyOps shrink. My apologies if that's too derogatory a term.

"Thomas, with his telekinetic power which have unlimited applications, will be utilized as the situation fits. The same thing can be said of Emily and Gavin. Their unique abilities drastically change the playing field that the world is used to."

Laura countered. "You want my children, who are only eight and ten, to put themselves through even more heartache and nightmares?"

"They would only be allowed to engage in what you both deem as acceptable levels of participation."

"Sounds fishy," Bill said.

Laura leaned back. "No. He's not lying."

"No, I'm not," the DCI replied.

"Please continue."

"Thank you." He turned to Sam. "You and your partner would be brought on as PsyOps security."

"And what would that entail?"

"Basically anything and everything security related, from keeping everyone safe to going on missions."

"Missions?" Julie snarled. "Our men have an agreement with us to do no such thing."

"To continue my bluntness and to apologize in advance Mrs. Paige, how's that worked out for them?"

Julie stiffened but remained quiet.

"Hobbes will be in charge of the technical side of the operation, assuming of course that he wants it."

Hobbes smiled.

"Here's the bottom line," the DCI said. "I can protect everyone and in turn you can protect each other. In all fairness, it's going to take a lot of effort to get Project Zelda, aka PsyOps, up and running. But the benefits from the idea of its success alone are breathtaking."

"And what about the significant problems we're currently facing?" Bill asked. "How do you propose we shed that weight and start all over working for you?"

"One step at a time, but I have some thoughts on that issue. In the meantime, none of this is a done deal unless the four core members," he said gesturing to the Clark family, "are in."

"And if we are," Thomas asked, "then what happens next?"

"You'll move to Virginia and remain together as a family unit in the coming weeks. SANDBOX is finished but I guarantee that each of your employees will be well compensated in their exit packets. Financially you're facing substantial fines which will basically drain your entire business and life savings, which are still frozen."

"And our wives and children?" Sam asked.

"Schooling and whatever they want to do. The sky's the limit. The important thing is that you'll all be together. Anyway," the DCI said as he stood up, "that's my pitch. The details will work themselves out on their own if you decide to move forward."

The DCI made his way towards the backdoor as a multitude of eyes followed his progress. He turned with his hand on the doorknob.

"I'm excited that this might be coming together and I think you are too. I await your decision."

"One more thing Mr. Duncan," Laura said.

He paused and turned around. "Yes?"

"What's stopping us from wiping your mind now or just making you disappear?"

"Absolutely nothing," he replied without missing a beat. "And yet I decided to come here anyway."

* * *

16

The DCI swiveled his leather chair around and leaned back in it as he looked out over the vast portion of the CIA campus that his office view provided him. *It's been three days. Did I misjudge them? I don't think so. But perhaps I did make a mistake by dropping in on them unannounced and potentially forcing their hand.* He rotated and stared out his windows at another portion of the campus. *What the Clark's bring to the table; those possibilities are mind boggling.*

The intercom on his desk suddenly beeped and a familiar voice began speaking. "Sir, there's a Mr. Thomas Clark on your private line for you. Shall I take a message?"

Robert Duncan whirled around in his chair and depressed a button. "No, thank you Patricia, I'll take his call."

"Very good, sir."

Patricia Reed, the DCI's executive admin, transferred the call and then paused. *I know that name. I wonder if that's the same Thomas Clark who came in here five years ago to see the former DCI, Victor Bannon when I worked for him? Strange.*

Patricia left her thought drift for a few more seconds and then went back to work.

Behind closed doors the current DCI picked up his phone.

"Thomas, this is Robert Duncan. I was just thinking about you. What can I do for you?"

"I believe you have a pretty good grasp on why I'm calling Mr. Duncan."

"I can only hope that it's good news. I'm assuming you've collectively reached a decision?"

"We have, but it wasn't an easy one to make."

"Life changes never are. So are you in or are you out?"

The other end of the line remained silent.

17

"Thomas?"

"We're in," Thomas finally replied.

A smile formed on Robert's face. "That's excellent news. I'll make sure everything is immediately prepared for your arrival. When do you plan on traveling?"

"How's Monday work for you Mr. Duncan?"

"That's fine. I won't be able to meet with you until after you've all settled in out here. Work has had me tied down to my desk for the past three weeks, as you can imagine. In lieu of my absence I will have my PsyOps assistant, Russell Washington, contact you immediately to work out the details of your trip. Is there anything you need from me in the meantime?"

"Discretion."

"Discretion happens to be my middle name, and even more so when it comes to PsyOps and the future you're going to bring the world Mr. Clark. Unfortunately I have a meeting I'm running late for but Russell will call you in the next few minutes. Keep him in the dark but know that he's been instructed to extend you every courtesy."

"Thank you Mr. Duncan," Thomas said.

"It is I who should be thanking you Thomas. I'll see you next week after you're all settled in."

The DCI ended the call and then buzzed Patricia.

"Yes, sir?"

"Have Russell get in contact with Thomas Clark immediately."

"In reference to…?"

"He'll know what it's about. Thank you Patricia."

He released the intercom button, picked up his phone and dialed home. After two rings his wife of twenty-seven years picked up.

"Hello?"

"Emma, I have good news."

"What is it Robert?"

"Thomas Clark and family will be here next week."

She smiled on the other end of the line. "That's fantastic news honey. I can tell how excited you are. I'll start on a roast tonight for dinner. We both know it's your favorite."

"You're a doll sweetie. Thank you. I have a meeting at the White House I need to leave for right this minute. Hopefully it won't be an all-nighter and make me miss dinner. I love you."

"I love you too. Bye."

"Bye sweetheart."

The DCI put his game face back on. He collected what he needed for his meeting and headed out his office door where Patricia Reed sat.

"I need…"

"Your car's waiting for you downstairs already, sir."

"You read my mind. Thank you Patricia."

"Knock them dead, sir."

* * *

Twenty minutes later the DCI passed through the White House's security and walked into the scheduled meeting right on time. Along with the DCI a number of other high ranking members were also in attendance. Kirk Nash, the Secretary of Defense; David Cook, the Director of National Intelligence (DNI), who was also Robert's boss; and Alan Holmes, the Director of the FBI.

The Secretary of Defense brought the meeting to order.

"In three days Operation Enduring Freedom commences. President Bush requests an update on our intelligence gathering of the region as well as our targets. Has anything changed in the past twenty-four hours?"

"We've been consistently monitoring chatter here in the states," said Alan Holmes. "The FBI currently does not foresee another attack on U.S. soil."

"Little good that did us three weeks ago," David Cook said as a dig.

Alan rolled his eyes. "That's funny, coming from the man who oversees the United States' entire intelligence operations."

"Enough," the SecDef commanded. "The buck stops with me so I'll be more than happy to replace both of you if you don't knock that shit off."

"Yes, sir," the FBI Director replied.

"Sorry, sir," the DNI added.

Satisfied the SecDef continued. "Robert. Anything new on your end?"

The DCI shook his head. "Satellite images still show our proposed Taliban and al-Qaeda targets in use."

"And what about one of our primary targets; Hamid Emal Habibi; one of the masterminds behind the 9/11 attack?"

"He still hasn't surfaced, aside from the video that was uploaded days after 9/11 on which he shared credit for the attack. Currently our sources still place him in Afghanistan."

"Very well," the SecDef replied. "As you all know President Bush demands action. The people of America are screaming for blood, for vengeance and for answers. Operation Enduring Freedom is the first step in our war on terror, and they will feel our wrath. Do not take pause in your obligations to our country gentlemen. Keep at this. You are our shields, our armor. Don't fail me again. This meeting is adjourned."

<u>3</u>
Friday Oct 5, 2001

A man, his right arm significantly scarred from fire, picked up his ringing phone.

"Yes?"

"The DCI has convinced them."

The man smiled. "Excellent. When will they arrive?"

"They're scheduled to leave as a family on Monday. The indictment hearing is on Tuesday, the following day."

"Good. Keep the updates coming while I continue to work on my own lab results."

"Of course," the female voice replied and ended the call.

Dr. Yamato Takuma Matsushita slowly placed the phone back on its cradle. "Welcome back Thomas, I missed you."

* * *

Four years prior...

Dr. Matsushita reached for his burning briefcase on the table just as something on the lab table exploded. The burning contents clung to his right arm.

"EEEooooWWW!"

He recoiled from the flames, pulled his lab coat off and smothered the flames. His right arm was covered in third degree burns and he did his best to cradle it.

Thomas saw his father on the floor and went to his side.

"Are you okay?"

Michael turned over. "I'm okay. Go get Em."

21

Betsy, his mother, had made her way over to Emily's gurney and stood up to check on her. The little girl was unconscious but otherwise unhurt. Betsy began to remove the sedation equipment.

Thomas nodded, stood up and helped his father to his feet. He watched the Dr. Matsushita hold his right arm and clench his teeth in obvious pain just six feet away.

"It's over you sick sonofabitch," Thomas hissed at him.

Dr. Matsushita turned away. "No! This is my legacy!"

"It ends here." Thomas took a step forward and raised his handgun. "Look at me."

Michael spoke up behind him. "Don't do it son. He's not worth it. Self-defense is one thing, but shooting him now would be in cold blood."

Thomas took another step closer and then another until the barrel was pressed against the doctor's head.

"You must have seen what he did to Emily! You must have seen what he did to me!"

Michael put a hand on his son's shoulder. "We saw everything. That's why we're here. It had to be stopped."

Thomas faltered for just a second.

Dr. Matsushita abruptly swiveled to his right, out of the way of Thomas' weapon. In his left hand he held a syringe. He stabbed Thomas in his right arm and injected a portion of the contents before Thomas pulled back.

"Sonfoa!" The gun fell from his hand and clattered to the floor as Thomas pulled his injured arm to his chest. In doing so the needle snapped off and left a jagged tear down his arm.

Michael stepped past his son and walloped the doctor in his face, who fell back on the floor and lay still. Flames licked at the briefcase as it hit the floor, still in Dr. Matsushita's grip.

"Are you okay?" his father asked.

"Other than my arm fucking hurts; yeah, I'll live."

"Let's get out of here before this place comes down around us."

Thomas sat down all of a sudden a little cross-eyed. "I'm not feeling too good."

Michael picked up the gun off the floor and placed it in his waistband. He helped Thomas up off the floor. "There's no time for this. We have to go."

Thomas nodded a little groggily and shook his head to clear it. "I'll be alright."

Betsy made her way across the room with Emily safely in her arms.

"Let's move," said Michael.

Dr. Matsushita, as he lay on his back, opened his eyes and observed Thomas, Emily, Michael and Betsy as they left the burning lab to escape the flames. He looked over and his leather briefcase that he held in his left hand was burning. He immediately let it go and pushed himself to an upright position with his right arm. He instantly regretted that decision and collapsed back to the floor.

"Fuuuuccccckkk!"

From the right shoulder down his lab coat had been burned away, and all that remained was charred and blistery flesh. Dr. Matsushita lay there surrounded by fire as it began to grow larger and larger, fueled by the contents of his lab. He was terrified and flashbacks, of when he was a young boy, flooded his mind.

"NOOO!" he screamed.

Gritting his teeth he rolled over on his left side and managed to get his feet under him. He stood up and then hunkered down as a number of ceiling lights exploded above him.

Escape. Flee.

23

He looked towards the rear of his lab, but a second thought gave him pause.

But this is my legacy.

Regardless of the absolute chaos a renewed determination washed over Dr. Matsushita. He turned and began to stomp on his leather briefcase until the flames extinguished. As he bent down to pick it up with his left hand he noticed one last syringe, the same type he'd stuck Thomas with, lying on the floor under the lip of the lab counter. He hurriedly snatched it up, shoved it into his left lab pocket and then took hold of his briefcase.

The last of the overhead lab lights burst and showered him with broken shards of glass. The doctor tried to exit the lab as he traversed through a wall of fire and a minefield of broken and destroyed equipment that was scattered everywhere. Smoke had quickly filled the facility and he choked as he breathed it in.

The fire had spread to the adjacent rooms of Facility Thirteen but hadn't begun to burn with the same intensity as the fire in the lab. Dr. Matsushita's original thoughts kicked back in as he finally exited the lab and emerged in the main facility's hallway. His hair smoldered but he maintained a desperate grip on his briefcase. His right arm dangled by his side, burned, useless and forgotten for the time being.

Escape. Flee.

He knew Thomas had headed towards the huge elevator and he wasn't about to confront Thomas again, knowing quite well that he'd been spared a bullet just minutes before. Dr. Matsushita turned left and headed down the hallway towards one of the storerooms in the rear of the facility.

Grimacing from the intense pain he finally found the door he'd been searching for. He placed his briefcase between his legs and then used his freed left hand to open the door before he took control of his briefcase once more. The storeroom was large and housed multiple racks which contained supplies, equipment and food. On the back wall Dr. Matsushita dropped his briefcase and used his left hand to push on one specific shelving unit. It swung inward forty-five degrees. He hastily retrieved his lab notes, contained within his briefcase, and stuffed them down his shirt. He entered the secret room and then pivoted the hidden door back in place behind him.

A ladder, bolted against the wall, rose up into the skinny shaft above him. He grunted, both in pain and exertion, as he slowly made his way up one rung at a time. To make matters worse he could smell the smoke behind him, as if it were coming for him.

No!

He climbed each rung with purpose, ignoring his pain as he climbed out of hell.

* * *

Friday Oct 5, 2001

Dr. Yamato Takuma Matsushita, now sixty-five years old, gazed down at his right hand. The months of treatments that had followed his escape had been just as, if not more, painful than the moment he'd been burned. But he had endured the treatments nevertheless. He had been lucky, in the overall picture, and over time had been able to recover sixty percent use of his right arm and hand. The skin grafts had done little to alter the extent of the scars he knew he'd be left to live with.

No matter.

Dr. Matsushita had come to terms with his debilitation quickly though. During his extensive recovery, overseas in his homeland of Japan, he'd come to the conclusion that he wasn't about to give up on what was going to be classified as man's greatest scientific achievement.

And when I say man's achievement, I naturally mean mine and mine alone.

He smiled behind his desk. Now he knew for certain that Thomas Clark and his family were coming to him and all he had to do was lie in wait in the shadows.

Still, Dr. Matsushita had remained perplexed for the past four years on the whereabouts of Victor Bannon, the former DCI and his previous collaborator. Victor had abruptly disappeared and never resurfaced. But, at least he still had access to the money he'd been using for the project.

Strange, but regardless of Victor's absence I'm now closer to my goal than ever before. I may have had to limp away like an injured dog to lick my wounds, but mark my words Thomas, I'm back and you have no idea I'm coming for you, especially after what you did to me and the memories you forced me to relive.

* * *

August 6, 1945

Monday morning, just after eight o'clock, nine year old Yamato was outside playing with his little sister in the garden. The family's small house lay on the outskirts of Hiroshima, Japan. Their parents were inside preparing breakfast as the air-raid sirens began to emanate throughout the region. Yamato and his sister stopped what they were doing and looked up in the sky, as did their parents as soon as they emerged from inside the house.

"Should we hide?" his sister asked her father in Japanese.

26

"No my flower blossom, we are safe right where we are."

The four of them looked up and watched a few bombers as they flew straight lines high above the city, but they did not drop their payloads.

"What are they doing father?" Yamato asked.

"I do not know."

"Perhaps we should go inside?" his mother cautioned.

"They have flown beyond us. They cannot hurt us here."

Two minutes later there was a large flash of light followed by a thunderous boom.

Yamato began to point. "What is…"

His father's eyes widened instantly in fear as he turned around and attempted to shield his family from the impending wave of destruction and fire. He pulled his wife down with his left arm and his daughter with his right. Yamato fell to the ground a second before the shockwave hit them. His father hunkered over Yamato as death and destruction rained down on their village.

"No!" Yamato cried out from underneath his father's body.

An equivalent of sixteen kilotons of TNT detonated at less than two thousand feet above the city. The resulting firestorm tore through the city and destroyed sixty-nine percent of Hiroshima's buildings. Eighty thousand people died instantly and another seventy thousand became injured.

Yamato's father and sister were part of the initial casualties as the debris and fire struck and ravaged their bodies. His mother survived, but two months later eventually succumbed to her own injuries. She had been a strong woman, but in the weeks that followed her strength continued to leave her. At her deathbed Yamato hardly recognized her.

It was then that Yamato vowed his revenge on the round eyes that had taken everything from him.

In the years that followed Yamato didn't know how to enact his revenge. He was alive and that's all that mattered. His grandparents took him in and as the world righted itself from the brink of destruction so did Yamato's life. He excelled at school and at sports. He eventually caught the eye of one of his teachers and was asked what he wanted to study. A doctor he responded instantly. In time Yamato was spirited away to medical school and poured his heart into his studies.

But he never forgot the vow that he made, nor would his heart ever let him forget.

Sunday Oct 7, 2001

Operation Enduring Freedom commenced as British and American forces began their campaign in Afghanistan. That evening President Bush addressed the nation.

On my orders, the United States military has begun strikes against Al Qaeda terrorist training camps and military installations of the Taliban regime in Afghanistan. These carefully targeted actions are designed to disrupt the use of Afghanistan as a terrorist base of operations and to attack the military capability of the Taliban regime.

We are joined in this operation by our staunch friend, Great Britain. Other close friends, including Canada, Australia, Germany and France, have pledged forces as the operation unfolds.

More than 40 countries in the Middle East, Africa, Europe and across Asia have granted air transit or landing rights. Many more have shared intelligence. We are supported by the collective will of the world.

More than two weeks ago, I gave Taliban leaders a series of clear and specific demands: Close terrorist training camps. Hand over leaders of the Al Qaeda network, and return all foreign nationals, including American citizens unjustly detained in our country.

None of these demands were met. And now, the Taliban will pay a price.

By destroying camps and disrupting communications, we will make it more difficult for the terror network to train new recruits and coordinate their evil plans.

Initially the terrorists may burrow deeper into caves and other entrenched hiding places. Our military action is also designed to clear the way for sustained, comprehensive and relentless operations to drive them out and bring them to justice.

At the same time, the oppressed people of Afghanistan will know the generosity of America and our allies. As we strike military targets, we will also drop food, medicine and supplies to the starving and suffering men and women and children of Afghanistan.

The United States of America is a friend to the Afghan people, and we are the friends of almost a billion worldwide who practice the Islamic faith.

The United States of America is an enemy of those who aid terrorists and of the barbaric criminals who profane a great religion by committing murder in its name.

This military action is a part of our campaign against terrorism, another front in a war that has already been joined through diplomacy, intelligence, the freezing of financial assets and the arrests of known terrorists by law enforcement agents in 38 countries.

Given the nature and reach of our enemies, we will win this conflict by the patient accumulation of successes, by meeting a series of challenges with determination and will and purpose.

Today we focus on Afghanistan, but the battle is broader. Every nation has a choice to make. In this conflict, there is no neutral ground. If any government sponsors the outlaws and killers of innocence, they have become outlaws and murderers themselves. And they will take that lonely path at their own peril.

I'm speaking to you today from the Treaty Room of the White House, a place where American presidents have worked for peace.

We're a peaceful nation. Yet, as we have learned, so suddenly and so tragically, there can be no peace in a world of sudden terror. In the face of today's new threat, the only way to pursue peace is to pursue those who threaten it.

We did not ask for this mission, but we will fulfill it.

The name of today's military operation is Enduring Freedom. We defend not only our precious freedoms, but also the freedom of people everywhere to live and raise their children free from fear.

I know many Americans feel fear today. And our government is taking strong precautions. All law enforcement and intelligence agencies are working aggressively around America, around the world and around the clock.

At my request, many governors have activated the National Guard to strengthen airport security. We have called up reserves to reinforce our military capability and strengthen the protection of our homeland.

In the months ahead, our patience will be one of our strengths--patience with the long waits that will result from tighter security, patience and understanding that it will take time to achieve our goals, patience in all the sacrifices that may come.

Today, those sacrifices are being made by members of our armed forces who now defend us so far from home, and by their proud and worried families.

A commander in chief sends America's sons and daughters into battle in a foreign land only after the greatest care and a lot of prayer.

We ask a lot of those who wear our uniform. We ask them to leave their loved ones, to travel great distances, to risk injury, even to be prepared to make the ultimate sacrifice of their lives.

They are dedicated. They are honorable. They represent the best of our country, and we are grateful.

To all the men and women in our military, every sailor, every soldier, every airman, every Coast Guardsman, every Marine, I say this: Your mission is defined. The objectives are clear. Your goal is just. You have my full confidence, and you will have every tool you need to carry out your duty.

I recently received a touching letter that says a lot about the state of America in these difficult times, a letter from a fourth grade girl with a father in the military.

"As much as I don't want my dad to fight," she wrote, "I'm willing to give him to you."

This is a precious gift. The greatest she could give. This young girl knows what America is all about.

Since September 11, an entire generation of young Americans has gained new understanding of the value of freedom and its cost and duty and its sacrifice.

The battle is now joined on many fronts. We will not waiver, we will not tire, we will not falter, and we will not fail. Peace and freedom will prevail.

Thank you. May God continue to bless America.

4
Saturday October 6, 2001

All three families spent the week packing their respective houses in preparation for their move for their new life in Virginia. Robert Duncan, the DCI, had dropped in on them five days prior and proposed a collaboration of sorts. Once he departed a number of subsequent discussions had broken out later that same evening.

* * *

"Good night. We'll talk tomorrow."

Laura closed the door behind Julie, Kim and their families as they left their house. They were all staying at Bill's house for the time being due to the fact that Sam's house had been shredded by gunfire. Hobbes had also been bunking with them and retired already for the evening. Laura turned and met Thomas' gaze from the family room.

"What?" she asked.

"You're still on the fence about all this, aren't you?"

"Hold that thought," she told him and walked down the hallway to the kid's rooms. "Bed time," Laura announced to both Emily and Gavin as she opened her son's door. Inside she found her children sitting on his bed talking. Stir lay next to them alongside Stickers, curled up and purring next to his playmate. When Laura opened the door Stir's wispy tail began to thumb against the bed. The two of them looked over at their mother as she entered.

"Bed time you two. You have school tomorrow."

"But we're moving to Virginia," Emily replied. "What does school have to do with anything right now?"

"Well, for starters, it keeps us all in a routine."

"A routine? If you haven't noticed, mom, a routine is the last thing we have around here."

"Now listen here..."

"No," ten-year-old Emily stated. "It's not fair. None of this is fair. Rebecca's dead because of us."

Stir's tail stopped whapping the comforter as the mood shifted.

Laura deflated. "Oh honey…" She made her way over to the bed and sat down.

"I miss her," Gavin said softly. Stir scooched over and laid his head on Gavin's leg.

"I do too sweetie." She pulled her eight-year-old son into her lap and gave him a hug.

Emily spoke up again. "Bad people want to hurt us and I want to do something about it."

"Robert Aleman is dead," Thomas said from the doorway. "We're safe now."

"Bullshit," Emily shot back.

"Em, watch you language," her mother warned.

"But it's true. We're not safe. We're never going to be safe, are we?" Emily turned to her father. "Are we?"

Thomas didn't know how to respond to his daughter's worries. She was right and he knew it. "Your mother and I are working on that. Right now please do what your mother has asked you and get ready for bed."

"Fine. Whatever." Emily sprung off the bed and stormed past her father.

Laura gave Gavin another hug and then he and Stir slipped out the bedroom door as well. Thomas watched his son leave and looked back over at his wife.

"Do you think they're going to be okay?" he asked her.

34

"In time. Losing Rebecca was a major blow. They don't feel safe and I don't know how to get that back for them."

"That's exactly why we need to take the DCI's offer."

"To move to Virginia and be part of his new group? What was it called? PsyOps?"

"Alright," Thomas replied. "But do you have a better plan of action?"

"I don't know. Buy an island?"

"So hiding out is our solution? Wait for whoever it is to come find us while we look over our shoulders for the rest of our lives?"

"I don't know dammit. Is that any worse than getting our children involved in the CIA? To use or abuse their abilities for the good of the country? Where will it stop? Who draws that line in the sand, him or us?"

Thomas crossed the room and sat down on the bed. "I don't have all those answers right now. However, for the record I think you're right."

"You only think I am?"

"You are. We're between a rock and a hard place. Em and Gav aren't children anymore. They've seen and done things that will stay with them for the rest of their lives. Could we run and hide? Sure, we have the means. But what kind of message does that send them?"

"The type that keeps their children safe."

Thomas nodded. "Agreed. But when will it end? Maybe we get another four years of peace. But it's not going to be peaceful. Around every corner we'll expect a new enemy, a new threat to our family."

"And yet you're so willing to throw in with the DCI, to share our DNA so our abilities can be replicated and reproduced?"

"No. We take what he has to offer us day by day. If we don't like what this opportunity ultimately turns into, well, we just walk away. But, in the meantime we'll be under his protection and be given the means to take the fight to those that want to do us harm."

"In the grand scheme of things," she cautioned. "The DCI was talking about threats to the United States and not specifically about the ones just against our family."

"I know sweetie. But if we run and hide then it'll feel like I'm back in Running Springs all over again."

Laura gave him her 'are you shitting me look'. "That's totally different. But, I can see where you're coming from."

"And what about what 'we' want to do?"

Thomas and Laura looked over to the doorway. Gavin and Emily stood there as Stir rubbed against Gavin's legs.

"Eavesdropping?" Thomas inquired.

"You're in my room," Gavin responded.

Thomas put his hands up. "Fair enough, son. What was your question again?"

"What about what 'we' want to do?" he repeated.

"Alright," Laura relented. "We're all ears."

"Em and I have been talking."

"I see," Laura said."

Gavin continued. "And we want to go to Virginia. We want to be part of something."

"You're part of this family," Thomas stated.

Gavin shook his head as Emily took over. "What Gav means is that we want to be part of something larger. When we were younger our powers were strange and scary. But we're older now. Do you really think buying an island and keeping the world at bay is going to be the right choice for us?"

"So you were listening in."

36

"Maybe what the DCI has in store for us will be exactly what we want to be a part of. I know it's difficult for both of you to open up to new possibilities, especially given what we've all been through already, but we're going to do this as a family. Instead of running away we should really face this challenge head on."

"Besides," Gavin added, "if we don't like it then we'll figure something else out together."

Thomas and Laura sat there in awe of their children. They turned their heads, and as their eyes met the choice had already been made. They nodded slightly to each other.

* * *

"I need a drink," Julie said as they walked through the front door into Bill's house.

"Make that two, sis," Kim added.

"Hey now, don't forget about us," Bill stated.

Kim smiled. "We could never forget about you two. Tell you what, why don't you make sure the kids are ready for bed, tuck them in and then make your way back here for your drinks."

Sam and Bill took the strong hint and herded their four children that consisted of Amanda, Craig, Sarah and Edward off to get them ready for bed. Ten minutes later they rejoined their wives in the kitchen and were each handed a beer.

"Thanks babe," Bill said.

"So what's the plan?" Julie stated matter-of-factly.

"Yes," Kim added. "Why don't you both enlighten us?"

Sam took a long swig of beer. They knew this wasn't going to be easy. For years they knew where their wives stood when it came to their men being in harm's way. When Robert Duncan, the DCI, had proposed that Sam and Bill would run security for

PsyOps as well as execute missions for the new group, Julie and Kim had picked up on that immediately and were none too pleased.

"So what's on your minds?" Sam asked. "You're obviously unhappy."

"Unhappy?" said Julie. "A more accurate word would be disappointed."

Shit. Here we go. "Go on," Sam said as he took another sip of his beer.

"The Director of the Central Intelligence Agency walks in and basically announced he wants to hire the two of you."

"That's what has you two in a twitter? That Bill and I might be back out in the field again?"

Julie and Kim nodded in unison. Sam slammed his beer bottle down on the counter hard enough that they were surprised it didn't shatter.

"Everything Bill and I worked for since we launched SANDBOX in eighty-five is fucking gone! It's just gone!"

Julie and Kim were stunned by Sam's sudden outburst. Bill knew his lifelong friend all too well and knew this blowup was coming.

"Robert Aleman, aka The General, took everything from us. He took our children. He took our reputation. He took our company. And now, early next week, unless a fucking miracle happens, he'll have taken all of our money as well. Everything we've worked for and have will be gone."

"That might be true but it's not the complete truth and you know it," Julie retorted in her husband's face. "I think the real issue is that you've never wanted stop playing soldier."

"Oh what the hell, Jules. We've been down this road before, too many times. We compromised and moved to Hawaii to appease the two of you."

"And all we've ever wanted is for you two to be safe. But time and time again you've come home, injured, shot up and bloody. We're not stupid. We know that's the life you chose for yourselves, but you're not on your own anymore. You have your children and us to think about. You PROMISED your action days were behind you and now it seems you can't wait to get right back in the thick of things."

"What other choice do we have Jules? We're financially ruined."

"Don't think for a second that Thomas and Laura wouldn't take care of us."

Sam roared. "I will NOT ask him to support our family. He helped us start SANDBOX but I will not go to him with my hat in my hands begging for money this time. The downfall of SANDBOX had nothing to do with him. That responsibility falls squarely on my shoulders. We got played and now my dream has been crushed."

Julie softened her tone. "I know you're hurting but Kim and I still want the same thing, and that's for the both of you to be safe and out of harm's way. To us it seems you're very eager to say yes to the DCI's proposal and throw all caution, and promises, to the wind."

Sam didn't reply. Bill and Kim had remained quiet as they watched the heated interaction. Sam eventually opened his mouth.

"We owe him."

Julie didn't understand. "What are you talking about? You owe who what?"

"We owe Thomas for being there in our hour of need. When we needed the money, to start our company, he came out of nowhere with an outstretched hand."

"What does that have to do with moving to Virginia?"

"Everything." Sam finally toned his own voice down. "This is twofold Jules. First off we have to start over. That's the hand that's been dealt to us right now. With that said you can't bench Bill and I and then somehow magically expect the two of us to provide for our families. Bill and I don't know how to do anything else.

"Secondly, Thomas and his family need us. Fate, or whatever you want to call it, has come a 'calling and the abilities they possess are absolute game changers. Do you really expect me to let my friend, and yours, to brave this new endeavor on his own?"

Julie and Kim looked at each other.

"I'm not happy."

"Trust me," Sam said, "neither am I. But let's see where this is going to take us. There are a lot of unknowns we're still dealing with." He paused for a few seconds before he spoke up again. "But I do have something that should bring a smile to your face."

Julie looked at Sam without responding. He continued anyway.

"When we were putting the kids to bed they told us they're excited about moving into a new house."

"I understand where they're coming from," Julie responded. "A house that isn't full of bullet holes. I'd be excited too."

Sam's face dropped. "There's no pleasing you, is there?"

"Not at the moment. Now, if you excuse me, I'm off to bed before we start packing tomorrow. In the meantime I'm sure my sister wouldn't mind giving you some blankets so you don't freeze on the couch overnight."

40

Monday October 8, 2001

The bulk of the families boxes were being handled by a moving company which would pack everything in a large truck and then drive from California to Virginia. The morning of October eighth a large Super Shuttle arrived to take the twelve family members, Hobbes and Stickers to San Francisco International Airport. Thomas and Laura hadn't slept much the night before so Thomas had dozed off during the ride. They were headed to a private hanger where SANDBOX's plane resided. It would take them to Virginia, and from there their new life would commence.

Bill turned around in his seat. "Hey, Thomas, wake up brother."

Thomas sleepily opened his eyes and looked out the van's window. They had just pulled off the 101 and were entering the airport. Before long the shuttle took them to the private hanger where they all disembarked, offloaded their carry-ons and a weeks' worth of clothing. Just enough to get by on until the moving truck was scheduled to arrive.

Sam and Bill began to head towards the plane when security called them back.

"What's the problem?" Bill asked. "This is our plane? We never go through security."

"Yes sir," the supervisor told him. "However, I regret to inform you that your permits have been pulled. We've been instructed to treat you like any other commercial passenger which includes baggage screening and a walk through the metal detector."

"You've got to be shitting me."

Sam put his hand on his friend's shoulder. "Roll with it. This is only the beginning and it's not going to get any easier."

Bill dropped his aggressive posture and nodded in compliance. Within minutes everyone had placed their gear on the x-ray belt and filed through the metal detector. Bill was the last one to come through and the detector sounded off as he passed through.

"What the hell?"

"Sir. Do you have anything in your pockets?"

Bill searched his pockets and came up empty. He finally realized he'd forgotten to take off his watch. He took it off, placed it in a small basket and walked back through the metal detector uncontested.

"Way to make a scene," Sam kidded as his friend as everyone boarded the private jet in front of them.

"Eat me," Bill said with a smile.

Gavin hefted Stickers' crate in front of him and repeatedly rebutted any help on making sure his cat made it onto the plane and into a seat next to him. Laura, Julie and Kim made sure everyone was properly buckled in. They also made sure that carry-ons were tucked away in preparation for takeoff.

Ten minutes later the two pilots secured the outer door, went through their pre-flight checklist and were cleared for takeoff. In no time the jet had roared down the runway and quickly shot up into the morning sky.

SANDBOX's Cessna Citation was forced to take a more southern flight path to avoid a large mid-western storm front. Currently it was cruising over the Gulf of Mexico with all family members safely on board, although very anxious about what they had agreed to. On top of that the indictment hearing was scheduled for the next day and Sam and Bill were thoroughly dreading it.

"They're going to bury us brother," Bill said.

"Probably."

"I just don't like it. This is all wrong."

"Tell me something I don't know. But unfortunately this is the hand that we've been dealt. We can either run from it or face the music."

Bill half smiled. "Running doesn't sound like that bad of an option right now."

"I'll see what I can do," Sam joked.

Sam got up from his seat and began to walk down the aisle to check on everybody.

"Daddy?" Amanda asked as he approached.

"What is it sweetie?"

"Are we there yet?"

"Don't make me turn this plane around young lady," he teased.

She laughed and then said, "Are you sure we're going to be okay?"

From the mouths of babes. "We're going to be just fine. It's going to take some time to adjust of course, but in time you'll make new friends. We have each other and that's what's important."

She nodded and he kept moving down the aisle. He stopped at Thomas' seat. Laura was across the aisle.

"You good?" Sam asked.

"I think we made the right decision, but only time will tell."

"I hear you."

"You nervous about the hearing Sam?"

"More than you know. It's going to be fun to get crucified on national television."

"Ugh. That sounds horrible."

"Yeah, I'm sure it will be. Anyway, can I get either of you anything?"

Thomas shook his head. "I'm good, thanks."

"Nothing for me Sam," Laura added.

"No problem."

Sam stopped at Hobbes' seat. He had the armrest in a death grip.

"You okay?"

Hobbes nodded. "I don't like flying."

"You'll be fine, trust me. Just think about the new opportunity. You're going to be great at it."

"Thanks."

As Sam left Hobbes behind the plane jolted violently to the left and dropped a good hundred feet. Sam was thrown off balance and barely managed to avoid injury.

"WHAT THE HELL IS GOING ON!" Bill yelled at the pilots.

The children began to scream as the jet continued to bounce around haphazardly.

"WE'VE GOT MULTIPLE WARNING LIGHTS ALL OVER THE BOARD!" one of them yelled back.

The jet suddenly veered right and tipped over into a dive. Magazines and refreshments went careening off the inside of the plane as the strong inertia yanked at each person's body, trying to yank them out of their seats. Sam' body flew past everyone and smacked into the rear bulkhead.

"MAYDAY! MAYDAY! THIS IS SB845 DECLARING AN EMERGENCY! I REPEAT, THIS IS SB845 DECLARING AN EMERGENCY! OVER!"

"SB845, this is Houston. We have you on our radar and see that you're rapidly losing altitude."

"NO SHIT HOUSTON! WE'VE LOST HYDRAULICS AND RUDDER CONTROL IS NOT RESPONDING!"

"25,000!"

"SHIT! WE'RE LOSING IT!"

"22,000!"

"19,000!"

"COME ON, WORK GODDAMMIT!"

"15,000!"

"SB845, you need to pull up! Pull up SB845!"

"WE'RE IN A STEEP DIVE THAT WE CAN'T PULL OUT OF!"

"10,000!"

"6,000!"

"MAYDAY! MAYDAY! THIS IS SB845! WE'RE GOING IN HARD! BRACE YOURSELVES BACK THERE!"

"Roger that SB845. We're right here with you. God bless."

"DADDY!" Gavin yelled as he clutched Stickers' cat carrier in a death grip.

Thomas was paralyzed in his seat, as was every family member on board. The intense inertia pinned each of them painfully to their chairs. Movement of any type was absolutely impossible. Sam, who had been walking around, had been slammed into the rear wall of the plane and was bleeding profusely from his head. All that any of the adults heard were the screams of their children as the plane plummeted out of the sky.

There had been no warning before the plane malfunctioned and in no time the front end of the plane had tipped over in to a steep dive as the hydraulics malfunctioned and froze up completely.

"1000!" one of the pilots managed to yell.

Thomas forced his head to twist as he looked across the aisle at Laura. Her eyes were wide open in utter terror and fixated on him. She mouthed *I love you.*

Thomas opened his own mouth.

"NNNNOOOOOOOOOOOOOO!"

The plane crumpled on impact, instantly killing everyone onboard.

Thomas woke up in a start.

"Hey, Thomas, wake up brother."

What the fuck was that?

Thomas sleepily opened his eyes and looked out the van's window.

"You okay?" Laura asked.

"I don't know," Thomas replied. "I think I just had a horrible nightmare."

Her eyes softened. "Anything you want to talk about?"

"No. No, I'm okay."

They had just pulled off the 101 and were entering the airport. Before long the shuttle took them to the private hanger where they all disembarked, offloaded their carry-ons and a weeks' worth of clothing. Just enough to get by on until the moving truck was scheduled to arrive.

Sam and Bill began to head towards the plane when security called them back.

"What's the problem?" Bill asked. "This is our plane? We never go through security."

"Yes sir," the supervisor told him. "However, I regret to inform you that your permits have been pulled. We've been instructed to treat you like any other commercial passenger which

46

includes baggage screening and a walk through the metal detector."

"You've got to be shitting me."

Sam put his hand on his friend's shoulder. "Roll with it. This is only the beginning and it's not going to get any easier."

Bill dropped his aggressive posture and nodded in compliance. Within minutes everyone had placed their gear on the x-ray belt and filed through the metal detector. Bill was the last one to come through and the detector sounded off as he passed through. Thomas watched as Bill was stopped.

"What the hell?"

"Sir. Do you have anything in your pockets?"

Bill searched his pockets and came up empty. He finally realized he'd forgotten to take off his watch. He took it off, placed it in a small basket and walked back through the metal detector unmolested. Thomas stood there and watched Bill put his watch back on.

"Way to make a scene," Sam kidded as his friend boarded the private jet in front of him.

"Eat me," Bill said with a smile.

Sam looked over at Thomas who had a blank look on his face. "You coming?" he asked in jest.

When Thomas didn't respond Sam's smile faded and he walked over to his friend. "What's up? You okay?"

"Something's wrong with the plane."

"What are you talking about?"

"I don't know exactly. I had a nightmare in the shuttle on the way over."

"A dream?"

"Yeah," Thomas replied. "But it felt so real."

47

Bill stuck his head out of the plane's doorway. "Are you two coming or what?"

"Give us a minute," Sam said without turning. "What are you saying Thomas?"

"I don't know but I think something's wrong with the plane."

"What's wrong with the plane? What are you talking about?"

"In my dream Sam. In my dream something went terribly wrong. The plane plummeted out of the sky and we all died."

"That isn't fucking funny bro."

Thomas locked eyes with Sam's. "No. No it isn't." He was dead serious and Sam picked up on that immediately.

"Okay. I'll play along. What went wrong?"

Thomas' face contorted as he tried to recall pieces of his dream. Eventually he spoke up again. "Hydraulics. Something about the hydraulics freezing up or not responding."

"What do you want me to do?" Sam asked.

"Can you have them check the plane?"

"You're serious? You want to postpone our trip to check the plane out? You know our indictment is tomorrow."

Thomas didn't respond. He only stared at his friend. Sam finally relented and walked over to the phone on the wall. He dialed an internal airport number.

"Mikey. It's Sam Paige. Good, and you? Listen, how long would it take for you and your crew to come over and check out the jet? Yes, I know it's up to date on maintenance but I'd like to have the hydraulics checked out nevertheless. Yes, right now would be ideal. My entire family is here in the hanger. Twenty minutes? Thanks Mikey. See you then."

Sam hung up the phone and walked over to the plane's doorway. He updated the pilots and the family that there'd be a minor delay on takeoff. As the family began to debark Sam walked back over to Thomas.

"My mechanic is on the way."

* * *

Two hours later Mikey motioned Sam over to his side. Bill and Thomas joined him.

"What's up Mikey?" Sam asked.

"I don't know how to tell you this Mr. Paige, but you were right on the money about the hydraulics."

"What?"

Mikey shook his head. "No one on my crew, or I for that matter, caught it right away."

Sam's face turned serious. "Explain."

Mikey cleared his throat. "There was a cut in the hydraulic line that leads directly to the rudders. It was a small breach and in no way could have occurred naturally over time or through normal wear and tear. This was an intentional cut. Now, my best guess is that after a few hours of flight that breach would have torn open and bled the line dry within ten to twenty seconds."

Sam's face turned white. "You said intentional."

"Yes sir, Mr. Paige. The only other term I have for it is sabotage, plain and simple. Someone didn't want this plane getting to its next destination, that's for damn sure."

"Fuck. Mikey, ground the plane and I want it every inch of it gone over, do you understand?"

"Yes, sir. I understand."

"Thank you Mikey. Thank you."

Mikey walked off to make a call as Sam turned to Bill and Thomas.

49

"What the fuck Sam?" Bill said. "Sabotage?"

"Yeah," Sam replied. "At this point I have to assume that Robert Aleman, The General, thought we might be on this plane sooner than later. Perhaps much sooner than him heading to SANDBOX to blow it up."

"But we never took the jet again," Bill said.

Sam nodded his head in agreement. "No we didn't and that backfired for us."

"How so?" Bill asked.

"If we had it might just have been us that died. But today we had our families onboard."

It was Bill's turn for his face to become white. "Oh shit."

"No shit." Sam slowly shook his head in disbelief as he trained in on Thomas. "How in the hell can you explain this?"

Thomas shrugged his shoulders. "I can't. It was just a dream."

Bill put his hand on his friend's shoulder. "Well, whatever it was brother we owe you."

"Yeah," Sam added. "Thank you."

* * *

Former General Robert Aleman, previously known as Raven when he was alive, watched the events in the hanger unfold from the comfort of the shadows. He knew he could walk amongst the living unseen, but he lingered towards the back of the hanger nevertheless.

"Damn you Thomas. How the hell did you figure out that I had the hydraulics tampered with? If all of you had only gotten on that plane…"

Raven's shoulders slumped as he came to terms that Sam, Bill and their families wouldn't be joining him anytime soon. However, a wicked smile slowly spread across his face.

"I want Sam and Bill to die by my hands. But right now that doesn't matter. My sights are on you Thomas Clark; you and your little boy." Raven continued to talk to himself. "Oh yes, I've seen what he can do. Your little Gavin will make his way back to my neck of the woods one of these days, and when he does I'll make sure I'm ready for him. In the meantime, I do believe I have some new friends I need to become acquainted with."

5
Monday October 8, 2001

Two hours after the sabotage was discovered the entire family was booked on a private charter that immediately took off towards Virginia. While they were boarding Thomas contacted Russell Washington, the DCI's assistant, and informed him of the change in plan. Six hours later the charter safely landed at Ronald Reagan Washington National Airport and taxied to a private hanger. As they began to disembark Russell was there to greet them.

"Mr. Clark," a six foot, brown haired mid-thirties man said as he extended his right hand towards Thomas. "I'm Russell Washington."

Thomas shook Russell's hand. "Thanks for meeting us. This is Sam Paige and Bill Nicholson."

Sam and Bill also shook hands with Russell.

"It's an honor gentlemen," Russell said genuinely. "I'm sorry to hear about SANDBOX."

"It's not over yet," Bill said.

"No, of course not. I meant no disrespect. What I should have said is that your reputations precede you."

Laura, Julie and Kim exited the plane and joined them.

"Russell, this is my wife Laura, Sam's wife Julie and Bill's wife Kim. Ladies, this is Russell Washington, the DCI's…"

"Liaison, or assistant, if you will." Russell smiled as he shook each one of their hands. "It's a pleasure to meet all of you."

"Likewise," Laura replied.

Hobbes followed the gaggle of children off the plane and was immediately waved over by Sam.

"Russell, this is Hobbes."

53

"Ah yes, Mr. Charles Hillburg," Russell replied. "You come highly regarded."

Hobbes smiled. "Please, no one calls me Charles anymore. But you can call me highly regarded again if you'd like."

Everyone chuckled and then turned around as Gavin hefted Stickers' cage down the plane's steps on his own. Stickers meowed from inside as Emily went and helped her brother before he potentially tripped over himself.

Russell paused for a second as he refocused on the adults. "The plan, for what's left of today, is to transport you to your new house and get you settled in. I've got a private bus parked right outside the hanger. How's that sound?"

Thomas took the lead. "That sounds good Russell. Thank you."

"Do you have any other questions or concerns at this time Mr. Clark?"

"Undoubtedly we all will, but for the time being why don't we just load up our family on the bus and get under way. Oh," Thomas said as another thought entered his mind, "you wouldn't happen to have any snacks onboard, would you?"

Russell smiled. "Absolutely Mr. Clark. It's fully stocked with plenty of kid friendly food and drink."

"You read my mind."

* * *

With their luggage stored, and everyone in a seat, the bus departed the airport and headed west to its final destination in Falls Church, Virginia. They drove through downtown and then continued on until the bus stopped at a large, and somewhat remote, property on the outskirts of town. The house stood in the

54

middle of four acres of wooded land and their closest neighbor was a thousand feet away. The children were pressed against the windows as the bus pulled up the long driveway and came to a stop. The house that stood in front of them was humongous.

"Wow."

"Neato."

"Is this where we're going to live?"

"It's huge!"

The bus door opened and all six kids rushed outside onto the driveway. They turned and started harassing their parents.

"Hurry up!"

"Come on slowpokes!"

"Let's go!"

With agonizing and deliberate slowness the adults took their time getting off the bus, much to the dismay of their excited children. Once they were all on the driveway it didn't take long for the kids to drag their parents by the hand towards the front door. Their reactions were priceless and the adults smiled at their antics.

Russell made his way towards the front of the group and unlocked the front door for everyone. In a somewhat controlled whirlwind of chaos the children began to immediately explore the vastness of the estate while the adults lingered in the entryway.

"This is a beautiful house Russell but it's so huge," Kim commented. "Which family gets to stay here?"

"My apologies Mrs. Nicholson. I was under the impression you were already aware of the...well, no matter. This estate was chosen so all three families would coincide under one roof. That decision was made by the DCI himself in an attempt to alleviate any fears you all may have about being separated in this new location."

The adults nodded along with his reasoning.

"With that said, let me go over the fine details of your new residence. This estate, or mansion if you will, is located roughly in the center of four acres surrounded by woods. The interior boasts ten bedrooms, eight bathrooms, a media room, a game room, a state of the art kitchen, family and dining rooms, a large outdoor pool and a six car garage."

"What are you trying to do, bribe us?" Thomas said. "Because it's working."

Russell smiled and then continued. "The estate is fully furnished and has already been stocked with food. In your rooms you'll find that clothing has already been purchased for each individual family member. Tags have been left on the clothing in case you want to go to the store and make any exchanges."

"That's impressive," Laura said, "and very thoughtful."

"Indeed," Julie added.

"On top of that you'll find there are six new vehicles in the garage. They keys are on the island in the kitchen."

"Jesus," Bill said, "where does it end?"

"Last, but not least, there is a cat box and food for Stickers located in the laundry room, which is right off the kitchen."

"Very thorough, Russell," Thomas admitted. "I'm very impressed."

"Thank you. The DCI means to extend you every courtesy."

"What about security?" Sam asked.

"The edges of this property are crisscrossed with motion and thermal tracking cameras. The house itself is wired and has multiple cameras. All that is piped into the Panic Room, which is where I have additional perks to show you. Please, follow me."

Russell led the seven adults into the Media Room. It consisted of stadium seating that filled the room in front of a large screen.

On the right side of the room Russell walked up to one of the many bookcases, popped a hidden switch and then swiveled the bookcase on an axis. Behind it they could see a spiral staircase that headed down beneath the house. Russell didn't look back as he took the stairs. One by one they all followed him down below to the spacious thirty by thirty foot security room that easily fit all of them and left plenty of room to spare. On the walls were multiple computer screens that displayed live pictures of their house and the grounds that surrounded the estate.

"Nice setup," said Hobbes as he checked out the setup.

"Is this the Panic Room?" Bill asked.

"No," Russell replied. "This is just the security portion of the hidden room. There's more." He turned and on the back wall pressed on a specific section of brick. That brick silently sunk in and the wall swung inward to reveal the Panic Room.

"It's like Scooby Doo with hidden walls and shit," Sam quietly said under his breath.

"Woah," Hobbes uttered as the smile on his face instantly broadened.

Russell stepped inside and they all followed. What they saw was nothing short of amazing. The interior of the Panic Room contained ten bunk beds, a kitchen, a full bathroom, a large television, bookcases filled with books and board games and a caged armory. Sam and Bill gravitated towards the armory without even thinking. Behind its locked doors were half a dozen MP5's and another half dozen CAR-15 assault rifles lined up side by side. On another shelf an array of Glock 17 9mm pistols were positioned. They noticed an extensive number of preloaded magazines were carefully stacked in easy to grab pull-out drawers. Extra ammunition was stored off to the side in sealed containers.

"Welcome home," Bill said.

Russell spoke up. "I hope this room meets your needs and answers your questions about our commitment to your security Mr. Paige."

"It's a start Russell and it's very much appreciated."

"Excellent. Now, why don't we head back upstairs so you can tour the house at your leisure."

"I have a few questions," Julie asked as they exited back into the Media Room and closed the bookcase behind them.

"Yes Mrs. Paige?"

"What are our children's schooling options?"

"In all honesty, that will need to be discussed."

"What do you mean?" Kim asked.

"Well, there's the local school here in Falls Church, of course. However, I've been authorized to offer you access to a few boarding school options here on the east coast that you may want to consider."

"Boarding schools?" Julie replied with some apprehension in her voice. "As in taking our kids away from us?"

Russell shook his head. "No one will do anything of the sort Mrs. Paige. It's merely an option to consider in the grand scheme of things. I have provided a number of information packets in regards to these schools that I will leave with you. However, if you do go that route please note that it will be completely paid for and the insertion of your children, into whatever boarding school you choose, has already been negotiated and approved."

As Julie mulled over what Russell had just said they found themselves back at the entryway. Everyone's luggage had been brought inside and was neatly lined up next to each other. Even Stickers had been brought in and carefully handled. Russell dug into his pocket, produced a set of keys and handed two to each adult.

"These are for the house and the armory. As I said before, car keys are on the kitchen counter and the fridge and pantry are fully stocked. Is there anything else I can do for you?"

Laura spoke up. "I hate to ask this…"

"Please, go on."

"Is there a paycheck that comes along will all of this?" she asked as she swept her arm around the house.

Russell smiled. "Those particulars will be handled when you meet with the DCI directly later this week. In the meantime I am at your disposal twenty-four seven." He turned to Sam and Bill. "Would you prefer a driver to pick you up tomorrow morning to take you to your indictment or to drive there yourselves?"

Sam and Bill looked at each other, raised their eyebrows and then turned back to Russell.

"A driver would be ideal," said Sam.

"As you wish. I'll make sure they arrive at eight in the morning." Russell then addressed everyone collectively. "Get some rest and please enjoy your new house. On Wednesday I'll take you on a tour of the facility where you'll be working."

Thomas interrupted. "Where is that by the way?"

"It's close by Mr. Clark."

"I see. And how far away is Langley, CIA headquarters from here?"

"Falls Church is nine miles due south of Langley. Is there anything else I can help you with before I pick you up on Wednesday morning?"

Everyone looked around at each other but couldn't come up with any additional questions.

"Thank you Russell," Thomas said. "Please let the DCI know how thankful and pleased we are."

Russell smiled. "My pleasure Mr. Clark. I look forward to working with you and your family."

Thomas faltered for a second. "You're going to be working at PsyOps?"

Russell nodded. "PsyOps is a need-to-know operation, so please watch the company you're in when you speak of it."

"Of course. Until Wednesday then."

Russell shook everyone's hand, closed the front door behind him. Shortly later the bus departed. The kids started filtering back in from various parts of the mansion.

"I think I need a drink," Julie said.

"Well," Laura added as she began to walk towards the kitchen, "Russell did say we were fully stocked. Why don't we test out that theory."

6
Monday October 8, 2001

It had been a long day of travel for everyone and they were having a difficult time comprehending just how large their new residence actually was. After settling in and assigning bedrooms Laura, Julie and Kim quickly whipped together an evening meal that consisted of pasta, meatballs and salad. At the large dining room table all thirteen of them sat down and ate their first family meal together in the new house.

"This was delicious," Hobbes said as he devoured his plate. "Thank you."

The ladies beamed.

"Yes," Thomas added, "thank you sweetie."

Sam, Bill and their children also said thank you. The children scooched their chairs backwards away from the table.

"And where do you think you're all going?" Laura collectively asked the youngsters.

All of them froze in mid push.

"If you're done with dinner then please take your dishes to the sink and rinse them. After that you need to start winding down for bed. We've got a busy week ahead of us."

"But mom, it's only eight o'clock," Emily assured her mother.

"That's true, but it's been a long day. On top of that there's a three hour difference that your body is going to instantly realize tomorrow morning. When you open your eyes at seven it's going to feel more like four in the morning."

"Do we have to?" Amanda asked her mother.

"Laura's absolutely right," Julie replied. "You'll have plenty of time to enjoy the house tomorrow."

"Dishes. Sink. Go. Now. Thank you," Kim added.

The six children picked up their plates and departed.

"Gav," Laura called out after him. "Don't forget to feed Stickers before you head upstairs, okay?"

"I will," he assured her without turning around.

The adults barely had time to suppress their smiles as their kids left the dining room and filed into the kitchen. Various clanks were heard followed by the sound of running water. Shortly thereafter five of them ran out of the kitchen, into the family room and noisily stomped up the stairs towards their new bedrooms. Gavin, on the other hand, took his time to prepare Stickers' food as his cat spun around his legs in anticipation. Gavin put the dish down for Stickers in the laundry room and then walked back through the dining room on his way out.

"Good night," he said to everyone.

"Night little man," Bill replied.

"Don't let those bed bugs bite," Sam added.

"They can try," Gavin quipped back.

"We'll be up in a bit to tuck you in," Laura said.

Gavin disappeared around the corner and headed up to his bedroom. Along the way Stir appeared out of nowhere, next to his side, and accompanied Gavin to his room.

Laura spoke up. "Would anyone like a beer?"

A multitude of affirmations arose from the remaining adults at the table and within a minute they all had a cold one in their hands. The adults were exhausted and the overhanging dread of the Congressional indictment, in the morning, was definitely on their minds.

"It's all going to work out," Thomas tried to assure his friends.

Sam half-smiled in return. "I appreciate where you're coming from but we're looking at a shot in the dark on coming out on top."

"Don't say that," Julie said to her husband.

"No offense," Bill interjected, "but I'm afraid Sam's right. It's going to be a cold day in hell before they let us off the hook."

"And it's that attitude that brought us to Virginia," Kim indicated before she drank more of her beer.

Bill paused and looked over at his wife. "Something on your mind?"

Kim put her beer down on the table. "Fine. I'll just come out and say it. Is this something we really want to go through with? I mean, really. What are we doing here? To me it feels like we were chased out of our home and grabbed on to the first lifeline that was extended to us."

Laura cut in. "Perhaps we should table this for another time."

"No," Bill replied. "This has been an ongoing discussion on our end Laura. I think it's about time it became public knowledge. What do you think Sam?"

Sam slowly nodded. "I'm afraid we have a slight division in our thought processes."

"Slight?" Julie mocked offhandedly. "That's an understatement. Kim and I are not happy with this situation whatsoever."

Thomas and Laura quickly glanced at each other and Hobbes looked downright uncomfortable.

"What are the issues?" Laura gently probed.

Julie continued. "Well, for one thing our damn lives are upside down. I close my eyes and all I can see is SANDBOX crumbling in on itself. That happened right after we found out Roberta had been selling us down the river for the past decade which in turn decidedly funnels our future into shitsville. Then, because of some lifelong loyalty, our men decide it's a great idea to follow your family, Laura, out here so they can redeem their honor, or some shit."

Laura had seen Julie livid before, but this was an entirely different level of frustration.

"You know Jules," Sam spat out, "if it wasn't for 'their family' you wouldn't even be alive."

"And if it wasn't for their family we'd never been in danger in the fucking first place."

Thomas and Laura recoiled in their seats as if they'd been struck in the face, Julie's words cutting deep. Kim and Bill reacted similarly.

"I…I didn't know you felt that way Julie," Laura whispered.

"Neither did I," Thomas added as he pushed back from the table. "Laura, I think we should give them some time to think about what they want to say next, AND how they want to communicate it."

Sam stood up. "It's not like Julie said…"

Thomas put his hand up. "Sam. We've been friends since we were kids and we've all been through some seriously fucked up shit over the years. However, there are some things that just can't be unsaid and I'd rather stop the conversation right here, right now before something like that actually happens." Thomas turned to Julie. "You're right Julie. Maybe none of this would have happened if it wasn't for me and my family. But I can't change that. You're not the only one that's scared right now. This is new for everyone." He turned back to Sam. "Good luck with the indictment tomorrow."

Laura stood up and Thomas put his arm around her as they walked out of the dining room and upstairs to their bedroom.

Sam sat back down with a huge scowl on his face as he looked around the table. Hobbes quickly stood, appeared as if was going to say something, changed his mind and departed.

"Seriously sis," Kim started, "what the fuck?"

"What I said was the truth."

"But the way you said it was categorically appalling."

"Was it? If it wasn't for the Clarks then none of this would have happened."

Sam had had enough. "Stop talking Jules."

"But…"

"Just close your mouth and listen. You're not the only person hurting at this table, got it? What Bill and I created will more than likely be taken from us tomorrow. How do you think we feel about that? And to top it off that shit had absolutely nothing to do with Thomas and his family. So take your anger out on me rather than lashing out at our family."

Bill spoke up. "I'll admit that the circumstances around what happened to Thomas have steered the course of our family's lives over the years. Yet the abilities they have they never asked for, nor the attention it bought from outside parties. Thomas and Laura are good people. Sam is right, be mad at us for wanting to go back to doing what we do best. But unless a miracle happens at our indictment tomorrow I'm afraid we're taking the DCI up on his offer. We will provide for our family, it's as simple as that."

Kim put her hand on Bill's. "I don't have to like it, but I understand where you're coming from now. The only thing I've ever wanted is for you to be safe because my sister and I are worried sick about you two being back in harm's way."

Sam took over the conversation. "We don't want to be back in harm's way, that's just part of our job. But that's currently not up for debate until we know how tomorrow shakes out."

"Fine," Julie finally said, still with a slight edge to her voice. "Then I want to bring up sending our kids to boarding school."

"What?" Sam responded. "We just got here. Where is this coming from?"

"It's coming from a position of safety," Julie snapped back. "Look what we just went through. Our children were kidnapped and Rebecca was killed. And that hasn't been the first time they've been put in a dangerous situation."

"What are you trying to say sis?" Kim asked.

Julie exhaled. "I know I fucked up tonight, alright. And I know I'm a huge ball of stress right now. All I'm trying to say is that I'd feel better if our kids were someplace safe. Would I miss them? Absolutely. But they need a break from what they've been through just as much as we do."

"Look around this house," Sam said. "There's plenty to do here."

Julie nodded. "Yes, there is. But the best thing I want for my children is to actually be children. At a boarding school they can be themselves, in a safe and controlled environment as well as play and interact with kids their own age. If we keep them here then who knows what they'll see, hear or potentially be subjected to."

"You realize the irony of your statement, right?" Sam stated. "We're here because of Thomas and his family. This house we're in is because of them. The boarding school offer is because of them and yet you just shit all over them."

"I get it Sam," Julie said. "I'm angry and scared. And because of that I don't want our children subjected to that environment. I don't know what's coming because of the Clarks arrangement they have with the DCI. What if we're targeted again? What then? Maybe next time our children won't be so lucky to have Gavin around to portal them out of danger." She paused. "I won't take that risk Sam, I just can't."

It was Kim's turn to weigh in. "I was initially against it, but Julie just convinced me. There are too many unknowns that we're dealing with right now and the kids need a stable day-to-day environment."

"Honey," Bill said.

"No Bill, Julie's right. Think about it. I'd rather have them away and safe than in my arms based on the history we've been through as of late. Wouldn't you?"

Bill opened his mouth to object but then closed it as his mind connected the obvious dots. He eventually looked over at Sam who met his eyes.

"You're onboard with this now too?" Sam asked.

"I hate to admit it but it makes sense, at least for the time being. It's not an all or nothing decision brother. Look at what they've had to experience. We're having a hard time as adults working through it. Think about how they're dealing."

"I do," Sam replied, "and I don't like what I come up with." He turned his head back over to Julie. "This is what you think is best?"

"My sister and I aren't stupid."

"What does that…"

Julie held up her hand to stop Sam. "Hear me out. We know that you're going to be out on missions and doing who knows what for the CIA. It's abundantly clear that that's what you know and what you do. But after everything that's happened I know that Kim and I want nothing more than to hold our children close to us. We want to smother them and let them know that everything's going to be alright. But the sad reality is that we haven't been able to keep them safe and that bothers me." She took a breath. "They need to be children, Sam. So yes, I think this is the best thing for them."

Kim nodded in agreement and Bill joined along.

Sam capitulated. "Very well, but there's no telling how they're going to react to this decision."

7

Tuesday Oct 9, 2001

Early the next morning Sam and Bill walked out of the front door and climbed into a town car that was waiting for them in the driveway. They had both dressed in business suits and appeared a bit haggard from anxiety.

"Good morning gentlemen," the driver said as he welcomed them.

"Morning," Bill said.

"Morning sir," Sam added.

"You'll find fresh coffee for each of you in front of you as well as an assortment of danishes."

"You read my mind…"

"Albert," the driver responded as he drove down the driveway.

"You read my mind Albert," Bill repeated. "Thank you."

"Yes, thank you Albert."

"You're quite welcome. Go ahead and sit back. It's going to take about thirty minutes to get where we're going."

* * *

Sam and Bill were ushered into the large room, led to a table that contained two microphones, and asked to sit down. Strangely enough, as they both took in the room, they noticed that no media were present. In fact, the large room was extremely empty except for members of Congress that were lined up and seated in front of them. Some aides stood up along the back edges of the room, but aside from that it was desolate.

Bill leaned over and whispered to Sam. "What the hell is going on?"

"Good question. I can't tell if the lack of press works in our favor or not."

A lone stenographer waited with her hands poised over her machine for the indictment to begin. Congressman Sutter, presiding over the indictment, spoke up.

"I'm Congressman Bill Sutter. We're here today in regards to the indictment brought upon the Private Military Company known as SANDBOX. For the record, gentlemen, please identify yourselves."

"Here we go," Sam whispered back to Bill. He adjusted the microphone in front of him. "My name is Sam Paige, owner and co-founder of SANDBOX Enterprises."

"And I'm Bill Nicholson, owner and co-founder of SANDBOX Enterprises."

"Very well," Sutter replied. "Let the record show both responsible parties are present and have identified themselves before this Congressional hearing. Now, Mr. Paige, Mr. Nicholson, before we begin I would like to talk about the history leading up to the creation of SANDBOX."

"Yes, sir," Sam replied. "In nineteen-seventy-five Bill and I joined the Army straight out of high school. Throughout the following eight years we strove to become the best we could be and to serve our country. Together we worked diligently to join the Airborne Rangers. And from that elite group we were tapped into the Special Forces community."

Congressman Sutter spoke up. "Yes. From your records in front of us it's very clear that you both have exemplary military records. Please, continue."

"At the end of our military contract we decided to strike out on our own, forgoing the military chain of command we wanted to get away from."

"Are you saying, Mr. Paige, that the chain of command is something to be scoffed at?"

"Not at all, Congressman. But I can say that it's not for everyone."

"I see. Carry on."

"Bill and I left the service in eighty-three and two years later, in eighty-five, SANDBOX was off and running. That was sixteen years ago."

"And in those past sixteen years how did you develop your business?"

Bill interjected. "Through hard work. We put everything we had into our business to make it the defining company it is today."

Congressman Sutter raised an eyebrow. "That's an interesting statement, Mr. Nicholson, seeing how your headquarters is in ruins and the two of you are sitting here."

Sam and Bill shifted uncomfortably.

"I find it ironic, according to your military records, that you were both involved in the United States war on drugs and yet today you're here because of that very reason itself, drugs."

"Now, sir, let me…"

Congressman Sutter held up his hand and cut Sam off. "Mr. Paige, you have to admit that there are some significant discrepancies in regards to how your company was operated."

"It was only recently that Bill and I became aware of how our company resources were being utilized behind our backs."

"Explain."

Sam continued. "I'll try to sir. Back when Bill and I were stationed at Fort Benning, Georgia, it was run by our company commander, Robert Aleman. As Bill and I moved on to Special Forces, Robert Aleman also advanced and obtained the rank of General. Now, unbeknownst to us, Robert Aleman was heavily involved in the trafficking of narcotics from various parts of the world. He, along with a conglomerate of other high ranking officials, smuggled those drugs into the United States using the US military infrastructure as its mules. It was during our time at Fort Benning that we were approached to participate in the theft of military grade weapons, from the base's armory. We brought this to the attention of Robert Aleman, a Colonel at the time."

"And what did he have to say about it?"

"He listened to us and shortly thereafter we were issued orders to try out for the Special Forces."

"And why do you think that occurred?"

"At the time, sir, it didn't feel like a concidence. It wasn't until years later, when the General, attempted to murder in us San Francisco, that the truth was revealed."

Congressman Sutter leaned back in his chair. "You're telling this hearing that General Robert Aleman attempted to kill you?"

"Yes, sir," Sam adamantly replied.

"For what reason?"

"He'd been instructed, by the conglomerate he worked with, to silence us years prior. However, instead he'd let us live with the plan that he would then recruit us later."

"That seems a bit farfetched. But regardless of how it appears, why try to kill you?"

Bill spoke up. "Because he did try to recruit us. We refused and the tone of the meeting immediately turned violent."

"There was a gunfight, sir. We defended ourselves but were shot in the process."

"And yet you both survived," the Congressman quipped.

"Sir?"

"Nevermind. Continue."

"We tracked down the General, subdued and handed him over to the military. In the General's possession was a briefcase that contained damning evidence that..."

Congressman Sutter cut Sam off. "That information has been coded top secret. The stenographer will erase the previous sentence Mr. Paige uttered."

"But sir," Sam pressed.

The Congressman waved Sam off. "Get to the point Mr. Paige."

Sam gritted his teeth as Bill seethed in silence next to him.

"In May, of this year, Robert Aleman escaped from a Black Site detention facility and proceeded to come after our families. He utilized SANDBOX personnel to help in that process."

Congressman Sutter flipped over a few pages from the binder in front of him. "You're referring to Roberta Constance, a founding employee of SANDBOX?"

Sam nodded. "There were also four other team members that he tapped."

"And why would Ms. Constance, or any of your other employees, do anything Mr. Aleman asked of them?"

"We discovered that Roberta had been a plant from day one, sir. Over the years she oversaw and managed what occurred at every level of our company. Bill and I had full confidence in her from the get go and never thought for an instant that she was working against us."

"And the reason behind her betrayal?"

"She was under the impression that Bill and I were responsible for her son's death."

"I see. And were you?"

"No, sir. She had been manipulated into believing it and ultimately used our company resources to enable what you're accusing us of today."

"Drug smuggling," Congressman Sutter stated matter-of-factly.

Sam and Bill remained quiet.

"Well gentlemen, that's quite a story. But ultimately that's all this hearing is left with, isn't it?"

"Sir?"

"Well, Robert Aleman, Roberta Constance and your four alleged team members that you say turned on you are all dead, aren't they?"

Sam and Bill didn't like where this was headed. "Yes, sir. But Robert Aleman blew up our building. My family and I barely escaped with our lives."

"That's either convenient or luck. Either way it leaves you both in the same situation. Your company was complicit in the smuggling of illicit narcotics, from foreign lands, into the United States. Now, as the owners of SANDBOX, are you not responsible for anything and everything that happens within your company?"

"Yes," Sam said with some trouble.

"Speak up Mr. Paige, for the record."

"Yes," Sam said louder.

"Good. This hearing is pleased to hear that you own up to your company's involvement regarding these crimes."

"Son of a bitch," Bill said inaudibly.

"There is another point of inquiry that needs to be addressed before we render our decision."

"What now?" Sam whispered over to Bill.

"When the FBI froze your financials, and began their audit, they discovered a staggering sum of money. It would appear that nearly half a billion dollars had been recently issued to you from an overseas bank. From Switzerland if I'm not mistaken. Now, we know that SANDBOX had become an international company in the past years, but that doesn't begin to explain who sent you that money, where it came from or what it was for. Would you care to explain, Mr. Paige?"

Oh shit. Sam shifted in his chair ever so slightly. He knew he could never talk about the five hundred million dollars that Michael Clark had gifted his company four years prior. How could he explain that the money had come from his friend's father, who in turn, had stolen it during the Cold War era from a Russian who'd been skimming off the top of his own smuggling enterprise.

"No sir, I can't explain it," stated Sam.

Congressman Sutter wasn't pleased. "Can't or won't?"

"Can't."

"You're aware that your silence in this matter makes you look more complicit. In fact it makes you look like you were very much involved."

Sam and Bill didn't respond.

"Your silence is noble, but ultimately foolish. The truth of the matter is that your business and personal reputations, that you've spent the better part of your lives cultivating, have been severely tainted. It is the ruling of the committee you see before you that SANDBOX Enterprises will immediately cease any and all operations, business related or otherwise."

Sam and Bill's jaws clenched.

Congressman Sutter leaned forward. "Your assets that were previously frozen will be seized. A portion of them will be utilized as severance to your employees, towards the cleanup and demolition of your headquarters and to the substantial fines levied against you. Ignorance is not a defense and drug smuggling has a hefty price tag which you are going to feel. You will be made an example of. The United States government will not sit idly by and let its people's minds become polluted as we desperately battle illegal drugs from crossing our borders and landing in the hands of our children.

"Now, Mr. Paige and Mr. Nicholson, we're not finished. Your complicity does not extinguish the facts that you both have exemplary military records and served your country well. In fact, you took that ideal and created SANDBOX with it."

He then leaned over and addressed the stenographer. "Stop typing."

She removed her hands from the machine and placed them in her lap.

The Congressman continued. "Suffice it to say we are aware of your involvement in the removal of one Nikolay Dmitriev in Cuba, the same man who orchestrated multiple bombings throughout our country that resulted in the loss of untold innocent lives. You are to be commended for that service to our country. We are also aware that you have copies of the documents found within General Aleman's briefcase."

Sam and Bill shared a quick glance.

"But all of this has to be off the record, doesn't it?" Sam said.

The Congressman nodded. "Some truths do not see the light of day. You may start typing again."

The stenographer placed her hands back on her machine.

"Sam Paige. Bill Nicholson. SANDBOX has been effectively shut down. The only reason you're not looking at incarceration is due to your impeccable reputations. With that being said it is the decision of this committee that each of you will retain one million dollars, in cash. You will also be able to keep any proceeds you make from the sale of your Marin homes. All other business assets, which include property, equipment, vehicles and accounts are now the property of the United States.

"We're done here gentlemen. You are dismissed."

*　*　*

A stunned Sam and Bill managed to make their way back to the town car and climb inside. As Albert drove them home Sam and Bill began to whisper to each other in the back seat.

"We just got fucking railroaded," commented Bill, very pissed off.

"That and we were played from the beginning by Roberta and Aleman's organization."

"What hurts the most is that all of our work has been for nothing. Everything we've done to build our company up over the years is gone. Our reputation is fucked."

Sam nodded. "Yeah brother, we're on some seriously unfamiliar ground right now and I don't like how it feels."

8

Tuesday Oct 9, 2001

As everyone gathered for lunch the tension between the remaining adults was still palatable. Julie's accusations the night before were fresh and the lack of communication as lunch was consumed was all too evident, especially to their children who immediately picked on their parent's odd behavior.

"What's wrong with you guys?" Amanda asked. "You haven't said a word since this morning?"

Julie looked over at her thirteen-year-old daughter. "What do you mean?"

"Oh please, mother. It's like you're all walking on eggshells."

"I've noticed it too," Emily added.

Laura and Julie exchanged a quick glance and then averted their eyes.

"Well, the good news is that you don't get to worry about that. However," Julie said as she looked around the table at all the children, "what you do get to worry about is changing in to swimming suits so you can go test out the pool."

"Oh boy!" Gavin squealed.

"Hell yes!" Edward let slip in excitement.

"Edward," Kim, his mother warned. "Language."

"Sorry," he called out over his shoulder as their children bolted out of the kitchen to get changed.

Thomas and Hobbes cracked a smile at the youth's anticipation but quickly faded once the kitchen emptied.

Hobbes stood up. "I'll, uh, head out back and be the lifeguard." He hastily left without waiting for a response.

Thomas, Laura, Kim and Julie remained at the table nursing their coffees. The silence between everyone was deafening.

"Soooo…" Thomas tried to say.

Julie cut him off. "I'm sorry. Okay."

Laura and Thomas were shocked by her admission.

"I was angry and I overstepped my bounds last night."

"But you weren't lying about what you said," Laura stated. "You truly believe our family is responsible for putting you in danger."

Julie sighed and nodded her head. "Part of me does, yes."

"And the other part?" Laura asked.

"The other part is pissed off at my husband."

"Why?"

"The normal reasons about false promises. Just when I think we're going to get out of this it all comes back. I just want a normal life for me and my kids. Is that too much to ask?"

"Look who you're asking."

"Shit. You're right. Sorry." Julie put her hands on her forehead. "I don't know what I'm thinking but here we are in Virginia, in a strange house and I'm still expecting the worst to happen." She lifted her head and turned back to Thomas and Laura. "But in all honesty, I apologize for what I said last night. I shouldn't have taken my frustration out on you two."

"Apology accepted. Thomas and I know what it's like to be afraid and not know what's around the bend. Like you said, did we expect to be where we are today, in Virginia, making a deal with the CIA? I don't think so."

"Definitely not," Thomas added. "So you're not alone in your thinking Julie. All we're worried about is keeping our kids safe."

"Speaking of our kid's safety," Kim interjected, "we have something of an announcement to make to tell you."

"Oh?" Laura replied.

"After my sister's rude behavior last night we decided that due to our current situation about not feeling safe or in control that we're going to send our four children to boarding school."

"Wow," Laura replied as she took the information in. "That's quite a decision. Do they know yet?"

Kim shook her head. "No, not yet, but soon."

"Is it just about safety?" Thomas asked.

"No," Julie replied. "I feel they need to be kids and have a normal routine. I mean, look at us and what we've been through. Your daughter had to wipe memories of the Hawaiian attacks out of our children's minds, and that's only one example I can come up with that convinced me to get them out of harm's way sooner than later."

"And you Kim," Laura asked. "Where do you stand?"

"Well," Kim responded, "I know there's no reason to try and lie to you."

"You can try," Laura joked knowing full well that her power allowed her to know when anyone was telling a lie.

"At first I was doubtful about my sister's idea to send our children away. But the more I thought about it I was swayed. I don't know what to expect here or what dangers potentially lie in wait for us. All I know is that I don't want my children to go through what happened at SANDBOX ever again."

Thomas nodded. "I understand. However, on a side note, we'll need to have a family discussion with them before they leave to ensure they know to keep our secret safe."

Before the conversation could continue the front door opened and Sam and Bill entered the house. The door closed and the two men, still in their suits, walked into the kitchen.

"Uh oh," Kim said as she instantly read Bill's body language. "What happened?"

"Are you okay?" Julie asked.

Sam and Bill took off their jackets and sat down at the table. Within minutes they had relayed that they had been screwed over and the judgment that had been levied against them.

"I'm sorry babe," Kim said as she tried to console her husband.

Julie reached out and held Sam's hand. "I am too."

"Damn," Thomas whistled at his friend's rehashing of the hearing. "All of the money. Wow. That's crazy."

Bill's long face told the entire story. "They took everything from us."

"Yeah they did," Sam added.

"But you're not responsible," Julie insisted.

"Not directly," Sam replied, "but that's not how they see it. We were complicit because we're the owners. And in that naivety, of obviously not knowing what was happening in our own company, the committee sent a very strong message. They took everything and gave very little back. In the end it was only our reputation that saved us from going to prison."

"And having copies of Aleman's briefcase."

"That too. But speaking of our reputation," Bill added, "it's now extremely questionable."

"So what does all of this mean?" Kim asked.

"SANDBOX is gone," Bill stated. "It's as simple as that. They tossed a million dollars each at us and basically told us to walk away with a smile."

"But that's not fair!"

"It is what it is," Sam dejectedly said. "When it comes right down to it we helped fund the war on drugs." Sam looked over at his friend. "Thomas. I'm sorry we lost your father's money."

"Sam, what happened to the both of you is nothing short of unfortunate. And even that word doesn't begin to describe the injustice."

Sam nodded.

"But, to your concern over the money, it's just money. Besides, the way my father obtained it was dubious at best." Thomas looked up at the ceiling. "Yes pop, I don't know if you can hear me or not but I said it." Thomas looked back over at Sam and Bill. "The real issue isn't the money. We have that and there's no way we would ever ignore family. What the real issue is that your good names have been tarnished. Even though Robert Aleman died in that explosion he really did succeed in fucking you over."

"Yeah, he did," Sam replied.

"Are you going to be alright?" Laura probed.

Sam and Bill both shrugged. "In time, I suppose. Right now the wound is fresh. Seeing what the DCI has in store for us might help us take our mind off of things."

"Jump right back into work?" Julie asked offhandedly. "That's the plan?"

Kim put her hand up. "Ease up sis."

Julie closed her mouth. Sam decided the best course of action was not to engage his wife. He knew they both had their issues to deal with in private.

Bill took up the slack. "I guess we'll know more tomorrow when we take the tour. Until then I think I'll change out of this suit and we should go join the kids in the pool. I have to find some way to relax."

9

Wednesday Oct 10, 2001

Russell Washington knocked on the front door and twenty seconds later Thomas opened it.

"Good morning Mr. Clark."

"Morning Russell. Would you like to come in?"

"No, thank you. I've got a van to transport everyone, well most everyone, for the tour of the facility."

Thomas nodded. "I think we're almost ready. Give us five minutes."

"Alright."

"You're sure you don't want to come inside and wait?"

Russell mulled it over for a few seconds and decided to accept Thomas' invitation. "Thank you."

"No problem," Thomas said as he headed towards the kitchen with Russell in tow.

As they entered Sam and Bill looked up from the table to greet him.

"Morning Russell," Sam said.

"Good morning Mr. Paige. Mr. Nicholson."

Bill cracked a smile. "You're so formal Russell. Is there anything we can do to break you of that habit?"

"I'm afraid not Mr. Nicholson. I take my job seriously and prefer to conduct myself with an elevated level of professionalism. I hope that won't be a problem."

Sam chuckled. "He's got you there."

"There's coffee if you'd like some," Thomas offered.

"No, thank you."

"Your loss. The blend you stocked for us is excellent."

"I'm happy to hear that," Russell answered. "Speaking of, do you have any complaints about the house?"

"No," Sam told him. "Everything's fantastic."

Russell smiled. "Good. Good." He looked around. "I don't mean to rush you but there's a schedule to keep and…"

"Say no more," Thomas countered. "I'll go see what's holding up my family."

Thomas left the kitchen just as Hobbes walked in.

"Good morning Mr. Hillbu…I mean Hobbes."

"Hey Russell. So we're getting the grand tour this morning, eh?"

"Yes, sir."

"Well I, for one, am excited. I can't wait to see the tech you have for me."

"I'm sure you'll be very pleased with it."

"I wish I could say the same thing about my wife right now," Sam whispered to himself.

"Did you say something Mr. Paige?"

"Oh. I was just mumbling to myself."

Hobbes decided to stand and wait rather than join Sam and Bill at the table. The past two days had been somewhat uncomfortable and he couldn't wait to get out of the house.

Sam asked a question. "So Russell, how long have you worked for the DCI?"

"Three and a half years now."

"And what's your role?"

"I'm one of his assistants."

"One of them?" Bill asked.

"Well, the one specifically tasked with the oversight of PsyOps."

Sam and Bill's eyebrows both rose with Russell's answer.

"So this project has been in the works for the past three and a half years?"

Russell nodded. "Yes, sir."

"Interesting."

"What's interesting?" Laura asked as she, along with Thomas, Gavin and Emily, walked into the kitchen.

"Russell was just telling us that he's worked for the DCI for the past three and a half years, directly for the PsyOps project the entire time."

"Is that so?" Laura began to probe as Thomas poured a glass of orange juice for each of his kids.

"Yes, ma'am."

"And what has kept you busy?"

"Construction, for the most part," Russell answered.

"Of what?" Thomas asked.

"The secret facility," he replied. "But I think you'll be very pleased when you see it."

There was a pause as they took in what he'd just acknowledged.

Laura spoke up again. "And building this 'secret facility', on behalf of the DCI, can be construed as a normal request?"

Russell shrugged. "This country is full of secrets, both public and private. I did what I was instructed to do."

"I see," Laura responded. "Well then, what are your thoughts about us?"

"I don't understand the question."

He's not lying. "Okay, I'll reword it. Why do you think we're part of PsyOps?"

"I haven't been made aware of that part of the project yet."

Laura nodded to everyone else there to let them know he was telling the truth.

"Alright Russell, then will you tell us what you assume we'll be contributing to the project?"

Russell looked around the room. "I'd rather not offend anyone."

"Go ahead," Thomas assured him. "I think we're all interested in what you have to say."

"Very well, Mr. Clark. My initial thoughts are that Mr. Paige and Mr. Nicholson are here to head up security. The obvious placement for Hobbes will be running the computer systems. However, I can't come up with any viable answers for the four of you."

"And why's that?" Thomas pressed.

"Well, and I mean no offense of course, but why would this project need an ex-children's book writer and an ex-psychologist? The other major item that baffles me is your children. Why are they necessary? Once again, I mean no offense."

"None taken," Thomas replied. "In fact those are all valid points. Perhaps in time the DCI will read you in."

Russell regained his professional composure. "If he deems that information necessary I'm sure I will. Until that time I have a job to do. Are you ready to depart?"

Sam and Bill stood up while Emily and Gavin placed their empty glasses in the sink. Everyone began to walk towards the front door.

"I'm sorry I didn't get a chance to say hello to your wives this morning."

"It's probably better that you didn't," Sam began to explain. "Right now Julie isn't too happy with me and this situation."

"Oh. I'm sorry to hear that Mr. Paige."

"Don't worry about it. It is what it is. Why don't we get out of here and see what you have in store for us."

* * *

Russell drove them just outside of Falls Church, a few miles away from the estate, to a farm. The van turned in the long driveway and made its way up to the main house. On the property was a single family farmhouse and adjacent to it was a large barn. Several horses and cows grazed in the pasture alongside the barn.

"That's a pretty horse," Emily said as she pointed at a mare in the distance.

"What are we doing on a farm?" Gavin asked.

"I think it's much more than that Gavin," Hobbes said. "On our way in I noticed security cameras in the trees and, if I'm not mistaken, a T-three data line running alongside the electrical lines."

Russell tapped the horn as he pulled up to the front of the barn and two men dressed in farmer's clothing, although both armed with rifles, opened the doors and allowed the van inside. Russell waved to them on the way in. The two men closed the doors behind them as the van came to a stop in the center of the floor. For all intent and purposes the interior of the barn looked like the inside of a typical barn. Bales of hay were stacked up in various locations and the floor was covered in it.

"Hold on," Russell cautioned everyone.

Soundlessly the van began to lower itself into the ground down a large elevator shaft.

"You've got to be shitting me," Bill said in delight. "This is awesome."

"Woah," Gavin exhaled as he watched the cement walls of the elevator shaft rise up past the van's windows.

After twenty feet their downward descent stopped and Russell gently pulled the van forward and parked in one of the empty available spaces while the barn floor ascended behind them.

"So the facility is all underground?" Laura asked as they disembarked.

Russell nodded. "Yes, Mrs. Clark."

Laura held up her hand. "If we're going to be working together then you're going to have to stop with Mr. and Mrs. We all have first names and I can guarantee that we all want to be called by them. In fact, we'll all get along much better if you do so."

The group collectively nodded to Russell's dismay.

"Alright, I understand. I'll see what I can do about that."

Laura smiled. "Good. Now, where were you?"

"Right," Russell replied. "This facility is entirely underground and consists of a number of separate wings each dedicated to their respective practices. Please, follow me."

He led the group down the only corridor out of the parking area. Cameras lined the walls and in fifty feet they came upon the main security station. Two men, both armed with side arms, manned the desk. Behind them was the actual entrance to the facility that was secured behind thick doors, which were currently sealed shut.

Russell greeted both men. "Good morning Chuck. Dave."

"Morning, sir," they both replied.

"I'd like to introduce the Clark's. This is Thomas, his wife Laura, their daughter Emily and their son Gavin. Then, on the other side, we have Sam Paige and Bill Nicholson. Last but not least is Hobbes."

"Nice to meet all of you," Chuck said.

"Likewise," Dave added.

Russell continued. "I'm taking them on a tour of the facility. I expect their access badges to be ready when we're done."

"We're on it, sir," Chuck replied.

The group left the security booth behind and approached the security doors. Russell produced his badge and swiped it through the reader that was attached to the wall. The doors slid open and they entered. Inside they discovered a circular hallway. Branching off the hallway, at various points, were corridors that led to separate yet specific outshoots of the facility.

"How large is this place?" Thomas asked as they turned right and began the tour.

"It's extensive, Mr. Cla...Thomas. Overall the size of this underground facility weighs in around four acres, or approximately one-hundred and seventy thousand square feet."

Bill whistled. "That's impressive. And what's all that space include?"

"I'm glad you asked."

For the next fifteen minutes Russell walked the family around the facility. In the various wings off the main circular hallway he showed them Interrogation, which included holding and questioning rooms; the Laboratory, stock full of medical equipment and medical bay; Testing, a few empty rooms with odd holes all over the walls; Tech, filled with servers, computers and communication equipment; and Tactical, a floor below the main hallway that had been built out with an armory, long distance shooting range and a Hogan's Alley. Back in the main level Russell ended the tour in the facility's break room that included a kitchen. The room also doubled as a gym and a side room contained bunk beds and a large bathroom. There was a sealed door, with a card swipe on the wall next to it, in the break room as well.

"So what do you think?" Russell asked them.

"Impressive and a little scary," Laura honestly answered.

Sam spoke up. "I'm guessing this facility is off the grid."

"Naturally," Russell replied. "It had to be given the constraints the DCI gave me."

"What does off the grid mean?" Gavin asked.

"It means that no one knows about this place," answered his father.

"That's probably for the best," Emily added.

Russell cocked his head slightly to the side at the ten-year old girls answer. He had a multitude of questions he wanted to ask them but he knew he couldn't. *Why are you here? What's so special about you? What is your purpose? What's going to transpire in this place now that you've arrived?*

"And all this is for us?" Thomas asked.

Russell regained his focus. "Yes."

"And when do we start working?"

"Tomorrow. The DCI will meet you here in the morning. Your house is close enough that my assumption is you'll drive yourselves here."

"We can do that," Sam assured him.

"Excellent. If there aren't any more questions or concerns then why don't we head back to security and pick up your badges then."

As they group left the break room, and filed back into the large circular hallway, Thomas asked Russell another question.

"So, what's your role in PsyOps now that we've arrived?"

"Honestly Thomas, I have no idea yet. The DCI hasn't broached that subject with me."

"Fair enough. Hopefully we'll see you around then."

92

Russell thought about that for a second. "You're all very pleasant to be around so I think I'd like that."

"Be careful what you ask for," Thomas told him with a grin.

10

Wednesday Oct 10, 2001

That evening, after an afternoon of playing in the pool and relaxing, Sam, Julie, Bill and Kim sat their four children, Amanda, Craig, Sarah and Edward down in the family room.

"What's going on?" nine-year-old Edward asked his father. "You all look so serious."

"Yeah," his thirteen-year-old sister Sarah added. "What's up?"

Since it was Bill's children that had broached the question he was the first adult to answer.

"Well, your mother and I have discussed schooling options."

"And your mother and I have as well," Sam added to solidify a unified front.

The children looked on in anticipation. They knew they should be in school already but were thoroughly enjoying the large new house and the distractions it had to offer.

"There's no easy way of saying this," Bill started," so we'll just come out and say it. There's a boarding school two hours north of Falls Church, in Harrisburg, Pennsylvania. It's called Culver."

"Boarding school?" Amanda stated.

"What do you mean?" Sarah asked. "We all thought we'd be going to school around here?"

"What's boarding school?" Craig inquired.

"A place where parents send kids they don't want around," Amanda said.

"What?" Craig responded with tears in his eyes. "Why don't you want me around?"

"You don't love us anymore?" Sarah pressed.

Sam and Bill rolled their eyes knowing full well there was a chance that their children were going to react this way.

Kim interrupted them straightaway. "This decision to send you to boarding school has nothing to with loving you or not loving you."

"Then why?" Craig continued.

"Yeah," Edward added. "Why?"

"Which one of you remembers daddy's building blowing up?"

Four of their hands shot up.

"I remember it too. And you know what, it scared me and I know it scared you too. And now that we've moved out here to Virginia, we," Kim said as she referenced the adults, "don't want you to be scared ever again."

Julie finally opened her mouth. "The truth is kids, we don't know what to expect yet and the last thing we want is for you to go through anything like that again. The boarding school is filled with kids your age and it's only two hours away. It'll be an adventure for each of you."

"So you're not mad at us?" Craig asked.

Julie motioned to her son so he came over and sat on her lap. She looked right at him. "No. No we're not mad. We just want you to be safe, that's all. Do you understand?"

He nodded his head.

"Besides, it'll be fun. The co-ed school is aggressively involved in water sports, hikes, camping and other activities."

"And what if we don't want to go?" tested Sarah.

Kim looked at her daughter. "You're going to have an amazing time."

"So when do we leave?"

"This Sunday."

"Sunday? But we just got here."

"I know sweetie, but you've all been out of school for so long. Everyday isn't about splashing around in the pool. There are laws we have to follow."

"It'll be good," Sam assured them. "In fact, you'll probably never want to come home once you're there."

"Does this have anything to do with Emily and Gavin's powers?" Sarah questioned.

"Yes," Julie answered without hesitation.

"It's partially the reason," Kim articulated. "Like we said, we just want you all to be safe."

"So, any more questions?" Bill inquired.

All of the children shook their heads no.

"We'll know more about the boarding school later this week in case you do. In the meantime, go wash up for dinner."

The children got up and scampered off.

"Well that was tougher than I thought," Julie whispered.

"Yeah it was," Kim agreed.

"They're going to be just fine," Bill said as he stood up. "Sam's right. Once they get a taste of parental freedom they're never going to want to live with us again."

* * *

After the kids were in bed it didn't take long for Emily to sneak across the hallway, open her brother's door and enter his room. A pair of red eyes stared at her from the bed but the thump from Stir's tail gave him away. Stickers stood up, stretched, turned around a few times and flopped back down in the same spot, away from the tail that had wacked him in the face.

"Gav, you awake?"

"Yeah," he replied as he sat up.

97

"Did you want to go to the…"

"Of course."

He pushed back the covers and slid out of bed. In an instant a portal formed, illuminating and casting shadows in all corners of his room. Emily stepped through and then Stir hopped off the bed and bounded through. Gavin followed behind and the room returned to darkness.

On the island Stir ran around on the sand sniffing everything. He circled the skeleton remains of Victor Bannon a few times and then left it alone before he returned to examining the rest of the small island.

Gavin sat down in the sand in his favorite spot and looked out over the tranquil water. It seemed to go on forever and ever. Emily avoided the skeleton, made her way over to her brother and sat down as well.

"It's really nice here."

Gavin nodded.

"You're lucky to have this power."

"Maybe. Maybe not. What do you think of the place we saw today?"

Emily shrugged. "I don't know. I guess I'm excited and hesitant about it at the same time."

"Why?"

"Well," she said, "I don't really know what we're going to be doing in that place. That's the scary part."

"And the excited part?"

"That's easy. I'm excited because we'll be able to use our powers."

Gavin nodded. "I think I feel the same way."

They looked out over the water together while the soft sun warmed their faces. Stir finally made his way over to them and he plopped down in the sand next to his master. Emily and Gavin closed their eyes and just enjoyed it. A few minutes later Gavin opened his.

"Em?"

"Yeah," she replied without opening her own.

"Do you think we've grown up too quickly?"

"What other choice have we had?"

Gavin bobbed his head up and down next to her. A few minutes later he made a statement.

"I wish Rebecca was alive."

Emily opened her eyes and looked over at her brother. "Yeah, so do I. I know we both miss her."

Gavin abruptly stood up and yelled. "REBECCA! REBECCA!"

Stir and Emily jumped a bit.

"What are you doing?"

"Maybe she'll come and visit."

"Don't you think if she could she'd be here already?"

He just stared back at his sister until he finally relented. "Yeah, probably."

"I don't know how this place works let alone the rules. All I know is that we haven't been able to summon grandma and grandpa since they helped rescue dad and I from that awful Dr. Matsushita."

"I miss them."

Gavin sat back down and Emily put her arm around his shoulder. Stir resettled and laid his head on Gavin's leg.

"All I know," she stated," is that it's up to us to protect our family. I may not have completely understood the danger we were in before, but it's clear to me now that our family is and always will be in danger."

"I'm right there with you sis. I'll do whatever it takes to keep us safe."

11

Thursday Oct 11, 2001

The following morning Sam, Bill, Thomas, Laura, Emily, Gavin and Hobbes drove in three separate vehicles out to the farm. Each of them, aside from the children and Hobbes, had armed themselves with a Glock Seventeen. As they arrived each vehicle took the hidden barn elevator door below the ground and parked. Collectively they walked down the hallway towards the security booth. Chuck and Dave were there and greeted them with warm smiles.

"Good morning. I'll let the Director know you've arrived." Chuck picked up the phone and dialed an extension. "Sir. They're here. Yes, sir, I'll send them in." He addressed them again. "Please, use your security badges and head inside. The Director is expecting you."

"Thank you Chuck," Laura said as they exited security.

"You're welcome."

Thomas swiped his badge and the thick doors parted in submission. As the group entered the secret facility Russell and Robert Duncan appeared from around a bend in the hallway. A smile instantly sprung up on the DCI's face.

"Good morning and thank you for being here." Robert began to shake hands of every single one of them, especially the children's.

"Morning sir," Sam and Bill replied.

"Mr. Duncan," greeted Thomas.

"Please, call me Robert. We're going to toss out any formalities within these walls, okay? We have a lot of work to get done and I won't bog it down with any customs." He turned back to Emily and Gavin. "You have no idea how much of a pleasure it's going to be to work with both of you."

Emily and Gavin returned the handshake as Robert turned his attention to their parents. Behind the DCI a confused look washed over Russell's face and Laura caught it.

"Mr. Duncan...," Laura began.

"Robert."

She acquiesced. "Robert. It's our understanding that Russell has not been cleared for this project."

The DCI nodded. "That's correct. I brought him along today so your family could ultimately make that decision."

"Sir, I don't understand," Russell stammered.

Thomas caught on. "It's all or nothing?"

"Something like that," the DCI replied.

"Before we talk that over would you please tell us how many people, in total, are aware of this project?"

Robert responded instantly. "Two people."

"And they are?" Thomas asked.

"Myself and my wife."

"Your wife?" Laura replied in surprise. "Why?"

"We've been together for twenty-seven years. I trust her implicitly. I believe you will too when we have you all over for dinner next week."

Thomas, Laura, Sam and Bill became uncomfortable.

"You asked us out in here in good faith, sir," Thomas said. "And now you're telling us your wife knows about us. Our safety is paramount and yet you put us at risk."

"I won't lie to you," the DCI said. "And it's not like I could even if I wanted to." He paused. "I'm sorry. I shouldn't have blind-sided you but the truth is, if this project moves forward we're going to have to bring more people in that know about you. From the interrogations, to testing and the lab work alone; all those positions require staffing, do they not?

"This facility was built with secrecy in mind. The surveillance cameras are limited to the security booth, hallway, garage and the entire exterior of the farm. All facility phones are on a closed line and can only communicate to other stations within the facility. The only exception, of course, is in the Tech wing.

"Now, that brings us full circle back to Russell. Would you like him to be part of this project or not?"

Russell uncomfortably shifted from one foot to another as if he were going to be blindfolded and stood in front of a firing squad.

"Give us a moment," Thomas said as he pulled the group aside to talk.

"Of course," the DCI replied.

The family members huddled up in the hallway out of earshot.

"So what are your thoughts?" Thomas asked everyone.

Bill spoke up. "So what I'm getting is that Russell's either in or he wants Em to wipe him?"

"That's how I read it as well," Sam said.

Thomas pressed on. "So I guess the question is can we trust Russell?"

"Why don't we recap what led us here first," Laura said.

Thomas nodded. "Go ahead."

"We've been on the defensive for years because people wanted to take and exploit our children's powers. But we decided that the best course of action was to take the DCI's offer of protection. Now, do we know if that was the right choice? No, not yet. But he hasn't lied once about his intentions or direction he'd like to take us. Sure, I'm not happy that his wife knows what we can do, but there's nothing to be done about that now. The DCI is also correct when it comes to this project moving forward. We can't sit back and stay naïve that only a limited number of individuals are going to know about us and what we can do. Do I want the world to know? Absolutely not. What I do want is that we ultimately maintain control over the project's goals. Why not go all-in and see where this takes us. If we don't we might as well just run and hide for the rest of our lives."

"I agree," Sam said. "Bill and I just want to keep you safe."

"Thanks brother," whispered Thomas.

"So what about Russell?" Bill asked. "In or out?"

"I like him," Emily suddenly said. "He's a little strange, but that's okay."

The adults chuckled a little.

"And what about you little man?" Thomas asked his son.

"I think Mom's right. We've been hiding too long and I think it's time to go big or go home."

Their chuckles turned to laughter. Robert and Russell renewed their interest with what the group was going to decide.

"Heh. Where did you hear that Gav?" Sam asked.

"Something I saw on television."

"Well, wherever you heard it," Thomas said, "that was well said. All in favor of Russell coming into the fold?"

"Aye."

"Aye."

"Yup."

"Alright then," Thomas grinned. "Then we should initiate him properly. Gav, when we turn around I want Stir to appear at your side. I'll do the rest. If he doesn't faint then he'll witness the extent of our powers in due time."

They broke their huddle and turned back towards Russell and the DCI.

"Have you come to a decision?" Robert asked them.

"Now Gav."

As Russell watched them walk back over something strange happened. In an instant, next to Gavin, a small shape suddenly appeared on the ground beside him. *What is that?* It had red eyes and was surrounded by wispy black smoke. *Is that an animal?* Russell took a step back as they approached. He attempted to take another but couldn't feel the floor through his shoes anymore. He looked down and realized he was floating.

"HOLY SHIT! WHAT'S HAPPENING!?"

Robert smiled at Russell's predicament.

"Why am I floating!?"

Emily and Gavin giggled as Thomas used his power and rotated Russell in the air three-hundred and sixty degrees, head over heels.

"Enough. Enough."

Thomas gently lowered Russell back to the ground. The look on his face was categorically priceless and it took him a few moments to recover.

"You...you did that?" he asked Thomas.

"Yes."

Russell then pointed at the thing next to Gavin. "And...what's that?"

"His name is Stir," Gavin proudly told him.

"What is it?"

"Stir's my friend and my protector. Do you want to pet him?"

"Um, I don't know. Will it hurt?" Russell hesitantly replied.

Gavin shook his head. "Not unless you try to harm one of us."

Russell slowly bent down and extended his hand out towards Stir, who in turn took a few steps forward and sniffed his hand. Russell relaxed a little when Stir's black tail began to wag back and forth. He swallowed hard and pressed onward. *I can do this.*

He carefully touched Stir's head and was pleasantly surprised at the texture.

"Woah, this is amazing."

Everyone looked on as he moved down to Stir's body as the black wisps tickled his hand. He was left speechless.

The DCI broke the silence. "I think I can safely assume you've been cleared as the third person in the know Russell. Congratulations."

Russell stood up but had a difficult time regaining his composure. "I…I don't know what to say. This is all…I mean, what you can do is…, well downright amazing. How is this possible?"

"I'm sure the answer to that question you'll learn in time," Thomas replied. "Right now you have a lot to take in and I don't have the time to go down that road of explanation."

"I can see why this is such a secret and I'm humbled to be a part of it. What can I do? I mean, what are we going to do here?"

The DCI patted Russell on the back. "We're figuring that part out on the fly. But thanks to your oversight this facility is just about ready to be put through the paces. Why don't we all get out of this hallway and have a chat in the break room."

The DCI led them around the circular hallway until the logo for the break room appeared. They turned down that wing, walked in and all took a seat.

"First off I want to extend my profound thanks to each of you. I have an idea of how frightening it's been out there in the real world for you. At the same time I don't want you to feel patronized when I say that you made the right decision by coming here. It was a leap of faith on your part, and in no way must have been an easy decision." He looked around at all of them. "Here's my pledge to you. I promise to keep you safe and together.

You're in charge of how things develop in this facility. I want you to feel comfortable with that progress but I also want you to own it."

"What's the ultimate goal here, sir?" Sam asked.

"Thank you Sam, that's an excellent question. My long term goal is to make America a safer place to live in. I know that sounds like a grandiose and impossible idea, and I wouldn't blame you for thinking that. What can the seven of you do to change the world, right? The answer is more than you know. My idea is this. We could start small but that's not the hand that America's been currently dealt. September eleventh was a huge wake up call for the intelligence community and the people of the United States paid the price for our government's complacency. Now, I know the people of the world aren't going to sit around a campfire and hold hands anytime in the future. But, that doesn't mean we can't make the world a safer place one step at a time. However, that first step is going to be a big one and I need you all to be on you're A-game when that happens."

"First step?" Bill asked.

Robert was in his groove and was very excited. "I'll break everyone's roles down and see what you have to say about it."

They were all ears as the DCI continued.

"Hobbes. Your job is to become familiar with the computer systems, satellite communications, CIA information database and the drones. You have full authorization to make any changes you deem necessary. If there is any equipment that hasn't been provided you will make that request to Russell and he will make sure it gets handled."

"Did you say drones?" Hobbes asked.

"There's a manual. I think you'll like them."

"Yes sir."

The DCI turned to Sam and Bill. "You two are going to have your hands full."

"With what?" Sam asked.

"Hamid Emal Habibi."

"We were questioned about Hamid by Colonel James at the Pentagon a month ago," Bill said. "They told us that Hamid was one of the men that were responsible for the planes striking the twin towers."

Robert Duncan nodded. "And, as you both know, he was the same man you trained in Afghanistan years ago to fight against the Soviets."

"So what about him?" Sam inquired.

"I'd like to send the two of you to the Middle East, specifically Afghanistan, to hunt and capture him."

"Sure," said Bill, "like we're going to just drop in, find him and pull him out as easy as that."

"You will have the full resources of the CIA at your disposal, including satellite coverage and communications. Tell me what else you need."

"Well," replied Sam, "if this was to happen we'd need personnel; seasoned professionals. With the war already underway you can bet that Hamid will be harder to locate. But, if his location could be discerned, a small group would be ideal, say six men total. After that we'd need detailed planning of the mission which would include both infiltration and exfiltration routes at the minimum."

"Done," the DCI replied. "I'll make sure Hobbes has access to the personnel dossiers from SAD, the Special Activities Division, and SOG, the Special Operations Group, who conduct covert missions for the CIA. They work for me gentlemen which means they work for you. You'll go through those dossiers and choose four operators."

"You're serious?" Sam probed.

"Completely."

Sam looked over at Bill. "What'ya think?"

"I think our wives are going to be royally pissed off, but other than that I'm in."

Robert continued on around the room. "Moving on. Laura. Emily. Your unique skillsets are perfect for interrogations."

"I'm sorry to interrupt, sir," said Russell, "but what skillsets are you referring to?"

"With your permission ladies?"

Laura nodded.

"Laura knows when someone is lying. Emily can bend people to her will, plant and remove memories and, to top it off, can summon the dead relatives of whomever she's touching."

Russell's face turned pale. "Seriously?"

"Would you care to try?"

"No no. I'm good."

Robert turned back to the women. "As I was saying, I'd like to utilize your skills in interrogations while we question people of interest. If Sam and Bill are successful in their mission to obtain Hamid Emal Habibi, then your skills in questioning him will be invaluable."

"We'll need to talk more about this," cautioned Laura. "We'll need to go over procedures and practice them."

"Of course, you're in charge. I'll set something up."

Robert finally turned to Thomas and Gavin. "As for the two of you I was hoping we could start with some non-invasive testing to see how proficient you are with your abilities."

"Like a test?" Gavin asked.

"Yes, exactly like a test. By engaging in these tests we'll be able to start mapping out your potential. As your abilities become honed, in this facility's controlled environment, we could eventually move on to DNA and RNA sampling."

Thomas immediately put his hand up. "One thing at a time."

"Of course," the DCI replied. "I absolutely understand. Let me assure you that nothing happens here unless you want it to. Now, aside from Hobbes who I'm sure can't wait to delve into the new tech at his disposal, I will need a few days to set up everything else before we get started. This facility is open to all of you twenty-four hours a day. If you have any concerns, complaints or needs please don't hesitate to inform Russell and he'll make sure they're handled."

Gavin pointed at the locked door against the back wall of the break room. "What's in there?"

"Through there is a tunnel that leads up to a secret door in the farmhouse. It's secured with a card reader and by the men stationed up top who guard this location."

Robert looked over at Sam and Bill. "If there aren't any other questions, perhaps you'd like to return home and be with your children before they leave for boarding school on Sunday. We'll make next Monday the project's first official day. Go, enjoy your weekend and rest up, we're all going to need it."

12

Sunday Oct 14, 2001

By the weekend Sam and Bill's children had come around and were excited to be headed off to boarding school to make new friends. Julie and Kim, on the other hand, were now coming to grips with the reality that they wouldn't be involved in their children's day-to-day lives anymore; a small oversight in the overall scheme of keeping them out of harm's way.

Instead of dwelling on it they spent their time playing in the pool together and concentrated on being a family. On Saturday evening, after dinner, everyone gathered together and celebrated Bill's forty-fourth birthday. In reality his birthday was on Sunday but Julie and Kim were headed out early in the morning to drive the kids up to their new school. The candles were blown out and the cake was cut as the family reunited once again.

Saturday night, right before bed, Thomas sat down with the four children with their parents in the background, and talked about the secret they all needed to keep.

"I want to take a brief moment and talk to you about my family's abilities. Now, I don't mean to bring up a scary memory, but you all remember what happened at SANDBOX, right?"

Amanda, Craig, Sarah and Edward all nodded back at Uncle Thomas.

"So do I and I don't like to think about it. But here's the point I'm trying to make kids. The world isn't ready for what my family and I can do. The reason we came to Virginia is to learn more about our powers while keeping them a secret from the world." He leaned forward. "It's imperative that you don't talk or tell anyone else about what we can do. If you do all of us will be placed in danger so I need you to promise me."

Sarah spoke up. "We've been talking and we'll all make that promise only if you'll do something for us."

Thomas and the other adults were taken aback but Thomas was curious.

"What?"

"We want you to spin us around in the air again."

"Have there been talks of blackmailing, young lady?" Sam asked.

"Maaayybbee," his daughter replied with a grin.

Thomas relented with his own smile. "Alright, alright. It's a deal."

And for the next ten minutes the room was filled with flying and laughing children, like a scene out of Peter Pan.

When Sunday morning rolled around a few tears were shed, and not just by the children, as they packed up the large Suburban and piled in. Julie and Kim sat in the front while Amanda, Craig, Sarah and Edward found room in the back for the two hour drive up to Culver School located in Harrisburg, Pennsylvania. Sam and Bill waved goodbye along with Thomas, Laura, Emily and Gavin as they watched the Suburban pull away and disappear down the long driveway.

"There they go brother," Bill said as he patted Sam on the back. "They're off on a new adventure just like we're about to be."

"That's for sure, on both counts. Oh, and in case I forget, happy birthday old man."

Bill laughed. "Yeah right. Fuck you too. I'm the youngest one out of the three of us and don't you forget it."

"The youngest, but certainly not the prettiest."

"What can I say, brains before beauty, which would make you the beauty."

Sam smiled. "At this point in my life I'll take it. And seeing as this is our last day of freedom before the shit hits the fan, anything in particular you want to do?"

"Just try and relax. After today the tone changes dramatically."

Sam nodded. "Yes, it will."

* * *

"Are we there yet?" Craig asked from the back seat.

"Almost," his mother Julie answered. "Are you getting nervous?"

He shrugged. "A little. What if the other kids don't like me?"

"Why should they?" his sister Amanda teased.

Sarah and Edward snickered.

"Hey. Be nice to your little brother."

"Mom, I'm not little," Craig complained.

"Right. Sorry sweetie. Amanda, be nice to your 'younger' brother."

"Aww. He knows I was just messing around."

"There's going to be plenty of other kids your age at this school," Kim declared. "Your mother and I were nervous when we went to school for the first time."

"Why?" her daughter Sarah asked.

"Well, for one thing, when we told the other kids that we were twins they didn't believe us. They thought that twins could only be identical."

"So what did you do?"

"The only thing we could do, be nice and smile. And before we knew it we were all running, playing and having a grand old time together."

113

"It sounds like you just made that up Auntie Kim," Amanda stated.

"Who knows," Kim responded. "Maybe I did, maybe I didn't. The fact remains that you're going to be a new face at a new school. Being nice goes a long way."

Twenty minutes later the Suburban pulled into a visitor parking spot at Culver School, just outside the main office doors. On their drive in what they had seen so far of the campus had perked the children's interests, which included kids riding on horseback in one field and playing soccer in another. As they drove farther into the campus the school's large and magnificent buildings presented themselves.

"Beautiful," Julie whispered.

After they parked the six of them made their way up the front steps of the main building. Inside a woman looked up from her desk as they approached.

"May I help you?"

"I'm Kim Nicholson and this is my sister Julie Paige. We're here to enroll our children. You should be expecting us."

"Of course," the woman said. "Welcome to Culver Boarding School. If you'll have a seat I'll locate our Headmistress. She takes pride in greeting every single parent and familiarizing them with the school grounds. I'll be right back."

The woman departed.

"So what do you all think so far?" Julie asked.

"Did you see the horses?" Sarah excitedly said. "I can't wait to ride one of them."

"Well, we'll have to see about that," Kim countered nervously. "I don't want you to get hurt."

"What? You can't expect us not to ride the horses. Are you crazy?"

114

"Now listen here young lady..."

Before Kim could continue they heard the sound of heels coming towards them on the hardwood floors. All of them watched as an older woman, with white hair and a stern look on her face, made her way over to them with a clipboard.

"My name is Headmistress Jones, or Ms. Jones if you prefer," she said with an air of superiority.

The children recognized her as an authority figure right away and unwittingly straightened their backs in compliance. Ms. Jones scrutinized her clipboard and then eyeballed each child individually, sizing them up before she addressed the two mothers.

"Ms. Jones," she said to Julie with an outstretched hand.

"Julie Paige," and was rewarded with a single pump handshake.

"Kim Nicholson." The same efficient greeting was repeated.

"And these must be your children, Amanda, Sarah, Edward and Craig."

Each child wasn't sure how to respond as their names were vocalized.

"Very nice to meet you all," Ms. Jones conveyed without a smile. "I do feel the need to express that it's highly unusual for any students to be admitted to Culver once the school year has commenced. Each of you," she said fixing her eyes on the children, "will need to work very hard to catch up to our current curriculum. Now, with that said, let me welcome you to Culver." She checked the clipboard again. "We have two third graders, Edward and Craig, and two seventh graders, Amanda and Sarah. I do hope you enjoy each other's company because you will be rooming with each other, in separate dorms of course.

"Now, without further ado, it's time to take you all on a quick tour of the campus and then get you settled into your respective dormitories." Ms. Jones abruptly left them in the entryway and opened the front door. "Time's a wasting. No dawdling children."

The four children looked up at their mother's with a 'what have we gotten ourselves into' look. Julie and Kim motioned for them to follow Ms. Jones out the door. Once they had Julie leaned over and whispered to her sister.

"I think I'm even afraid of her."

Kim chuckled as they followed Ms. Jones and their children. The first stop on the tour was the dining hall.

"Meals are eaten in the dining hall three times a day. Schedules, along with the following day's menu, are posted nightly. Food is to be eaten in the dining hall and not outside of it, unless specifically permitted. Any food discovered on your person or in your dorm room will result in an infraction."

"What's an infraction?" Craig asked her.

"Young man. An infraction will be levied on you if you break the rules. Too many infractions will result in punishment. Do you understand?"

Craig and the rest of the children slowly nodded.

"Excellent. Carrying on then."

Kim softly spoke in Julie's ear. "Are you sure we didn't bring them to a military school?"

Julie snorted as she tried to suppress her reaction.

"Is there a problem ladies?" Ms. Jones inquired without missing a beat or turning around.

"No," Kim answered.

"No, what?"

"No, Ms. Jones."

"Good."

Julie and Kim looked at each other and Kim mouthed the words 'holy shit' to her sister who responded with both a nod and a smirk.

Fifteen minutes later, after pointing out the pool, extracurricular activities and where their classrooms were located, Ms. Jones finished the tour outside the dormitories. They stood in the large courtyard that separated the boy's dorm from the girls.

Ms. Jones extracted a schedule from her clipboard and handed a copy to each of the mothers.

"Here are your children's class schedules along with their dorm room assignments and a list of rules we expect them to uphold. Also, there are extracurricular activities that we encourage our students to sign up for, including horseback riding, archery, canoeing and the like. Our primary goal is to teach and provide an education. The rest, as you are well aware, is whether each student is up for the challenge that's presented them. Now, if you'll excuse me, I have other matters to attend to. It was a pleasure meeting you." Ms. Jones turned to the children. "Good luck."

And with that Headmistress Jones turned on her heels and strode away. Everyone breathed a collective sigh of relief as she departed.

"Wow," Edward said, "she's intense."

Julie and Kim smiled. "Alright everyone. Why don't we go check out your dorm rooms and then go unpack the car. Sarah and Amanda, you're in room five-fourteen. Edward and Craig, three-sixteen."

As their kids took off to check their rooms Julie and Kim finally had a moment to themselves.

"They seem happy."

"And excited," Julie added.

117

"I really like the smiles on their faces. I think this is going to be one hell of a learning experience."

"For them or for us?" Julie asked.

Kim smiled. "Both."

"Yeah. You know what though."

"What?"

"I'm really going to miss them."

"Yeah, you can say that again."

13

Monday Oct 15, 2001

The house was much quieter than the night before, as well as during breakfast the following morning. To add to that sense of calm Gavin asked where Hobbes was. As it turned out no one had seen Hobbes since Wednesday's meeting with the DCI. A check of the garage, as they were headed out to work, indicated that his car was still missing. When they arrived at the farm they discovered his car was parked underground, along with a few others they hadn't seen before.

"Now that's either dedication or a problem," Thomas joked.

"I'm sure he's fine," Sam replied. "Let's go see what he's up to."

The group greeted Chuck and Dave as they made their way through the security booth and into the facility. Russell met them as they walked in.

"Where's Hobbes?" Bill asked.

"He's in Tech. Is something wrong?"

"He never came home," Laura told Russell.

"I know. He's been camped out here since last week fiddling with everything. You should go talk with him. He looks pretty frazzled."

With Russell in tow they walked around the circular hallway and took a right at the Tech wing. At the end of that corridor they found Hobbes in the midst of rearranging the entire room. The floor was littered with equipment.

"Hey. Hobbes."

Hobbes looked up as they all walked in. His hair was a bit disheveled and his clothes were wrinkled from use.

"Oh hey guys. What's up?"

"You tell us," Sam replied.

"I've been busy."

"We can tell. But busy for the past five days? You had us worried."

Hobbes stopped what he was doing and sat down. "Sorry about that. Once I set my mind on a task I just keep plugging away at it. You're saying it's Monday?"

Thomas chuckled. "Yeah. We're just glad you're okay. What have you been up to in here?"

"Just putting this place together so it works for me, that's all. Besides, they also have some seriously neat technology they made available to me. I just wanted to be ready for you so I'm not scrambling at the last minute."

"What do you have left to do?" Sam asked.

Hobbes looked around. "Not much actually. I just need to rewire a few consoles, initialize the backup system, test out the communications array and a few other odds and ends."

"You need to rest," said Bill. "Well, take a shower and then get some sleep."

Hobbes nodded. "Probably. But first I need to print out the dossiers that Russell sent over for you and Sam to look through. After that I'll take some down time."

"Fair enough," Sam replied.

Laura spoke up. "Hobbes?"

"Yes?"

"Thank you for taking this seriously."

"Are you kidding me? You're the only people that give a shit about me, pardon my French. I know you trust me so I'm absolutely taking this seriously. If it wasn't for you I'd be in jail alongside Calvin right now. You changed my life and this is the least I can do to say thank you. Besides, when it comes down to it your lives may depend on me at some point."

"Hobbes," Thomas said, "you're a good man. Carry on. Gavin and I are headed over to the Testing wing."

"Speaking of, "Russell said as he addressed Laura, "I would like to take you and your daughter over to Langley."

"CIA headquarters?" Laura asked. "Why?"

"Testing. We have some candidates coming in today that we're putting through the polygraph. We'd like you both there, if you don't mind."

"Okay."

Russell turned to Thomas and Gavin. "As for you two, you'll find someone new in your neck of the facility."

"What? Why?" Thomas asked somewhat concerned.

"This project is growing. I can't be everywhere at the same time to record your progress. Just go easy on her. I don't think she knows entirely what she's in for."

"And we can trust her with our secrets?"

"That's up to you to determine. She's been fully vetted but you get the final call."

Thomas nodded and then kissed and hugged Laura and Emily. "Be safe."

"We will," Laura replied as she hugged her son. Afterwards the two of them left with Russell.

Thomas looked over at Sam and Bill. "You guys have this under control?"

Bill smiled. "Get out of here and go play around with your powers. We all know you're dying to do so."

Thomas grinned. "Well, maybe a little."

He and Gavin left Tech and headed off to Testing. Sam and Bill turned back around and looked at Hobbes.

"The dossiers?"

"Shit, right. Sorry."

Hobbes turned in his chair and began accessing the information on the computer. Thirty seconds later the printer began to spit out paper.

"You might have to add more paper," Hobbes explained. "There's going to be sixty full dossiers coming out of there. It looks like you have your work cut out for you."

"Thanks Hobbes," Bill said. "No go take a shower and relax, you've earned it. You can finish putting this place together later."

Hobbes smiled as he stepped around piles of equipment he hadn't found a new home for yet and headed towards the bathroom.

Sam and Bill looked around at the clutter and finally cleared off one of the tables for them to work on. Bill grabbed what the printer currently had ejected and somehow managed to find a stapler. He sat down at the new work area and began to create ad hoc files of the SAD, Special Activities Division, personnel. They knew it was going to be a long day as they began to sift through sixty top notch operators to narrow that list down to just four men.

14
Monday Oct 15, 2001

Thomas and Gavin left the Tech wing to let Sam, Bill and Hobbes to do their thing and made their way around the circular hallway until they entered the Testing section of the facility. Thomas was on the lookout for the new female employee that Russell had just given him a heads up about. As the two drew closer to the control booth, which controlled the events in the actual testing area, a woman suddenly stepped out to meet them. She appeared to be in her early thirties but what caught Thomas and Gavin off guard was her shoulder length purple hair along with a long tattoo of a dragon that jutted down out of her left shirt sleeve. Its body wrapped around her arm and its head encompassed her forearm and hand.

She smiled and extended her right hand. "Hi. You must be Thomas."

Thomas shook her hand. "I am. And you are?"

"Oh right. Sorry about that. I get distracted when I'm excited sometimes. It happens all the time." She bent down and left Thomas with a confused look on his face. "And you must be Gavin. How cute are you?"

Gavin smiled. "You're funny and I like your hair."

"Aww, thank you cutie. I think we're going to get along just fine."

"Is that a dragon?" he asked pointing to her arm.

She nodded. "Do you like it?"

"It's cool."

"Miss?"

She straightened back up and looked at Thomas. "What's up?"

123

"You were about to tell us your name?"

"Yes. Sorry. It's Gabbi with an 'I'."

"Well, Gabbi with an I, what do you have in store for us today?"

"Wellll, that's the thing. I don't entirely know why I was transferred here. I mean, don't get me wrong or anything, this underground facility is waaay cool but he didn't tell me anything other than to keep an open mind."

"Who did?"

"Mr. Washington. You know, Russell."

"How about this then, Gabbi. What group were you working with before?"

"R&D. That's Research and Development," she clarified as she gave Gavin a wink. "Believe it or not I'm an engineer. A little quirky, some say, but an engineer nevertheless. It's a fun job and I never knew what the next project was going to be. I mean, it could range from…, well, I can't talk about it of course, but there were some neat projects. Wait, what were we talking about?"

"And you have no idea what you've been asked to be a part of or why you're here?"

Gabbi shook her head back and forth. "Although the NDA, non-disclosure agreement, I signed was crazy thick. It said that if I discussed anything that my life would basically be over. Now, that should probably scare away any normal person, but not me. I enjoy a challenge even though I don't know what I'm getting myself into." She paused. "What are you saying? What am I getting myself into?"

Thomas smiled. Anyone could tell that Gabbi was eccentric but aside from that she seemed to have a good head on her shoulders. To top it off Thomas had already come to the conclusion that she was friendly and had an open mind, which is what she'd absolutely need for this assignment she'd signed up for.

"I can see why Russell chose you Gabbi and I know we're going to get along just fine."

She visibly relaxed. "Soooo, the only thing I was instructed to do was to test the two of you, acquire baselines and then go from there. There's just one problem, I don't know what I'm supposed to be testing. I mean, no offense or anything, but both of you appear out of your depth. You can't work for the CIA, so what could a father and his young son be doing in this underground facility anyway?"

"How open minded are you?" Thomas asked her as he sidestepped the question.

She cocked her head to one side. "Have you 'not' seen my hair and body art? I'm not a traditionalist in any sense of the word."

"Alright," Thomas replied. "Then if that's the case you're about to find out exactly why you were brought on board."

Gabbi's eyes grew inquisitive. "Okay. Tell me."

"Oh, I think it'll just be easier to show you."

Before she could react Thomas lifted her body off the ground by thought alone.

"Holy crap! What the hell!"

He then moved her in a slow circle around himself and Gavin while they watched her wrap her mind around the phenomenon.

Gabbi's face quickly changed from fear to utter joy. "This….this is amazing. Holy shit this is awesome."

Thomas ended the demonstration as he gently lowered her back to the ground. Her eyes were wide open in amazement and delight.

125

"How did you…I mean…holy shit…I, uh…that was…how did you seriously just do that?"

He smiled. "Would you like to sit down for a moment?"

"That's probably a good idea."

The three of them entered the control booth. Gabbi took a seat at the console while Thomas and Gavin observed her brain work through what she'd just experienced. It didn't take long for her to recover.

"So you have the power of telekinesis?"

"I do."

"How?"

"All in good time Gabbi."

"Okay. That's fair." She looked over at Gavin. "And I don't suppose you're here just to look handsome?"

Gavin blushed a little. "No. I can do stuff too."

"Do you need me to stand up?" she asked.

Gavin shook his head. "No. Just don't be scared."

"Why would I be sca…"

The words hung in her throat as a small, black four-legged creature materialized next to Gavin's leg. Tendrils of black smoke, or at least what appeared as smoke, hung over its entire form. Its red eyes bore into hers. To Gabbi's credit she didn't react negatively at all. In fact, she bent forward in her chair to get a better view.

"Hello little thing. How are you?"

In response Stir began to wag his tail.

"Oh, it's adorable. May I touch it?"

Gavin nodded. "His name is Stir."

"Is that short for monStir?"

"You're the first person to get that," Thomas told her.

"Well, I'm kooky that way I guess," she replied with a grin.

126

Gabbi left the chair behind, got on the floor on all fours and approached Stir as close to his level as she could.

"Hello Stir. Aren't you a cutie pie. Yes you are. And you know it, don't you?"

Stir laid down as she made her way to him. His tail thumped against the concrete floor. She slowly reached her hand out and petted his head.

"Oh wow. That's really neat. He's solid but not dense at the same time. What a trippy feeling."

Stir began to purr as Gabbi continued to pet him.

"Soooo, where does he come from?"

"I don't know," Gavin replied.

"What do you mean?"

"When I want him he's just there for me."

"Huh. Interesting. Well, maybe we'll get to the bottom of that mystery. Can you guys do anything else?"

Thomas was floored. "You're okay with this, just like that?"

"This is a dream come true."

"Why?"

"Are you kidding me? All my life I've been an outcast. It's tough to grow up smart and into nerdy things like Star Trek, comic books and science fiction without being bullied about it. When I joined the CIA's R&D division I thought I was in heaven creating gadgets and shit. But this...holy crap....this is beyond any expectations I ever had. You're like Jean Grey, but a man. Well, you get what I'm saying. Oh, and I'm sorry for swearing in front of your son. It's just when I get excited I can't help myself."

"That's okay. He's heard worse."

"Dad, who's Jean Grey?"

"Gav, Jean Grey is a comic book character in the X-Men. She's a mutant and can move things with her mind just like I can."

"Oh. Okay. Cool."

Gabbi smiled, stopped petting Stir and stood up. "I'm totally freaking out right now, but in a tremendously good way. What else can you do Gav?"

Gavin looked up at his father. Thomas grinned and nodded.

"Well, I can heal people and I can also make a portal to another world."

Gabbi's mouth opened wide. "Shut...up. No way."

Gavin couldn't help but giggle. "Way."

"Seriously?"

He nodded.

"That's fricking awesome. You have to show me."

"Which one do you want to see first?"

"Well, in all honesty it really sounds like this portal thing of yours is the main event. Why don't we start smaller with your healing?"

"Kay."

"What do you need me to do?"

"Do you have an owie?"

Gabbi's eyes lit up. "Well, I cut myself shaving my legs this morning. You know, I wanted to make a good impression, and then duh, I'm wearing pants so that was a waste of time." She caught herself. "Sorry, rambling again." She rolled up one of her pant legs until they saw the band aid. She ripped it off and exposed a minor cut before either one of them could say anything. "Tada. Now what?"

Gavin took a few steps over to her and placed his hands over the cut on her leg.

"Watch."

He closed his eyes and concentrated. A few seconds later he removed them and stepped back.

"Are you shitting me right now?" Gabbi uttered in complete disbelief. "How did you do that?"

The cut on her leg had completely disappeared. There was no trace of her injury whatsoever.

Gavin shrugged. "I don't know. I just know I can do it."

"Well, young man, I am very impressed. That is one hell of a gift." She took another long look at her leg, shook her head in amazement, and then rolled her pant leg back down. "Okay. I'm trying to contain myself after my mind just got blown wide open, again. What's this portal thing you say you can do?"

"It's where I summon a portal. It takes me to my island."

"An island? Like an island in the ocean?"

"Uh huh."

"But didn't you say it was a portal to another world?"

Gavin nodded. "It is. I've been visited by dead people there, but recently I was shown that I could travel to other islands, recreate my portal and reappear someplace else on Earth."

Gabbi squinted. "So let me get this straight. Wherever you happen to be, when you make your portal, you always end up on your island?"

"Yes."

"Fascinating," she said as she mimicked Spock's favorite line. "What else can you tell me?"

"Tell her about the time issue," Thomas suggested to his son.

"That's right."

Gabbi looked back and forth between the two. "What time issue?"

"No matter how much time you spend on my island, when you return only a few seconds will have passed."

"You're talking about time displacement. That's incredible." She stood up and began to pace. "I mean, I don't even know

129

where to start with all this. I'm so excited right now that I feel like I just want to jump right in. Sleep? Hell no. I don't think I'll ever want to sleep again." She stopped and looked at them. "Do you have any idea how mindboggling this is? Oh yeah, now that I think about it you must, seeing that you're in a secret underground bunker with me blowing my mind wide open," she said as she used her hands to mimic explosions from her head.

"Let's just say," Thomas began, "that my family and I have been through more than you can ever realize."

"Your family? You're telling me there are more of you that can do things? Sorry, I didn't mean it like that of course. What I meant was…"

Thomas put his hand up. "It's okay. Really. You're excited. Why don't you sit back down?"

Gabbi nodded. "Right. Good idea." She plopped down on her chair and began to spin it around and around in three-sixties as her mind came to grips with what she's seen.

"The answer to your question is yes. My wife and daughter also have abilities."

She stopped spinning. "This day just keeps getting better and better. What can they do?" She quickly put up her own hand. "Never mind. I'd rather be surprised." Gabbi looked back over at Gavin. "Would you mind showing me that portal now?"

15
The Other Place

Rebecca stood in the corner of the Testing room and watched as Gavin summoned his portal. Gabbi's eyes opened wide in shock and disbelief. The shimmering gateway sparkled and radiated with an unknown energy. At its core the portal seemed to throb ever so slightly, as if beckoning something to enter its depths.

As Rebecca stood there she realized she hadn't felt the necessity to eat or sleep. *But who or what am I now? Am I plagued to roam this new existence for all eternity? What's my purpose?* It was then that movement, from across the room, caught Rebecca's attention. *What is that?* Before she could react four individuals, a pair of male and females, emerged out of the shadows and walked with purpose across the room towards her. As they approached Rebecca knew they were coming for her so she immediately turned around and walked away down the hallway. She didn't get very far before one of them called out to her.

"Rebecca."

She spun around ready to defend herself. "Who are you? What do you want?"

The same aged woman spoke up again. "We mean you no harm."

Rebecca relaxed a little. "Who are you? Wait. I think I recognize you, from the photos they had on the wall. You're…"

"Betsy and Michael Clark. Behind us are Thomas' grandparents, Ed and Claire Clark."

The four migrated over to Rebecca and she dropped her guard completely. Rebecca regained her composure as they all exchanged hugs.

"It's a pleasure to meet all of you. I...I don't know what to say really other than how unexpected this is."

"We didn't mean to frighten you," Betsy said. "We're all very much aware of how this new environment takes some getting used to."

"I still feel alive. Is that normal?"

Michael nodded. "It takes some adjusting. It's a combination of incredible freedom, even though we reside inside a very large prison. Well, at least it feels that way to me."

Rebecca digested that for a moment. "Thomas shared some stories with me on how each of you passed away. I'm sorry."

"We know dear," Claire said. "We've been watching."

Betsy spoke up again. "To clarify, we've been watching you watch over our family for some time now."

Rebecca was taken aback. "Really? To what end?"

"We've scrutinized your commitment and the sacrifices you've made," Michael told her. "You may not be blood, Rebecca, but you are unquestionably a member of this family."

"Well thank you, but how long have you been keeping tabs on me?"

"Since Hawaii," Ed clarified. "It began as soon as you became a part of our son's lives, and consequently the lives of his children, Emily and Gavin."

"I miss them," Rebecca said with sadness in her voice.

"We know, just like we're well aware that you've been shadowing them."

"I only want to protect them," she countered.

Betsy smiled. "As do we."

132

Something clicked in Rebecca's mind. "Is that why you're here? I mean, there were other stories Thomas told me as well, like four years ago when I tracked down where Thomas and Emily were located when they were being tortured and experimented on. I thought I was coming to their rescue."

"You were," Michael assured her.

"But I didn't get there in time, did I? Dr. Matsushita was about to do something to Emily but I was pinned down by the guards in the garage. That'…that's when the two of you, as Thomas explained, popped in and initiated a distraction. They escaped because of you two."

Betsy nodded. "And with your help. But we paid a price for our actions."

"A price?" Rebecca thought some more. "Is that why Emily was unable to summon either of you after that?"

"See. I told you she's smart," Betsy said to Michael.

"Yes," Michael replied, "you did."

"Why? What happened? What's preventing you from going back?"

"The Caretaker."

"The Caretaker?" Rebecca asked. "But why?"

"Because we broke the rules."

Recognition washed over Rebecca's face. "The rules. The Caretaker told me there were rules to follow but he only told me the first one. He said that direct interference isn't allowed; that no one alive should ever be made aware of my presence. He also said that others have broken that rule and paid the consequences. He was talking about you, wasn't he?"

"In part," Betsy replied.

"But you're here, talking to me now. What were the consequences?"

Michael sighed and finally said. "We can never leave the Other Place."

"I don't understand."

"Our energy is trapped here."

"Trapped? Where else would it go? Wait. You're saying there's more to the afterlife than this place?"

Betsy nodded. "Oh yes. Much, much more."

"So you're telling me that since you broke the cardinal rule of non-interference your punishment is to never move on."

"That's correct. The Membrane prevents us from ever returning."

"The Membrane?" Rebecca inquired.

"That's what it's called," Michael said. "It also prevents the undesirables from breaking the rules in the first place."

"The undesirables?"

"The ones whose energy are bound to evil. They must remain here for eternity."

Rebecca mulled that over. "Okay. So why are Ed and Claire still here?"

"We have unfinished business," Ed told her point blank.

Rebecca cocked her head to the side. "What does that mean?"

"No need to worry about that dear," Claire replied.

Betsy took Rebecca's hand in her own. "You're our last hope."

"I'm so confused. What are you talking about?"

"The Caretaker watches us, all of us. He's well aware that Emily and Gavin are anomalies and knows our relationship to them. The breach, as it's been termed, is the first of its kind into this world."

"So why am I your last hope?"

"Because a storm is coming and no one knows who you are yet. You need to use that to your advantage."

Rebecca withdrew her hand. "Storm? Advantage? You talk in riddles, just as the Caretaker did."

"It's up to you now Rebecca," Michael declared. "The children need your protection now, more than ever before. They are to be targeted and we can't do anything to prevent the harm that's coming to them. You, however, still can."

Rebecca didn't like what she had just heard. "Who's going to harm them?"

"They won't want to harm them. They're going to use them."

Rebecca was perplexed. "Who's they?"

"We have to go," Ed told them.

"But you can't leave. I have a million questions to ask you."

Ed, Claire, Michael and Betsy began to fade away, in front of Rebecca's eyes.

"Find a way to protect them before it's too late," Betsy managed to utter before they all disappeared.

And just like Rebecca was left alone in the hallway.

What the hell do I do now?

16

Monday October 15, 2001

Russell drove Laura and Emily off the farm and north to the headquarters of the CIA. Once there he escorted them through security, down a side hallway on the primary level, and stopped outside a door where he punched in a security code. It opened and he ushered them inside. The room contained audio and video equipment used to record everything that transpired in the adjacent room, which they saw through the one-way glass in front of them. Russell pressed a button on the console and shortly thereafter two people entered the room; an older male and a younger blond female. The young woman was asked to take a seat and the man adjusted the microphone in front of her.

"Russell, what are we doing here?" Laura asked.

"For the moment all we're doing is observing. That may or may not change, but if the subject lies I'd like you to tell me. Now please, why don't both of you please take a seat."

Laura and Emily sat down while Russell tapped on the glass. The man nodded in return, while the young woman briefly glanced over at the one-way glass, and he initiated the interview by opening the dossier in front of him.

"Miss. For the record, please state your name and age."

"My name is Cynthia Mack and I'm twenty-five years old."

"Thank you Ms. Mack. I want to start off by thanking you for coming back in. This is purely routine." He glanced down at the dossier. "It says here that you're applying to the CIA for an Operations Officer position."

"That's correct."

"And in your mind the definition of an Operations Officer is?"

137

"It consists of the gathering of human intelligence, in potentially high volatile situations, throughout any number of foreign countries."

"I see. And why do you think you'd be a good fit for the Central Intelligence Agency?"

"I'm intelligent, motivated and I'll do whatever it takes to get the job done."

Russell looked over at Laura for a reaction but didn't get one as the interviewer continued.

"Where were you born?"

"Spokane, Washington."

"And how long did you live there?"

"We moved to Los Angeles when I was seven."

"The three of you?" he asked.

"Yes."

"For what reason?"

"Excuse me?"

"I'll rephrase. Why did your parents move from Spokane to L.A. when you were seven?"

"I don't know. I was seven."

"She just lied," Laura stated from behind the glass.

Russell nodded.

The man carried on. "What line of work are your parents involved in?"

"My father is a lawyer and my mother stays at home."

"That's another lie, but it's wrapped in a partial truth."

Russell nodded once more.

"So it might be safe to assume that your family is well off, seeing that your mother doesn't work?"

"Yes."

"And your family's financial security allowed you to obtain a college education at USC, did it not?"

"Yes."

"Since your graduation, three years ago from USC, you found employment in the entertainment industry, furthering your budding acting career."

"That's right."

"And when that didn't pan out as you hoped, your next step was to apply for a position in the CIA?"

She smiled. "Is that a weird transition?"

He returned her smile. "No, not at all actually. As an Operations Officer I think you'd do very well with your qualifications. Living your cover to the n'th degree is exactly what's expected of you, don't you agree?"

"Absolutely."

"Good. So we can only assume that's why you passed the polygraph with flying colors?"

Cynthia's demeanor faltered ever so slightly. "What are you talking about?"

He pressed on. "You've been living your lie for so long now that it feels completely natural to you."

"Excuse me?"

"Who do your parents actually work for?"

"What are you trying to get at? I've already told you."

"No Cynthia, you haven't."

Her expression didn't budge an inch. It was a perfect poker face. "Well, I don't know what to tell you then."

The man placed her dossier on the table and stood up. "I understand. I do have one more question for you before we're done."

She remained silent.

"What if I told you your parents were detained three hours ago, in L.A., and are being held as suspected Russian sleepers?"

Cynthia slowly blinked but otherwise didn't react.

"And we believe you're a sleeper agent as well."

"That's ridiculous," she finally responded. "I want to leave now."

"She's lying," Laura said.

"We figured as much," Russell acknowledged. He picked up the phone and dialed an extension. "Detain her. I need five minutes prior to her being processed." He hung up.

As Cynthia got up to leave two guards entered the room. As the interviewer backed away she swung and hit the first guard in the face. The second one tackled Cynthia and within seconds she was subdued. They picked her up off the floor, handcuffed and walked her out the door.

"Let's go," Russell told Laura and Emily.

"Now what?" Laura asked.

"Well, you had your turn and now it's Emily's. We have five minutes with Cynthia and I'd like to make the best of it. Are you up for this Emily?"

Emily nodded. Russell led them out of the room and down the hallway to a temporary holding cell. Russell kept the two women out of sight until he knew Cynthia was secured and all alone.

"Let's go," he told them.

Laura and Emily stayed on the heels of Russell as he unlocked the holding cell. The three of them entered and Cynthia looked at them with tears streaming down her face.

"What am I doing here? Why are you holding me? I haven't done anything. This is all just a big misunderstanding, there's no other explanation."

"Lie," Laura whispered.

Russell bent down and spoke quietly in Emily's ear. "Will you do your thing?"

Emily nodded.

"Good. Once you control her I want you to ask her some questions for me."

"Kay."

Three minutes later Russell, Laura and Emily exited the holding cell with the definitive and incriminatory answers Russell needed to forward this case to the FBI. They left Cynthia with zero memory of their time with them. Russell couldn't wait to report back to the DCI on the absolute impact these two woman and their abilities had in nailing down a Russian sleeper agent who had nearly slipped into the ranks of the CIA. On top of that the information gleamed from the subject had been fast and efficient. He only wished he had more time with Cynthia but he knew that once the FBI got a hold of her, and her parents, it was only a matter of time before they'd break. Back in the car Russell took a moment to thank them.

"Listen. What you did back there was nothing short of amazing. I thank you and I assure you your country thanks you."

"You're welcome. But you already knew her parents were sleepers. Why not take her into custody at the same time?"

"That's easy. I wanted to see you both in action."

"So it was a test of sorts?"

"It was a dry run and you two knocked it out of the park."

"I'm hungry," Emily said as she interrupted them.

"We'll get something to eat when we're back at the farm sweetie," Laura said.

Russell spoke up. "I tell you what, if it's okay with your mother why don't I take you both out for well-deserved ice cream?"

17
The Other Place

Robert Aleman, the former General known as Raven, entered the region known as the Dark District. The hatred he held on to ebbed and flowed around his body in ripples. In fact, most of the inhabitants of the Dark District displayed similar indicators in this place and wore them proudly.

Raven's loathing stemmed from the simple fact that he was now dead. He'd reveled in the fact that after ten years in a hole, put there by Sam and Bill, he'd finally had the opportunity to extract his revenge. But his plan, time and time again, had been thwarted. He'd even kidnapped their children and was going to execute them, but they had disappeared out of that locked room somehow.

I don't understand. What the hell went wrong?

And then, after setting explosives throughout SANDBOX, he'd watched in amazement as Thomas diverted the live grenade he'd thrown at his family.

Was that divine intervention? How did he do that?

But Raven didn't get a chance to figure that out. Roberta betrayed him and before he could kill everyone she managed to shoot him in the shoulder. The timer on the detonator hit zero and that was the last thing he remembered.

But it wasn't.

After the building collapsed on him Raven found the will to stand up. The air was thick with dust and debris but for some reason that hadn't affected his ability to breath. He looked around and immediately laid eyes on the body of Roberta. Aside from her gunshot wound in her stomach, which he'd administered by his

143

own hand, her corpse was crushed. It was then that he glanced down and realized his body was in the exact same state.

What?

"Hello Robert."

A voice spoke behind him and Raven turned to face it.

"Who are you?"

"It is not who I am, but who we all are. However, you may call me the Caretaker."

"The Caretaker? What the fuck is going on?"

"Look around you. You know what's happening here so I'll be blunt and forgo the riddles. You didn't survive."

"Go to hell," Raven spat out.

The Caretaker smiled. "The world you left is better off without you and the hate that oozed from your pores. You were a blight. You brought misery to thousands of people with your poisons, your greed and your thirst for power. And for what? In the end it all meant nothing."

"Go away before I kill you." Raven began to walk away.

"Impossible. However, before you go let it be known, Robert Aleman, that I am imbuing you with the Membrane."

Raven turned around. "What bullshit nonsense are you babbling about?"

"You will be forever chained to the Other Place, eternally bound for all time."

Raven tried to shake that memory from his mind as he entered the Dark District, but it wasn't that easy. The Caretaker had left him there in the rubble, angry and full of rage. When Raven finally emerged from the rubble he saw the family, he'd tried to kill, gathering to take care of each other. He ran over and tried to attack Sam, but instead he just phased right through him.

144

Undeterred Raven began to shout and scream, but no one heard or acknowledged his presence.

"Frustrating, isn't it?" a familiar voice said beside him.

Raven looked over and saw his dead father, the man once known as Serpent; the same man he'd stabbed in the throat with a broken bottle and watched the life ebb out of him.

"Hello father. What the fuck do you want?"

Serpent smiled. "It's all over son."

Raven seethed. "For you perhaps. Go away old man before I kill you again."

Serpent faded away and Raven remained where he was.

He watched the emergency vehicles arrive.

He watched the families being treated.

He watched the television crews film.

He watched and watched and watched. Before he knew it all that was left was the sea of destruction, and he was alone.

Raven didn't know what to do. So he chose to pursue the one thing he'd always wanted, and that was Sam and Bill. So he decided right then and there to monitor everything they did. It was his new mission. Eating. Sleeping. Everything. He had to find a way to get to them and when the DCI arrived to speak to the family Raven was overjoyed at what he'd overheard.

Powers? Come work for the CIA? Secret project? Move to Virginia?

Raven couldn't believe his luck. And it was at that moment when he recalled ordering his men to sabotage SANDBOX's private jet. An evil grin appeared on his face and Raven's anticipation grew day by day as he watched them pack up their belongings.

In the van on the way to the airport Raven took an empty seat in the back.

Look at them. They have no idea what's in store for them. I'd weep for them if I wasn't eagerly waiting for them to die horribly.

At San Francisco International Airport the family went through the security and boarded the plane. Raven watched from the shadows as Thomas held back and Sam walked over to him.

What's the holdup? Get on the goddamn plane.

After they talked for a bit Sam walked over to a phone and made a call.

"Mikey. It's Sam Paige. Good, and you? Listen, how long would it take for you and your crew to come over and check out the jet? Yes, I know it's up to date on maintenance but I'd like to have the hydraulics checked out nevertheless. Yes, right now would be ideal. My entire family is here in the hanger. Twenty minutes? Thanks Mikey. See you then."

Fuck.

Two hours later Raven watched the events in the hanger unfold. He knew he could walk amongst the living unseen, felt or heard but he chose to linger in the back of the hanger nevertheless.

"Damn you Thomas. How the hell did you figure out that I had the hydraulics tampered with? If all of you had only gotten on that plane..."

Raven's shoulders slumped as he came to terms that Sam, Bill and their families wouldn't be joining him anytime soon. However, a wicked smile slowly spread across his face.

"I want Sam and Bill to die by my hands. But right now it doesn't matter. My sights are on you Thomas Clark. You and your little boy." Raven continued to talk to himself. "Oh yes, I've seen what he can do. Your little Gavin will make his way back to my neck of the woods one of these days, and when he does I'll make sure I'm ready for him. In the meantime, I do believe I have some new friends I need to become acquainted with."

146

It was at that moment that Raven headed to the Dark District.

* * *

As Raven entered the Dark District he was delighted to see so many other kindred spirits in one place. He felt absolutely at home here as serial killers, rapists, child molester, mutilators, and once powerful men and women shuffled to and fro along the district's roads. The Dark District was dim and was perpetually shrouded in black clouds.

The district hadn't always been like this, but over time, a term never utilized in the Other Place, the hazy outlines of this territory began to take shape. The Caretaker was all too happy to contain this shadowy enclosure at first, but the haze slowly changed to a blur. Then, as gloomier energy became trapped the area began to take shape, it grew larger. And when it did the Caretaker chose to concentrate on the energy he knew could move on, rather than the energy that remained. But the real crisis was the Membrane. It kept each and every single dark and wicked soul trapped within Other Place, and it was those souls that grew in number; seemingly endless additions.

As Raven entered the Dark District he strode down the main boulevard with an air of confidence until he stopped and breathed in the ambiance. The buildings were abstract and appeared somewhat blurry. The air was thick and tasted malevolent.

Now this is a place I could really get used to.

On one corner Raven saw a sign with the words 'Misery' over the doorway. On another corner a separate establishment was named 'Agony'. It wasn't until a block later that Raven saw a sign that caught his eye. It was called 'The Albatross'. From within its depths emanated the sound of glasses; glasses continuously being filled with whiskey, scotch and any other drink a lost soul could ever want. Raven was drawn towards the entrance and as he approached he pushed open the doors and disappeared inside.

18

Wednesday Oct 17, 2001

By Tuesday evening an exhausted Sam and Bill had narrowed down their top four picks from the sixty SOG operator dossiers they'd printed out on Monday. Every single one of the operator's jackets was top-notch and it had been a tough choice to come up with their top four. But, after they had, Sam had Hobbes sent their request to Russell who told them an offsite meeting would take place the following afternoon. There, a meet and greet would commence, individually to finalize group dynamics and team synergy.

Just after one p.m. Sam and Bill parked in the driveway of the address Russell had provided them. The location was designated as a safe house, and used by the CIA, but for the purpose of the meeting it provided a secure location for Sam and Bill to introduce themselves. The two opened the front door, entered the residence and came to a halt when Russell and their four top picks met them with stares. The four men were seated around a large table while Russell leaned against a wall.

Russell spoke first. "Good morning Sam. Good morning Bill."

Sam nodded.

"Morning Russell," Bill replied.

"I'll get right to the point before I depart." He turned and addressed the four SAD operators at the table. "Sam and Bill are working on a special operation that reports directly to the DCI. They have personally chosen the four of you for a unique mission."

"Which is?" one of the men asked.

Russell smiled. "First things first. Once Sam and Bill greenlight this team those mission details will follow. Until then consider yourselves under the direct command of these two gentlemen." Russell headed for the front door and opened it. "I'll sync up with you both later." He closed the door behind him and left the six men alone.

"Good morning," Sam began as they took a seat at the table with the other four. "My name is Sam Paige. This is my partner, Bill Nicholson."

"I know you," one of them replied. "You used to run SANDBOX. I saw on the news that it had been destroyed. What really happened?"

Sam nodded. "That's true, but it's a long story and something we're not going to get into at this time." Sam took a breath and continued. "I realize our meeting like this is unorthodox and that each of you has questions about why you're here. However, those will have to wait. Bill and I were tasked to create a six man team. Out of the sixty SAD operators we chose the four of you and here's our reasoning."

Sam began with the operator that sat to his left.

"Darius Hawkins. Twenty-eight. Expert marksman and proficient with any small arms platform."

"Carl Abney. Twenty-seven. Badass tech. I'm quoting of course."

"Eliot Marlow. Twenty-nine. Medic."

"And Jordon Marston. Thirty-one. Sniper."

"As for Bill and I, well, we're ex-Special Forces, and before that we were Airborne Rangers. We spent eight years in the Army and led numerous missions during that time. In eighty-five we founded SANDBOX, a Private Military Company. We started small, just the two of us, and grew it into an international business, which as you've all heard, does not exist anymore. After its destruction the DCI recruited us." Sam took a breath. "Now, if any of you think we're not qualified to run this team, or if you don't want to sign on without knowing what we're getting you into, then stand up and walk out of that door right now."

Sam and Bill waited while the four men glanced around the table at each other. None of them said anything or made a move to leave.

"Good," Bill said as he took over. "We don't have a lot of time so we all need to get on the same page right away. For the next nine days we'll be training together in preparation for our mission that departs ten days from now."

"What's our mission, sir?" Jordon, the sniper, asked.

"You'll know the answer to that in eight days," stated Bill. "Any other questions?"

The four SAD operators had been down this path before. They all knew what they had signed on for and reveled in the missions that took them overseas. With the memory of the two towers collapsing each of them individually came to the conclusion that they'd probably be conducting their exercise somewhere in the Middle East.

"Good," Sam said when no one spoke up. "We have a lot of work to do so let's get to it."

19
Wednesday Oct 17, 2001

Dr. Matsushita swiveled his office chair around and stared at the glass case that sat behind him. Inside were two thin glass rods that projected upwards, split off in forty-five degree angles and formed a 'Y'. Those two rods suspended a syringe and unless one looked closely enough it appeared to float in midair.

Yamato put his hands together in contemplation as he gazed upon the empty syringe.

It began with you Thomas. It all began with you. I know everything about you. And you remember why, don't you? It's because I made you tell me, at first anyway. But later, when you knew the pain was coming, you opened your life to me like a running river. But I understand; you just wanted me to stop the torture. Oh Thomas, the secrets you possessed. I took what you had and began to make it my own. But, you managed to take that away from me.

Dr. Matsushita looked down at his burned right arm and seethed.

I continued my research without you and tried to reproduce my results. But I failed, time and time again. That will end now that I have you where I want you. The time has come to fulfill my destiny and finally avenge my family. The United States will never know what hit it.

He swung back around to his desk.

The time has come to put the next step of my plan into motion.

He picked up his phone and dialed. "Get me his DNA samples."

20

Wednesday Oct 17, 2001

"Give it back," Craig demanded.

The older boy taunted him. "Or what? You gonna go call your mommmmmy?"

It was the third day of boarding school and the hazing had started. It had been unusual for the four children to start a month into the new school year, and in doing so they were the topic of the campus. That also meant the four of them had become targets, to students that either wanted to be friendly, or to students that insisted on making their lives more challenging.

The routine was to rise at six-thirty, eat at seven-fifteen and arrive to class by eight. Activities throughout the day were scheduled well in advance and everyone knew that the Headmistress roamed the hallways and courtyards in search of delinquent students. She often preached that 'punctuality is the key to respect and respect is earned'. Every student knew that to be a second late to class meant receiving a tardy slip, but more importantly it meant you would be punished; which included anything from washing dishes to cleaning out the horse stalls. And, to those unlucky students who wished to argue with the Headmistress, additional punishments would be issued on the spot.

Wednesday morning Craig, Sam and Julie's nine-year-old, had just been deliberately bumped into on his way to class by Tad, a hefty thirteen year old boy. As Craig was hit he spun around and was knocked to the ground. As he landed his backpack burst open and some of his schoolbooks spilled out.

"Watch where you're walking shit stain," Tad spat out.

"You did that on purpose," Craig shot back as he began to pick himself up.

Tad smiled. "Maybe I did, maybe I didn't. What're you going to do about it little man?"

Craig stood up straight, was dwarfed by the older boy and didn't reply to the bully's taunts. Other students, on their way to class as well, stopped and watched things unfold.

"That's what I thought." Tad bent down and picked up a fallen book.

"Give it back," Craig demanded.

The older boy taunted him. "Or what? You gonna go call your mommmmmy?"

"No," Craig said as he stood his ground. "But I might call my father and he will end you."

Tad laughed. "Brave words from a nine-year-old. Look around you. Look at everyone laughing at you. I bet you're a pussy, just like your old man." He extended a finger and poked Craig in the chest. "I own this school which means I own you."

Craig staggered backwards as Tad stabbed him with his fat finger. Some of the other kids watched as the school bully picked on one of the new kids. It was widely known that Tad's father was the school's top donor and Tad made sure everyone knew he couldn't be touched.

Craig recovered from the painful thrust, tightened his fists and stepped towards his attacker.

"Oh, how cute," Tad told the crowd in amusement.

What Tad didn't know is that Craig's father, Sam, had taught him a few self-defense moves. And the one thing that stuck in Craig's mind at this moment was the words his father had instilled upon him. *It doesn't matter how large your opponent is because every man is vulnerable in the same place.*

Craig stepped towards Tad, and with every ounce of strength he could muster, he kicked Tad square in the balls.

"OOoooo," the crowd collectively echoed.

Tad's face promptly transformed to an expression of pain, cupped his groin, slowly collapsed to his knees and then onto his side. The book he'd taken from Craig toppled to the pavement.

Headmistress Jones appeared out of nowhere and shadowed over Craig and Tad.

"What's going on here?" she demanded.

The students scattered as the word of the incident began to quickly spread.

"Mr. Paige," she said as she peered down at Craig and took in the obvious scene. This wasn't her first incident with Tad. "What do you have to say for yourself?"

Craig didn't know what to say so he only shrugged.

She eyeballed him. "Well, to me it appears as if the two of you accidently ran into each other and apparently Tad caught the raw end of the encounter."

"I don't know."

"And during the accident you must have dropped your backpack."

He shrugged again as Tad continued to writhe on the cold pavement; clutching his testicles.

Headmistress Jones continued. "Unless you tell me differently this clearly looks like an accident."

Tad mumbled.

"What was that Tad?"

"He…he…kicked…me…in…the…nuts…"

"You know Tad, it's tough to make out what you're trying to tell me. Did you just tell me that the two of you were fighting? If that's what you're implying then for the next two weeks you'll both be on shit detail. How's that sound?"

Tad shook his head back and forth. Headmistress Jones turned her attention back to Craig.

"And what about you, Craig?"

"I'd rather not."

She smiled. "Well good. I'm glad that's settled and all this was just an unfortunate incident. I'm sure in the future such mishaps won't be occurring."

Craig was unsure of what had just transpired but his brain screamed at him to flee the scene before she changed her mind. He collected and shoved his books back in his backpack. Tad rolled over to a sitting position and caught his breath; he knew he wouldn't be moving for some time.

Headmistress Jones watched them both mull over how she'd handled the situation and pulled a small notepad from her side pocket. She scribbled on one, ripped it off and repeated the process.

"Before you leave," she said as she handed the tardy slips to the two boys, "you know my policy on being late for class. You will both come by my office this afternoon where I will assign you a suitable punishment. Craig, you may run along now."

Craig took the tardy slip and vanished. He knew he'd just slithered out of a two week sentence by the skin of his teeth.

Headmistress Jones helped Tad to his feet.

"You know what I said," he declared. "My father is going to hear of this."

She smiled. "I hope he does. And you know who else is going to hear about this? Everyone. The entire campus will soon know that a nine-year-old took the mighty Tad down."

Realization hit the thirteen-year-old.

"So please, go ahead and tell your father because when you do I'll make sure two things happen. The first is that I'll tell him how

158

much of a shithead you are; like father like son. And second, I'll expel you so fast it'll make your head spin."

"You wouldn't."

"Try me. We appreciate your father's donations, but we don't require them. Your days of maliciousness are over." She held up a finger. "If just one more student complains about you it's over. Just one. Change who you are Tad, because this world has enough assholes in it already." She paused to collect herself. "Now, pull yourself together and make your way to the nurse's station. I'm sure they'll have a cold pack you can use."

21

Friday Oct 19, 2001

"It's very nice to meet you," Emma Duncan said as she greeted her guests. "Robert has told me so much about all of you."

Robert Duncan, the DCI, had invited the family over to his home for dinner. His wife, Emma, greeted them as they entered. All in all Thomas, Laura, Emily, Gavin, Sam, Julie, Bill, Kim and Hobbes were now in the house of their new boss, the Director of Central Intelligence. As they all entered the DCI appeared around the corner with a friendly smile and began to shake each of their hands.

"Welcome to our abode. I see you've met my wife Emma. Everyone, please come in and make yourselves at home. Coats go over there. What can I get each of you to drink?"

Five minutes later they'd found a seat in the spacious living room and settled in with glasses of beer and wine. Emily and Gavin were delighted with the Sparkling Apple Cider they'd been handed.

"So how long have the two of you been together?" Laura casually asked the DCI.

Robert gently squeezed Emma's hand. "Twenty-seven years. Before that we dated for three years before I popped the question. And you know what the secret to a successful marriage is? I'll tell you. It's communication. Open and honest communication. Secrets, as you know, are an essential part of my job, but not between my wife and I. And yes, before you ask, we tell each other everything."

The adults began to shift uncomfortably so Laura picked up where the DCI had left off.

"Everything?"

He nodded. "Of course."

"I see. And with our situation you deemed it necessary to potentially put our lives at risk by sharing our secrets with your wife?"

"Laura," Emma said, "I understand exactly where you're coming from."

"I highly doubt it."

Emma continued. "Let me assure all of you that your secrets are safe with me. My husband only wants the best for you and the amazing things you and your family can do. He sees the potential you offer the world." She paused. "What I'm sure you don't know is that Robert is at risk, just as you are."

"What do you mean?" Thomas asked.

"Do you think the house that you're living in or the underground facility were magically built overnight? No, they weren't. After my husband took over for the previous DCI, Victor Bannon, who needs no introduction, Robert came across Project Zelda. From that moment he protected you and your secrets from the rest of the world. For the past four years he's done nothing but plan for the day he could approach you Thomas." She turned and looked at Laura. "I know you can tell when someone is lying. My husband and I mean you no harm and only want to help. Do you believe me?"

As Emma finished speaking the group turned to Laura for her reaction. Laura took her time before she answered.

"Yes, I believe you. I'm just angry we weren't given a choice. As you can imagine we need to keep who knows about us to an absolute minimum."

Emma nodded. "I understand. I want you to know that I would never to anything to hurt you or your family. I also understand that your past experiences with those individuals who

162

wanted to exploit you have been just awful. I don't blame you for being angry and I want to take this moment to apologize for my husband. In his excitement to do the right thing he neglected to ask for your permission."

The DCI's face grew serious. "Laura, my wife is right. I trust her with everything because she's the only person I can talk to. But, in this case, I can see now that I was wrong. Thomas, Laura, my sincerest apologies."

The room remained quiet for a few seconds until Thomas broke the silence. "Alright."

"Thank you," Robert said.

"So where do we go from here?"

"Why don't we hear from you about how your first week went?"

"It was pretty awesome," Gavin interjected before his father could respond. "Gabbi's really nice and we've been practicing with our powers in the testing room."

"I'm glad to hear that Gabbi is working out," the DCI said. "She's definitely unique."

"Not to mention smart and fearless," Thomas added. "She jumped right in with the tests. To her this is a dream come true."

Robert smiled. "Excellent."

"Where do you stand on DNA sampling?" Emma asked.

"Truthfully, Mrs. Duncan…"

"Emma."

"Okay. Truthfully Emma, my wife and I are not comfortable with that aspect of the proposed project."

"Why's that?"

"It's too soon," Thomas replied. "I believe that you both have our best intentions at heart, but my family and I have been down this road before and we're very apprehensive. Right now I don't even think Robert knows where this is heading, big picture and all."

"Thomas is correct," conveyed the DCI. "Right now we're testing the waters to determine the extent of both your abilities and how they can be utilized. Would I like to initiate DNA testing to uncover the limitless potential you would bring to the world? Yes. But I can't force that upon you, nor would I. We're figuring this out as we go. But I can feel the excitement growing and it's only been a week."

"Excitement isn't the word I'd use," Julie said bitterly.

"Honey," Sam said. "Now's not the time or the place."

"It's okay Sam," Robert assured him. "We're all friends here. If Julie has an issue then I'd like to hear about it."

Julie continued. "While my sister and I appreciate the large house, and the boarding school tuition for our children, this situation has once again put our husbands and us in direct conflict."

"Go on."

"When we got married fifteen years ago we knew what our husbands did for a living. We lived with the possibility that they might not come home day after day, year after year, until we put our foot down. But, as history has shown us, we've all been placed in dangerous and unforgettable situations due to our husband's history as well as what Thomas and his family can do. And here we are again. It's as if Sam and Bill can't wait to take up arms, go to war and leave worrying whether they're ever going to make it home again."

Sam spoke up. "And what would you have me do Jules? The government shut us down and took everything we worked for."

"I don't know. But anything has to be better than what he's proposing," Julie said as she pointed her finger at the DCI.

"I apologize, sir," Sam said.

Robert waved him off. "There's no need Sam. Julie's concerns are my concerns." He took a breather. "Julie, I hear your frustration with this situation. All I can try to do to reassure you is to say that they're taking four elite operators on the mission with them. Throughout the entire operation they're going to have the full resources of the CIA helping them, from satellites, communications and drones. Now, I'm not saying you shouldn't be worried, but Sam and Bill understand the risk versus reward on this particular endeavor and have readily agreed to it."

"That's not reassuring at all," Julie rebutted. "If we're so open with each other why don't you tell me what their mission is, because they refuse to talk about it with us."

Sam rolled his eyes in embarrassment but kept his mouth shut.

"A fair point so here it is. I've tasked Sam, Bill and their team with the capture and extraction of Hamid Emal Habibi."

"Who's he?" Kim asked.

"He's one of the masterminds behind nine-eleven."

Julie and Kim looked at each other and then back at the DCI.

"I see. So it's even worse than I imagined. That's great, just great. I'm sure they'll just walk right into wherever this Hamid resides and snatch him up just like that. What was I thinking? This plan sounds foolproof." Julie stood up. "I'm sorry but I want to leave now," she said as she made her way over to the coat pile.

Everyone else placed their drinks on the coffee table and stood up during the awkward moment. There wasn't much else to say as the gathering came to an abrupt end.

Emma did her best to maintain her demeanor. "Why don't we take a rain check? We can do this again some other evening."

22
Friday Oct 19, 2001

"Well that was goddamn embarrassing," Sam shouted as the door to their bedroom closed behind them.

"Oh go to hell," Julie shot back. "You've always fought against getting out of this line of work and now look at you. Even though your company blew up, with us practically inside it, you can't wait to get right back out there. It's infuriating. When are you going to put this family's needs ahead of your own?"

"Are you kidding me right now? I'm doing this for our family."

She glared at him. "Don't kid yourself. You continue to wrap bacon around the dog shit you're feeding me but we both know it's dog shit."

"So you're making this about me?"

"Of course this is about you and your needs. There's a million other ways to make money out there, yet the two of you decide the best way is to put your lives at risk, again, regardless of the obvious fact that your family needs you around. So don't try and bullshit me again. I've looked the other goddamn way too many times already."

"What the hell does that mean?"

"Take it any way you'd like. Seriously, what the fuck are we doing out here? And why do you think it's a good idea to work for the CIA?"

"Dammit Jules. You know I can't sit idly by and let Thomas' family come under fire again."

Julie snorted. "Interesting choice of words. You use Thomas as an excuse but the reality is that you're going to be on the other side of the world and not here protecting him, like you said you were. No, I think you're never going to change Sam. You enjoy the action and adrenaline too much. Maybe you made a mistake getting married and starting a family. The kids and I should give you pause, but we don't. You've always done whatever you've wanted, so why shouldn't you stop now."

* * *

Bill slowly closed the door behind Kim and sat down beside her on the bed.

"So Julie's pretty pissed."

Kim nodded. "That's an understatement."

"And you?"

"Oh, I'm angry and disappointed, but not to the same extent."

Bill breathed out a quiet sigh of relief. "Okay. Talk to me."

"I have the same fears and worries that my sister has. This move to Virginia, the pampering and treatment we've been receiving; it happened all too quickly." She took his hand. "We were attacked, your company building was destroyed and everything you've worked for has been taken away. But look at you. You act like it doesn't matter. But the truth is I know you and I know how much this has affected you."

"I'm okay," he assured her.

"No, no you're not. And somehow your answer to it all is to gear up, trek halfway around the world to capture some bad guy. And for what? So you can redeem your reputation?"

"You'll never understand."

"What? What won't I understand?"

Bill dropped her hand, stood up and began to pace.

"What is it? What won't I understand? Talk to me."

He turned and faced her. "Our reputation is all we have. We built it up over eight years in the service, and then made it shine through our hard work at SANDBOX. But then, in one fell swoop, it was all taken away from us."

"And what about your family? We don't care about your reputation. We just need you to be around, safe and close, and not in some far away country."

Bill sighed through his frustration, both with the situation he found himself in as well the old argument he and Kim were once again engaged in.

"I can't change that now. Sam and I have already made the commitment. What I can tell you is we will talk about this when I get back." He took a breath. "Kim, I hear what you're saying and I understand where you're coming from. Somehow we need to come up with some sort of compromise going forward."

Kim slowly stood, walked over to Bill and put her arms around him.

"Thank you."

He returned her embrace. "We'll figure it out."

23
Sat Oct 20, 2001

Stir happily wacked his tail against the bedspread as Thomas tried to rouse his son early in the morning. Stickers yawned and stretched at the mild disturbance before readjusting and closing his eyes.

"Gav."

"Whhhhatt?" Gavin replied sleepily as he rolled away from his father's voice.

"Come on bud, it's time to get up."

"I don't want toooo. It's early."

"I know it's early, but today I want to test your portals."

Throughout the week Gabbi, Thomas and Gavin had initiated a series of basic tests to create a baseline of their abilities. Gabbi's goal, for the following week, was to build upon those newly established reference points and raise the level of complexity as she continued to test the limits of Thomas and Gavin's powers. During the week Thomas, watching Gavin and Gabbi's faces light up as he manipulated objects, he had finally felt himself start to relax and enjoy himself. It was if the huge burden of secrets he carried on his shoulders had begun to lessen, and he welcomed that relief. This morning, however, Thomas wanted to take the time and practice with his son's portal summoning so they'd be ready for Gabbi, and her enthusiasm, on Monday.

"But it's the weekend," Gavin whined.

Thomas nodded. "I know. And the quicker we do this the sooner you'll have to enjoy your Saturday. Now, move it kiddo."

Gavin gave his father one last look of distaste, reluctantly threw back his covers and slowly made his way out of bed. It was then that he realized that his father was wearing a t-shirt and swim trunks.

"Dad. Are you going swimming?"

"Maybe. I figured there's a good chance we'll both get wet on your island."

Gavin rubbed the sleep out of his eyes. "That only happens if you get in the water."

Thomas grinned. "Well, that could happen today. I want to try portal hopping from one location to another with you."

Gavin looked at him with a blank expression. "You know I've only done it that one time, and I had help from Uncle Sam's dad."

Thomas put his hand on his son's shoulder. "Yes, that's true, but you did do it. You were the one that rescued your sister and the other kids from that locked room after the General kidnapped all of you."

"I know."

"So we're going to try that again. Gabbi's going to want to see this in action so we'd better know what we're doing. Go change into your swimsuit and I'll meet you downstairs in a minute, okay?"

"Kay."

Thomas withdrew from his son's room and headed downstairs to wait. Shortly thereafter Gavin appeared at the top of the stairs wearing a t-shirt, trunks and bare feet. Everyone else in the house was still asleep as Gavin made his way down to his father with Stir on his heels.

"Ready?" Thomas asked.

Gavin nodded and immediately a portal formed in the middle of the family room. Thomas swallowed his fear, closed his eyes and walked through it. Stir leapt in and Gavin followed behind. Thomas instantly felt the warm sun on his skin as he emerged on the other side and the sand seeped through the cracks between his toes. He opened his eyes and regarded the small island that Gavin had utilized for years as his private place to get away from it all. The lone palm tree cast a shadow across the skeletal remains of Victor Bannon, the former DCI that had become obsessed with Emily and Gavin's powers and had wanted nothing more than to use Thomas' children for his own benefit. *And put my entire family at risk.*

Thomas snapped out of his meander down memory lane as Stir licked his leg. He looked down and smiled at the little monster that protected all of them. *Where do you come from anyway?*

"Dad?"

Thomas turned and looked at his son. "Yeah?"

"Are we going to do this or what?"

Thomas chuckled. "Alright, alright. I was just taking in the view Mr. Antsy. Hold your horses."

"You know I should be sleeping right now," Gavin reminded him.

"Fair enough." Thomas crossed the sand over to his son. "Okay. So let me get this straight. No matter where you are every time you make your portal you end up here on your island?"

Gavin nodded.

"Okay. And you said that Ray, Sam's dad, helped you cross the ocean the last time."

Gavin nodded once more. "In a boat."

"And where did that boat come from?"

Gavin shrugged. "Magic."

"Magic?" Thomas asked.

"I don't know. It just appeared. Come on Dad, this is a waste of time."

"Hold on. Don't be so hasty." Thomas thought about it for a few seconds. "Maybe you created the boat."

"No. I told you that Ray created it."

"Are you sure son?"

"Yes," Gavin adamantly insisted.

"Take it easy on your old man Mr. Cranky. I have another question for you. Have you ever tried?"

"I…" The words stuck in Gavin's throat and then a weird expression appeared on his face.

"Gav?"

"Umm."

"Gaaaav? You haven't tried, have you?"

"Welllllll…not really," he sheepishly replied.

Thomas smiled. "See. That's another reason why we're out here so we can figure this out on our own. Sooooo, if you've never tried then let's give it a shot. What happened last time?"

Gavin recalled the incident. "Well, Ray told everyone why don't we take the boat. And then I said, what boat? And then he moved to the side and there was a boat on the shore."

"Just like that?" Thomas asked.

Gavin nodded.

"It sounds like you could have made that boat appear."

"I've never been able to do anything like that before."

"And yet you just told me you've never tried, right? So let's give it a shot."

"Okay," Gavin said. "What should I do?"

"Try wishing for a boat."

"That sounds dumb, Dad. I don't think that will work."

"But you haven't even tried it yet. What are you worried about, that it won't work or something?"

"No, just sounding like a dork."

174

Thomas laughed. "Okay, I'll give you that one. But I suppose if I was on a deserted island with my father, and my pet monster, on an entirely different plane of existence, that phrase might be the one thing that gave me pause above all else."

Gavin chuckled. "Okay, okay. Sheesh. I'll wish for the damn boat."

"Thank you," Thomas replied with a grin.

Gavin collected himself and closed his eyes. "I wish for a boat."

As Gavin opened his eyes Thomas looked around. Neither of them saw a boat, or anything else. Nothing had changed.

"See, I told you it wouldn't work," Gavin exclaimed.

"Maybe you're doing it wrong."

"What? I've never even done this before. How could I be doing it wrong?"

"Then why don't we use the boat?" Thomas said.

"What boat?" Gavin asked with a slight edge in his voice.

It was then that Thomas turned around and moved off to the side. As he did so Gavin saw the boat that had materialized on the shore, obscured by his father's outline.

Gavin's face instantly changed from uncertainty to astonishment. "How in the hell…"

Thomas patted him on the back. "I knew you could do it."

"You tricked me."

"I just followed the same steps you told me worked the last time, right?"

Gavin couldn't argue with his father's logic. The boat was definitely here now. He scrunched his face up as he mulled everything over.

"If I did that then I want to try it again," Gavin finally stated.

"Excellent. I was hoping you were going to say that."

Gavin approached the boat and grabbed hold of its side. *I did this. I wished this into existence. I can do this again. It's got to be just like when I want Stir to appear.*

"I don't think I need to say anything," he explained to his father.

"What do you mean?" Thomas asked.

Before either of them could say another word the boat suddenly disappeared. Stir barked a few times in excitement.

"How in the…"

Gavin turned around and faced Thomas. "Watch this."

"What?"

Gavin motioned with his hand for his father to look. When Thomas turned around he saw another boat pulled up on the sand behind him. As he looked back at his son his eyes were filled with exuberance.

"Quick learner."

"Stubborn father."

"Guilty as charged. Shall we?"

Gavin walked into the water and then jumped up and in. Stir wasted no time and bounded over the boat's side. Thomas began to push the boat off the sand when Gavin spoke up.

"You don't need to do that. Just get in."

Thomas protested. "We're still stuck on the sand."

A second later the boat lifted up and floated in place a few inches above the water and the sand.

"Well shit."

Thomas climbed aboard and sat down.

"What do you want me to do now?" Gavin inquired.

"You said that Ray directed you to another island. Once there your portal took you back to the real world, but you ended up coming out in SANDBOX's motor pool."

176

Gavin nodded.

"Alright. Well, I don't have a map so I'm going to make another leap of faith and assume that you determined the destination."

"Me?" said in disbelief. "How? Ray did it."

"Or maybe he didn't. Maybe you did everything and he was only there to guide you. I mean, you just figured out you're the one that can make the boat appear and disappear on command. You did that, not Ray. So there's a chance that you know this next step as well."

Gavin went silent and chewed on the simple idea his father had just communicated to him. *Is it possible? Am I the one that did it? Was Ray with us just as my guide? I don't know. Maybe I can do it.*

"Okay," Gavin finally said. "I'm going to try."

"Excellent. Let's start with something simple. We entered from the family room. Can you try to take us to a place where your bedroom is the exit? I mean, we're only in swim trunks. I don't know about you but I'd like to keep the walk home as minimal as possible," Thomas joked.

Gavin smiled. "Let me see what I can do about that," he teased.

Gavin's smile retracted as he closed his eyes and began to concentrate. He opened them.

"Hold on."

Thomas gripped the side of the boat as they left the island behind and began to rapidly accelerate. Gavin's short hair rippled in the warm air as an island loomed in the distance.

"Is that it?" Thomas asked.

"Yeah."

Thomas was thrilled. "You know how fricking amazing you are, don't you kiddo?"

Gavin smiled proudly. The boat abruptly slowed and came to a halt fifty feet from the new island's shores.

"Over the side," Gavin said.

"We're swimming?"

"Unless you want to stay this is as close as the boat got the last time too. I don't know why. Race you!"

Gavin hopped out into the water and Stir followed right behind. Thomas took a look around and then followed suit. Twenty feet later he quickly discovered he could put his feet down and walked the last thirty feet to the beach. Gavin and Stir had already made it and were waiting for him.

"Slow poke," his son said as his father finally made it to the new island.

"You win," Thomas said. "Now, for the final test."

"Ready?" Gavin asked.

Thomas nodded and Gavin made his portal. Thomas swallowed hard and stepped through. His feet touched carpet as the portal's light illuminated his son's room. Stickers raised his head and looked over at Thomas in quiet contempt for disturbing him yet again. Behind Thomas Stir and Gavin also materialized. The portal disappeared and the room plunged into darkness. Thomas blindly made his way to the bedroom door, flipped on the light switch, turned and faced his son.

"You did it Gav," he said with a huge smile on his face. "That was amazing. Come here. I'm so proud of you."

Gavin walked over to his father, received a high five and then a huge hug.

"Thanks."

178

Behind them, on the carpet, Thomas saw the trail of sand that they'd left behind and smiled.

24
The Other Place

Unbeknownst to either of them, Rebecca had watched in fascination as Gavin worked through his mental complexities. She was delighted when Gavin realized he was the one that could summon the boat and was delighted as his frustration melted away. As Thomas and Gavin zipped away Rebecca felt something.

What is that?

She looked over her shoulder and gazed off into the vast distance. An unknown force pulled at her being.

What's happening?

Rebecca rose up into the air and sped off at incredible speed towards the peculiar sensation.

Something's different.

Obscurity loomed in the distance. Doubt, incomprehensibility, insignificance and oblivion hung thick in the air.

Why am I here? Why am I drawn to this place?

Below Rebecca, off in the distance, the Dark District materialized. Clouds of hate, repulsion and loathing filled the air.

Why this place?

A jolt of energy unexpectedly rippled down her body. As Rebecca lost control she plummeted from the sky and hit the ground so hard she formed a crater in the middle of the street. No one batted an eye or came to her rescue, nor should they. Rebecca was dead, as they all were, and her energy was unable to die again. She climbed out of the hollow her body had created in the street and stood up.

What the hell was that?

Rebecca looked down and the hole began to fill itself in. Moments later the street had repaired itself. Her body was unharmed and when she glanced around no one else appeared to remotely care what had just transpired. But as she began to collect herself she felt the strange pulling sensation once more, but stronger this time.

It's like a surge.

Rebecca took a moment and observed what was happening all around her. People seemed to be herding towards one particular location.

No. It's more like a gathering.

Rebecca began to walk, led by the sensation that pulled at her.

I don't belong here.

Her legs propelled her forward against her will, one in front of the other, again and again.

This place is evil so why am I drawn here?

Before she knew it she had placed her hand on the handle and pulled the door open. She looked up and caught the name of the establishment. It was called The Albatross.

25
The Other Place

Raven sat at the head of a large table within the confines of
The Albatross. He was particularly pleased with himself because
his effort to gather the individuals that sat at the table with him had
paid off. Raven viewed himself as the obvious leader, but so did
the majority of those that were now seated with him.

"Give us all one good reason we should stay and listen to what
you have to tell us," the late Victor Bannon stated with
decisiveness.

Victor Bannon was the former DCI who, after using Sam and
Bill to track down and capture Nikolay Dmitriev, took Thomas and
Emily hostage. That forced Laura, Gavin and the rest of the family
to flee to the Marine Base. On the way they were ambushed by
Alexei Vorobyrov, Nikolay's hitman. In the ensuing firefight Julie
was killed, along with Alexei and his crew, and she was
subsequently brought back to life by Gavin. When Victor
witnessed this he knew he'd stumbled onto something magnificent,
powerful and life changing. He immediately focused on capturing
the entire family so he immediately took Thomas and Emily
prisoner. The family, after leaving Rebecca in a coma at the
hospital, was able to escape Hawaii undetected on a luxury yacht.

Meanwhile, Victor kept Sam and Bill out in the field where
they eventually parachuted into Cuba and assaulted Nikolay's
stronghold. On the beach, as Sam waited for extraction with
Nikolay, Bill and their team, the attack in Hawaii led by Alexei,
commenced. Sam heard Laura's cries of sorrow when she realized
his wife Julie had been shot through the heart. With that
knowledge fresh in his mind, and Nikolay standing in front of him,
Sam put a bullet in Nikolay's head and left his body on the beach.

However, his entire team was detained and handed over to Victor. It was at that point that Victor made Sam and Bill do his bidding by insinuating that he held their family hostage.

It wasn't until much later when Thomas, along with Rebecca, was finally able to catch up to Sam and Bill and fill them in on everything that Victor had done. But by this time Victor had tracked down the yacht and sent a team to retrieve them. Everyone on board was slaughtered and the family was taken. Sam, Bill and Thomas mounted a rescue operation that backfired. Victor, with his gun extended towards Laura, pulled the trigger. Thomas reached out with his mind, as he discovered his new ability, and pushed Victor's arm which altered the bullet's trajectory just enough to miss Laura's head.

With Victor in custody the family made a tough decision. To keep their secrets safe Victor had to go, but he was still the DCI and therefore a very powerful man. So they had Gavin form a portal and Sam pushed Victor through, and he was never heard from again. Victor perished on that island, in a place and time he could never escape from. His skeleton remains are the only thing that proved he once existed. But as Victor died of dehydration his anger grew; he knew he'd been bested and as he died he vowed for revenge.

"Give us all one good reason why we should stay and listen to what you have to tell us," the late Victor Bannon stated with decisiveness.

Sitting at the table, along with Victor and Raven, were Nikolay Dmitriev, Alexei Vorobyrov, Anna Garland and Frank Russell, otherwise known as Yuri.

"You're all here for the same reason Anna and I are here," Raven replied. "And that's because we have unfinished business to contend with."

"And what business may that be?" Nikolay asked.

Raven took the time to look at each of them before he answered. "We're all here because of the same three people; Sam Paige, Bill Nicholson and Thomas Clark."

Victor scoffed. "So what? You brought us here to tell us something we already know?" Victor stood up from the table. "You're dead General. In fact, we're all dead. There's nothing we can do about that, or to them at this point. This is a waste of time. I'm leaving."

"What if there is?" Raven declared.

Victor paused and then turned back. "What?"

Raven smiled. "What if there's a chance to kill all of them? Please, sit down. I have an idea I'd like to share with everyone."

*　*　*

As the door to The Albatross closed behind her the pulling sensation that Rebecca was unable to fight against immediately faded. She looked around the large establishment and saw hundreds of people. As she walked around some of them seemed familiar.

What the hell? What is this place?

As Rebecca moved farther in she began to recognize more and more faces.

That's one of the guards I shot at Facility Thirteen, when I was trying to rescue Thomas and Emily. Wait, there's another one.

She kept walking as she scrutinized her surroundings.

That one seems familiar as well. That's right. He was one of Victor Bannon's bodyguards. I knew I recognized him from the surveillance cameras.

Further in she stopped short and just stared.

And there's the man that shot me in the head. He was killed during the assault on SANDBOX.

Rebecca began to have mixed emotions but there was nothing she could do about it. Every last person in here was just energy in the form of the body they used to inhabit. She knew she couldn't do a damn thing to any of them even if she wanted to. She finally averted her gaze from the man and relocated. It was then that she saw the large table and the specific individuals that were assembled around it. One in particular Rebecca focused in on right away.

Anna Garland. It was you who turned off my life support system. You're the one responsible for killing me.

Rebecca nearly jumped over the barricade and made a run at Anna, but her anger quickly faded as she realized who the other individuals seated with Anna happened to be. Rebecca slowly moved through the crowd until she was hidden by a wooden support column.

Shit. What the hell is General Aleman doing with Anna, Nikolay, Victor, Alexei and Yuri? It's like a meeting of the worst of the worst. I have to get closer.

Rebecca wove her way through the large crowd and used them to mask her approach towards the table. When she managed to get ten feet away she found an empty seat and quickly sat down with her back towards the group. She tried to focus on what they were saying.

"What if there's a chance to kill all of them. Please, sit down. I have an idea I'd like to share with everyone."

Victor slowly sat back down. "Very well. You have my attention."

"And mine as well," Nikolay added. "What exactly are you proposing General?"

Raven grinned. "If you all take a quick look around the room you're going to find a commonality. And do you know why that is?"

"Enough of your games," Victor warned him.

"I'll tell you," Raven continued undeterred. "Everyone you see around you was drawn to this place because they, in one form or another, have been affected by Sam, Bill and Thomas."

Rebecca couldn't believe she hadn't come to that conclusion on her own already. *That's why I was drawn here. It makes perfect sense. But how did he do it?*

"And you did this?" Yuri asked. "You somehow made them come here?"

Raven shook his head. "No. We did," he said as he motioned around the table with his hand.

"Explain," said Nikolay.

"The power that drew these souls here, that power comes from our collective strength. The six of us, together, pulled all these inflicted souls to us."

"For what purpose?" Anna asked.

"To prove to all of you that we're stronger together. And with that strength we will enact our revenge."

Victor leaned forward, very interested. "How?"

Raven couldn't contain himself. "I'm glad you asked."

26

Monday Oct 22, 2001

"I'm moving!" Sam yelled. "Covering fire!"

"Go!" Bill shouted as he leaned out and opened fire on enemy positions in the distance.

Carl and Eliot, who were next to Bill, kept their heads on a swivel in preparation for the next bound. Sam emerged from cover and sprinted towards the next protected barrier. Automatic gunfire erupted from a bunker two-hundred feet away and was quickly silenced as Jordon, the team's sniper, nullified the target.

"Nice shot," Darius said over comms even though he was stationed next to Jordon and acting as his spotter.

"I do what I do," Jordon smugly replied.

"Cut the chatter," Sam ordered. "We still have targets to engage. Focus."

The six man team was practicing in a mock-up urban environment. The four Special Activities Division men they'd chosen for this mission had readily agreed to work with Sam and Bill on a secret mission they still didn't know the details of. In the meantime they had been drilling nonstop together to enhance team cohesion and trust, and that included this current live-fire scenario.

"Preparing to move," Bill told his teammates.

Eliot stood right behind Bill, at the corner of the building, so that he could cover Bill as he advanced. Carl maintained his position at the opposite corner of the same building which prevented any enemy combatants to engage them from behind.

"Moving!" Bill declared. He swung out from the protection of the building and sprinted towards Sam's position.

Jordon's voice materialized in their ears. "Sam. Contact, two-o'clock. Fifty feet."

Sam tilted to his right as he simultaneously extended his weapon. He placed his iron sights over the target and depressed his trigger.

"Paper target down," Jordon confirmed from his elevated position.

A second later Bill finished his bound and appeared next to Sam.

"Miss me?" he joked.

"Funny," Sam replied. "Alright, Carl and Eliot, it's your turn to travel. Bill and I have you covered."

"Roger that," Eliot replied.

"No movement," Jordon said as he swept the area with his sniper scope.

"Confirmed," Darius added. "No targets."

"Go," Sam told them.

"Moving," Eliot broadcasted.

*   *   *

Sam handed out cold beers to each member of his team and then grabbed a final one for his own consumption.

"Good work out there."

"A few more drills like that and we'll know what to expect from each other out there in the real world," Bill concluded.

"Speaking of," asked Darius, "when are we going to get the mission lowdown?"

"Ditto," Carl added. "What's all this training leading up to?"

Sam put up a hand. "Patience. On Thursday we'll have a sit down with the DCI where we'll go over the details of our mission. Until then we have a few more days of group training, and trust me, we're going to need it."

27

Monday Oct 22, 2001

Monday evening, back at home, Thomas, Laura, Emily and Gavin sat down privately to have a family discussion. For the past week they'd all been actively engaged in Project PsyOps, staying busy and hadn't spent as much time together as they were used to.

"So Em," Thomas began, "how're things?"

"Good," she replied.

"And Russell's not having you do anything you're not comfortable with?"

Emily shook her head no.

"Okay. Are you feeling overwhelmed at all?"

"Daddy, I like it."

Thomas wasn't ready for that answer. "You enjoy what you're doing?"

"Uh huh," she nodded.

"Me too," Gavin added.

"Shhh," Thomas whispered to his son as he tried to conceal his grin. Thomas tried to compose himself as he looked over at Laura. "Would you care to expand on what your daughter is talking about?"

Laura smiled. "I see what's going on here."

"What?" Thomas replied in feigned innocence.

"Don't try and pull the wool over my eyes mister. You're having a good time, just like we are. It's completely obvious."

"That's crazy talk."

"Liar," she immediately said and then turned to her son. "Since your father can't help himself, what's the truth Gav? Have you two been having a good time testing your powers this past week?"

Thomas gently elbowed his son in the ribs and Gavin opted to play along. "Noooo. No. No. Of course not. It's been horrible, mom."

Laura couldn't help herself. "Liars, both of you."

Emily and Gavin giggled.

"It sounds like we're all in the same boat," Emily stated.

"It most certainly does," her mother answered. "And I think your father and I are more surprised at that than anything else."

Thomas nodded and took Laura's hand in his own. "It's like a weight has been lifted. I don't know, it's hard to describe."

"I get it sweetie. We're finally able to relax and be who we are."

"Yes. That's it completely. How're the two of you faring?"

"Really well. As weird as this sounds, especially coming from me, but I'm glad we're doing all of this." Laura looked over at Emily. "And Em's PTSD is under control, which was the main thing I was concerned about when I agreed to this endeavor. I was very reluctant to put her in a position where she'd take on more memories from other people which could back track her progress. But so far so good. She's really a trooper and I'm very proud of her."

"Mommmm," Emily said with some embarrassment.

"There's nothing to be embarrassed about," Thomas said. "I'm proud of you as well. You've come a long way in a short amount of time." He paused. "And speaking of going places in short amounts of time," Thomas said as he roughed up his son's hair. "This young whippersnapper's abilities are progressing nicely."

"Dadddd, quit it," Gavin said as he rearranged his hair.

"Ohh really," Laura said as she waited for her son to explain. "Do tell."

"Well," Gavin said, "for one thing I realized that I was the one that can create the boat."

"The boat?" Then it hit her. "Ohhh, the boat. You can do that?"

Gavin nodded. "And Dad and I took it to another island."

Laura leaned back. "Is that so? And when did that happen?"

"Saturday morning," Gavin stated. "He woke me up early."

"Interesting." Laura stared at her husband. "Care to explain?"

"Thanks a lot pal," Thomas whispered.

"Mom's sitting right there. What am I supposed to do, lie?"

"You could try," he teased.

"Yeah right."

Thomas knew he'd been caught. "Well, what can I say, it had been an exciting week and I didn't want it to end I guess."

Laura smiled. "It's okay, Em and I feel the same way."

"Yeah Dad," Emily said with a proud smile. "We even caught a Russian sleeper."

Thomas wasn't prepared. "Wait. What?"

Laura spoke up. "Oh shit, I totally thought I told you about that."

"No, it's okay. We've all been busy but I guess we should have these sit downs more often. What happened?"

"Well, Russell had us watch an interview with a potential female CIA candidate. I forgot her name."

"It was Cynthia," Emily said.

"Right. Thank you sweetie. Cynthia. Anyway, long story short Russell was already aware that her parents were sleeper agents but wanted confirmation that she was as well. She had passed the lie detector stage of the interviewing process with flying colors, but I was able to pick up that what she was shoveling was pure BS."

"Nice," Thomas said.

"She was detained and then it was Emily's turn. Our daughter made short work of her and Russell was very impressed."

Thomas looked at his daughter. "This is important. Are you okay with that Em?"

His daughter nodded. "I'm fine."

"And it wasn't scary?"

She shrugged. "Not really. Cynthia was restrained so she couldn't do anything to me. And after I was done she didn't remember we'd even been there."

"So you're good?"

Emily nodded. "Daddy, I'm fine. I told you I liked it."

"Why?"

"That's easy. I like it because I feel like we're going after the bad guys instead of them coming after us."

The truth of Emily's statement hung over the table for all of them to absorb.

"From the mouths of babes," Thomas finally said and then took a few moments to look at his family. "Alright, it looks and sounds like we're moving forward with the project. My only concern is that I need to make sure we all stay safe. Just keep alert out there. We may be enjoying ourselves but remember, we're still targets."

28

Tuesday Oct 23, 2001

Russell found Laura and Emily in the Testing wing of the underground facility. They, along with Thomas, Gavin and Gabbi, were all engaged in a friendly chat as he walked up.

"Good morning everyone," he said.

"Hey Russell," Thomas replied.

Laura returned his greeting. "Morning."

"Good morning, sir," Gabbi added.

Russell smiled. "You can relax Gabbi, we're all friends here."

"Yes sir. I mean, sure, no problem. You know, it's cool."

Gavin giggled.

Russell turned to address Thomas. "So how's Gabbi treating the two of you?"

Gabbi's eyes opened wide as her performance was suddenly the topic of discussion.

"She's been great. Gavin and I are having a fun time with all our testing, and that's due to Gabbi and her unique way she handles us."

"I'm glad to hear it." Russell looked down at Gavin. "And what do you think of Gabbi?"

"She's awesome," he immediately replied.

Gabbi visibly relaxed when Russell nodded. "Good good."

"Can I talk to you for a second?" Thomas asked.

"Sure," Russell replied.

Thomas motioned and the two of them took a few steps off to the side. He lowered his voice. "So I hear that you have a Russian sleeper agent, or family rather, in custody."

"I apologize that you didn't hear that from me or the DCI yourself. I should have made the time during this past week to bring you up to date on the CIA's progress into those investigations. Without your father's information on these sleepers that you personally brought to our attention four years ago, the United States would have continued to be at risk."

"So you've picked them all up?" Thomas asked. "All the sleepers have been accounted for?"

Russell shook his head. "No. But we've put a serious dent in how many remain on U.S. soil. However, with that said, we're operating under the assumption that any remaining sleepers won't be woken due to the fact that Nikolay Dmitriev's voice was effectively silenced on that Cuban beach. Since his death the bombings that occurred throughout our country immediately stopped four years ago."

"Unless someone else in the Russian hierarchy is just biding their time to activate them at a later date."

"Yes. That is a plausible alternative, which is why we're still actively tracking down and pursuing other sleepers like Cynthia Mack and her parents. Your wife and daughter are now instrumental in this process, for obvious reasons."

Thomas nodded. "Fine, but I expect to be kept in the loop from now on."

"Absolutely. And again, my apologies. This past week has been hectic and new for all of us. We'll iron out the bugs in no time, I promise."

Emily broke off from her mother and came over. "So where are you taking us today?" she asked Russell.

"As a matter of fact, I was just talking to your father about that very same thing. I'd like to take you and your mother to go have a chat with Cynthia's parents."

"Is that the same woman we had a discussion with last week?"

"Yes," Russell replied.

Laura joined the group.

"Kay. I want to make sure we get them."

"Get them?" her mother asked.

Emily nodded. "I know that the men who attacked us in Hawaii were sleepers." Her face took on a seriousness that they hadn't seen before. "That's a day I'm never going to forget. So yes, I want to get them."

* * *

Russell parked next to a nondescript building, in downtown Washington D.C., and turned off the motor.

"This is one of our safe houses. Traditionally we'd handle questioning outside of U.S. territory, but covertly flying both of you to a CIA black site would raise too many questions, and too many people would see you."

"Why didn't you bring them to the underground facility instead?" Laura inquired.

"The less people that know about that place the better. We're erring on the side of caution to maintain your family's anonymity and safety." He paused for a second and then continued. "Inside are Rick and Leslie Mack, the parents of Cynthia Mack. We already know from your time with their daughter last week that Cynthia was born in the United States. But, when she turned sixteen they revealed to her that that were Russian sleepers and from that moment on her ideology changed."

"What do you want us to do?" Laura asked.

"I'm looking to see whether they're aware of, or had any contact with, other sleepers in this country. Aside from that I want to gather a history of their time here in the U.S. and before."

197

"I'm guessing previous sleepers weren't terribly cooperative with this line of questioning?"

Russell shook his head but then smiled. "That's why I'm glad we have the two of you on our side. Shall we?"

* * *

Rick and Leslie Mack were seated side by side in a small room. They were secured by handcuffs with short chains, which were then fed through eyeholes in the metal table they sat behind. The two had been left alone for the past hour so when Russell opened the door he wasn't surprised when Rick lit into him.

"This is outrageous! I don't know who you are but you have no right holding my wife and me. I'm a lawyer and when I get done suing you for illegal detainment, amongst other charges, you'll wish you'd never been born. You will release us this instant. We've done nothing wrong."

Russell calmly pulled out one of the two chairs opposite them and sat down. "You are Rick and Leslie Mack, originally from Spokane, Washington."

"That's correct," Rick replied defensively. "So what?"

"Eighteen years ago, in nineteen eighty-three, you moved from Spokane and relocated to Los Angeles."

"And?"

"Why?"

Rick and Leslie glanced at each other before he answered. "I was offered a better paying job in L.A. so I took it. Look, I've answered all of these pointless questions before. I demand to know why we're being held and what we're being charged with."

Russell was undeterred. "Have you spoken to your daughter, Cynthia, lately?"

Leslie's eyes opened wider. "What do you mean? Has something happened to her?"

"She's been arrested."

"What?" Rick refuted. "On what charge?"

"Conspiring against the United States of America," Russell stated as he closely observed their reactions.

"That's ridiculous."

"Do you know she recently applied for employment at the CIA?"

"Yes," Leslie replied. "Of course I did, she's my daughter."

"So you're close to Cynthia Mrs. Mack?"

"She's my daughter. What kind of question is that?" she shot back. "Who do you think you are? What are my husband and I doing here?"

Russell pushed his chair back and stood up. "That is an excellent question and you'll be happy to know that we'll have a definitive answer to your question very shortly. Now, if you'll excuse me, I have some colleagues to confer with."

Russell left the room, closed the door behind him and walked into the adjoining room. "So?"

Laura spoke up. "The only question they lied about was when you asked them what their names were."

"Alright. And what about Cynthia?"

"They're close to their daughter, no doubt about that. Aside from that they're frustrated and it shows."

Russell smiled. "I know. But now it's time to get down to the nitty-gritty." He turned to Emily. "Ready?"

She nodded.

"Good. I'll be right there in the room with you. Which one do you want to do first?"

"Both."

Russell and Laura hadn't expected that answer. "Both?" he asked.

"I want to try something new," Emily said. "If it doesn't work then you can separate them."

"Are you sure?" Laura probed. "You haven't tried this before."

"It'll be fine, and if it works it'll make this process that much faster."

"I'm game if she is," Russell stated.

"Alright," Laura said. "Just be careful."

"I will mom."

Emily followed Russell to the door. He opened it, they both entered and he closed it behind them. The two sat down in chairs opposite the Mack's.

"What the hell is this?" Rick demanded. "Who's this little girl and what does she have to do with any of this?"

"I'm glad you asked," Russell replied as he pushed a button. Instantly the slack in their handcuff chains retracted into the table. Their bound hands were pulled forward and secured firmly against the table.

"Hey! What the hell!?" Rick yelled.

Before any further complaints could be aired Emily took the opportunity and put one of her hands on each of them. Rick and Leslie simultaneously relaxed and stopped struggling. Their faces went flaccid.

"How're you doing?" Russell asked Emily.

"So far so good."

He smiled and produced a typed list of questions. "This is what I'd like you to ask them."

"Kay."

Emily started with the first question.

"Is Rick Mack your real name?"

"No," Rick replied.

"I'm going to change these questions to plural now that my experiment is working."

"Go for it," Russell replied.

"Is Rick Mack and Leslie Mack your real names?"

"No," they replied in unison.

"What are your real names?"

"Yakim Anatoli."

"Katia Anatoli."

"Are you Russian sleepers?"

"Yes."

"How long have you been stationed in this country?"

"Twenty-five years."

"How old were you when you moved to the United States?"

"Twenty-five."

Russell leaned back in his chair and shook his head. *Damn. They're really playing the long game.*

"Where were you born?"

"Moscow."

"What year were you born?"

"Nineteen fifty-one."

"How old are you now?"

"Fifty."

"Where was your daughter born?"

"In Spokane, Washington."

"Where was she conceived?"

"In Moscow."

Russell quickly wrote a new question for Emily to ask them.

"So you were pregnant with Cynthia before you arrived in the United States?"

"Yes."

Russell pointed to the next question for Emily to ask.

"What's the name of your handler?"

"Nikolay Dmitriev," they both answered.

"Do you know the names of any other sleeper agents?"

"No."

"During your twenty-five years on American soil were you ever activated?"

"Yes."

"What was your assignment?"

"We were ordered to move to Los Angeles in nineteen eighty-three. We were told to embed ourselves into the new community and wait for further instructions."

"And did further instructions come?"

"Yes."

"Explain."

"We were contacted on thirty-two separate occasions to provide new identification documents for specific individuals. Once those documents were forged we would leave them off at predetermined drop points."

"That was the extent of your participation?"

"Yes."

Russell made some notations and then pointed to the next question.

"At what age did you reveal to Cynthia who you both really were?"

"Sixteen."

"Did she believe you?"

"Yes."

"Why?"

"She had her suspicions after catching us coming home late from a drop one night. She had been asleep when we left but had heard us leave."

"So your daughter accepted her new life?"

"She embraced it and Nikolay was ecstatic to hear about it. He told her that he had great plans for her."

"Is that why she wanted to join the CIA?"

"Yes," they both said. "We haven't heard from Nikolay in the past four years so Cynthia decided to join the CIA in hopes of making him proud."

Laura listened to audio from the adjacent room as Russell and her daughter continued to unearth Yakim and Katia's minds for information. It made for a long but very productive day.

29

Tuesday Oct 23, 2001

"Oh," Gabbi exclaimed, "so you think you're that good?"

"Bring it," Thomas replied with a grin.

In the Testing room, or the Arena as they now called it, Thomas stood in the middle of the room. Three of the walls, along with a portion of the wall that overlooked the Arena, were covered in various sized holes. Up in the control booth Gabbi oversaw Thomas' progression, for the past week, as she tested his reflexes. By pressing buttons she would shoot projectiles out of the holes, which in this case were limited to tennis balls. Sometimes they were aimed at Thomas and his goal was to deflect any of them before they made contact, and he had done well with single projectiles. He wore a specialized outfit that would electronically record any hits to his body. His instincts and awareness levels had steadily risen over the past week as Gabbi had upped the complexity from single to dual tennis balls. This was the first instance where Thomas was going to test himself against three or more targets at the same time.

Thomas calmed and prepared himself for the upcoming onslaught. *You got this.* Without warning three balls propelled themselves out of the wall his body was turned towards. Thomas, with his arms raised in a fighting stance, flicked his fingers and altered their trajectory. The balls bounced away harmlessly, rolled along the floor and came to rest along the edge of the Arena.

"Is that all you've got?" he taunted.

"Hardly," Gabbi's voice resonated from the overhead speakers.

An instant later a ball nearly connected with Thomas' head from behind as it flew by. He spun around.

"I guess you can't deflect what you can't see," Gabbi teased.

She pushed another series of buttons and three balls shot out of the walls, from various angles, at Thomas. *Damn, she's really keeping me on my toes today.* With his head on a swivel Thomas appeared to dance around the room as he deflected and intercepted the projectiles. Five minutes later Gabbi disengaged the system. The Arena floor was covered in tennis balls and Thomas in sweat.

"Take a break," Gabbi said over the loudspeaker.

Thomas exited the Arena and made his way up to the control booth.

"That was cool to watch," Gavin said as he mimicked the movements his father had made out on the floor.

Thomas smiled. "Thanks kiddo. How'd I do?"

Gabbi looked over at the computer screen which tallied the number of projectiles used verses the number of contacts the suit registered and came up with a percentage.

"Seventy-four percent."

Thomas shook his head. "Damn."

"I'm guessing your back is pretty bruised. Those balls shoot out at high velocity."

"Yeah, tell me something I don't know," he winced. "They smite when they hit, that's for sure. And you're right; I can't deflect what I can't see."

"Maybe I should turn the speed down," she said.

"No," Thomas countered. "The faster the better. I'm not going to be fed softballs out in the real world."

"I can make those bruises go away," Gavin offered.

"I think I'm going to take you up on that champ. Your old man feels, well, a little old at the moment."

Thomas pulled off the upper portion of his suit, turned around and knelt down so Gavin could work his magic. His entire back, as predicted, was filled with angry welts that were already bruising. Gavin placed his hands on his father's back and concentrated. Seconds later, and right before their eyes, Thomas wounds healed. His bruises grew smaller and smaller until there was nothing left. Thomas arched his back and let out a sigh of relief.

"Thanks Gav. That feels a million times better," he said as he stood up.

Gavin wiped his hands on one of the towels stacked on the counter. "Gross dad, you're sweaty."

"Yeah, yeah."

"I just can't look away," Gabbi said in awe. "Every time I see you do that Gav it amazes me."

Gavin smiled. "It's what I do."

"Well, not entirely," she replied. "It's one of the things you do and you do it quite well."

"Hey," Thomas kidded, "what about me? What am I? Chopped liver?"

"Your power, well, it's okay I guess," Gabbi teased.

Gavin laughed.

Thomas smiled. "I'll be sure to mention that to my daughter. I'm sure she'll be able to change your mind about that, whether you want to or not."

Gabbi grinned and put her hands up in surrender. "You win. Your power is awesome."

"You hear that Gav, she said my power is amazing."

"No, she said it was awesome and that was after you twisted her arm. My power is amazing."

Thomas chuckled. "Fair enough." He turned back to Gabbi. "I'm going to take a quick shower and then grab some lunch."

She nodded. "Gav and I will gather up all the balls and reset the room. We'll join you after we're done."

"Thanks Gabbi."

"Why do I have to help?" Gavin asked.

She smiled. "Because you're amazing, remember?"

* * *

After lunch Thomas suited back up and the three of them walked back to the Testing wing. Thomas took his place in the Arena while Gabbi and Gavin entered the control booth.

"Do you want to go with the same routine?" Gabbi asked over the loudspeaker.

"Mix it up."

"You got it."

Thomas began to swivel his head so he could catch any movement coming towards him. As the balls began to shoot out he began to twist and deflect them. Seconds later the Arena filled with a huge flash of light, the room went dark and the balls stopped firing. Thomas looked up at the control room and barely caught Gabbi and Gavin as they collapsed.

What the fuck?

Thomas rushed out of the Arena and up to the control booth where there, on the floor, he found them. In the shadows he could tell that neither of them was moving.

"Gav? Gabbi?"

Thomas swiftly knelt down by his son and pulled his limp body to his lap.

"Gav?"

No response. Thomas began to panic as he checked for a pulse on Gavin's neck. Nothing.

208

"Nononononononono. Come on Gav, wake up."

Tears welled up in his eyes as he opened his mouth and shouted.

"I need some help! Somebody help me! Please! Somebody!"

Thomas violently woke up and smacked his head on the bunk above him.

"Ouch! Fuck that hurt."

He rubbed his forehead as he swung his legs out and placed them on the floor.

Please! Somebody!

The echoes of his dream reverberated loudly in his head.

Gavin appeared in the doorway. "Dad. Are you done napping? Gabbi and I prepped the Arena for you and ate while you were passed out."

Thomas nodded. "I'll be right there."

"You okay?"

"Yeah son. Just a bad dream."

Thomas stood up from the lower bunk bed and put his testing suit back on. After that the three of them walked back to the Arena. Thomas took his position down below while Gabbi and Gavin entered the control booth.

"Do you want to go with the same routine?" Gabbi asked over the loudspeaker.

"Mix it up."

"You got it."

Thomas paused as a sense of déjà vu coursed through his body. The first projectile whistled past, barely missing his head.

"Heads up!" Gabbi said over the speaker.

He looked up at them. "Get out! Get out of the booth!"

Thomas sprinted out of the Arena. As he turned the corner a huge flash of light filled the control booth and the overhead lights flickered and died.

"Nononono!"

In his plight, and sudden loss of sight, Thomas bumped into Gavin and Gabbi. Thomas, off balance, plummeted head first into the wall.

"Oof."

Emergency back-up lights sputtered to life and illuminated the hallway.

"Dad? Dad? Are you okay?" Gavin asked as he picked himself up and went to his father.

Gabbi, having been knocked down as well, rolled over on her back and slowly sat up.

"Dad?"

Gavin managed to push his father on his side. It was immediately apparent that a huge gash had opened up on Thomas' forehead and that blood had already begun to pool.

"Dad!"

"Gav, what's wrong?" Gabbi asked.

Gavin wasn't listening as he put his hands on his father's head and then closed his eyes.

Gabbi pulled herself up and looked over. Her demeanor changed right away. "I'll grab some towels."

As Gabbi made her way to where the towels were in the control booth Gavin bore down. A few moments later Thomas groaned and opened his eyes.

"Dad?"

"What…what happened?" Thomas managed to say.

Gabbi returned with some towels and gently placed some under Thomas' head. She handed another one to Gavin when she realized Gavin's hands were covered in his father's blood.

"Are you okay?" Gavin asked as he wiped his hands clean.

"My head hurts. What happened?" Realization hit him. "Shit, are you both okay?"

Gavin nodded. "Yes, we're both okay."

The three of them heard the sound of running and Hobbes appeared around the corner.

"There was a power spike in this sector. Are any of you hurt?"

"Thomas banged his head," Gabbi told him, "but Gavin just fixed him up."

Relief washed over Hobbes' face. "Good good. Let me take a look in there and see what I can figure out."

Gabbi nodded and Hobbes made his way past them towards the booth. She looked back towards Thomas with an inquisitive look on her face.

"You yelled at us to get out of the booth. How did you know this was going to happen?"

Thomas shook his head. "I don't know."

"Bullshit. This can't be a coincidence so spill it."

Thomas mulled it over and finally opened his mouth. "I had a dream."

"A dream?" she asked.

"Yeah."

"You had a dream that the booth was going to get hit by a power spike?"

He slowly nodded.

"When?"

"When what?" he asked.

"When did you have this dream?"

211

"After lunch when I took my nap."

"Interesting." She thought for a bit and Thomas caught it. "What?"

"What you call a dream I want to label as some sort of premonition."

"Like being able to see in to the future or something? Is that what you're saying?"

Gabbi nodded. "It's plausible. Tell me, what happened in your dream?"

"I'd rather not," Thomas countered.

"It's important that you do."

Gavin spoke up. "Come on dad. Tell us."

Thomas relented. "Fine. In my 'dream' the booth filled with light and everything went dark. When I ran up to you, well…you both were just lying there and you weren't moving." He choked on the next sentence. "You'd both been electrocuted."

"Shit," Gabbi breathed out. "If you ask me that's one hell of a specific dream."

"Look dad, we're fine," Gavin pointed out. "You saved us."

"I didn't do anything. I panicked."

"No," Gabbi told him. "I think Gavin's right. Look, if my theory on this premonition is on the money then that means you did save us. If you hadn't told us to get out then we'd both be dead right now, electrocuted like you described, right?"

"Maybe," Thomas replied.

"So A, thank you. And B, you know what this possibly means, don't you?"

Thomas sat up against the wall and felt his forehead. The large gash was gone, as if his injury had never occurred. The only evidence to the contrary were the bloody towels.

"Tell me Gabbi, what do you think it means?"

She smiled. "I think there's a chance you're developing a new ability."

* * *

Emma Duncan, the DCI's wife, sat on a park bench within the boundaries of Falls Church's community center. It was late afternoon and the wind was beginning to pick up and it sent a slight chill down her spine. But Emma didn't react to the cold and instead waited patiently, as she'd been instructed to do, for someone to come by and hand her a package.

Ten minutes later a young woman, with purple hair, strolled over to Emma and dropped a wrapped parcel off on the bench next to her. The woman didn't glance at Emma as she continued her walk down the path and disappeared around a wooded bend in the distance.

Emma, with a blank look on her face, pulled the parcel to her and stood up. She casually made her way back to her vehicle, got in and drove out of the community center. Five minutes later Emma got off the road and parked behind a grocery store. She quickly exited, placed the parcel behind one of the dumpsters, got back in her car and headed back to her house as if nothing had happened. Fifteen minutes later another vehicle pulled up beside the dumpster. The man looked around and, after not seeing anything out of the ordinary, got out and retrieved the parcel. Dr. Matsushita got back into his car and ripped open the package. Inside he found exactly what he needed, bloody towels. He smiled and drove off.

* * *

One year before...

Dr. Matsushita agonized over his latest lab results. Since returning to the United States, from his time spent recovering from his injuries in Japan, he'd spent months pouring over the data he'd collected from little Emily Clark during the time she'd been a 'guest' of his. His ultimate goal was to take Emily's power of suggestion and not only make it his own, but to take it to the next level. Day and night, he worked tirelessly on splicing and recombining a portion of the syringe sample he'd saved from the fire, until he made progress. Then, one night, he was done.

"There, that's it."

Triumphantly he stepped back and marveled at his ingenuity.

"I think I've done it."

But Dr. Matsushita knew that there was only one way to test his creation and there was only enough serum left in the syringe for a single dose. He clumsily rolled up his left sleeve with his burned right hand, uncapped the syringe, took a breath and injected the contents.

Nothing happened at first aside from feeling nauseous and a bit lethargic so he mentally willed himself to be patient. Days later, after continually attempting to implement what he knew his ability should manifest itself to be, his genius and the thoroughness of his work finally presented itself.

Yamato sat and watched the tourists mill about around the Washington Monument from a distance. A family of four caught his attention.

Is that you and your family Thomas?

For a moment he lost himself in a flashback. When that passed he saw the family for who they really were. The young boy began to pull on his mother's arm in excitement when he saw a

214

stand that sold balloons. His older sister joined in the fun and before long their parents relented and headed over to the balloon man. The children each picked out the balloon they wanted and they were handed them as soon as the transaction was completed. The smile on their faces was the catalyst that Yamato had been waiting for.

Let it go.

The young boy's hand opened and his balloon rose swiftly into the sky.

Yes!

Yamato couldn't hear the conversation but as he watched the interaction he saw the boy start to scream and point upwards. The balloon man instantly came to the rescue and offered the boy another balloon which the boy readily accepted. The father pulled his wallet out and offered to pay but the balloon man shook his head no. The wallet disappeared back in his pocket and the two men smiled and shook hands. Yamato concentrated on the girl.

Let your string go.

A second balloon shot up and quickly disappeared. A grin slowly spread over the doctor's face as he watched the parents decide how to deal with a similar situation. The girl put her fists to her eyes and appeared to be crying. The father pulled his wallet out and pushed it towards the balloon man.

Drop it.

The young boy's second balloon took off after his sister's and confused faces appeared on all three adults faces. Yamato changed tactics.

Grab them all.

The balloon man stopped interacting with the two confused adults and in one motion gathered the remaining balloon strings on one hand.

215

Cut the strings.

The man deftly used his scissors until the only thing that moored the immense collection balloons to the ground was his hand.

Set them free.

The stunned family of four, along with a number of curious bystanders, watched as the balloon operator lessened his grip. The balloons leapt out of his grasp and soared into the air. The man looked up, as they flew away, terribly confused.

Yamato felt drained so he stood up from the bench and made his way back home. He was thrilled that his evolution of Emily's power of suggestion was initially very successful.

I didn't have to touch them, like Emily does, for them to do my bidding. All I have to do is command them from a distance. What absolute freedom this is.

In the weeks that followed Yamato practiced daily to strengthen his power of suggestion. During that time he had a multitude of ideas of how he should use his ability. Thoughts of revenge filled his brain.

I could make the President of the United States launch nuclear missiles at its own territory. I like that idea, but I have other pressing matters to deal with first. Thomas Clark. Yes, Thomas Clark. And money. I need my own source of money.

In the months that followed, in a variety of cities around the country, blatant and unexplained heists took place. In all of them large sums of money had disappeared right under the noses of the men and security systems that guarded it. In every single case each witness couldn't understand how the money had vanished.

Dr. Matsushita took that money, bought property and built a secret lab in Falls Church. He hoped that in the future Thomas would eventually come to him and he needed to be prepared for that day. In the meantime, to make that wish a reality, Yamato began to research Robert Duncan, the man who had replaced Victor Bannon as the Director of Central Intelligence. During that research he discovered Emma Duncan, his wife, and turned his attention towards her.

Control the wife, control the man.

Within a month he knew where Emma liked to go for coffee, the places she went for errands and her general schedule. Yamato used that to his advantage and stationed himself in a coffee shop she frequented. Once she arrived, and picked up her coffee, he commanded her to meet him around the corner at his car. She complied. He made her tell him everything and was happily surprised that she knew about the Clarks. It was then that PsyOps came up and he knew that the DCI knew what Victor had been up to. Yamato commanded her to forget about their meeting and to go about her day normally.

As the next few months progressed he tapped into her knowledge from time to time to obtain updates, each time forcing her to forget that they ever met. He used their meetings to plant suggestions in her head that she would then take back and whisper in her husband's ear. It was then that he got the idea to try something new. He implanted a future command that would activate. After the command was successfully followed she had been ordered to forget about the interaction entirely, effectively making her the perfect mole. And he did just that.

A week ago Emma had called him and informed Yamato about a transfer that her husband had just made. The girl's name was Gabbi and she had agreed to join Project PsyOps. Yamato thanked Emma for the information and hung up. Emma promptly wiped the phone call from her memory, walked back to her table and finished her coffee amongst the other patrons.

217

* * *

Tuesday Oct 23, 2001

Dr. Matsushita gripped the parcel with the towels that contained Thomas' blood and drove them back to his lair. Without a fresh supply of Thomas' DNA Dr. Matsushita had little chance to replicate his serum, but that hadn't stopped him from trying. After every batch he tested the results on men and women, typically homeless he commanded off the street, and then observed them post injection within the confines of his lab. So far none of his homeless abductees had ever survived.

But now, with fresh DNA in his possession, Yamato couldn't wait to take his work to the next level.

30

Wednesday Oct 24, 2001

It was lunchtime for the students but Ms. Jones, the headmistress of the Culver boarding school, had summoned Amanda, Craig, Sarah and Edward to her office.

"What's this all about?" Amanda asked.

"Take a seat and have some patience," Ms. Jones responded.

The four kids sat down on the bench together.

"Are we in trouble?" Craig probed.

Ms. Jones smiled. "Apparently patience does not run in your family. You're here because shortly that phone," she said as she pointed to the one on her desk, "will ring. When it does I'm to understand that your fathers will be on the other end and have requested to speak to you."

"About what?"

"That information I'm not privy to. In the meantime why don't we play the quiet game." It came out as a statement rather than a question.

Four agonizing minutes later the phone finally rang. Ms. Jones took her time to answer it.

"Culver School, this is Ms. Jones, how can I help you? Yes, Mr. Paige, they're sitting right in front of me. In private? No, I'm afraid I'm not prepared to evacuate my office. Unreasonable? Mr. Paige, your children are on a strict regimen and parental dialogue has always been scheduled during the early evening. Now, I'd be more than happy to put you on speakerphone and you'll need to make this a quick conversation. I understand your time is valuable but let me assure you that mine is even more so. Shall we continue this pointless argument, Mr. Paige, or shall I dismiss your children from my office?"

Ms. Jones nodded her head, pressed a button on her phone and placed it back on the cradle.

"Go ahead Mr. Paige, they can hear you," she said and then leaned back in her chair.

"Amanda? Craig? Can you hear me?"

"Yeah dad," Craig responded as he sat on the edge of the bench.

"And what about my Sarah and Edward?" Bill asked over the speaker. "How're you two doing?"

"Hey dad," Sarah replied, "We're good."

"You know, Sam and I miss you guys," Bill stated.

"We miss you too."

"So," Sam said, "the reason we're calling is to let you know that we're going to be away for a bit. And you all know that means we'll be out of touch. Bill and I just wanted to let you know that we're thinking about you and for you all to have an awesome Halloween next week."

"Where are you going?" Edward asked.

"You know how it is son," Bill replied. "Keep it in the family, alright?"

"Okay."

"So how's school?" Sam asked.

Ms. Jones perked up.

"It's okay," Sarah collectively answered for all of them.

"Just okay? Are you all making new friends?"

"We're fine," Sarah pressed with a slight edge in her tone.

"Got it," Bill answered. "The walls have ears."

"Something like that," Sarah responded.

Ms. Jones took that opportunity to speak up. "I think enough time from your children's schedules has been interrupted. Please wrap it up."

A few seconds of silence emanated from the other end of the line before Bill spoke up.

"Anyway kids, we love you and miss you."

"Yeah we do," Sam added.

"Love you too," the children said.

Bill continued. "And just as a final thought, that Ms. Jones sounds like a real ballbuster. Don't let her run any of you over. Gotta run. Bye!"

The line went dead. The four kids tried to do everything in their power to stifle their laughter as they left her office and headed to the dining hall.

31
Thursday Oct 25, 2001

The Special Activities Division operators had spent the last seven days drilling endlessly with Sam and Bill in preparation for their mysterious mission. It'd been a week since they'd been selected and it was finally time to inform each of them what they had been preparing for. Russell escorted Darius, Carl, Eliot and Jordon around the underground bunker's circular hallway and hooked a right down to the Tech wing.

"You may remove your blindfolds."

It became very apparent, as they took them off, that they were standing in a communication nerve center. On the walls were multiple monitors that displayed everything from live satellite feeds to streaming information. The men knew instantly that this is where their mission would be controlled from. Sam, Bill and the DCI were present, as was another man they hadn't met before.

"Gentlemen," the DCI began, "I want to start off by thanking each of you for embracing this opportunity sight unseen. You could have easily said no, but your dedication to this country's safety and security made your decision an easy one. I also appreciate your understanding that the facility you're currently in, along with its location, need to remain secret which is why you were brought here blindfolded." The DCI pointed at the one individual the men didn't know. "Alongside Russell, I'd like to introduce you to the man that will be overseeing your operation from start to finish. He goes by the name of Hobbes. He will be your overhead eyes and ears during this endeavor."

Hobbes haphazardly raised his hand. "Hey."

The men nodded their heads towards Hobbes.

"Now I know you're all very interested in the exact mission specifics so I'll turn this briefing over to Sam who will run you through it. Sam."

Sam stepped forward and approached the large table. "Thank you, sir. Gentlemen, please take a seat."

Everyone pulled out a chair and sat down around the table as he began the rundown.

"As you're all very aware on September eleventh four airplanes were hijacked. Two of them hit the twin towers, one took out a portion of the Pentagon and another one crashed after the hijackers were overpowered."

Sam motioned to Hobbes and the picture of a Middle Eastern man appeared on the large monitor.

"This is Hamid Emal Habibi and he is one of the men responsible for those attacks. Now, before any of you ask, the reason Bill and I were tasked with this particular mission is that we have history with Hamid."

"What kind of history?" Darius asked.

"The kind that involves training him and a number of other Afghans to fight against the Russians back in the eighties. We were embedded with him in Afghanistan for nine months."

"And you think there's a chance you still know this man and how he thinks?"

Sam shook his head. "No, but we know him better than anyone else, and that's enough of an edge. Are there any other questions?"

No one spoke up.

"Okay then. The U.S. is two and a half weeks into Operation Enduring Freedom and that means a carrier fleet is stationed in the Gulf of Oman. After we meet up with that carrier group we will be airlifted north through Pakistan and eventually turn northwest high

224

above the Afghan mountains. Current intel places our target in a village just outside the Panjshir Valley. We will execute a night drop, parachuting north of the valley where we will land in the mountains and traverse south for two to three days. We will then locate our subject. Once we confirm he's on site we will make a night approach, make contact and detain our subject. Blackhawks will exfiltrate us once we have secured Hamid, under the cover of darkness. Questions?"

"Parachuting into that type of terrain is risky," Eliot, the team's medic, stated.

Sam nodded. "Yes, it is. But there's little other choice. Panjshir Valley is surrounded by miles of mountains on all sides. If we dropped directly into the valley we'd immediately lose the element of surprise, and we can't expect Hamid to be out there alone. He'll have plenty of security with him which means we have no choice but to hump through the mountains. A night drop is risky, but we'll have overhead eyes and ears watching out for us, right Hobbes?"

"Absolutely," Hobbes replied. "In addition to real time satellite imaging I'll also task a MQ-1 Predator drone to your AO, or area of operation. For those of you who are unfamiliar the Predator is an unmanned aerial vehicle and this particular drone will be outfitted with two Hellfire air-to-surface missiles. Communications between your team and this facility will also be conducted in real time through encrypted headsets via satellite uplinks."

Hobbes finished his spiel and handed the floor back to Sam.

"This past week we've trained together on small arms tactics and maneuvering. Tonight in preparation, and to make sure all of you receive a refresher, we will be conducting a night drop."

One of them men put his hand up.

"Yes Jordon?"

"When do we leave to join the carrier group?"

"Direct and to the point. I like it. We leave Saturday morning, bright and early. I expect us to have boots on the ground Sunday night or Monday morning at the latest."

"What equipment will we be packing in?" Carl, the team's tech, inquired.

"We'll try to keep it as light as possible, but you know how this works. M4's with side arms and Jordon will be hefting his Remington seven-hundred sniper rifle. Grenades, smoke, ammo, food, water, med kits and communications gear at a minimum." Sam paused for a few seconds and looked around at the four operators. "Each of you needs to take the time and get yourself in the right frame of mind. This mission, while risky, will be a game changer. The information we'll extract from Hamid will be invaluable. With that said, do any of you wish to back out at this time?"

Silence fell over the room.

"Good," Sam finally said. "Let's get it done. Bill and I will see you tonight."

32

Thursday Oct 25, 2001

Kim and Julie sat at the kitchen table together, alone in the large house. Their husbands had called and informed them that they'd be home late, tell them that their mission was a go and they'd be departing Saturday morning. The two wives knew it was coming, and hadn't taken the news well, but Julie seemed overly dejected by it. After hanging up the phone Julie extracted a bottle of white wine from the fridge, opened it, poured a glass and sat down.

"Talk to me," said Kim. "We knew this was happening. What's going on?"

Julie drank from her glass and looked over at her sister. "Here we go again. That's what the hell is going on."

"And you think I'm happy with this?"

"Well you're certainly not doing anything about it, are you? I mean, look at us. We sit in this house all day while everyone else is out doing something."

"That's right," Kim said," our husbands are doing something. And no, I'm not happy about it but what am I supposed to do, brood, like you are?"

Julie let her sister's jab go. "This isn't what I signed up for and for years I've begged Sam to stop and reconsider."

"It's what they do."

Julie slammed her fist down on the table and nearly knocked her glass over. "No! It's what they want to do rather than do what's best for our family, plain and simple." She took another sip. "And now this. Now they're headed off across the world to put themselves in harm's way all over again. And for what, to regain his reputation? What about my needs? What about our children's needs? It's as if we don't fall into his thought process whatsoever, and I'm sick of it."

Kim gently placed her hand on her sister's free one. "It's going to be okay."

Julie glared at her. "Oh really? How do you know? Can you honestly sit there and predict that 'everything' is going to magically be okay? No, you can't, and neither can I and that's the problem." Julie took another mouthful and swallowed. "I know I knew what I was getting into when I married Sam, just as you did with Bill. But that was a long time ago. I thought he'd grow older and grow wiser with age. No. The fact is he's as stubborn as I am and I love him to death, but I can't go through this again. When I really think about it, this isn't the life that I wished for when I decided to marry him."

Kim didn't know what to do. "What...what are you saying?"

Julie finished off her glass. "I think I have to divorce him."

33
Thursday Oct 25, 2001

Emily gazed out over the vast ocean and let her skin soak in the tantalizingly warm sunlight. Stir, on the other hand, was busy running around in the sand, scampering close to the water's edge and then bolt away before it could touch him. Gavin watched in amusement as he sat next to his sister, his back against the island's lone palm tree.

"So you and mom have been making people spill their guts or something?"

Emily nodded. "Yeah. It's been pretty crazy actually."

"What do you mean? Like scary?"

"No, not really. More like crazy good. Oh," she said excitedly, "did I tell you what I can do now?"

Gavin shook his head. "What?"

"I was able to control two people at once and make them talk at the same time."

"Seriously? That's pretty cool."

"I know. It felt good."

Gavin was happy for his sister. "Well, apparently you're not the only one whose powers are expanding."

She turned to him with excitement. "Really? What new thing can you do?"

"Actually, it's not me."

"Dad?"

Gavin nodded. "Yeah. It has something to do with premonition."

"That's like seeing things before they happen, right?"

"I think so. Anyway, I don't think he wants to talk about it."

"Why not?" she asked.

He shrugged. "I don't know. But something happened."

"About the power surge in the booth?"

"Yup. I think it scared him"

"It probably did. I'd be scared too if I somehow experienced a death before it happened."

"But dad says he prevented it from happening."

"Maybe he did. But think about it, to know that it happened he had to have gone through it before. And that means he still has the memory of it stuck in his head." She paused. "And I know exactly how that feels."

Gavin mulled over what his sister had just told him. "That makes sense."

The calm water lapped against the shore and provided a measured breather in their conversation.

"So, how're you doing?" she finally asked.

"Okay I guess. Since the Arena's broken we're going to start experimenting more with my portals."

"And are you worried about that?"

"No, not really."

"Then what's wrong?"

"I dunno. I guess I just miss us hanging out as a family."

Emily agreed. "Yeah, I get that. Ever since we started this program, or whatever you want to call it, it does seem like we've been somewhat separated."

"I thought that was something I wanted, but now I'm not so sure. I mean, don't get me wrong, it's fun to hang with dad and play with our powers, but it's just not the same."

"Then we should make an effort to do just that this weekend."

Gavin brightened up. "Yeah?"

She nodded. "Yeah."

"Cool. Thanks."

"You got it baby brother."

"Hey now, don't make me leave you here," he teased.

She smiled. "You wouldn't dare!"

Gavin scooped up a handful of soft sand and tossed it in his sister's direction. It didn't take long for her to return the favor. Stir, catching the interaction and not wanting to be left out, ran over and began to leap over the two of them. They laughed at his antics and their amusement echoed across the open water and into the distance.

34

Friday Oct 26, 2001

President Bush entered the secured command center and sat at the head of the table.

"Take a seat," the President ordered.

The men who stood around the table, which included Kirk Nash, the Secretary of Defense; David Cook, the Director of National Intelligence; Robert Duncan, the Director of Central Intelligence; and Alan Holmes, the Director of the Federal Bureau of Investigation, did as they were instructed.

"Brevity is the term of the day gentlemen," the President said as he turned to his Secretary of Defense. "Kirk, where are we with Operation Enduring Freedom?"

"Sir, the Northern Alliance has successfully bombed dozens of terrorist training camps and specific infrastructure installations throughout Afghanistan. We've also seen massive defections from both the Taliban and al-Qaeda which in turn has allowed us to capture a few of their leaders. Currently the Taliban are heading north towards Kabul. We estimate that we should recapture that city within two to three weeks as we push the fleeing Taliban forces into the mountains."

"Excellent. Our war on terror seems to be working. Keep me informed."

"Yes sir."

The President looked to the Director of National Intelligence. "David, you're up."

"Yes, Mr. President. As Kirk mentioned, we have captured a number of al-Qaeda leaders."

"And what information, if any, have we gleaned from them?"

"That process is ongoing Mr. President. The less you know about it the better."

"Very well. So, by your omission, you have zero updates regarding the individuals responsible for the nine-eleven attacks?"

"Well, sir, I…"

Robert Duncan spoke up. "I believe I can field this one, Mr. President."

"Well someone had better tackle it," he stated with some annoyance. "What do you have for me Robert?"

"We have the location of Hamid Emal Habibi, one of the masterminds behind the attacks. I already have a team prepped and they will depart in the morning to join up with the carrier group in the Gulf of Oman."

The President leaned back as he took the information in, clearly engaged.

"From there they will fly north over Pakistan and then turn north west and fly over the northern mountains of Afghanistan. At that point my team will night drop, by parachute, and then spend the next few days heading south until they reach the Panjshir Valley region."

"And that's where Hamid is holed up?"

"Yes, Mr. President."

"How big is this team?"

"It's a six man team, sir."

"Continue."

"Once they arrive they will dig in, observe and locate the target. Once Hamid's been found they will capture and extract him from the area."

The President mulled what the DCI had said for a bit. "This mission sounds extremely risky, almost suicidal. Who's on the team?"

"The team is being led by Sam Paige and Bill Nicholson, the former owners of SANDBOX Enterprises. The other four members were handpicked from my Special Activities Division."

"I know them," the FBI Director said. "What the hell are they mixed up in this for?"

"That's a good question," the President said. "The last I heard they had been charged with drug smuggling and their company was stripped from them."

Robert nodded. "That's partially true."

The President sat forward. "I'd say that's what happened."

"Sir, they were framed and hug out to dry. Regardless of what anyone might think, they're good men and even better operators. The reason they're involved in this mission is that they trained Hamid, and his men, for nine months back in the eighties to fight against the Soviets."

"And you think this gives them an edge?"

"Yes sir. They know the terrain and they know the man."

"Or they used to know him," countered the President. "It's quite a change going from fighting Soviets to masterminding an attack on American soil, don't you think?"

"Yes sir, I do. But at this point we need every advantage we can get our hands on. Besides that, Sam and Bill are motivated."

"How so?"

"They're hungry to reinstate their reputations, which at this point have been extremely tarnished, if not ruined."

The President nodded. "So if we know where Hamid is, why don't we just send a drone and be done with it?"

"The village he's hiding in is filled with civilians, sir. A strike like that would kill innocents."

"How many?"

"Sir?"

"How many civilians would be killed in the strike?"

The DCI shifted in his seat. "Dozens, sir."

The President mulled those casualties over in his head before he responded. "Very well. Thank you for that information. I hope you can pull it off successfully."

"So do I Mr. President," the DCI replied.

"Anything else?" the President asked.

Alan Holmes, the FBI Director, spoke. "Yes sir. In conjunction with the CIA the FBI has been actively following up and pursuing leads in regards to Russian sleeper agents residing within the United States."

"What is this, the Cold War era all over again?" He looked at Alan. "I can't believe this level of incursion is still occurring. How credible are these leads?"

"Very, sir. We've already detained a number of suspected sleepers. They're naturally being questioned."

"Thank you Alan." The President looked back over at Robert. "It seems like you've been staying busy."

The DCI nodded. "Yes sir. There are plenty of threats to the United States out there that need to be dealt with."

"Indeed there are. Good work." He abruptly stood up and the other men followed suit. "Keep me informed if anything new surfaces."

And with that the President left the room and the door closed behind him.

David Cook, the DNI, instantly turned and glared at both Robert and Alan. "What the fuck? Why wasn't I informed? I sat here in front of the President with my dick hanging out because you two assholes didn't keep me in the loop. I should suspend both of you right now."

236

"The less people that knew about our investigation into the Russian sleepers the better," Alan told his boss. "At this point we don't know how extensive their network has become as well as how embedded they are within our own system of government."

"Oh bullshit," David replied. "You're just using that as an excuse. The reality is that you fucked me today and it's going to come back around and bite you in the ass. There's a chain of command for a reason."

The DNI stormed off and left the three men behind.

"Don't worry about him," the Secretary of Defense told them. "He'll get over it even though his ego may not. If he tries anything I'll take care of it."

"Thank you sir," Robert replied.

"Yes, thank you," Alan added.

"My pleasure. Now get the hell out of here and go catch us some bad guys."

35
Saturday Oct 27, 2001

Before the sun was up Sam, Bill and the rest of their team were taken to Andrews Air Force Base. Once they arrived the 89th Airlift Wing directed them to board a Gulfsteam IV which would take them, and their gear, to an airbase in Saudi Arabia. With everything secured and the six men in their seats the jet flew down the runway and disappeared from view into the dark sky.

"Sit back and relax," Sam told them. "We've got fifteen hours until we land in Saudi Arabia."

"And then a chopper out to the carrier group," Bill said.

"Negative," Sam replied. "That was misinformation in case there's a leak someplace up the chain of command."

"What? Seriously?"

"Yeah. Instead we'll deplane when we land and board a C-5 which will take us where we need to go."

"So you're worried about our information getting out?"

"It's probably nothing, but the DCI made this slight change to lessen the amount of personnel that will see us. Our mission is to get in and out. Even the Blackhawk pilots, who will extract us, don't even know about their involvement yet. The DCI's keeping this one close to the vest."

"And that doesn't worry you?"

Sam shrugged. "No. We have a job to do and we have the tools to get it done. Once we land we're effectively on our own except for Hobbes, our eyes in the sky. I'm not stressing over how we get there because I know we'll tackle whatever problems that may arise as a team, and that's all that matters."

"Roger that brother, roger that."

36
Saturday Oct 27, 2001

Laura quietly, so not to wake Thomas, slipped out of bed, put on a robe and headed downstairs to the kitchen. The previous night the families had dinner together knowing full well that Sam and Bill were going to be wheels up first thing. As much as Julie and Kim acted normally throughout the evening Laura picked up on the fact that neither of them seemed very happy. It'd been a while since the three of them had talked so Laura made it a point to get up early in the hope that she'd catch Julie and Kim alone, especially since their husbands had already departed that very morning.

As Laura walked into the kitchen the conversation between Julie and Kim abruptly stopped.

"Morning," Laura said as she went to pour herself a cup of coffee.

"Hi," Kim said. "What are you doing up so early?"

Laura finished and walked over to the table and sat down with them. "Honestly? I'm worried about both of you."

"And why's that?" Julie asked.

"Because I know you've both been trying to hide the fact that you haven't been happy."

"Must be easy to get to the bottom of anything with that power of yours," Julie remarked snidely.

"Jules," Kim told her sister, "that's not very nice."

Laura took a deep breath and said, "So what's going on?"

Julie didn't hesitate. "Why don't you tell us?"

"I'm sorry Laura," Kim said, "my sister is…"

"Obviously stressed out," Laura said as she finished the sentence. "And lashing out is a common symptom. But, to comment on your comment Julie, the two of you have been unhappy ever since we moved out here. And trust me when I say I didn't need my power to figure that out. So I'll ask again, what's going on?"

"It's none of your business," Julie said between clenched teeth.

"Really? After everything we've been through?"

Julie didn't waste any time. "And maybe that's exactly what the issue is."

"Sis…"

"No," Laura said, "she's on a roll, why stop her now. Julie apparently has something to get off her chest."

"Very perceptive," Julie sarcastically replied.

Laura slammed her fist down on the table which visibly startled the other two. "Drop your fucking attitude Julie. If you don't want to talk to me, fine, no problem. But what I don't get is why you're clamming up now?"

"You might as well tell her," Kim told her sister.

"No," Julie declared.

"Maybe it'll help."

"Whose side are you on?"

"Side?" asked Kim. "We're all on the same side."

"Not for me."

"Fine. Forget it, I'll tell her then." Kim addressed Laura before Julie could object. "Julie's seriously contemplating divorce."

Laura wasn't prepared for that explanation. "What? Seriously? Why?"

"I can't take this anymore."

"Can't take what? I thought we're a family and that we're all in this together?"

Julie deflated in her seat. "We are, or at least we used to be. Everything's changed."

"Okay," Laura calmly said. "Like what?"

"For one thing it feels like we were chased out of our homes. The business gets yanked out from underneath us and our husbands, in their infinite wisdom, are back in the field doing the only thing they think they can do to make any of it right. But you know what, none of this feels right. We've been thrust into a new life; a life that I didn't ask for and a life that doesn't make me feel safe. I've got you Laura, a best friend, and your family, a team of superheroes. And you know what I have? I'll tell you exactly what I have. I've got nothing left. My husband thinks he's making the right decisions, but he's not. I've got my children that I shipped off to boarding school just so I can keep them out of harm's way. And you know what that leaves me? It leaves me alone, with my sister, in this large strange house and in a place I never wanted to come to in the first place."

"Okay. So let me ask you this," Laura said. "What do you want?"

Julie shook her head. "And that's just it, I don't know. But I do know that I've tried time and time again to make Sam see that his family needs to come first; that I need to come first."

"And so divorce is the answer you've arrived at?"

"Don't patronize me," snapped Julie. "I know I sound like a crazy person, ranting and raving."

Laura put her hands up. "Okay. I hear you."

Julie calmed down a bit. "But you know what the truth is…, the truth is that I'm tired. I'm just so tired of all this and I don't want to be a part of it anymore, and I don't want my children to be either."

Twenty seconds passed before Laura spoke up.

"Can I tell you a secret?"

Julie stopped and looked Laura in the face. "What?"

"I don't know what I'm doing either. What I do know is that people keep coming after us, which has put both of our family's at risk. Did I want to come here and work with the CIA? No. Do I feel safe? No, but I'm getting there."

"What are you trying to say?"

"I'm telling you that you're not alone in how you feel."

Julie tried to smile but it just came out as a weary look on her face. "I appreciate what you're trying to do here Laura, really. But the reality is that our lives are completely and drastically diverse. Thomas is there for you, and has been each and every day. He'll continue to be there for you and your children. I can't say the same for Sam even though I desperately want to. I feel like my voice isn't heard. I need time away from this situation, a situation that I don't see changing anytime soon, and that's exactly what I'm going to do. This is my life and I'm tired of feeling like I don't matter."

37
Saturday Oct 27, 2001

Craig and Edward pulled their canoe up to the dock. They'd spent the last fifteen minutes paddling around the large pond that was located adjacent to the horse stalls. One of the teachers steadied the canoe as the two boys got out, removed their life jackets and handed them off to two other students who were anxiously awaiting their own turn. The two nine year old boys walked past the line of students on the dock and headed back towards the main building in the distance.

"So what do you want to do now?" Edward asked.

Craig shrugged. "I dunno. We could go kick a ball around the soccer field?"

"Nah."

"Basketball?"

"Nah."

"Then you come up with some ideas," said Craig.

"I know."

"What?"

"Swimming in the pool."

"But you know they covered it up already for the season."

"Yeah," Edward replied, "I know. I guess I miss the pool at the house since it was heated all the time."

Craig smiled and nodded. "Me too."

They strode past the horse stalls and Edward got a gleam in his eyes. "I have an idea. We should sneak in and see what the horses are up to?"

Craig took that moment to look around to see if anyone was watching them.

"Just for a minute," Edward pressed. "We'll be in and out in no time."

Craig nodded and smiled back. With their scheme in place the two quickly hopped the fence, ran across the enclosure and slipped into the darkened stable. Their sudden appearance spooked a few of the nearby horses, in their stalls, and one of them reared up as it cried out. The other horses quickly became agitated and within seconds their loud neighing could be heard.

"We need to get out of here before we're caught," Craig urged.

Edward didn't need any additional encouragement. The noises the horses were making would warrant a response from someone sooner rather than later. As the two boys turned around to leave they stopped short. There, in the doorway, was Tad. Craig and Edward froze as he advanced with a smile on his face.

"Well well well. What do we have here?"

"Get out of our way Tad," Craig demanded.

"Not this time little man. You kicked me in the nuts, so now I'm here to return the favor," he said as he clenched his fists.

Craig and Edward looked behind them for a way out but there wasn't one. More horses spooked and began to reel up in their stalls.

"Come here you little shit," Tad threatened as he advanced on them. "You're dead."

As Tad bore down on them one of the horses suddenly kicked. The door to its stall swung open with force, barely missing Craig but startling him nevertheless.

"What the…!"

Moments later the large animal burst forth, glanced off Craig and ran headfirst into Tad. All three boys were sent sprawling as the agitated horse bolted out the stable doors and into the large fenced enclosure.

"What the hell is going on in here?" a voice boomed.

Craig, Edward and Tad, now covered in bits of hay and manure, looked up at the large man the school employed to care for their horses.

"You know this area is prohibited to students and yet here you are, scaring my horses. What do you have to say for yourselves?"

Tad was the first to speak up. "They came in here first and when I saw them I followed to tell them to get out."

"That's bullshit and you know it," Edward shot back.

"Yeah," Craig added.

"Oh fuck you," Tad shouted back.

"Enough!" the man hollered. "I don't give a crap what your excuses are. All I know is that right now we're all taking a walk to see Ms. Jones, and she'll determine what happened."

All three boys knew what that meant.

"After she's done with you I'll make sure you're back here working for me for the next month. How does that strike you? Now, get up and wait by the outer fence while I calm this mare down that you spooked. As soon as I get her back in her pen we'll take that walk. And don't think about running away either unless you want to spend more time with me than what's already coming to you."

38

Sunday Oct 28, 2001

Since Tuesday, after his acquisition of Thomas' blood, Dr. Matsushita had been diligently working on a synthetic variation of the serum he'd successfully created four years before. It was a time consuming endeavor and Yamato was exhausted. In the bowels of his lab he'd labored night and day to duplicate the meticulous conditions, but had run into problems right from the start. Once Dr. Matsushita opened the package and saw the bloody, but now dried towels inside, he knew there was a good chance that the blood was tainted, but that hadn't prevented him from soaking the towels in a solution to separate it. From there his process to isolate Thomas' DNA was just a matter time, but he knew there were still risks involved. Ideally he required fresh blood from Thomas, extracted straight from his vein.

Like before, when I had him under my control.

Yamato had hardly slept all week as he worked in a frenzy to replicate the serum. Once he created a new batch Dr. Matsushita took the time to properly scrutinize the serum. But, after five consecutive lots, his latest was still thick with contaminates.

"Dammit," he said as he pulled his eyes back from the microscope.

Yamato tore off his protective glasses and threw them across the room where they bounced off the glass barrier between his lab and his containment area. Four individuals, secured and in their beds attached to IV's, sluggishly rotated their heads towards the clatter. Unsure whether they had hallucinated or not they quickly dismissed the noise and returned to their induced state of relaxation, brought on by the illicit drugs Dr. Matsushita used to keep them docile. Of the four, three were male and one was a female. The one thing the four had in common was that they were homeless and had been recently abducted off the street from various city streets in the area. To any potential witnesses that saw the homeless individuals, each of Yamato's test subjects appeared to be a willing participant as they entered his van of their own volition. Yamato gazed through the clear glass at his captives. His plan was to inject all of them, wait and see what abilities they developed and then take control of their minds.

As he stared at them he suddenly changed his mind. "I have a better idea," he said out loud.

Dr. Matsushita immediately went to work and prepared four syringes with the tainted serum. He picked them up with his left hand, walked out of his lab around to the containment area, punched in the door code, and let himself inside.

"Hello everyone. I hope you've all been having a pleasant time in whatever blissful adventure land you're currently tripping out in."

He made his way to the first bed.

"Where…where…am….I?" the man barely managed to articulate.

"Well Clyde, you're in the hospital of course."

"I…I…am?" Clyde blinked his eyes in confusion as the drugs in his body vehemently worked against him. "Wh…why?"

"You were injured during the time you spent living on the street. I've been nursing you back to health. Don't you feel better?"

Clyde couldn't think straight. "I…feel…good."

Dr. Matsushita smiled. "Good Clyde. That's good. Now, I'm going to give you another shot. This one should make you feel a whole lot better."

"O…okay…doc. Thanks."

250

"You got it Clyde. I'm only looking out for your wellbeing."

As Clyde dozed off again Yamato took one of the four syringes and injected the contents directly into Clyde's vein. With that taken care of he wasted little time doing the same to Mary Ann, Peter and Hank. None of them put up a fight and two minutes later Yamato had secured the containment door and was back in his lab. He began to talk to himself.

"Contaminated serum or not I still went to a lot of effort to make this all happen. If something adverse happens to them then who cares, I'll just incinerate their bodies, like I've done before. There will always be more homeless people out there to fill my beds. But, that reminds me, I need a real blood sample from Thomas so I can really move forward with my work."

Yamato picked up the phone but was disrupted by a commotion in the adjoining room. He looked over as Clyde began to convulse and thrash around in his bed.

"So soon?"

He put the phone back, stood up and walked towards the glass partition. Clyde's face was twisted in horrible agony, his fingers bent in abnormal directions, distorted and misshapen while his entire body began to alter itself. Puss-filled nodules jutted out from his cheek and around his neck. Clyde's bones began to snap loudly from his violent contortions as his screams filled the room.

Yamato was captivated at the transformation Clyde's body was going through and wasn't able to look away until Mary Ann, the second subject he injected, started to thrash around in her bed. Her cries of agony immediately mixed with Clyde's as her body began to perversely distort.

Yamato was grossly captivated as he monitored their body fluctuations from the other side of the glass.

Clyde abruptly went quiet as Mary Ann's cries worsened. Yamato glanced back over at Clyde and knew he was no longer alive.

There's time for that later.

As Mary Ann's body and limbs grotesquely bent her face began to transform unnaturally; monstrously. Her chin jutted forward, audibly popped out of its socket and hung loosely to one side. Her eyes bulged as her brain expanded, but Yamato could still hear her scream. And then she went limp, her face and body an unrecognizable mess.

Peter and Hank weren't far behind as their bodies reacted to the tainted serum they'd been injected with.

Three minutes later their screaming came to an end as well.

Yamato slowly sat down and took in the grizzly scene before him. What he'd just experienced he'd never seen before and was utterly unexpected. Silence washed over his lab as he unconsciously stroked his disfigured right arm with his left hand as he contemplated his next move.

He cocked his head to one side. *What was that?*

A faint murmur emanated from one of the beds in the containment area. Yamato stood up and peered intently through the glass. It didn't take him long to discern that Peter was still breathing. He rushed out of his lab, punched in the code and rushed over to Peter's side, ignoring the three other twisted bodies. At first glance Yamato was able to discern that Peter had fared better than the others. Yes, he was deformed but not to the same extent. Peter's forehead had protruded and 'caveman' was the first word that popped in Yamato's head. His arms had expanded and the majority of his fingers had extended, making them noticeably longer than usual. Multiple hives, as if from an allergic reaction, covered Peter's chest, portions of his arms and legs. But, regardless of his extensive transformation, Peter was still breathing.

He's alive. What does this mean? What does any of this mean? Worry about that later.

Yamato wasted no time as he took tissue samples, from multiple areas, from all four specimens. He labeled each one so in the coming days he'd know exactly who and what he was testing to determine what had occurred. After the samples were taken he wheeled each corpse, individually, to the incinerator. Once there he adjusted the bed's height to the appropriate level so he could easily dispose of the scientific material that was now useless to him.

Throughout the entire process Yamato remained excited about his new discovery. He didn't know what it meant, at the moment, but he was sure that it would help him towards his ultimate goal.

With the containment room cleared and cleaned up Dr. Matsushita turned his concentration to Peter, or more realistically, what was left of him.

"Peter? Can you hear me?"

One of Peter's malformed eyes half opened and blankly stared at the man who had asked the question.

"Peter? How many fingers am I holding up?"

Yamato held up two fingers but Peter only grunted in return.

"How many fingers?"

This time Peter didn't reply at all and closed his one good eye.

"Do you understand me at all?"

Peter's right hand shot up and caught Dr. Matsushita by the throat. His long fingers wrapped around his neck and began to squeeze. Yamato, caught off guard, tried to pull the hands away but Peter's strength was like steel. Peter opened his one eye and stared at the man who had done this to him as the doctor weakened in his grasp.

No! Not like this!

Yamato stared back at Peter.

Let me go! Release me!

Peter instantly pulled his enormous hands away as Yamato coughed and took his time to recover. Once he did he looked back down at his hideous creation.

"I understand your pain Peter. They did this to me, and I did this to you. But, I'm going to give you the chance to take your rage out on the world. I'm going to put you back where I found you; back on the street."

39

Sunday Oct 28, 2001

"One minute!" one of the C5's crew yelled at Sam's team with a single finger held up. "One minute!"

Sam reiterated the time left to his other five operators as the rear cargo door began to lower.

"One minute! Final gear check!"

Each of the six men performed a safety spot check of the parachute in front of them. When the last man was finished he turned around so the fifth operator could inspect his own chute. Six thumbs were then held up.

"Thirty seconds!" the same crew member yelled.

All six of them were dressed in desert camouflage, tactical vests, side arms and a very heavy rucksack filled with the necessities they needed to complete their mission. Strapped to their right leg was a quick release weapon's bag and attached to each of their helmets were night vision goggles. On each man's left wrist was a GPS and altimeter unit. They all knew that extra weight wasn't going to get them back on the ground any faster once they launched themselves into the blackness miles above the northern mountains of Afghanistan.

Each man's anticipation of what they were headed into now came to a head as icy wind whipped through the aircraft's hold and it tugged at the absolute reality of what they were all about to embark on. But they were ready, willing and able.

The red light changed to a blinking green and all of them knew it was only a matter of seconds before they would all plunge out the back of the large plane and disappear into the darkness below.

The green light stopped blinking and remained on. Without hesitation Sam hobbled the last ten feet, with his team on his heels, and leapt. The freezing air instantly enveloped each man's body and simultaneously yanked on their gear as they plummeted towards the ground together. On the way down each operator constantly checked their elevation. When they hit nine-thousand feet they fanned out from each other. At eight-thousand feet each man pulled his drogue chute, which quickly inflated and extracted their main chute from its housing. As they slowed all six pulled their night vision goggles down over their eyes and immediately looked up to confirm their chute had deployed correctly.

"Check in," Sam's voice ordered through their headsets.

"Good to go," Bill said.

"I'm here," Darius replied.

"Bring it," said Carl.

"Good chute," confirmed Eliot.

"Tally ho," Jordon added.

"Roger that team. That first step was a doozy. Now check your GPS and line up on my six. This is the easy part."

Within thirty seconds the other five operators had formed a line behind Sam, who in turn controlled the angle and direction of his descent. As the team drew close to the ground they were finally able to make out the terrain in the dark below them. The landing, a treacherous part of their mission, was about to commence.

"The mountain's coming up too quickly, "Sam told his team. "Turn fifteen degrees south to parallel the slope."

Sam pulled down on his right handle. He and his parachute dipped as they changed angle. Sam, and his team, had just missed slamming into a mountain top and were now swiftly gliding a mere forty feet above the angled ground.

"We're running out of space," Sam said as he looked around. "That looks like shale right below us."

"It does," Bill said.

"Drop bags and flare," Sam ordered.

In the pitch black the six operators let their quick release bags drop off their legs and pulled back hard on both parachute handles. In unison they quickly decelerated, raised their legs and landed ass first on the mountain shale. The sound of loose rocks cascading down the mountain filled the once silent air as all six of them came to a grinding halt, some facing up and some down amidst the sliding rocks. They began to slough off their parachute harnesses.

"Everyone okay?" Sam whispered. "Any injuries?"

Ten seconds later everyone reported back that, aside from a few bruises, that they were mission ready.

"Well that was a first," Bill softly uttered. "Remind me not to do it again."

Less than a minute later their primary weapons were out and pointed in all directions, scanning for threats. Once they were secure all six parachutes were collected and easily disposed of under a massive amount of shale.

"Checking in," Sam said over his headset. "Hobbes, checking in."

"I hear you Sam," Hobbes replied from the other side of the world. "That was one hell of a landing. Glad to hear you're alright."

"Tell me something I don't know. What's our immediate area look like? Any contacts?"

"No," he told the team as he worked his computer magic. "The closest thermal contact is a mile east of your current location." Hobbes zoomed in on it. "I've got four guys lying around a campfire at that location. Other than that you look pretty clear."

"Roger that," Sam answered. "Thanks."

"No problem. Also, the drone is on standby. If you need it I can have it overhead in about thirty minutes from your say so."

"Understood Hobbes." Sam addressed his team. "Is everyone good to go?"

Five affirmative responses sounded off in Sam's ear.

"Good. As we all know, we'll head towards our target location during the night and dig in during the day. We do everything we can to avoid contact and that should be relatively unproblematic with Hobbes looking out for us overhead. With that said, silence and stealth are our primary goals. Move out."

40

Monday Oct 29, 2001

It had been a week since Gabbi and Gavin had narrowly escaped electrocution in the Arena's control booth. Since then Hobbes had freed up some time, out of his busy schedule, and corrected the problem. In the meantime, Thomas and Gabbi had begun to focus on Gavin's portal ability and she had been absolutely awestruck the first time she stepped through and found herself on the small island beach. Today was no exception. All three of them wore bathing suits because they knew they were going to get wet.

"I don't think I'll ever get tired of this place," Gabbi said as the sun warmed her face and illuminated her smile. "It's amazing."

Gavin closed the portal behind them while Stir excitedly began to run around the island's perimeter. Thomas watched Gabbi as she glanced over at Victor's skeleton.

"Does it bother you?" he asked her.

"What?"

"The skeleton. I've seen you eyeball it more than once since you started coming here."

She shrugged. "To be honest it's a little creepy, but hey, this isn't my slice of paradise so who am I to complain."

"You don't have to be scared," Gavin assured her.

"I'm not scared. If anything I'm a little envious, that's all."

"Envious?" Thomas stated. "What do you mean?"

"Seriously?" she replied as she swept her arm around. "Look at where we are right now. I mean, we're on a different world or plane of existence or something. How freaking awesome is that? It blows my mind that I'm really here and trust me, I've spent a lifetime indulging in Star Trek, sci-fi, fantasy and other distractions with the faintest of hopes that one day I'd stumble in to one of their worlds. And, blam, here I am. So yeah, I'm envious of what Gavin, you and the rest of your family take for granted."

"I'm not sure 'granted' is the right word though Gabbi."

She cocked her head to one side. "Okay. Why not?"

"Well for starters our abilities, as unique and fascinating as they may be, have consistently placed my entire family in peril." Thomas motioned towards Victor's bones. "That skeleton is a constant reminder that we're never going to be safe. I mean, look at what my family has agreed to in an effort to alleviate our fears. And the worst part about it is that I don't know if it's all for nothing. Working with the DCI could be a futile chapter in our lives and it's just a matter of time before someone takes my children from me again."

"I'm sorry," Gabbi said. "I have no idea the sacrifices you've all had to make over the years. All I know is that I feel like the luckiest person in the world to work with you guys."

Thomas relaxed and the tension flowed out of his shoulders. "No, you're right Gabbi. It's all too easy for me to dwell on what's happened to us in the past rather than what we're going to do to prevent it from reoccurring in the future. It's a pleasant surprise that you're not as jaded as we are."

She smiled. "Like I said, I find it incredibly fascinating. But that doesn't mean I can't find that skeleton a little disconcerting."

"Fair enough."

"Are you two finished yapping," Gavin kidded, "or should I come back later?"

"Very funny," Gabbi replied. "I'm going to get you."

She took off after him across the sand. Gavin screeched in delight as he avoided her outstretched hands. Thomas stood his ground and watched the two of them interact. He was happy to see his son smiling and having a good time for once.

"Okay okay," Gabbi finally said a minute later as she made a 'T' with her hands. "Time out. I need a break."

She plopped down in the shade, provided by the island's lone palm tree, and rested. Gavin and Stir went over and sat down beside her as well, a grin still visible on his face. Thomas walked over.

"Funny. I was under the impression we were going to get some work done today."

"Dadddd. In a minute."

The previous visits to the island, in the past week, were initially designated to map out Gavin's portals. However, the three of them quickly came to the conclusion that creating a map, using the island as a constant point of reference, was going to be impossible. Unfortunately the reasoning was simplistic. Every time Gavin made his portal, and then entered it from the real world, he ended up on his island. In other words, to create a map that would differentiate the distances to known destinations, based on Gavin's initial location before entering, would be impractical. But, it didn't take Gabbi long to come up with a new idea which was to record the time it took to reach specific destinations using Gavin's boat. Using that information they could chart each destination, in real world miles, and then correlate the time it took to arrive there. Gabbi planned on creating a straightforward algorithm that would apply the distance required to travel and then spit out the time it would take to arrive on the other end. It was an easy solution to the problem and it was brilliant. So far the three of them, and Stir, had made fourteen round trips, each one a little farther than the next. Today the plan was to portal clear across the country, the farthest they'd ever recorded.

Gabbi and Gavin stood up and brushed the sand off. He looked at the water and, like so many times before, and the boat materialized.

"That never gets old by the way," Gabbi declared.

Gavin smiled and made his way to the boat, with Gabbi and Thomas behind him. Stir jumped in and took his normal position upfront looking out over the ocean. With everyone situated the boat rose out of the water a few feet.

"Ready?" Gavin asked.

Gabbi readied her stopwatch, nodded and pressed start. The boat promptly accelerated and made a beeline towards their destination. With Thomas looking on Gabbi watched the seconds tick by as they flew over the endless ocean.

Ten seconds.

Twenty seconds.

Thirty seconds.

And there, in the distance an island rapidly approached; an island that Gavin directed the boat towards.

Thirty-one.

Thirty-two.

Thirty-three.

The boat slowed and hovered fifty feet from shore before it lowered into the water where it gently bobbed up and down.

"Thirty-four seconds," Gabbi told them as she hit the stop button. "Although, sorry for asking Gav, but why do we always stop fifty feet away? Why can't you park this thing on the beach so we don't have to get wet?"

"I don't know. Each time I can't make the boat go any closer than this."

Thomas spoke up. "Maybe the answer isn't as complicated as we think it is."

"Okay, it sounds like you have a theory." Gabbi indicated. "What're you thinking?"

"Well, it's just an idea, but maybe the boat can't go any closer because it doesn't belong there."

"You mean something like trespassing?"

Thomas shrugged. "Maybe. It's just a thought."

"I like it," Gabbi told him. "And you may be on to something. In any case we should get out so we can finalize this leg of the trip for our records."

As Gabbi slipped over the edge of the boat, with her waterproof stopwatch hanging around her neck, Stir suddenly began to growl and became very agitated.

"What is it Stir?" Gavin asked his best friend.

Thomas turned his head and followed Stir's gaze. There, off in the distance but rapidly approaching, was a dark cloud, menacing in nature.

"What the…?"

"Hey," Gabbi said from the water as she noticed the same thing, "what is that?"

Thomas squinted and put his hand up to block the sun in his eyes. It wasn't a cloud. The impending blackness that surged towards them was filled with a myriad of shapes that Thomas had a difficult time discerning from one another.

Stir's growls became guttural, loud and menacing.

"Oh Shit, no no no no!" Thomas sputtered. "Go! Out of the boat and go!"

"What is…"

Gabbi didn't have a chance to finish as Thomas tossed his son into the water next to her.

"FUCKING MOVE!"

The look on his face convinced her to swim to the island as if her life depended on it. Stir jumped in the water and Thomas was right behind him as the four of them frantically closed the gap to the island. Behind them the sun was abruptly blotted out as a tremendous shadow overtook them.

Gabbi was the first to get a solid foot underneath her some twenty-five feet from the shore. As she went to scoop up Gavin she froze. The pure magnitude of creatures that filled the sky nearly forced her to her knees in fear. She was able to blink once before Thomas pulled her back up in one arm as he dragged his son by the other.

Shadowy wings beat the air.

Horrific faces emerged from the smoke, faded away and then appeared once more, horrible and filled with hate.

Fire saturated the air, burning it.

Gabbi turned away, planted her feet under here once more and reached the island just before Thomas and Gavin.

Stir was beside himself and was in a desperate frenzy.

Gavin wasted no time as he made his portal. Thomas took both Gabbi and his son's hands and rushed through. Gavin cried out as they entered.

"STIR!"

The three collapsed on cold concrete inside a building, the portal still open behind them. Gavin cried out again in a desperate voice.

"STIR!!"

"Close it!" Thomas commanded.

"Not without Stir!"

Before Thomas could convince his son otherwise a dark shape flew through the portal. It landed on all four feet, turned and stared at them with its glowing red eyes. It was Stir.

A shadowy hand, distorted, long and tipped with sharp razors pierced the portal. The hand, attached to a long dark arm, emerged.

"CLOSE THE PORTAL!" Thomas screamed.

Gavin instantly snapped the portal shut and the smokey arm was cut off from the other world. It instantly collapsed in on itself and within seconds had dissipated completely leaving the four of them were wet and alone on the cold concrete floor. It took them a good twenty seconds to begin to slow their breathing, and another twenty finally to stand up.

"Shit on me," Gabbi exclaimed. "What the hell just happened?"

Thomas shook his head and just stared at where the portal had been. That long arm; the claws; coming for them.

As they adjusted to the interior light of the building Thomas bent down and picked up his son. He immediately noticed that Gavin had tears in his eyes.

"It's okay bud. We're safe now."

Stir wound around Thomas' bare ankles nonstop.

"Why...why did those things come for us?" Gabbi asked in a shaky voice. "We've never seen that before."

"But I have," Gavin indicated.

"Wait. What? What are you talking about?" Thomas asked as Gabbi looked on in rapt attention. "When?"

"The time when Uncle Sam's dad helped us escape from the General's locked room. I saw the same thing then. They were after us too."

"Did you see them any other time?" his father asked.

265

Gavin shook his head no. "This was the second time."

"But why now?" Gabbi pressed. "Why this trip and not the fourteen other trips we've taken?"

"Sam's father told me I was immune, that I could never be discovered. But the last time I saw them there were more people with me."

Thomas got it. "The children. Your sister plus Sam and Bill's kids. You had five others with you."

Gavin nodded. "And that was the farthest I'd ever traveled, at the time, until today."

Gabbi interjected. "So you're saying they, whatever they were, can sense us in their world?"

"It would appear so," Thomas replied.

"But if that's the case then why come at us now, today? We've been traveling quite a bit over the last week."

"Your scent," Gavin said. "I think they have your scent now."

"That's disturbing," she murmured. "Fuuuccck. Hey, sorry for the language but I almost crapped my shorts." Gabbi looked around. "Where the heck did you take us anyway? It's dark in here."

"Home," Gavin whispered. "Back home."

What? Home?

With Stir hot on his tail Thomas began to recognize where they now were.

Oh man. I get it.

"Gabbi, open that door so we can head outside."

Gabbi followed Thomas' instructions and the four of them walked through the open door and found themselves outside SANDBOX's motor pool, now abandoned and defunct. They saw a humongous pile of rubble off in the distance and the entire

266

property had a new chain link fence erected around it. Signs were posted every thirty feet that stated the area was off limits.

"Where are we?" she asked. "This can't be Virginia. Wait, is that the ocean?"

"It's not Virginia," Thomas answered. "This is where SANDBOX used to be. California. Marin. Home."

She turned back to face them. "Seriously? Shit, I'm sorry."

"It's okay. Let's just concentrate on how we get back to Virginia because we're certainly not going back through there," Thomas said as he pointed back towards the motor pool and the experience they had just gone through.

"No argument from me there," Gabbi said. "But you do realize we're standing here, wet and in our bathing suits, right? No cash. No phones. No clothes."

Thomas nodded. "We'll figure it out. All we have to do is make it to a phone." He turned to his son. "Hey Gav, sorry to bring this up but could you, well you know, have Stir disappear. We're out in public and that's the last kind of attention we need right now."

Gavin was unhappy about the request but he completely understood. Stir vanished.

"Thanks bud. I'm going to put you down now so we can find a way out of here and get to a phone."

The three of them made their way to the fence and spotted an opening a hundred feet away, closer to the rubble. As they made their way there Gabbi poised a new question.

"Soooo, I know this experience is fresh on our minds buuutttt, did anyone else recognize what some of those things that were after us looked like?"

Thomas and Gavin shared a long look before Thomas answered.

"Yeah, they looked like the same essence that Stir is made out of."

41
The Other Place

Within the confines of The Albatross, Robert Aleman continued to go over his plans with the others, who sat at the table with him; Anna Garland, Nikolay Dmitriev, Victor Bannon, Frank Russell and Alexei Vorobyrov.

"The power that drew these darkened souls here, that power comes from our collective strength. The six of us, together, pulled all these inflicted souls to us."

"For what purpose?" Anna asked.

"To prove to all of you that we're stronger together. And with that strength we will take our revenge."

Victor leaned forward, very interested. "How?"

Raven couldn't contain himself. "I'm glad you asked. Now as I'm sure you're all aware, the Caretaker has decreed that our souls, or however you'd like to view your present state, cannot leave this place. We're stuck."

"Stop wasting our time General," Yuri stated. "Make your point."

"Patience Frank," Raven replied. "Now, I believe the revenge we all seek might well be within our grasp, but to obtain it we have to work as a collective unit."

"Specifics," Victor said, "we need specifics or otherwise I'm leaving."

"And yet time is exactly what we're all afraid of, isn't it? In this place, where time doesn't exist, all that's left for each of us is our eternal contemplation of what could have been, or should have been. Those options were taken away from us. In fact, why don't we recap exactly how each of us ended up here, shall we?" Raven turned to Yuri and started in. "You were captured, placed in federal custody and interrogated for two years before you died of a heart attack. Alexei, your attack on the families in Hawaii didn't quite turn out the way you wanted it. In fact, your head came clean off thanks to Thomas Clark's young son and his imaginary pet, if I'm not mistaken."

"Otebis'," Alexei told Raven in Russian. "Fuck off."

"Moving on. Nikolay, as safe as you thought you were in Cuba with your group of ex-Spetsnaz soldiers, Sam and Bill made short work of them. Of course, you couldn't keep your mouth shut on the beach and ended up with a bullet in your head courtesy of Sam himself."

Nikolay didn't reply but his face clearly showed his displeasure.

"Anna, my sweet Anna. As honed as your assassin skills were you eventually failed me, and yourself, when you tried to kill Sam and Bill. In fact, you received a taste of your own medicine and died by your own hand, literally. That was one heck of a bloody puddle you left on the floor."

"Go to hell General," she told him.

"Moving on. I myself, having Sam, Bill, Thomas and their families at gunpoint, was unable to take them out. I was shot and died when SANDBOX, the building I planted explosives throughout, exploded and crushed me to death." Raven turned towards Victor. "And that just leaves you Victor."

"Yeah?" the previous DCI said. "What about me?"

"Well, your death was imaginative to say the least. You had the children and the men's wives in your grasp. Hell, you practically killed Laura until Thomas stumbled on the fact that he had his own power. Then it turned bad for you, really bad, didn't it?"

Victor chose to remain silent.

"Instead of killing you outright for your atrocities, not to mention explaining why you were dead, they pushed you through Gavin's portal. At first you probably thought they'd made a mistake, but in time you realized that they weren't coming back. How long did you have to endure the agony brought on by hunger and dehydration? I bet it built up, hour after hour, until your thirst and the realization what you were going to die overwhelmed you."

"What's your point?" Victor finally said as he grinded his teeth.

"My point is that I believe your body, or what's left of it, is the key to our current predicament."

"How so?" Anna asked.

Raven smiled. "Thomas' kid, Gavin, has the ability to create a portal to this realm. Now, I've heard rumors rumbling in the Dark District for some time that the child visits from time to time."

"I've heard the same," Nikolay added, "but so what."

Raven continued. "What I'm trying to get at, and the point of gathering all of you all here, is that I propose we use that portal to go back."

None of them expected what he'd just told them and their faces reflected it.

"Is that even possible?" Yuri asked.

"It's never been attempted because an opportunity like this has never before presented itself," Raven clarified.

"So what," Victor said, "you're just saying we walk through and miraculously we're alive again back on Earth? That sounds absurd."

Raven nodded. "Perhaps. But think about it. There's no reason for us not to try, is there? Do any of you have something better that's occupying your time?"

"So even if we wanted to go along with your plan," said Alexei, "there's still a huge hurdle ahead of us."

"And what do you think that is?" Raven asked him.

"Locating the boy. We don't even know where to begin looking for him. Without his portal this plan is over before it even begins."

"Actually, that part of the plan is the easiest part."

Alexei chuckled. "Fine. Enlighten us then."

"And that's why we need Victor."

"What are you talking about?" Victor retorted.

Raven pressed the issue. "You have something none of us have."

"What's that?"

"We all have the ability to go back to where we died. However, your body is here because you died somewhere in this world. Maybe it's time you showed us exactly where."

42
The Other Place

"We all have the ability to go back to where we died. However, your body is here because you died somewhere in this world. Maybe it's time you showed us exactly where."

Rebecca eavesdropped with her back towards the group and couldn't believe the conversation she'd just overheard.

Oh shit. What the hell do I do now? What they're planning to do sounds crazy, but what if it works?

A multitude of expressions washed over her face.

What if Gavin's portal is a loophole? What if they go through it and appear on the other side? If they succeed then everyone in the Dark District will desire the same thing. A multitude of evil will follow, enter that portal and spew forth on an unsuspecting Earth. In essence it will become hell on Earth.

She took a moment to glance over her shoulder and noticed that the six individuals had stood up. She watched them begin to walk towards the entrance of The Albatross.

Shit! I'm dead. They're dead. What am I supposed to do to stop this?

Without having an answer to her question she slowly stood up, as to not attract any attention from the numerous individuals she had recognized on her way in.

Nice and casual.

Rebecca walked cautiously, but with purpose, after General Aleman and his new collaborators. As they exited a strong hand suddenly landed on her shoulder and spun her around. It was one of Aleman's men, the same man who had shot her in the head.

"Hey, don't I know you?"

"I don't think so," she instantly replied and tried to turn away.

273

He pulled her shoulder back once again. "I do know you. You're that bitch that…"

Rebecca brought her left knee up as hard as could and solidly connected with his groan. He collapsed instantly and she took that opportunity to escape.

I didn't expect that to work. In fact, he shouldn't have been able to touch me at all. I guess that means I'm still holding on to my past life tighter than I want to admit.

Rebecca shook off that thought as she looked around the Dark District streets outside the Albatross. The six were nowhere in sight.

Damn.

Rebecca gazed upward and launched herself off the ground and into the sky.

I may have lost them for now but I definitely know where they're going.

43

Wednesday Oct 31, 2001

Three days before Dr. Matsushita abandoned Peter under a bridge in Washington D.C.. Yamato had used his ability to command Peter, now nothing more than a hideous creature with incredible strength, to stay out of sight for three days. After those seventy-two hours he instructed the creature to make his presence known to the world, and that's exactly what he did.

Officers Davis and Hicks rolled their patrol car to a stop near a well-known homeless encampment.

"What's that over there?" Davis said as he pointed towards the trees in the distance.

"What are you talking about? I don't see a thing," Hicks replied as he followed his partner's finger.

"Shit. It's gone."

"It's gone? There are homeless all over the area. You probably just caught one of them taking a shit or something."

Davis shrugged. "I'm not sure." He put the vehicle in park and stepped out. "I'm going to go check it out."

"Come on Davis. Just because you're a rookie it doesn't mean you have to go traipsing after every little thing to prove you're a good cop. It's Halloween and my wife's been busting my balls to be home in time to take our boy out. Let it go."

Davis was undeterred. "It'll just take a second," he said as he turned and headed through the underbrush towards the underpass in the distance. "I'll be right back."

Hicks shook his head as he watched his partner vanish into the foliage.

"Fucking impatient rookie. I'm never going to hear the end of this." Hicks opened his door, stepped out and yelled, "Davis, hold up!"

A deafening and dreadful bellow sliced through the afternoon air. It instantly sent a chill up Officer Hicks' spine. He pulled his service weapon and aimed it in the direction he heard the sound come from.

"Davis!? Talk to me Davis!"

In the distance Hicks heard the unmistakable sound of branches breaking as if someone was barreling through them.

"Davis!?"

Twenty feet.

Fifteen feet.

Ten feet.

Hicks prepped his weapon and took aim at the unknown individual.

"Take cover!" Davis screamed as he burst through the undergrowth, vaulted over the hood, and took defense next to his partner as he pulled his own weapon.

Hicks didn't buy it. "Come on, how'd you manage to scream like that? You really had me goi..."

The horrific sound emanated once again, thunderous and closer than ever. Hicks barely had time to turn as a humungous individual charged out of the bushes. It rammed the other side of their cruiser with such force that it clipped both officers and sent them flying. As they landed hard on the pavement Davis and Hicks lost their grips on their side arms and they skidded out of reach.

Hicks couldn't turn away as whatever it was jumped effortlessly on top of their patrol car, caving the roof in under its weight. Hicks finally got a good look and sensed that the creature used to be a man. But now the individual attacking them had large arms, long fingers and sharpened nails. It's enlarged body was covered in boils and barely looked human.

"What the fu…"

The creature, on top of the patrol car, lifted its head and let out a guttural roar. Hicks was paralyzed in fear as he continued to stare at the unholy monstrosity. Four rapid gun shots rang out from Davis' weapon and tore into the creature's hide. It screamed, fell backwards and landed on the far side of their vehicle.

"I…I think you got it," Hicks said as he slowly got his feet under him and stood up. He quickly retrieved his own side arm.

"What the hell was that thing?" Davis asked.

"Shit if I know rookie. But whatever it was its dead now, thanks to you."

Davis began to edge around the front of the car. "We'd better call it in," he said as he cautiously approached from one side.

"First thing's first," Hicks reminded him. "Check on it and whatever you do, go easy."

"I hit it four times center mass," as Davis approached the creature lying on the ground. "It's not moving. It's dead."

"You don't know shit rookie. I said go eas…"

One of the creature's hands lashed out and grabbed Officer Davis' leg. Before Hicks could react the creature plunged all five sharp and elongated fingers, from his other hand, into Davis' chest. Davis' eyes opened wide in surprise and blood spurted from his mouth.

"NOOOO!" Hicks heard himself yell as he brought his weapon up to bear.

As the creature dropped the lifeless officer to the ground Hicks depressed his trigger over and over, lost in his own rage at the senseless death of his partner. The creature took the first two bullets from Hicks' weapon before he fled into the bushes. Hicks emptied his weapon into the trees until its slide locked open. It took a few moments before he realized he was out and quickly dropped the empty mag and replaced it with a full one. But by then the creature was gone and all that was left behind was a scene from a horror movie.

Hicks looked down at Davis' body, gutted and lying in a vast pool of blood.

"Fuck me." He pushed the button on radio microphone. "Ten thirty-three. Ten thirty-three. Officer needs assistance. I have an officer down."

* * *

Peter, or what he'd been transformed in to, bolted from the scene, driven away by the barrage of gunfire. Very little blood trickled out of his wounds as he darted out of the woods and ran into afternoon traffic. Horns blared and people angrily shouted as Peter made his way up the highway towards downtown D.C., leaving a multitude of crushed hoods and roofs in his wake.

* * *

"Nine-one-one. What's the nature of your emergency?"

"A monster just ran over the roof of my car. It's heading north up South Capitol Street."

"Sir. It's illegal to call nine-one-one with a false report. You could be arrested."

"I'm not fucking lying goddammit. I barely survived as my roof caved-in, and you're dicking with me?"

"Sir, please hold for one moment."

278

The operator muted the line and noticed the increased volume of calls the other operators were involved in.

I'm going to sound like an idiot but oh well.

She cleared her throat. "Has anyone else taken a call about a 'monster' on South Capitol Street?"

* * *

"Team Three," the dispatcher voice said over the intercom, "Hot call."

"What've you got for us?" the team lead radioed back.

"We've got multiple reports of a deranged man that's headed north along South Capitol Street. The description fits a ten thirty-three call made five minutes ago. Your team is north of the suspect's position."

"Did that officer make it?"

"Negative. The officer died on the scene. Suspect was last reported at N and Capitol. I've got Team Two coming in from the south and local police are beginning to block off the side streets."

The team leader grimaced. "Roger that. Team three in route from the north. Keep us apprised of any new information."

"Will do Team Three."

* * *

"This is Wendy Williams of WJLA 'News at Five'. I'm currently coming to you live, from the corner of K and Capitol Street, where just seconds ago members of the SWAT team arrived and appear to be in the process of blockading the street. In the past ten minutes nine-one-one has been flooded with calls of what some are describing as, and I quote, 'a monster'. Apparently whatever it is may be causing havoc on the streets of Washington D.C. at this very moment. Some of the reports talk of the 'monster' that crushed their cars, seriously injuring some of the people and trapping them inside their own vehicles. I don't know about you but its Halloween, and as we all know this day always seems to bring out the crazies."

* * *

Peter plunged full speed up the middle of Capitol Street. He was furious, confused and not in control of his actions. The only thing he did know was that his body had warped; transformed in to a repugnant entity that now demanded as much attention as it could muster.

He looked up and immediately discerned that the road was obstructed ahead with flashing red and blue lights. A quick glance behind him spurred him on as he noticed additional police on his tail.

Peter let out a fierce and bloodcurdling roar as he charged ahead.

* * *

Hobbes keyed the facility's intercom. "Everyone needs to come to the Tech wing immediately!"

Within a minute Thomas, Laura, Emily, Gavin, Gabbi and the DCI, who was checking up on everyone's status, made their way over to Hobbes.

"What is it?" the DCI asked. "Is something wrong with the mission?"

"No no no. Nothing like that. But shit, you have to look at what's on the news."

Hobbes unmuted the large monitor on the wall and the sounds of automatic gunfire instantly filled the room. On the screen a television crew appeared to be taking cover behind their van but had extended their camera outward to capture the shaky footage that they were all now watching. The events that appeared on the monitor were chaotic at best.

"That's downtown Washington," the DCI stated.

Multiple SWAT members aimed and shot at something that moved very quickly.

Whatever they were shooting at suddenly stopped and picked up a police vehicle. It stood on long legs and its sharp claws were seen protruding off to one side.

"What the hell is that thing?" Thomas questioned.

Round after round peppered the creature, leaving blood specked holes in its skin, but bullets didn't slow it down. The creature threw the vehicle at the SWAT van with such intensity that two SWAT members couldn't get out of the way and were crushed.

"Jesus Christ!" the news reporter screamed from off screen. "Oh my God! We need to get out of here or we're all going to die!"

Not one of them knew what to make of what they were watching. The creature roared so loudly that even Thomas and Laura cringed.

More automatic gunfire filled the screen as SWAT and police officers rallied together. A barrage of bullets ripped into the creature and disrupted its howl. The camera man took that opportunity to zoom in and the world got its first real glimpse of the creature. It had long bulging arms, elongated fingers topped with sharp razor looking claws. Its head was a misshapen, bulging mess and a lone eye stared back at the camera with an intensity that couldn't be measured. Patches of boils littered the rest of its body and the creature looked as if it had just stepped out of a Wes Craven horror film.

"Holy shit," Thomas said. "Where did that thing come from?"

As the creature continued to soak up bullets from the police something else became very apparent.

"No way," Gavin muttered in disbelief. "Are you seeing this?"

"Yeah, I think we're all seeing it son, and I don't know what to say."

On the monitor they all watched as the creature's wounds began to heal, the bullets tumbling out of the mended holes and on to the street.

44

Wednesday Oct 31, 2001

Uniformed bodies littered the street alongside a multitude of broken and battered vehicles, tossed haphazardly amidst the carnage. The firefight had intensified as additional police and SWAT swarmed the scene. With the added firepower Peter's tissue was torn apart faster than it could possibly repair itself.

Two news helicopters diverted to the area and filmed the incident from the sky. The news camera, on the ground, continued to capture the horrific events as well.

Seconds later the footage was broadcast by national affiliates and streamed over the internet to the world. Within a minute the amount of people that had tuned in was staggering, and not one of them knew what to make of the creature they saw battling the police in downtown Washington, D.C.

As additional weapons were brought to bear the creature took the brute of the punishment. A seemingly endless supply of bullets shredded his body and people around the world witnessed the monster's final moments. Peter wasn't Peter anymore, but deep inside his humanity still lived on. He knew his time was over so he lifted his head and howled. His sorrowful cry was heard by millions as his body gave in and collapsed to the street. Some people cheered but others felt only sadness for the creature. And even though it had been taken down by the hands of those men and women, who swore to protect the city and its inhabitants, the world collectively asked one question; what was that thing?

Thomas and his family asked the same question as they turned away from the television and stared at the DCI. Hobbes muted the sound.

"What the hell is going on?"

"I have no idea," Robert Duncan replied as he met each one of their eyes. "Honestly. I'm as shocked as you are."

"He's telling the truth," Laura stated.

"Great," Thomas said with frustration. "So if you don't know what's going on then why do I get the impression that someone else must?"

"I…"

"I'll tell you why. This," Thomas said as he pointed at the screen, "isn't a coincidence. You bring me and my family out here and now, suddenly, there's a misshapen man running around the streets with what appears to be incredible strength and healing powers. So I'll ask it again Director, what the hell is going on?"

"Thomas, I had nothing to do with this, I swear. I will lock down this facility and you can question everyone. I've been absolutely straight with you from the beginning. This didn't come from our camp."

Thomas looked over at Laura.

"He's telling the truth."

"Shit." Thomas began to pace, somewhat in a panic. "How could this have happened? I mean, this isn't going away. The whole world is going to see this, if they haven't already."

"Honey…"

"They're going to go over the footage frame by frame. They're going to talk about the healing, the visible healing that we caught on to right away. Then they're going to dissect it; learn from it. What we all saw, it just can't be explained away. The public is going to demand answers." He stopped and looked at all of them. "And after that it's just be a matter of time before we're all exposed."

"Thomas, you're reaching," the DCI told him.

"Am I? Am I really? Someone else is out there, right now, and look what they created; a fucking monster."

"I can't deny what we all just witnessed. It's obvious that at least one person is out there, experimenting, and not for a positive outcome, obviously. And you're right, the public is going to want answers, but they're not the only ones. Multiple government agencies and research companies are going to want their hand in the cookie jar on this one, that's for sure."

"And this can't be covered up?" Gabbi asked.

The DCI shook his head. "That's impossible at this point so there's nothing I can do in that regard. However, I will tap my contacts and make sure we know where its body will be taken."

"So they can experiment on it?"

"Most likely."

Thomas didn't like it. "And then who knows what they'll discover. What we explicitly asked to keep secret is now out there in the world. This is exactly what we needed to contain and somehow it's out there. We blew it and it's all my fault."

Laura put her arms around her husband. "It's going to be okay."

"I only wish I could believe that."

"Listen," the DCI finally said after a few seconds of silence. "I know it's raw right now, but this could be an opportunity for us."

Thomas saw where he was headed. "You're going to take this incident and try to capitalize on it?"

"No, not capitalize. The word is combat. The bad news is that some other group is experimenting and for whatever reason decided to make their progress public."

"You call what we just saw as progress?"

"Not from our perspective," the DCI replied. "What we witnessed was the exact opposite of what I've wanted for you and your family. We can do good, but we can't do it without your consent or willingness. The ugly reality is that we're behind the eight-ball and now we're on the defensive. I would strongly suggest that we take a proactive stance while we root out whoever's behind the experiment the entire world is currently talking about."

"But to what end?" Thomas asked. "Why should I submit?"

It was the DCI's turn to point at the television. "Do you honestly think that's the last time the world is going to witness an attack like that?"

Thomas and Laura remained silent.

"Neither do I."

It'd been hours since he'd started watching but Dr. Matsushita couldn't tear his eyes away from the television. Every station was airing footage from the incident. An endless string of witnesses wanted their fifteen minutes of fame in front of the camera, each one recounting things from their perspective. Expert after expert expressed their opinion but many of those opinions were quickly rebuked. It didn't take long for the global debates to develop.

Yamato was overwhelmed, and thrilled, at the amount of mayhem his creation had brought to the city, the United States and ultimately the world. The success of his endeavor was currently immeasurable because the fallout of it was in its infancy. He watched as analysts concentrated on the creature's healing ability, commenting over and over that what they were seeing was unbelievable; the next stage of human evolution.

The world will never be the same again.

Ding.

Yamato, extremely giddy, turned his head towards the sounds that came from his lab and got up from the chair he was sitting in.

"Excellent. It's time to see what really went wrong with my test subjects."

Days before, when three of his four homeless abductees died from their injections, Dr. Matsushita had taken tissue samples from each of them. Dr. Matsushita had been running computer tests to analyze those samples. He needed to narrow down the specific reasons why three of his subjects had died, and why Peter was the only one that had dramatically altered.

Yamato sat down on a lab stool and accessed the computer's conclusions.

"Interesting."

Their tissue was too old; damaged. Well that makes sense, they were homeless. The good news is that I saved them from the harsh winter that's just around the corner. They should thank me that I put them out of their misery. No more suffering for you. Now, what else do we have? Hmmm. The blood sample obtained from Thomas was contaminated, but I knew that already. Still, the side effects weren't what I was expecting.

Dr. Matsushita scrolled down and skimmed through the data. *Wait a second. What's this?*

He stopped and thoroughly read the rest of the analysis. When he was done he leaned back from the monitor and slowly spun on his stool.

"Thomas Clark, what a wonderful paradox you continue to bring to the table. And because of it I'm now torn; torn between staying with my original course of action or diverting down this new path you've presented me with. What to do, what to do."

Dr. Matsushita stood up and contemplated his two options. As he did he brought his right thumb up to his mouth, as he often did, and lightly began to chew on his thumbnail. The sleeve on his lab coat slid down slightly as his brain methodically worked on the problem. But then he caught a reflection of himself, a shimmer in one of the lab's glass walls. Without realizing it he walked towards his likeness until his eyes focused on the scar tissue that ran up and down his right arm.

The fire. Can't get out. Burning.

His breathing intensified as panic coursed through his body.

The explosion. Loud. Death raining over us.

Yamato collapsed to his knees just as he'd done in Hiroshima decades before. He imagined his father, sister and mother all

288

beside him; covering and protecting him from the brutal explosion. The wave of fire washed over them.

"NOOOOOOO!"

He fell to one side and lay there, panting and sweating on the floor. Five minutes passed before he moved a muscle.

I know what I need to do now.

Yamato rolled to one side and righted himself.

I wanted the United States to know what fear tasted like by perfecting the abilities that Thomas Clark possessed and manipulating them to fit my needs. But now I will achieve that same goal without the complications I'm facing. I've been given a means to the end; a gift horse; a sign. America will tremble for a time, and the world will follow. Then everything will be quiet. Very quiet.

Dr. Matsushita smiled as he stared at the computer screen. On it he reread the following:

Smallpox sequence detected

Utilizing my own personal bio-weapon, which also happens to be the world's deadliest disease, will be entirely more satisfying.

He turned and began to jot down, all with a renewed kick to his step, a list of bullet points he'd have to attain to move forward with his new plan.

Recreate previous lab results. Identify and isolate smallpox sequence. Augment strain. Create delivery system. Test subjects. Additional lab equipment. Test runs.

Yamato paused in thought. His eyes moved back a few lines.

Test subjects. Yes. I will need both young and old guinea pigs for my plan to work. And if I happen to get lucky with another result like Peter, well, the world will be thrilled to have another plaything to gawk at.

46
Thursday Nov 1, 2001

Overnight the government, by executive order from the
President of the United States, swooped in and took possession of
the creature's corpse. Questions of where its body had been taken,
both by the press and by foreign leaders, were outright ignored.
That quickly led to public speculation that the creature had either
escaped from a government research lab, or was currently in the
process of being dissected in a secret government facility, much
like Area 51. Regardless of the creature's whereabouts, the raw
footage captured from the D.C. incident was consistently replayed.
Scientific experts were interviewed to get their opinion on what
was obviously, at least to most, the creature's ability to self-heal.
That was heavily scrutinized and had become the topic of
conversation throughout the world. Newspaper and internet
websites printed similar headlines like 'Human's next evolutionary
step?' and 'Scientific breakthrough or scientific debacle?'. Rag
newspapers printed titles similar to 'Where did this man-beast
come from?' and 'Alien attacks D.C.'.

* * *

The following morning both Thomas and Laura sat down with
Emily and Gavin in the family room.
  "How'd you two sleep last night?" Thomas asked.
  "Dad," Emily said, "Gav and I slept just fine. But from the
look of it you two were the ones that had a hard time sleeping.
Mom has bags under her eyes."
  "Yeah," Gavin added. "So do you dad."

291

It was true. Thomas and Laura had been up all night watching the news and worrying about how it could affect them. In a matter of hours their anxiety levels had risen to new levels as they agonized over how, as a family, they should react if at all, to the knowledge the world was now energized about. It inevitably ended up as a long night for both of them.

Laura spoke softly. "How do you two feel about what you saw last night?"

Emily and Gavin looked over at each other and then back at their parents.

"I don't know," Emily replied. "I feel bad I guess."

"Why bad?"

Gavin answered for his sister. "Because someone did that to that person; turned them into a creature and then set it loose."

"I agree with Gav. Someone did this on purpose. The question is why." Emily paused for a few seconds. "But I don't think that's what you're asking us. I think you're more interested in whether or not we're scared of what we saw on television. And if that's your real question then my answer is no, I'm not scared."

"And neither am I," Gavin added.

"And why not?" their father asked.

"Its eyes," Emily told him.

"What about them?" Laura probed.

"They were sad, like if it was in pain."

Gavin nodded. "I don't think it wanted to do what it was doing."

Thomas and Laura were somewhat surprised at their children's unified response.

"Your mother and I are proud of you. Not everyone saw the situation like you have."

292

"Why should they?" Gavin said. "They aren't like us. No one is."

"Until now," Emily observed.

"Exactly," Thomas said. "And that leaves us with an extremely difficult decision to make which is why we wanted to discuss this as a family. How do you think we should proceed?"

Emily shifted in her seat. "You're referring to what the DCI has wished-for from the very beginning, right?"

"Yes, to cultivate my DNA in an effort to recreate similar abilities, like both of yours, in other human beings."

"So why ask us then? Last time I checked you're the adults."

"Yes, of course," Laura replied, "but what we decide will affect us all. It's important to your father and I that you're involved in this decision."

"Fine. But what are you really talking about? Are you suggesting that you're going to have another child or something?"

Laura shook her head. "No, nothing like that."

"Then what are we talking about then; the pros and cons of sharing our abilities with the rest of the human race? Is that it?"

"Something like that," Thomas answered.

"You were up all night watching the television; you must know the rest of the world has figured it out already." Emily looked back and forth between her parents. "Whether either of you wants to admit it or not, the entire world's perception shifted last night. So now the question changes from what we should do to what we have to do about it."

"Have to?" Laura tested.

"Mom. Seriously. Let me do the math for you. First, we've got the creature. His body is gone and who knows where it is now or what's going to happen to it. No one has to be a genius to

293

conclude that it's going to be sliced open and the government is going to start dabbling."

"Gross Em," Gavin said.

"Second, whoever let that creature loose did it for a reason, or maybe they didn't. In either case that's another group that's already been experimenting, and obviously with some success."

"So what are you saying sweetie?"

"I know you both have been doing everything you can to keep Gav and me safe. But I can't believe for a second that we're going to just sit back and let the world get their answers from someone else; especially considering the fact that we don't even know who publicized it the way they did in the first place. I don't want to expose our family; that much I get. But what I do want is for us to find a way to fight back."

* * *

"I'm thrilled with what you've decided Thomas," said the DCI on the other end of the phone. "I'll send a few white coats to the facility."

"How soon?"

"Two hours. I'd be there in person but yesterday's events really stirred up one hell of a shit storm within the various government offices, if you can imagine. The level of intrigue has skyrocketed."

"I have a pretty good idea about that, sir."

"Of course. My apologies if I came off as flippant."

"No apologies necessary. It's not every day that the President of the United States appropriates the one thing that the entire world is talking about. Do you know where he sent the body?"

"Not yet," the DCI replied. "And currently I'm not in a position to ask. The President is keeping this one close to his vest which is all the more reason for us to move forward before we end up that much farther behind the eight-ball."

"Agreed. Anyway, we'll be there in a few hours."

"Thank you Thomas."

* * *

After they arrived at the underground facility Emily and Gavin splintered off to spend time with Gabbi while Thomas and Laura made their way towards the Laboratory wing. In the distance they saw a guard stationed outside the entrance to the lab.

"Are you ready for this?" Thomas asked his wife.

"As ready as I'll ever be. The world is gaining speed and our daughter is right. We need to fight back before it's too late."

Thomas smiled at Laura as they paused in front of the lab doors. "I just hope we're doing the right thing."

"So do I. I love you."

"I love you too."

The guard opened the door for them. Laura stepped though and Thomas followed behind. Inside they were immediately greeted by two new faces, a male and a female, both dressed in white coats.

"I'm Dr. Joseph Brown," a man in his sixties said as he approached, his right hand extended.

Thomas and Laura both shook his hand.

"And this is Dr. Ming Sung."

"A pleasure to meet you," Dr. Sung said as she shook the Clark's hands as well. "Do you have any questions for us before we begin?"

Laura addressed the two doctors. "Do you know why you're here?"

"We've been specifically tasked, by the DCI, to analyze your DNA for genetic anomalies."

"And are you aware of the purpose for this analysis?"

They both shook their heads. "The DCI said that answer to that question would present itself in due time. What did he mean by that? Why go to this level of secrecy? Why do we have a guard stationed at the door?"

Laura nodded to Thomas which indicated that the doctors weren't lying.

"All in good time," Thomas told them. "In the meantime, my wife and I would like to get this over with."

And so, for the next few hours, Thomas and Laura subjected to the process of having multiple vials of blood drawn, skin and hair samples categorized. To top it off, they also subjected themselves to the careful extraction of their semen and eggs. By the end they felt like pin cushions and hoped that their sacrifice would ultimately lead to a positive outcome. But, they knew only time would tell.

47
Thursday Nov 1, 2001

In the rugged mountains of Afghanistan Bill was on point, which meant that out of the six team members he was currently up front, cautiously leading their advancement. Bill stopped, brought his left arm up and made a fist. The five men, staggered behind him, immediately dropped to one knee, brought up their weapons and, using their night vision goggles, scanned the darkness for danger. Sam inched towards Bill and whispered.

"What'ya got?"

Bill pointed out in the distance and spoke softly in return. "I thought I caught some movement on the ridge we're coming up on."

"Roger that." Sam activated his radio. "Team. Hold. Hobbes, you with us?"

"I hear you."

"We need a thermal scan."

"Stand by Sam," Hobbes replied.

"Roger that. Standing by."

Back at the underground facility Hobbes feverously typed away on his keyboard while his eyes darted back and forth between multiple computer monitors. Thirty seconds later a new image overlay popped up. He worked the controls until the satellite image zoomed in towards the Afghan mountains at an alarming rate. Hobbes made a minor adjustment to the coordinates and six human figures appeared on his screen.

"Okay, I'm zeroed in on your team Sam. It looks like a clear night in your neck of the woods. What can I do for you?"

"Survey the ridge that's south of our position."

"On it."

Hobbes zoomed out a bit and then manipulated the satellite camera controls to sweep south. There, on the ridge, three human shapes were clearly evident.

"Sam."

"Go ahead Hobbes."

"You were right. I'm counting three, I repeat, there are three soldiers on the ridge two hundred from your position. One is moving around. In fact," Hobbes said as he zoomed in, "it looks like he's smoking. The other two haven't moved and appear to be sleeping."

"Acknowledged. Thanks."

"Do you need anything else?" Hobbes asked.

"If something changes then let me know. Sam out."

Sam raised his forefinger, twirled his hand in a circle and the rest of the team rallied on his position.

"We've got three tangos ahead. One is active and the other two have been designated as sleeping." Sam pointed at Darius and Jordon. "Both of you drop your gear. You're with Bill and me. Silent takedowns. Carl. Eliot," he said to the remaining two, "Stay here."

Quickly and quietly the four men shrugged out of their heavy gear. In the darkness they unsheathed their combat knives and, with a nod to the two left behind, snuck off into the night. Back at the facility Hobbes watched the four men slink away on his computer screen towards their unsuspecting targets in the distance. It took an agonizing five minutes for the four men to silently creep up the ridge and get into position.

Thirty feet from the camp Sam's team spread out, encircled it and came in from all sides at once. The smoker had finished his cigarette and now cradled his AK-47 in the crook of his arm as he continued his watch. As Sam crept closer he hoped his target's night vision hadn't fully corrected itself due to the cigarette ember, but he was prepared either way.

Sam waited until the soldier turned his back and then rushed ten feet towards him. The Taliban soldier began to turn around but before he could Sam's left arm hooked around the man's neck like a vice grip. A split second later Sam's right hand arced in an overhead motion and his knife plunged deep into the man's chest.

Hobbes watched in morbid fascination as Sam and his team decidedly eliminated the three Taliban soldiers. The two men that were asleep never woke up again, but Hobbes knew that there were no gentlemen rules when it came to war. Long gone were the days of soldiers lining up in rows to take turns shooting at the opposing army. Now it was kill or be killed. And if you weren't ready, well, that was your problem.

Sam, Bill, Darius and Jordon lay the bodies next to each other, wiped the blood from their blades on the dead men's clothing and sheathed them.

"Hobbes?" Sam said into his radio.

"Still here."

"Do you see anything else out there?"

"Negative. You're clear, although you're practically on top of your objective."

"I know. We're heading to our final overwatch position once we gear back up."

"Understood. I'll keep an eye out for any patrols in your vicinity."

"Much appreciated. Sam out."

The four men traversed the terrain back to where they had departed from, hefted their gear on their backs and continued on into the night.

Two hours later, as the remnants of night were threatened by the light of dawn; Sam's team reached their overwatch position above Panjshir Valley. They knew that they had another hour before daybreak and they utilized that time to dig in and camouflage their position.

"To up and four down," Sam ordered. "Bill and I will wake two of you up in a couple of hours for your turn at watch. In the meantime, get some rest. We're all going to need it."

* * *

It was late in the day when Sam and Bill were tapped for another watch.

"Anything?" Sam asked Carl and Eliot.

"It's all been written down. Movements. Number of men. Small arms. The usual."

"Thanks. Get some sack time."

"Roger that."

Sam and Bill took up prone positions behind their camouflaged desert netting and then placed high powered binoculars up to their eyes. They began to sweep the village in the distance for Taliban movement, new areas of interest and their primary target, Hamid Emal Habibi.

"Feels weird to be back here," Bill whispered.

"Tell me about it." Sam said in agreement. "The nine months we spent training the Mujahideen back in the eighties was enough time in this particular part of the world for me. These past four days, making our way to this village, have been grueling."

300

"Really? I'm glad to hear I'm not the only one. Apparently we're not as young as we used to be."

"No shit. I'm going to have bruises and a sore back for weeks after this is all over."

Sam and Bill continued to scan the as they continued their quiet conversation from halfway up one of the village's adjacent mountains.

"Listen Sam, there's been something on my mind that I wanted to talk to you about."

"Okay. What is it?"

"I don't really know how to begin."

"Just say it."

"Fine. What the hell are we doing out here?"

"You know what we're doing Bill. We're tracking down one of the men who masterminded nine-eleven."

"That's not what I meant. I mean, why was it so important for us to come out here; to prove ourselves?"

"What are you saying?"

"Listen, you know I've got your back, no matter what happens. You know that. But our business, SANDBOX, it was ripped away from us before we could do anything about it. Everything we worked for just slipped through our hands."

"I know. I was there. Your point?"

"And now here we are in the middle of a mission we should have passed on, and in doing so we've left the people that really matter to us back home."

"We worked with Hamid for nine months. We have the edge."

"That's a load of shit and you know it. I followed your lead because I wanted what you wanted, redemption; a chance to prove to everyone out there that we weren't traitors to our country. And here we are."

Sam put down his binoculars and turned his head towards Bill.

"Where's all this coming from? You've had plenty of opportunities to bring this up before."

Bill nodded. "Yeah. But now that I'm looking down at Hamid's village I can't help but think that we acted too quickly."

Sam let this tumble around his head for a few seconds.

"Alright, I'll give you that one brother. Maybe I've been blinded by my own hatred and grasped at the first chance that came along for redemption."

"Well, we both did," Bill added.

Sam nodded. "Let's just concentrate on the success of this mission and then we'll take the time to figure out our future." He brought his binoculars back up and started to scan the village again.

"Sounds good brother. I'm sure our wives will be happy to hear thi...hold it."

"What?" Sam asked.

"Pan right. The second story building towards the back. Balcony."

Five seconds later Sam zoomed in and focused on the same location.

"Shit."

"I know," Bill replied. "That's him."

There, on the balcony, stood Hamid Emal Habibi.

"He looks older, but it's definitely him," said Sam.

"I guess we'll see if he remembers us when we meet with him later."

"Oh, he will, and he's not going to like it." Sam activated his radio. "Hobbes? Hobbes?"

"Sorry," Hobbes replied. "Was just getting a little shuteye. What's up?"

"We've got eyes on the package. Positive identification. The mission is a go for zero two-hundred."

"Understood. I'll relay the message."

48

Thursday Nov 1, 2001

Kim pulled the car into an available parking spot and killed the engine. She looked over at her sister Julie and let out a sigh.

"Are you sure you want to go through with this?"

"What other choice do you think I have?'

"How about anything else other than this?"

Julie shook her head. "Sam's left me with no other options. I feel like he's abandoned me. He's doing what he thinks is best for our family without even listening to my opinion. And now our kids are away at boarding school, for their safety, while he and your husband are on the other side of the world playing soldier."

"Come on sis, you know that's not entirely fair."

Julie stared at her sister. "Oh really? What part?"

Kim was stumped. "Oh, I don't know, okay? But this isn't the right course of action to take."

"Why not?"

"Because it's drastic. You'll blindside him and your kids. And speaking of Amanda and Craig, what do you think they'll think of you, eh?"

Julie frowned and looked away. "It doesn't matter. What matters is that I take them away from this insanity before it swallows us whole."

"Are you talking about Laura and her family or the shit that we saw on the television that the world is going berserk about?"

"They're one and the same," Julie adamantly replied. "It's beginning all over again and it's only a matter of time before one of us either gets kidnapped, injured or worse."

"You mean like dying again?" Kim asked, knowing full well she was referring to the incident in Hawaii.

"Yes, like Hawaii. I don't want to go through that again. I'm done putting my family in harm's way. And now look, a self-healing monster ravages downtown D.C. and I'm supposed to calmly think that it doesn't have any connection to Thomas? I don't fucking think so. We're going to be put in danger again."

"Alright. I get that part."

Julie shot Kim a bullshit look.

"No. Seriously Jules, I get it. We've all been through the ringer, time and time again and you and I clearly don't have any super powers. So, I get it. You feel helpless, but you're not the only one."

"I know, but I think that's the part I don't understand."

"What do you mean?" Kim asked.

"The part where you don't want to get away from all of this as well."

Kim put her hand up. "What? You think I'm going to let my twin sister just up and leave without my support?"

Julie was stunned. "But...you..."

"I'm not finished. Just because I don't want to divorce my husband, like you do, doesn't mean I don't agree with where you're coming from."

"Really?"

Kim smiled. "Really. I'm not going to let you go through this alone and I'm certainly not letting you leave me alone in that house all by myself either."

Julie leaned over and gave her sister a hug. "Thank you."

"You're welcome. We'll figure this out together, but first we need to put a plan together. What do we need?"

"Divorce papers. Packing. Money. Pick up the kids. Travel to someplace safe."

Kim was silent for a few seconds. "I still think you should give this divorce another thought."

Julie slowly shook her head back and forth.

"Alright. I've said my peace about that. You ready to get it done?"

"Yes."

Kim opened her door and stepped out and Julie did the same. They walked towards the large building, through the doors and into the spacious lobby.

"May I help you ladies?"

Julie and Kim looked towards the young woman at the front desk and then walked over to her. The woman spoke up again as they approached.

"Good afternoon. How may I help you?"

Julie spoke up. "I have an appointment with the law offices of Foley and Winston."

"Yes ma'am. Their offices are on the fourth floor." The receptionist pointed towards the bank of elevators.

"Thank you."

Julie and Kim left reception and headed across the lobby to them. Kim pushed the call button and a few seconds later one of the doors opened. They got in, hit the 4th floor button and waited patiently until the doors reopened. The two of them walked out, opened the door to Foley and Winston and headed inside.

"Good afternoon," greeted the law firm's receptionist.

Julie and Kim approached her. "Hi. My name is Julie Paige. I have an appointment with Mr. Monroe."

"Very good Mrs. Paige. I'll let Mr. Monroe you're here. Please have a seat."

"Thank you."

Five minutes after they sat down a man, dressed in a suit, emerged from the office area and approached them.

"Mrs. Paige?"

Julie and Kim got up from their seats.

"Yes," Julie replied.

The man offered up his right hand and smiled. "I'm Mr. Monroe. It's a pleasure to meet you."

Julie shook his hand. "And you as well. This is my sister, Kim Nicholson."

He swiveled and shook Kim's hand as well. "Also a pleasure."

Kim nodded politely.

"Why don't we take this meeting to my office? Please, if you'll follow me."

Mr. Monroe led them to his office. The two sisters sat down in his visitor seats while he made himself comfortable in his high back leather chair.

"Now, Mrs. Paige, how may I help you today?"

Julie cleared her throat. "I'd like to have divorce papers drawn up," she said with some discomfort in her voice.

"I see. Well, I can definitely help you with that," he said as he pulled out a legal pad to write on. "I'll need to ask you some pertinent questions before I can move forward with this. Is that alright with you?"

Julie nodded.

"What's your full name?"

"Julie Paige."

"Age?"

"Forty-one."

"What is your husband's name?"

"Sam Paige."

"His age?"

"Forty-four."

"And what does he do for a living?"

"Well…uh…I guess you could classify him as a soldier."

Mr. Monroe gave her a skeptical look. "You don't sound sure of yourself, Mrs. Paige. I should have prefaced this meeting by informing you that anything and everything you tell me is covered by client confidentiality. In other words, please speak freely. I'm your lawyer, not your husband's."

"Of course," Julie replied.

"Now, your husband's line of work?"

"He's a private military contractor that's currently working for the CIA."

"Interesting. How long have the two of you been married?"

"Fifteen years this past July."

"Is this your first marriage?"

"Yes."

"And for your husband as well?"

"Yes."

Mr. Monroe continued to jot down the relayed information. "Children?"

"Two."

"Ages and names?"

"Amanda is thirteen and Craig is nine."

He stopped writing and looked up at Julie. "And the reason you'd like to file for divorce?"

"Irreconcilable differences," she told him.

"That's it?"

"What do you mean?"

"You don't suspect him of having an affair or anything of the sort? I'm sorry to be so frank but that's my job."

"No. Never. We just don't see eye to eye anymore, that's it."

"Very well. Now this next part is a little tricky so please excuse me in advance. Are you going to request full custody of your children?"

"Absolutely," Julie stated.

"Do you think he'll fight you on that?"

"I…I don't know."

"Fair enough. Don't worry about it for now; we'll cross that bridge when we get there. In the meantime, first thing's first. When would you like to move forward with filing your papers?"

"As soon as possible."

"Alright. I can have the preliminary papers drawn up and available by tomorrow morning. If you sign off on those then I can file them in the afternoon. Once that occurs you have two options."

"Options?"

"Correct. The first is that you can have an officer of the court serve the papers to your husband. The second option is that you can do that yourself."

Kim squirmed in her seat a little as she took everything in. She wasn't pleased with the situation but she had already told her sister that she was here to support her regardless of her personal feelings in the matter.

"I hadn't really thought of that part," Julie admitted.

Mr. Monroe nodded. "That's alright. It's understandable during these proceedings that there's a lot to take in and process. Why don't you think about it and let me know tomorrow morning when you come back. Will ten o'clock work?"

"Yes," Julie said. "That'll be just fine."

Mr. Monroe stood up and the sisters followed his lead. "I'll walk you out. Katrina, our receptionist, will walk you through my invoice."

49

Friday Nov 2, 2001

Thomas and Laura walked into the Tech wing Friday morning. Hobbes was engrossed in something and Russell stood over his shoulder.

"Hey Hobbes," Thomas said in greeting. "Russell."

Hobbes looked up from his computer screen. "Oh hey Thomas. Laura."

"Morning," Russell replied.

"You both look tired," Laura told them.

Hobbes yawned. "I am. Or rather, we both are. It's been a long week making sure the mission is on track."

"Speaking of," said Thomas, "how're Sam and Bill?"

"They're at their final mark and will be executing the last phase of the mission later this afternoon. Well, afternoon for us but it'll be the middle of the night for them."

"And everything's been alright?" Laura asked. "No surprises?"

"So far so good," Hobbes relayed. "And with my help it'll stay that way. Anyway, unless there's something you need I really need to stay focused on this."

"No," Laura told him. "We're just killing some time."

"Thanks for the update."

"Anytime Thomas. Anyway, I'll catch up with you both after this is all over, okay?"

"You got it."

They left Hobbes and Russell behind as they walked down the corridor and hung a right. Thomas and Laura wound around the circular hallway and eventually made their way back to the break room. They found Gabbi, Emily and Gavin sitting at the same table they'd been at a few minutes prior.

"So what's everyone up to?" Thomas asked as he and Laura entered the room. "Hey Gabbi."

Their children turned and looked at them.

"Hi Thomas," Gabbi replied with a smile. "Laura. Your kids have been keeping me company."

"And how's that coming along?"

"I'm booooorrred," Gavin told his parents as he melodramatically put his head down on the table.

"Me too," Emily added. "What are we doing? I thought we weren't supposed to be here today?"

"Technically you're right sweetie," Laura began to explain, "but after they took samples from us yesterday we wanted to check in and see how the doctors have progressed."

"And?" Emily pressed, openly impatient.

"Nothing yet," Thomas told her.

"Then why are we still hanging around? I could be at home in the pool."

Thomas smiled at Gabbi. "So it's been a real pleasure to look after them."

Gabbi chuckled. "They're adorable and we get along great. But patience is definitely not one of their strong suits."

It was Laura's turn to smile. "No, and especially not when they're hungry. How about this. Your father and I will go visit the Lab real quick, and when we get back we'll all go out for pizza? Gabbi, you're invited and more than welcome to join us. How's that sound?"

Gavin's head popped up. "Pizza!"

"That's one," Thomas said.

"I'm in," Gabbi told them.

"That's two. Em?"

"Okay, I guess."

"Excellent. Your mother and I will be right back." They turned to walk out.

"Gav," Emily said, "can we go visit to your island while we wait?"

Thomas turned on his heels as both he and Gavin responded simultaneously to Emily's request.

"No."

"I don't think that's a good idea," Thomas added.

"Why not?" Emily asked.

Laura immediately picked up on the situation as she watched Thomas, Gabbi and Gavin's facial expressions. She put her hands on her hips. "Okay, what's going on?"

Nobody opened their mouth. Laura walked back to the table and sat down next to her son. Thomas reluctantly did the same.

"Talk to me."

"You're not going to like it," Gavin answered.

Laura glanced over at Thomas. "I'm assuming you know exactly what's going on?"

He nodded. "Yeah. There was an incident earlier this week."

"What day?"

"Monday."

"Alright. So it's been four days since this 'incident' occurred." Laura paused. "Wait, this has something to do with why you had to charter a plane from San Francisco back here, doesn't it? What else happened? What haven't you told me yet and why?"

Thomas sighed. "It's my fault. I told Gavin and Gabbi not to mention it."

"Mention what?"

"They came after us," Gavin told everyone.

Emily and Gabbi leaned in.

"Who came after you?" Laura asked.

Gavin shook his head. "Not who; they."

"It's tough to explain," Thomas tried to tell her.

"Well, I can't remember the last time you lied to me, so whatever this is you need to do better than that. This is our family and we don't have any secrets."

Thomas put his hands up as he relented. "You're right. You're right. I apologize, I should have told you all about it."

"And you will start right now," she stated.

"As you know, Gavin, Gabbi and I have been mapping out the time it takes to portal from one location to another based on distance."

Laura nodded.

"Well, on Monday we continued that trend and decided to head to the west coast. It was the furthest we'd traveled."

"What happened?"

"I'm sorry we didn't tell you Laura," Gabbi said with sincerity. "But what we saw was absolutely horrifying."

"Terrifying," Thomas told her. "As we came to a stop, fifty feet from the new island, Stir began to growl."

"Growl?" Laura asked.

Thomas nodded. "I looked over my shoulder and a huge dark cloud was rapidly approaching. At first we didn't know what it was, but seconds later I could tell that the cloud was made up of shapes."

"Shapes?"

Gabbi answered. "Horrific shapes. Shadowy wings. Dark things."

"Fire," Gavin said. "Lots of fire."

"I was petrified and your husband," Gabbi told Laura, "took control of the situation and got us out of there. But it didn't end there."

Laura looked around at each of their faces. Their fear was real. She softened her voice. "Tell me."

Thomas finally spoke. "We got through the portal but Stir hadn't come through yet. I yelled at Gav to close it but he wouldn't do it without Stir. A few seconds later Stir burst through the portal but a long arm followed behind him. The hand...the thing's hand was tipped with sharp blades and it reached out for us. If Gavin hadn't closed the portal I think it would have come through."

Laura couldn't believe what she'd just heard. "I understand why you were so reluctant to talk about it, but in the same breath I can't believe you chose to hide this from me. Although this does explain why I haven't seen Stir around the house this week." She took her time and looked at each one of them. "I'm disappointed that you kept this from me. We're a family and we don't keep secrets from each other; not ever."

"I'm sorry sweetie."

"Sorry mom."

"I apologize, Mrs. Clark."

"Accepted," Laura said. "Now where do we go from here in regards to Gavin's portal?"

Thomas instantly responded. "I say it's off limits."

Gavin shook his head. "No. I still go there all the time.

Thomas was shocked. "You still go there? But why son?"

"My ability masks my presence. It was only when I took you and Gabbi on a long trip that those creatures had time to hone in on us."

"I want you to stop visiting that place," Thomas told him.

"No," Gavin replied indignantly. "And besides, you can't make me."

Emily half smiled.

"Now listen here son, I..."

Laura placed her hand on Thomas' arm. "I think we should table this discussion for the time being, don't you honey?"

Thomas took a deep breath. "You're right. Sorry Gav, we don't know what those things were or what they'd do to you. I'm just worried about your safety, that's all."

* * *

Dr. Joseph Brown and Dr. Ming Sung had been working diligently on the genetic samples they'd extracted from the Clarks the day before. They had spent all day Thursday segregating and cataloging the samples into groups for testing. It was a long and detail oriented process. They'd both left exhausted and even after a night's sleep they were both tired when they arrived to continue their work on Friday. The guard, stationed at the Lab's entrance, was there to maintain the integrity of the Lab and to verify that nothing had been or could be removed from the premises.

"I'm starting the sequence for lot two, section three-B," Dr. Brown told Dr. Sung.

"What's the cycle duration?" she asked him.

"Two hours."

She nodded. "Then maybe I'll take an early lunch and then come back and grab a nap in the break room."

Dr. Brown smiled. "That sounds tempting, but I think I'll stay here and continue to work."

"Okay. Did you want me to pick up something for you while I'm out?"

He shook his head. "Nah, I'm good. After yesterday I decided to brown bag it. Besides, these initial readings I'm seeing are pretty interesting and I still don't know what we're even looking for."

"Quite the mystery, isn't it?"

Dr. Brown nodded. "Indeed. Well, enjoy your lunch and your nap."

She smiled and maneuvered closer to him. "Hey, before I go can you do me a favor?"

"Sure."

"Can you keep your area clean?"

"What do you mean?" he said with a puzzled look.

Dr. Sung pointed behind him towards the floor. He swung around as he followed her gaze.

"I don't see what you're talki…OUCH!"

As he turned around Dr. Sung slipped a syringe out of her coat pocket and had deftly injected him with the contents straight into his rear end. Moments later he silently collapsed to the floor as the sedative coursed through his body. Dr. Sung swung her head towards the Lab door and waited for five seconds; then ten seconds.

Good. The guard didn't hear a thing.

She headed to the refrigerator that contained small vials of Thomas' blood and quickly withdrew two of them. She closed the door and shifted over to her purse. She withdrew one of the three wrapped tampons from inside and, using a scalpel, carefully made a slit down the seam. Afterwards she pulled out the innards and carefully dropped the two vials of blood inside. Dr. Sung packed the vials tightly and then replaced the tampon back in the packaging. She looked down at her work and compared it to the other two tampons in her purse.

It'll pass.

She delicately put all three in a side pocket, took another look at her sleeping counterpart, and exited the Lab. The guard stood up as she walked out.

"Hello Dr. Sung. Please place your purse on the counter for me."

"Of course," she replied with a smile and put her purse down. "I may be new but I already know the drill."

The guard nodded. "Arms up please."

She complied and the guard patted her down. Afterwards he opened her purse and rummaged through it. While he was doing so one of the packaged tampons was jarred loose from its side pocket and hit his hand. He instantly put her purse down.

"I apologize. I didn't mean to…"

She continued to smile. "It's alright. Accidents happen and there's no harm done. You know how it is, a woman always has to be prepared."

"Yes ma'am. You're clear to go."

"Thank you. Oh, and Dr. Brown is knee deep in a new round of tests and he doesn't want to be disturbed."

"Of course Doctor."

"Thank you. I'll see you in a couple of hours."

Dr. Sung walked away. Her smile faded once her back was to the guard. She rounded the corner and made her way to the break room to grab a quick drink on her way out.

Thomas took a deep breath. "You're right. Sorry Gav, we don't know what those things were or what they'd do to you. I'm just worried about your safety, that's all."

Dr. Ming Sung entered and five faces who sat at the table turned in her direction.

"Oh, hi," she told them. "I just wanted to grab a drink."

Laura spoke up. "I'm glad you're here Dr. Sung."

"Oh?" *Does she know something?*

"You saved Thomas and I a trip to the Lab. Is there anything new to report?"

"Nothing yet. We're running tests on the samples we took. As soon as we have something to report we'll let you know."

"We figured as much. Sorry if we keep disturbing you."

"Of course, it might help us if we knew what we were looking for?"

Laura shook her head. "If the Director hasn't filled you in then I'm afraid I can't comment."

Smile and get out of here. Dr. Sung forced a smile. "I understand." She pulled her purse tight over her shoulder and began to leave.

"Doctor?"

Dr. Sung turned and looked back at Laura. *Shit, what is it?* "Yes?"

"Aren't you forgetting your drink?"

Stupid. "Yes, of course. I'm still tired after working late." She walked over, opened the fridge and pulled out a Gatorade. "Thanks. See you later."

Laura watched the doctor leave and then turned back to Thomas, Emily, Gavin and Gabbi. "She's lying."

"About what?" Thomas inquired. "Being tired?"

"I don't know exactly. I just know that something's off."

"She's new. Maybe it's just jitters."

"And this coming from someone who doesn't believe in coincidences."

"Okay. What do you want to do about it?"

"Well, we are heading out for pizza so we should try and follow her."

"Why not just tell Russell about your concerns and let him handle it?"

Laura shook her head. "There's no time. Dr. Sung will be gone by then." She stood up. "Let's go. If it ends up being nothing then so be it. But right now, with everything that's happened recently, can we really afford to take any chances?"

* * *

After they exited the underground garage, and climbed into their Suburban, it took them a couple of minutes to catch up to Dr. Sung's car. Thankfully the road was relatively devoid of traffic so when Laura pointed out the doctor's vehicle Thomas was able to maintain a degree of distance.

"Where do you think she's going?" Gabbi asked from the back seat next to Gavin and Emily.

"Well," Laura replied, "she said she was going out to lunch but that doesn't explain why she's pulling into the park's parking lot right now."

Thomas pulled over to the side of the road as they watched Dr. Sung, get out of her car and begin to walk through the park.

"We have to get out and see what she's up to," Laura told her husband.

Thomas shook his head. "We'll be too exposed. Look, there's nowhere to hide. If she turns around she'll see anybody behind her."

Laura frowned. "Then what the hell do we do?"

Thomas pointed at the glove compartment. "Open it. There are some binoculars in there."

Laura popped the catch and extracted the binoculars. "How? I mean why were they in there?"

Thomas smiled. "It pays to be prepared."

"And paranoid," Laura said as she raised the binoculars to her eyes and swiveled the focus knob.

"That too," Thomas said. "What'ya see?"

Laura traversed her head slightly. "Got her. She's still walking, but she's not even looking around." The car grew quiet as Laura zoomed in. "Wait. It looks like she's headed towards one of the park benches. Yup, she's bee-lining right to it and there's someone else sitting on it already. I can't see the person's face."

"Let me see," Thomas said.

"No. She's almost there and I don't want to miss anything." Laura paused for a few seconds. "Okay, she just sat down on the opposite end of the bench. She's…she's unzipping her purse…rummaging through it…and just pulled out a….no, that can't be right." Laura zoomed in as far as she could and readjusted the focus. "She just pulled out a tampon."

"A tampon?" Thomas asked. "Seriously?"

"What's a tampon?" Gavin asked.

"It's something that ladies use," Gabbi told him. "Bathroom stuff."

"Ohh. Yuck. Nevermind."

Laura picked up her commentary. "She just put it down on the bench and now….and now she just stood up and she's retracing her steps."

"Go back to the bench," Thomas told her.

Laura panned back just as the other individual scooted over, plucked the tampon up and put it in their own purse. The unknown female stood up and Laura finally got a good look.

"Holy shit."

"What is it?" Thomas asked.

"It's Emma Duncan, the DCI's wife. She took the tampon, put it in her own purse and now she's walking away."

"What?"

Laura lowered the binoculars and looked at her husband with a shocked look on her face. "But she wasn't lying when I questioned her. What the hell is going on?"

Thomas' head began to swim is disbelief. His worst thoughts that the DCI had betrayed him began to permeate and flood his mind.

"This can't be happening," Thomas mumbled. "Not again."

"Then what are we waiting for?" Emily declared. "Let's go get her."

"Yes, seriously," Gabbi added. "Let's go grab her so we know exactly what's going on."

"Yeah," Gavin added. "Come on dad!"

Thomas shook his head to clear it, put the Suburban in gear and then flipped around as he drove towards the far side of the park where Emma had headed.

"What about Dr. Sung?" Gabbi inquired.

"First thing's first," Thomas replied. "We'll follow the package, retrieve it and hope we're not imagining things."

Thomas took the next right and paralleled the park.

"There she is," Laura said.

She pointed towards Emma and all of them watched Mrs. Duncan step into her own car and pull away from the curb.

"Plan?" Laura asked.

"I'm going to wait until she comes up to a stop sign. When that happens I'm going to pull in front to block her. You and I will then pop out and surprise her. Kids. Gabbi. I need you to stay in the car."

"Kay dad."

"Fine."

"No problem."

"You good?" Thomas asked Laura.

She nodded. "I'm ready."

Thomas accelerated down the street and caught up to Emma's sedan. At the corner Emma rolled to a stop. Thomas took that opportunity and pulled the Suburban around diagonally in front of their target. Laura opened her door, jumped out and quickly approached the driver's side while Thomas ran around the front of the Suburban to join her.

"Laura?" Emma said in surprise. "Is that you?"

Laura yanked open the door just as Thomas arrived on the other side of her car.

"What are you doing?" Emma exclaimed.

"Where is it?" Laura demanded.

Thomas pulled open the passenger door and reached for Emma's purse, but Emma managed to get her hand on the strap and held on for dear life.

"What the hell are you doing!?" she screamed. "That's my purse!"

Thomas pulled again and the strap broke. He took it and began to rummage through it.

Emma was in tears. "Give it back! What are you doing? What's wrong with you?"

"What were you doing at the park?" Laura insisted.

Emma turned back at looked at Laura. "What?"

"I said what were you doing at the park?"

"I...I wasn't at the park."

Laura was caught off guard.

"It's not here," Thomas exclaimed as he tossed it back towards Emma. "It's not in her purse."

325

Laura tried again. "Who did you meet in the park?"

"Laura," Emma asked, "what's this all about?"

"Who did you meet in the park Emma?"

"I...I don't know what you mean. I haven't been in the park."

"We saw you," Laura insisted even though she already knew that Emma wasn't lying.

Emma regained some of her composure. "I don't know what to tell you but this certainly isn't the way I like to be treated."

"Where is it?" Thomas questioned.

Emma turned her head. "What are you talking about?"

"The tampon. Where's the tampon you picked up off the park bench?"

"Was that what you were looking for in my purse? That's incredibly rude of you. I can't wait to tell my husband how you've accosted me."

"Why are you lying!?" Thomas demanded with an edge to his voice.

"I'm not!" Emma shot back.

"I don't beli..."

Laura cut him off. "Thomas."

"What?"

"She's not."

"What?"

"She's not lying?"

He was confused. "But then how...I mean...what...how?"

Laura nodded. "Yeah. Exactly."

"I demand that you let me go."

Laura looked back at Emma. "We're sorry Mrs. Duncan but this isn't over."

"I'm going to call my husband."

Laura nodded. "In a minute. But first I need you to do something so we can clear this all up."

"I will not be dictated to."

Laura leaned in and got right in her face. "You were in that park to pick up a package left by one of the new doctors at the facility, a Dr. Sung."

That caught Emma off guard. "You mean Dr. Ming Sung?"

"Yes. Do you know her?"

"Yes, of course. I've known her for years. In fact, I was the one that suggested she work there to my husband."

"And you don't remember meeting her five minutes ago when she left a tampon on the bench?"

A puzzled look washed over Emma's face. "There you go again. I don't know what you're talking about."

Laura nodded. "That's okay. I believe you and we don't mean you any harm. Please stay here, I'll be right back."

Thomas gave Laura a questionable look and she put her hand up for him to hold on. Laura walked back to the Suburban and opened the back door.

"Em, you're up. She doesn't believe she was in the park and I believe her. Something's not right."

Emily climbed out and walked back over to Emma with her mother.

"Laura, I know what your daughter can do," Emma said with a twinge of fear in her voice. "Why did you bring her over here?"

"Because we don't have any time to wait. Something's obviously going on without your knowledge."

"So you say," Emma shot back.

"So I know," Laura reminded her. "Now give me your hand."

Emma reluctantly stretched her left hand out. "Is this going to hurt?"

Emily shook her head and placed her own hand on top. Emma instantly became rigged.

"What were you doing in the park?" Emily asked.

"Waiting."

"Waiting for whom?"

"For Dr. Sung to give me something."

"And did she give you something?"

"Yes."

"What was it?"

"A tampon, but it wasn't."

"Why?"

"It was too heavy, like something else was inside it."

Emily looked at her mother and Laura whispered in her ear. Afterwards Emily continued.

"Where is the tampon?"

"I put it where I was instructed to."

"And where's that?"

"In the park, by a tree."

Thomas' eyes opened wide. "Ask her exactly where."

"Where is this spot?"

"Thirty feet from where I was parked. There's a trashcan. I put the tampon inside."

Thomas wasted no time and took off running down the street in the direction they'd come from. Laura whispered in her daughter's ear again.

"Why don't you remember these instructions?"

"I was told to forget them."

More whispers.

"Told how? It's impossible to forget a conversation."

"I...I don't know. He just told me to forget what I'd done after I'd completed the task."

"Who did?"

Emma cocked her head to one side. "I don't know his name."

"What did he look like?"

"He's Japanese. Older." Emily flinched slightly as Emma continued. "He tried to hide the scars."

"What scars?" Emily pressed.

"On his right arm. I don't know how far they went up, but they were pretty significant."

"And you said this man was Japanese?"

Emma nodded. "Educated and very sure of himself."

Emily lowered her head and shook it somewhat.

"What is it?" Laura asked her.

"It's him. It has to be."

Laura didn't like what her daughter had just told her. "You mean HIM him; the doctor that kept dad and you hostage?"

Emily nodded and let Emma's hand go. "He did other things to us as well. He wasn't a nice man."

Emma's eyes cleared and her body relaxed. "What did you just do to me?"

"Oh honey," Laura said as she pulled Emily close. "I'm so sorry. He can't get you now. You're safe."

Thomas ran back and rejoined them just as Laura pulled Emily close.

"What's going on?"

"In a second," Laura told him. "Was it there? Did you get it?"

Thomas shook his head. "It's gone goddammit. I turned that garbage can upside down and it wasn't there. Someone must have been waiting and already took it."

"And I think we know who that person was."

"Really? What'd I miss?"

"With Emily's guidance Mrs. Duncan recalled who gave her the instructions, except you're not going to like it."

A frown appeared on his face. "Shit. Tell me anyway."

"It was an older Japanese man with scars on his right hand and arm."

Oh fuck me. "But...but he died in the fire." Thomas put a hand to his forehead. "I mean, I assumed he did. And besides, it's been four years since then. If he was alive why hasn't he come for us since then? It doesn't make any sense." Thomas paced back and forth. "What was Emma's reason for forgetting everything she had done? Hypnosis or something?"

"That's a good question. We skipped over that."

"Well ask her then."

Laura turned to Emily. "Can you sweetie?"

Emily nodded. "I have to." She grabbed Emma's hand again. "You said you were told to forget the conversations you had."

"Yes."

"How?"

"I'm not sure."

"How did he make you forget your conversations?"

"He...he commanded me."

"Commanded?"

"His voice...it was in my head...it told me to do things."

"Wait," Emily said. "You told me that you had conversations with him."

"They were more like directions and they were all in my head."

"And where did this take place?"

"At the coffee shop I go to. He was always on the other side of the room."

330

Emily let Emma's hand go and Thomas, Laura and Emily all looked at each other with disbelief.

"He's alive," Thomas finally admitted. "The asshole is alive and he has an ability. And from the sound of it it's extremely powerful."

Laura nodded. "To bend someone else's will to do your bidding. Yeah, I'd say that it's formidable skill and downright terrifying."

"We have to circle the wagons," Thomas said. He turned to Mrs. Duncan. "Call your husband Emma and tell him to drop whatever he's doing and meet us right away. We'll all head to the facility and you're coming with us."

* * *

"What do you mean my wife was being mind-controlled?" the DCI shouted. "Do you know how ridiculous that sounds?"

"No more ridiculous than my ability to manipulate objects or Emily's powers to take control of someone just by touching them."

Robert Duncan relented. "You're right. Sorry. I'm just having a difficult time putting this all together."

Everyone had gathered in the break room.

"We followed Dr. Sung to the park where she left a package on a bench. Your wife, who was already sitting there, picked it up and departed. Now, by the time we caught up with Emma she had already dropped the package in the trash for someone else to retrieve."

The DCI looked at his wife. "Is this true?"

"It must be. I didn't remember doing any of this but when Emily did her thing even I couldn't believe what came out of my mouth. I've been used and I wasn't even aware of it. I'm so sorry."

"Dammit. And what you're telling me Thomas is that this Dr. Matsushita, who used to work for Victor Bannon, is behind this?"

Thomas nodded. "It all makes sense. He survived and escaped the fire somehow. He was the only other one that had any evidence about my children's abilities. It's been four years but he must have spent that time developing something new for himself, and apparently it's working as intended. And based on what he's capable of, he's got to be responsible for what happened the other day in downtown D.C., hands down. Who knows what his end game is. He's a sick fucker and he has to be stopped."

The DCI nodded. "So what did Dr. Sung take out of the Lab and hand off then?"

"Why don't we go ask Dr. Brown that exact same question?"

"Good idea." The Director's phone chirped. He pulled it out and tapped a few keys. "My guys have picked up Dr. Sung. She's going to be transported here."

"Good," Laura said.

The group headed out of the break room and around the hallway towards the Lab. The guard outside stood up as they approached.

"Sir."

"Is Dr. Brown still inside?"

"Yes, sir."

"Very good," the DCI responded. "Open the door."

The guard did as he was instructed and instantly noticed something wasn't right.

"Shit, he's down." The guard rushed up to the doctor and checked the pulse on his neck. "He's alive."

Laura took Gavin's hand and walked inside. Along the way she whispered to the DCI. "You should have him leave."

The DCI immediately understood. "We'll take it from here."

"But sir, I…"

"He's alive. You're dismissed. Now."

The guard straightened. "Yes, sir." He left the room and closed the door behind him.

Gavin went over and placed his hands on Dr. Brown's temple and concentrated. A few seconds later the doctor came to and rolled over on his own.

"What…what happened?"

Gavin stepped back as the DCI helped the doctor to his feet. "We were hoping you could tell us. What's the last thing you remember?"

Dr. Brown scrunched his forehead. "Well, Dr. Sung said she was going to head out for an early lunch and then grab a nap while this latest batch ran through the system." His eyes opened wide as his hand went to his butt cheek. "Sonofabitch, she injected me. Why would she do that?"

"What's missing?" the DCI insisted instantly. "What did she take?"

"Whatever it was would have been small," Laura told the doctor.

"How small?"

"Small enough to fit in a tampon."

"I see. Give me a second to look around."

"I'm guessing it's blood," Thomas announced.

Dr. Brown took the hint and went to the refrigeration unit. He opened it up and quickly counted the remaining vials.

"You're right. Two are missing from your collection Mr. Clark."

"Thank you Dr. Brown," the DCI said. "Are you well enough to continue working?"

"Yes, sir."

"Good. We'll leave you to it then."

The group exited the Lab and paused just outside. "When he wants to leave you let me know."

"Yes, sir," the guard replied.

They all went back to the break room to further discuss the issue in private.

"What's Dr. Matsushita's endgame?" the DCI asked. "I can only assume he needed your blood to continue whatever the hell he's been working on."

"Maybe," Thomas told him. "I don't think we can guess what Matsushita is up to. If he was willing to torture my daughter and I then he's capable of anything."

"So what do you want me to do?"

"Don't you see, we're compromised. I want you to shut it all down and destroy whatever genetic materials you extracted from my wife and I."

"Done."

"Do I have your word on that?"

"Absolutely."

Thomas looked over at Laura and she nodded her head.

"Good. That gets taken care of immediately, before we leave this facility. After that we're going back home."

"And then what?" the Director asked.

"I don't know. We need to discuss, as a family, whether we run away or stay and fight."

Friday Nov 2, 2001

"I'll have these prepared and ready to be served on Monday, if that's alright with you Mrs. Paige?"

Julie and Kim were back at Mr. Monroe's office Friday morning to finalize the divorce papers. The meeting turned out to be brief, much to Julie's surprise.

We spent so much time cultivating our relationship. The planning; the decisions; the children; the vacations; everything. And after fifteen years of marriage it all ends with this, a piece of paper. I have a hard time thinking that some document is supposed to make me feel better about myself; as if it's something tangible that sums up our entire experience together.

Julie stared off into space, seemingly fixated on some speck on his office wall.

"Jules?" Kim whispered.

What am I doing? I know I'm furious with Sam but is this really the only answer? Who am I really trying to punish, Sam or myself? I don't know. And the kids. Our children won't understand so what the hell am I doing?

"Mrs. Paige?"

"Jules?"

Julie finally blinked and turned her attention back to Mr. Monroe.

"I'm sorry, you were saying?"

"Will having these papers served to your husband on Monday be alright?"

"No."

"Alright, that's not a problem. What day would you prefer Mrs. Paige?"

335

"I've changed my mind," Julie told him.

Mr. Monroe cocked his head to one side. "I see."

"Thank you for your time Mr. Monroe but I want you to destroy those documents. My sister and I will show ourselves out."

Julie picked up her purse, stood, walked to the door and then exited his office. It didn't take long for Kim to catch up with her sister.

"What's going on?" Kim asked as they entered the elevator and the doors closed.

"You mean why my change of heart?"

Kim nodded enthusiastically.

"Well, for one thing I realized I was being selfish. I don't like how Sam has reacted and the choices he's made, but blindsiding him with a divorce isn't going to make our situation any better."

"So what's your plan?"

The doors opened and they stepped out into the lobby.

"Sam and I used to be a team, just like you and Bill, like Laura and Thomas. He and I need to get back what we've lost, and if we can't, well then at least our divorce will be a mutual decision."

"I'm proud of you sis. You really had me worried there."

"Don't be. I didn't have an epiphany. I know I'm lonely, and you are too, especially after our move to Virginia and sending our children off to that boarding school."

The two exited the building and headed towards their parked car.

Kim nodded. "Yeah, you're right about that. But, I have an idea."

"What?" Julie asked.

"Why don't we call them from the car?"

"You mean our kids?"

Kim nodded. "Exactly. It might help cheer you up."

Julie smiled. "We could try, although I don't see Ms. Jones allowing any of them to come to the phone."

Kim chuckled. "Yeah, she did come across as quite the authoritarian."

Julie unlocked the car door and they got in. Before Julie started it up she paused and turned to her sister.

"Thanks for being there for me. I know I've been incredibly difficult but you've stuck by me the entire time. So thank you."

"That's what sisters are for. We'll figure it out."

"You know it's not going to be easy, right?"

"When has it ever?" Kim replied with a smile.

Julie turned the key and the engine came to life.

"I tell you what, why don't we go out and get something to eat?"

"Sounds good. We'll toast your non-divorce."

Julie snickered. "You're hilarious."

"I do what I can. Besides, maybe after we eat we can get hold of our kids."

"That sounds nice."

* * *

"No mom," Amanda said as she tried her best to reassure her mother, "I'm doing just fine, honest."

Julie leaned back in the restaurant's booth and smiled. "I'm really happy to hear that honey. And how's your brother?"

"Well, you know Craig."

"Okay, what happened?"

"You mean you don't know?"

"Know what?"

337

"Oh crap. Well, he's right here so he can tell you. Gotta go. Bye."

Amanda immediately handed the phone to her brother as he hit her in the arm. "Thanks a lot sis."

She shrugged and sat down on the wooden bench next to Sarah and Edward. Craig put the phone up to his ear.

"Hi mom."

"Tell me exactly what happened," Julie instructed.

"Welllll…"

"Craig, would you rather I drove up there right now and make a scene in front of all your classmates?"

"No."

"Spill it then."

"I got in a fight."

"I see. With who?"

"A kid named Tad. He's thirteen."

"A boy and you, who is four years older, got in a fight? Is that what you're telling me?"

"Yeah." He paused for a few seconds. "Are you mad?"

"That depends," Julie told her son. "Did you start it?"

"No."

"Okay. Did you finish it?"

"I don't know; kind of, I guess."

"Craig, what do you mean you don't know?"

"Well, Tad bumped into me and knocked me down on purpose. When I stood up he wouldn't give me back one of my books and starting talking shit. Oops, sorry."

"That's fine. Go on."

"So I did what dad showed me and kicked him in the nuts."

Julie covered the cell phone and suppressed her giggle so her son wouldn't hear it. Kim gave her a 'what's going on' look and Julie held up her finger.

"So why is this the first time I'm hearing about this? Didn't you get in trouble?"

"No, that was the weird part. Ms. Jones interrupted us and insisted that everything was an accident. She said if it wasn't that for the next two weeks we'd be shoveling out the horse stalls."

Julie laughed but quickly coughed to try and mask it.

"You okay, mom?"

"Fine honey, just fine. Your Aunt Kim and I are eating and something didn't go down right."

"So I'm not in any trouble?"

"Well, I'll need to talk to your father first. When you come home for Thanksgiving we'll discuss it then."

"Okay. But there's something else."

"Something else?"

"Yeah."

"Spill it."

"Wellll, Edward and I snuck into the stables. Tad saw us go in there and wanted payback, but before anything could happen a horse kicked its way out of its stall and knocked us to the ground."

"And then what happened?"

"And then we were caught and the three of us have been shoveling shit, uh, I mean manure since."

"Good."

"Good?"

"Sweetie. The two of you knew you weren't supposed to be in there. However, this Tad person sounds horrible. Is Ms. Jones there? I'd like to speak to her about this."

"She's in the other room with Tad right now actually. I'll go get her although it might take a minute."

"That's fine. I love you sweetie."

"I love you too," Craig practically whispered.

"Can you put Sarah on the phone please?"

"Sure. Hold on."

Julie handed the cell phone over to Kim.

"Hello? Sarah?"

"Hi mom. What's up?"

"Aunt Julie and I are just checking in on you guys. Are you having a good time? Do you need anything?"

"Mommmm," Sarah said with a little impatience, "I'm thirteen. Everything's fine."

"Okay, okay. No need to get snippy. A mother has the right to worr…"

Kim suddenly heard a deafening explosion on the other end of the phone and jerked the phone away from her ear because it was that loud. Then she instantly began to panic.

"Sarah?"

"Sarah!?"

"SARAH!?"

* * *

"Mommmm," Sarah said with a little impatience, "I'm thirteen. Everything's fine."

"Okay, okay. No need to get snippy. A mother has the right to worr…"

The office windows exploded and all four children were tossed to the floor. Glass cut into their exposed skin and the floor was littered with its jagged shards.

Alarm bells rang all over campus.

Sarah, who had been standing, had been propelled into the adjacent wall. The phone she once had in her hand now lay on the floor alongside her unmoving body.

"SARAH!?"

The sprinkler system sprang to life and quickly drenched each of the four inert forms. A trickle of blood ran down Sarah's head, across her cheek and mixed with the water from above.

A humongous fire began to ravage the main building and two others. Smoke filled the air and billowed into the sky.

Children's screams could be heard throughout the campus, and the fear those cries generated were even louder.

51
Friday Nov 2, 2001

Just past midnight, on a mountainside in Panjshir Valley, six men made their final preparations and geared up to capture Hamid Emal Habibi in the Afghan village. They'd spent the day watching and observing; waiting in anticipation for the long day to finally fade to night.

"Hobbes?" Sam transmitted. "Are you there?"

"I'm here. I've got you and your team bracketed. I'll follow you in the entire time."

"Good. We're about to move out. I want that Predator drone up and available ASAP."

"Sam, Russell already tasked it to your area of operation."

"How long till its overhead?"

"Twenty minutes."

"And our extraction?"

"The Blackhawk helicopter is ready to disembark from the carrier in the Gulf of Oman on your go ahead."

"Roger that."

"Anything else you need Sam?" Russell asked.

"Just a little luck, if you can spare some."

"I'll see what I can do about that. In the meantime, good luck."

"Thanks."

Sam turned to his team. Bill, Darius, Carl, Eliot and Jordon stared back at him.

"You ready for this?" he asked.

His team nodded collectively in the darkness.

Sam reminded them once again about their mission. "Our goal is to penetrate the village and silently make our way to that two

343

story structure where we know Hamid is located. Once we have him detained we egress the same way we came in. Once we're clear, and out of the area, we'll signal the bird to come pick us up. Questions?"

"Are we there yet?" Bill joked.

"No shit," Sam retorted. "Let's just finish this mission and get the hell out of here."

* * *

Thirty minutes later the six man team had successfully snuck to within fifty feet of the village's northern perimeter wall.

Hobbes' voice filled their ears. "The satellite shows minimal movement from your current position all the way to the target building."

"Roger that," Sam replied and gave the hand signal for everyone to move out.

The team split into two three-man units. Alpha team consisted of Sam, Bill and Jordon which meant Bravo was Darius, Carl and Eliot. Alpha team moved from their position and moved the last fifty feet to the exterior wall. Bravo team did the same but positioned themselves thirty feet to the east of Alpha.

"A two-man patrol walked by twenty seconds ago," Hobbes told them. "They're gone. You're clear."

"Switch to silent," Sam told his team.

Simultaneously they slung their rifles, extracted their side arms, withdrew silencers from their tactical vests and screwed them on. Sam, with his night vision goggles in place, slowly peeked over the low wall, scanned left to right to make sure it was clear.

"Go," he whispered.

The three members of Bravo hopped the wall. As soon as they were over they crouched down, handguns extended and scanned for any threats as Alpha took their turn. The team had chosen this spot to breach the village for a few reasons. The first was that this part of the village offered the most direct route to their target. The second was that the team knew they could keep to the shadows and away from the various fires that were lit throughout the village. Third, this section of the village contained a high concentration of dwellings which allowed them to bypass the majority of the village's populated zones.

Silently the two groups moved forward as they proceeded down a narrow alley that ran behind the houses, each team staying close to the walls. All six knew they were deep in enemy territory and any mistakes would wake this unsuspecting village and rain hell down on them. Knowing this they moved cautiously, but also with purpose. The longer they were here the more likely they could be discovered.

"Target building is two hundred feet from your position," Hobbes said.

The two teams, with silenced weapons up and ready, continued to move down the alley towards their destination when a large dog appeared ahead of them. Alpha and Bravo instantly froze as the dog cocked its head to one side and sniffed the cold, still night air.

Fuck. Good doggy. Nice doggy.

The dog snarled and let out a large bark. Bill depressed his trigger, his weapon coughed and the round struck the ground in front of the dog. It immediately turned and ran away. A moment later a back door, in front of Alpha, opened with a creak and two Afghans with AK-47's emerged into the alley. Darius, on the opposite side of the alley, swiveled and shot the first man in the

345

head. A split second later Carl silenced the second man. Both Taliban instantly dropped to the ground as lifeless heaps.

Bill entered the house through the open door, with Sam on his heels while Eliot and Jordon immediately scanned for additional threats as Darius and Carl moved the bodies inside. Sam and Bill quickly cleared the house, and, with the bodies now inside, headed back to the alley.

"Hobbes. I'm sure you saw that. Is there any new movement within the village?"

"Scanning," Hobbes replied. "Negative. Nothing."

Sam breathed out and gave the hand signal to move. Luck had been on their side. The two teams continued to move in parallel down the alley as quickly and quietly as they could while their NVG's illuminated the night. They reached the end of the block without further incident. Across the intersection, sixty feet away, was the two story building; and within it resided Hamid Emal Habibi, one of the men responsible for the nine-eleven attacks. The two teams crouched and hid as they scanned the outside of the structure. The street around the structure was partially lit and traversing it would leave them vulnerable for a few seconds.

"It looks like three men, with rifles, are guarding the exterior," Hobbes explained. "Unfortunately I can't see inside. The walls are thick which means I'm not getting any thermal readings."

"Understood," Sam replied. "Is the Predator overhead?"

"It is."

"I want one of its Hellfire missiles locked on to that building."

"On it."

Sam motioned to Bravo. With one last scan the three men ran crouched across the intersection and took up positions along the outer wall of the target building.

346

"Jordon," Sam whispered, "I need you here to provide overwatch with your sniper rifle. You're now designated Charlie."

Without speaking Jordon holstered his side arm, took his Remington 700 off his shoulder and carefully climbed up to the roof of the single story house they were next to. Sam and Bill took a quick look up and down the intersection and then bolted across the street and joined up with Bravo.

"Bravo, cover us. Charlie, we're heading in."

Sam and Bill vaulted over the stone barricade and instantly moved to the side of the two story house, their backs against the wall.

"Two in the front and one in the rear," Hobbes coached.

Bill moved to his left and gently came around the corner, weapon up and saw the guard ten feet away. The Taliban's face barely acknowledged Bill's presence before a silenced bullet entered the front of his forehead. As he collapsed Bill retraced his steps to join Sam as the two of them made their way down the side of the house towards the front. Using hand signals they materialized around the corner, Sam going high and Bill going low, and wasted no time double tapping each guard in the chest.

"Clean kills," Hobbes told them. "No external movement."

"Bravo," Sam ordered. "Move up to our position."

Darius, Carl and Eliot made their way over the stone wall and came to the front. All five stacked up next to the door and prepared to enter.

"Making entry."

Sam raised his leg up and kicked the door in.

* * *

347

Russell and Hobbes couldn't take their eyes off the monitor as they watched the team advance through the village and up to their target.

"They're good," Russell said under his breath.

Hobbes nodded. "Yeah, they're professionals."

On the screen they saw Bravo bolt across the street while Charlie took an overwatch position on the roof. Alpha then crossed the street and joined up with Bravo.

"Bravo, cover us. Charlie, we're heading in."

Two thermal white outlines jumped over the wall and took up positions alongside the houses exterior.

"Two in the front and one in the rear," Hobbes coached.

Ten seconds later the three guards were down. Hobbes zoomed the satellite out and looked around.

"Clean kills," Hobbes told them. "No external movement."

"Bravo," Sam ordered. "Move up to our position."

Bravo moved from its location and joined Alpha at the front of the house where all five team members stacked up at the front door.

"Making entry," they heard Sam say over comms.

As Sam struck the door Russell and Hobbes heard the door give way. A few seconds passed before the heard the team speak.

"First floor is clear."

Hobbes' tranquil view of the village changed in a heartbeat as the satellite displayed a horde of Taliban pouring out of their houses that surrounded the two story structure the team was inside.

"Holy shit!" Hobbes yelled. "You've got a massive amount of enemies incoming!"

* * *

348

Sam booted the door and as it swung inward he and his team aggressively entered. Sam went straight; Bill instantly hooked left; and Darius went right searching for targets. Carl and Eliot followed behind.

The front room was empty; devoid of people or furniture.

"First floor is clear."

Sam then pointed up to the ceiling and the team converged at the base of the stairs. Together they advanced up to the second floor, weapons trained on the doorway at the top.

"Holy shit!" Hobbes yelled. "You've got a massive amount of enemies incoming! Estimating fifty men closing in on your position."

"Confirmed," Charlie said from behind his sniper scope. "Orders?"

Fucking hell. "Charlie, hold. Bravo, keep moving," Sam ordered.

Five operators reached the second floor and encountered a closed door. Sam used a hand signal and pulled a flashbang out of his tactical vest. He pulled the pin as Bill kicked the door open and tossed the flashbang in the room. Gunfire erupted from inside the room and peppered the landing, narrowly missing the team.

The flashbang detonated, sending a concussive blast, mixed with a concentrated flash throughout the enclosed space.

"Danger close!" Hobbes yelled in their ears.

Sam, Bill, Darius, Carl and Eliot rushed through the doorway and began to dispatch the ten disoriented men they encountered inside. One of the Taliban had his finger held down on his AK and, in his confused state, spewed bullets into the ceiling.

Sam shot the closest man in the head and then traversed slightly to the right as his target fell over.

349

Bill's handgun coughed as he entered the room. His first bullet caught a Taliban in the neck but he immediately followed that up with a second shot that put his target down.

Darius, hot on the heels of Sam, nullified two enemies, which included the sprayer as his weapon issued a death sentence.

Before anyone else could do anything the room imploded.

* * *

"Holy shit!" Hobbes yelled. "You've got a massive amount of enemies incoming! Estimating fifty men closing in on your position."

"Confirmed," Charlie said from behind his sniper scope. "Orders?"

"Charlie, hold. Bravo, keep moving," Sam ordered.

Hobbes and Russell watched in horror as the large courtyard began to fill up with Taliban, their weapons aimed at the front of the house. Additional Taliban had begun to encircle the location.

"What do we do?" Hobbes asked Russell, panic in his voice. "They're dead if we don't do something."

"Use the Predator!"

"I'm not shooting the house!"

"No, aim outside!"

Hobbes nodded and adjusted the drone's target. He hit the master arm switch that deployed the weapon. One of the two Hellfire missiles launched off the Predator's wings and rocketed towards the ground.

Five.

"Oh shit, this is going to be close."

Four.

Three.

350

"Danger close!" Hobbes yelled over comms.

Two.

One.

The center of the courtyard vanished as the enormous explosion destroyed it. The shockwave emanated outwards, in all directions, from the point of origin and slammed into the two story house.

Dozens of dead bodies littered the ground; a huge crater where the courtyard used to exist. Dozens of other Taliban, who had been behind the house, hadn't been harmed and were now flocking to the front.

"Sam?" Hobbes said. "Sam, come in."

Hobbes and Russell heard sniper fire over comms and watched on the monitor as Jordon, the team's sniper, began to pluck off individual Taliban in an attempt to save his team members lives.

* * *

"Sam?" Hobbes said. "Sam, come in."

The air in the room was filled with dust and debris as Sam rolled over on his stomach and pushed himself up on his hands and knees. He coughed and spat out thick phlegm on to the floor.

My weapon, where's my weapon?

Sam frantically searched for his handgun but spotted an AK-47 next to him. He grabbed it and brought it to his shoulder as he leaned back on his heels to scan the room.

Four dead Taliban. Six remain.

Sam cocked his head as he heard sniper fire outside.

Bill. The team.

Sam turned and saw Bill and three others were down. They were stunned but moving. They had been closer to the blast and had been hit harder.

Sam didn't waste any time and immediately used the AK he'd scrounged to dispatch the remaining six Taliban without hesitation. With the current threat handled Sam went to the doorway and peered out. At the base of the stairs were a number of enemy combatants. Sam pulled his head back just before their gunfire riddled where his head had just been.

Fuck!

A constant rhythm of sniper fire continued from outside as Sam helped his team to their feet.

"Hobbes? Hobbes?"

"Sam! Oh shit, am I glad to hear your voice!"

"What the fuck just happened?"

"I'm sorry."

"What happened?"

"Wellllll, you know that Hellfire missile…"

Sam understood immediately. "How many did you get?"

"I don't know. Maybe thirty. But there's at least that many, if not more still active."

"No shit. The first floor is flooded with them and there's no sign of Hamid upstairs here in this bedroom."

Sniper fire was followed by sporadic AK-47 bursts.

"Is everyone okay? The Taliban are regrouping. They're circling behind Jordon."

His team had gotten back on their feet and rearmed themselves. Some of them were bleeding, but nothing that would be considered life threatening.

"We're good." Sam turned his attention to what was happening outside. "Jordon? Talk to me."

More AK fire, both outside and from the first floor directed at the second floor doorway.

"Thinning them out for you," Jordon replied over the headset.

"I want you to disengage. Fall back!"

"Negative sir, I'm not leaving you behind."

"Get out of here right now!" Sam ordered.

More automatic gunfire was heard outside.

"Oh shit," Hobbes said. "Oh shit oh shit oh shit."

Sam, or any of the other team members, didn't need to ask what had happened. The tone of Hobbes' voice told them everything they needed to know.

"Dammit." Sam shook it off and took charge. "They're going to rush us so barricade the door right now!"

Bill and the others moved dead bodies out of the way, shoved the bed across the room and against the door. After that each man checked to make sure their rifle was working as they took defensive positions around the room. They all knew they were in a precarious situation and nobody needed to voice it.

Five long minutes passed without gunfire or additional activity. Sweat poured down five faces as each second of anticipation ticked by.

"They're just grouped up outside in defensive positions," Hobbes said, "but they're not advancing."

"What the hell are they waiting for?" Bill asked.

"No fucking clue," Sam replied. "This mission is over. Just be prepared for anything so we can carve a hole through these assholes and make our escape."

Even though they were all professionals they were rattled with this dire situation they found themselves in.

The headset in each man's ear came to life. "I don't know who you are but you made a grave mistake invading my territory. Your transgressions, for my village, will be paid for in blood."

Sam brought his finger up to his lips.

The new voice spoke up again. "You see, my people and I have lived in these mountains for generations. And although I must admit you're skilled at what you do, it would have been a smarter choice if you had just bypassed my three lookouts rather than kill them in cold blood. When they failed to check-in the entire valley went on alert. Who knows, maybe you would have succeeded in your mission if it wasn't for your short sidedness.

"Now, as you can tell, I'm using your teammate's headset to converse with you. I'm sure he doesn't need it anymore due to the fact that he's no longer alive."

"Fuck you," Bill replied.

"Oh good. I thought for a second that you were all dead up there. Who do I have the pleasure of talking to?"

"You first asshole."

"Very well, since it hardly matters at this point. My name is Hamid Emal Habibi. And you are?"

Sam and Bill looked at each other.

"Why don't you come up here and we'll tell you in person?" Bill taunted.

Hamid paused. "Your voice, it's familiar, is it not? Do I know you soldier?"

"You know us both Hamid," Sam said.

"I do? Who are you?"

"It's Sam and Bill. I'm sure our names ring a bell."

They couldn't see as Hamid smiled outside. "My old friends, if I had known it was you I would have invited you in with open arms. But it appears that you are here for more nefarious reasons.

It's unfortunate that we now find ourselves on the opposite sides of this conflict."

"Cut the shit Hamid," Sam told him. "You were behind nine-eleven. You have blood on your hands."

"And you Sam, my old friend, are you saying you don't? We fought together once, you and I, against the Russians. But your America, your country is just as guilty for the atrocities it continues to commit. But what happens to you and your government? Nothing. Nothing happens. You're the world's bully, demanding whatever you want and expecting every other country to step in line. And then there's me; a nobody. Compared to the United States I'm a mosquito, in a locked room, that's constantly annoying you. But this mosquito bit down on your country when it wasn't looking; when it was asleep. I struck back against the world's oppressors and now here you are, enacting revenge as if that will change anything. I pity you. You're being used by your government and you don't even realize it."

"Why don't you come up here and we can talk about that face to face?" Bill asked. "For old times' sake."

"A moment," Hamid said over the headset.

Bill looked back over at Sam. "Do you really think he's thinking about coming up here?"

"I don't know."

A minute later there was a knock outside the barricaded door.

"It's Hamid. I'm unarmed and alone. Would you care to open the door for me?"

"Cover the door," Sam ordered. "Carl. Eliot. Pull the bed back and get ready to shove it back in place."

The two did as requested as Bill extracted his handgun. When they were ready Sam nodded and Bill eased the door open slightly. In the tattered hallway Hamid stood with his hands over his head.

355

He looked older; worn down by the sand and his life as a rebel. Bill let him in and closed the door as Darius patted Hamid down. They pushed the bed back and Darius nodded to them that he was unarmed. Hamid put his arms down.

"As-salamu alaykum," Hamid said. "Hello."

Sam was bewildered. "What are you doing Hamid?"

"May I sit?" Hamid sat down on the edge of the bed. "I wanted to look you in the eyes when I told you. I owe you both that much from our past lives together."

"Tell us what?" Bill pressed.

"That you're my prisoners."

"Get fucked," Bill replied. "You think we're going to let you walk out of here now?"

Hamid shook his head. "No, of course not. But I expected that. Truth be told, I'm safer with you than I am outside, right?"

Sam rolled his eyes. *Sonofabitch.* "He's right. He doesn't think we'll sacrifice ourselves to make sure he's dead."

"The Hellfire," Bill stated.

Sam nodded.

"So why don't we kill him now and make a break for it?"

Hamid smiled. "You could do that Bill but my death would only rally our cause. I'd be a martyr and all of you will still be killed. Every second you're trapped in this room is another second additional Taliban, from all over the region, flock here. You thought there were thirty men outside. Try one hundred. In twenty minutes that number will double, then double again. None of you are leaving here."

"Hobbes," Sam asked through his headset, "what's it look like outside?"

"Not good."

"Define not good please."

356

"The site is overwhelmed. Satellite imaging shows multiple inbound vehicles vectoring in on your position."

"And armed men outside?"

"Just like he said. Their number has already doubled."

Sam sighed and lowered his weapon. *Checkmate.* "Hobbes, lock and fire on my position."

"Wait, what? You're still inside."

"Don't think," Sam told him, "just do it. That's an order."

Hobbes didn't respond.

"Hobbes? Confirm."

"I'm…I'm not doing that. I won't sacrifice you. That's not the mission."

"Dammit Hobbes. Lock on and fire."

"Absolutely not."

Sam shook his head. "Then we're going to die by their hands; slowly. Think about that for a second and then fucking push the button, okay? You'll be doing us all a favor."

Tears began to run down Hobbes' face as he struggled with Sam's decision. Russell moved away and made a phone call.

"I'm…I'm sorry. I can't."

"Forget it Hobbes. I understand. It's okay."

Sam motioned for his team to put their weapons down, step back, get on their knees and put their hands on their heads. After that he took off his headset, placed it on the floor and assumed the position.

Hamid smiled, pushed the bed to one side and hollered to his men. A dozen Taliban rushed up the stairs, AK's at the ready and entered the room. They collected the loose weapons and waited for their leader's instructions. Hamid took an AK out of one of his men's hands and walked over to Sam, who looked up at him as he approached. Hamid bent down and whispered in Sam's ear.

"You will not die today, my old friend. But, rest assured, I will look weak if I don't kill you. When the time comes I will make sure it's quick."

Hamid stood back up and swiftly cracked Sam's head with the wooden stock. Sam fell over on his side, unconscious.

52

Friday Nov 2, 2001

Julie and Kim let themselves in through the front door, late at night, and were immediately greeted by Thomas and Laura, who embraced the two emotionally, wrought sisters. The four adults sat down in the family room as Laura began to console them. It had been an incredibly trying day for everyone and this had been the first opportunity for the family to bring each other up to speed. As Thomas sat down he knew his mind was far away, mulling over the infinite scenarios that could be played out in the coming weeks. He tried to reel those anxieties in and concentrate on the immediate problem in front of them.

"What happened?" Laura gently asked the sisters, clearly in pain.

Both Julie and Kim were exhausted, both mentally and physically. At the restaurant, after Kim heard the loud boom over the phone and lost contact with her daughter, she began to panic. Julie tried calling the school's main office but it wasn't answered. Instead the phone endlessly rang over and over. Julie hastily plunked money down on the table, grabbed her distraught sister and hurried back to the car. Once there she handed the phone back to Kim and instructed her to dial 911, drove out of the parking lot headed north to the boarding school in Harrisburg, Pennsylvania that was only two hours away.

"By the time we got there," Julie said, "the fire had been put out but the police weren't letting any of us through."

"Us?"

"Kim and I weren't the last parents to show up. We learned that the local news had already broadcast a live report which meant that additional parents, completely frightened, continued to arrive after we did."

"What about all the students? What happened to them?"

Julie looked towards her lap as tears ran down her cheeks. "We heard that most of them got out."

"Most?" Laura glanced over at Thomas and then back at Julie. "Where are they Julie? Where are your children?"

"They…they don't know…"

The sisters couldn't hold their emotions back any longer as a flood of anguished tears streamed down their faces. Julie and Kim held each other as their sobs wracked their bodies to the very core. Laura and Thomas could do very little other than wait for their heartbreaking wave of emotions to pass. Kim eventually managed to speak.

"The students…the kids that escaped the fire have already been reunited with their parents. They wouldn't give us any other details."

Laura was worried. "So you don't know where they are?"

Julie and Kim both shook their heads. "We were instructed to go home and wait."

"That's unbelievable," Laura told them. "What can we do to help?"

"I don't know," Julie replied. "Our kids….our kids are everything to us." She began to plead. "Where are they Laura? Where are they? I just want them back. I just want to hold them tight and tell them I love them and that everything's going to be all right."

Laura turned and whispered to Thomas. "Why don't you head to the kitchen and see if there's an update on the television."

Thomas nodded and stood up.

I'm as helpless as they are right now, and I can't help but feel for them. They don't know what's happened to their kids, and that has got to be driving them insane, whereas I happen to know exactly who my enemy is.

He headed to the kitchen and turned on the news. Laura joined him a minute later.

"Anything?" she asked as she walked in.

"They're just getting to that now."

On the television a female news reporter moved on to the next story. "Thank you Vicki. Now, we return to a heart wrenching story that's gripped the east coast. Earlier today a massive fire broke out at Culver boarding school, which is located in the community of Harrisburg, Pennsylvania. We now go live to the scene with Beth Brown who has the latest update on this tragic event."

"This is Beth Brown with WPMT. I'm here at Culver, a boarding school that houses just over three hundred children in dormitory buildings. Earlier today a fire consumed two of those structures and so far investigators have been extremely tight lipped on how these fires may have started. But what has been leaked is that nine bodies have been recovered from those two structures; two adults and seven children. The grim truth is that there may be more yet to be discovered. The headmistress, Ms. Jones, has informed the media that she is overwhelmed with grief. She praises her staff for their quick response and says that if it wasn't for them the school may have suffered additional casualties. Ms. Jones goes on to say that her prayers are with the families that are suffering from this terrible loss.

"Now," Beth continued, "I questioned a number of parents about what happened here today and an overwhelming amount of them informed me that their children heard explosions. Currently it's unclear whether these explosions were an accident or a case of arson, but we do know that innocent lives were lost today. We'll have updates on this story first thing in the morning. I'm Beth Brown with WPMT."

Thomas and Laura turned around when they heard Julie and Kim begin to cry again. The two had come in and heard the majority of the news report.

"They're dead, aren't they?" Kim sobbed.

Laura shook her head, went to her side and put her arm around her. "We don't know that."

"Then why...why... are they missing?"

"I don't know."

The television boomed. "Breaking news. The Taliban have just released a video on YouTube in which they claim to have captured five American soldiers, while killing a sixth, when the Americans attacked a Taliban village within the Panjshir Valley region."

The four adults immediately turned to watch.

"I need to warn our viewers that what you're about to see is extremely graphic and very difficult to watch."

The video started with five men in a small room, black hoods over their heads. They were on their knees and had their hands tied behind their backs. Two Taliban soldiers stood on either side of them with AK-47's cradled in their arms. Another man appeared and spoke to the camera.

"My name is Hamid Emal Habibi."

"Oh shit no," Thomas barely managed to say.

"Is that...are they?" Julie uttered as she grabbed his arm.

Thomas didn't have a chance to answer as Hamid continued.

"The American soldiers behind me were captured when they attempted to assassinate me under the pretext of justice for you, the

American people." Hamid spat on the ground. "I spit on every American and the freedom you think you stand for. The truth is your country, and your government, are nothing more than a blight on this planet that needs to be exterminated. I took thousands of your lives on nine-eleven, and now I'll take one more to prove how serious my convictions are."

Hamid made a motion and one of his men pulled one of the hostages forward. Hamid removed his hood and a bloodied face stared back, a huge knot on the soldier's head and one of his eyes was swollen shut. Dried blood covered his face, neck and shirt.

"Tell them your name," Hamid demanded.

"Fuck you."

Hamid punched the soldier in the face, audibly breaking his nose.

"Tell them your name."

"Darius."

"Darius what."

"Darius Hawkins, you asshole."

Hamid removed a handgun from his waist, put it to the man's temple and pulled the trigger. Blood shot out the other side of his head, along with bits of brain and bone. As Darius' lifeless body collapsed the remaining four bound soldiers began to scream and yell.

"You fucker!"

"I'll kill you!"

Thomas, Laura, Julie and Kim froze. Time had halted for each of them. On the video Hamid walked down the line of hostages and removed each one of their hoods. There, on the screen, Sam and Bill's face stared back at them; their eyes hollow because they knew what was coming.

"NOOOOOOO!" Julie screamed at the television.

"Oh God, no!" Kim exclaimed as she covered her mouth.

Hamid put the gun to Sam's head and looked at the camera. "America, I have killed two of your soldiers. You have twenty-four hours to remove your troops from Afghanistan or I will execute my remaining four hostages, live, for the world to see. Failure to comply will result in their blood being spilled."

The video stopped playing and the reporter appeared visibly shaken by what he had just seen.

"SAMMMM!" Julie bellowed. She was beside herself and couldn't stop. "SAMMMM! SAMMMM! SAMMMM!"

Kim fainted and collapsed on the kitchen floor. Thomas went to Kim's side as Laura tried to console Julie, but she wasn't listening, her mind had already checked out.

"SAMMMM! SAMMMM! SAMMMM!"

Emily and Gavin appeared in the doorway, woken up by the commotion. Laura frantically motioned for her daughter to come to her side.

"Make her sleep!" she yelled so Emily could hear.

Emily grabbed Julie's ankle. Thomas barely had time to catch Julie as she toppled over, asleep on the floor. Laura stood up and clicked off the television.

"What's going on?" Gavin asked.

"It's complicated," Laura replied immediately.

Emily pressed the issue. "What happened?"

Laura slowly shook her head.

"We're not young or innocent anymore mom. Gav and I have seen terrible things, but you said we handle everything together. Don't try and hide it and tell us what's going on."

Laura couldn't answer her daughter so Emily turned to her father.

"Dad?"

Thomas took a few seconds before he answered. "Uncle Sam and Uncle Bill were captured. One of their team was killed during the mission and another one was just executed in front of the entire world."

"Are they going to die?" Gavin asked.

"I don't know. The man on the video, the same man they were sent to capture, told us they have twenty-four hours before he's going to kill them."

"We can't just wait for them to die, right? They're family."

"Gavin's right," Emily added. "What's the plan to save them?"

* * *

President Bush slammed the door to the Oval office after Robert Duncan, the Director of the CIA, entered the room.

"Mr. President, I..."

"No Robert, you listen to me. Look at the GODDAMN position you've put me in!"

The President paced back and forth, clearly aggravated.

"What am I supposed to tell the American people, huh? Answer me that. I can't back out of this war, which means I certainly can't save those men you sent in. Either way I play this I come off as weak to the world."

"Mr. President, we need to mount an immediate rescue operation."

The President waved his hand as if he were swatting a fly. "Out of the question. Denied. I won't put more men in harm's way just to rescue four of yours. It'd be suicide and I'd never hear the end of it. The press is already going to eat me alive over this, thanks to you, and when I end up doing nothing to rescue them the rest of the world will loathe me even more."

"But sir…"

"You will take zero action in this matter, and that's an order. Do I make myself clear?"

"Yes, sir."

"Dismissed."

53
Saturday Nov 3, 2001

It turned out to be a long night. Thomas and Laura lay in bed and stared at the ceiling whil they agonized over the situation. Dr. Matsushita had survived the fire. He was alive; had an extremely powerful ability; was in possession of Thomas' blood and was actively experimenting. They didn't know what to expect from him and that was just a sample of the overall problems they now faced.

Amanda, Craig, Sarah and Edward's bodies hadn't been identified yet so they were still officially listed as missing. Julie and Kim were beside themselves with anxiety, terror and dread. They didn't know where their children were, aside from watching the body bags as they were removed from the buildings burned out husks; and they had shouldered that fear by themselves because they couldn't turn to their husbands for emotional support. The two were at their breaking point and Hamid's video pushed them straight into the abyss. Laura had made sure Julie and Kim were comfortable in their beds, forced to sleep by Emily to alleviate their tortured state of minds.

In bed, Thomas and Laura shuffled their bodies in an attempt to find a comfortable position, but their thoughts kept them wide awake. They knew they had to deal with the reality that Sam and Bill had been captured and were going to be executed the following day.

It was the middle of the night when Thomas rolled for the millionth time.

"I can't sleep either," Laura stated.

"Sorry, but I just can't get the condition we saw them in out of my head."

"Neither can I."

Thomas sat up and swung his legs out to the side of their bed. "I have to do something. I'm going to call the DCI and see what his plan is."

"It's the middle of the night."

"I don't give a fuck," Thomas shot back and then calmed down. "Sorry, I didn't mean to snap at you."

Laura slid over on the bed and wrapped her arms around him from behind. "I get it. Call him."

Thomas picked up his cell phone, off the side table, and called the Director's private number. It rang three times before it was answered.

"Listen Thomas, before you say anything you need to know that I tried."

A confused looked washed over his face. "I called to ask when the rescue mission is proceeding. What are you talking about?"

"We're talking about the same thing," the DCI told him. "I went to the President but he wasn't interested in what I had to say. He's decided to leave them there."

"What? What are you saying?"

"I'm saying there isn't going to be a rescue mission."

Thomas' mouth opened in disbelief so he stood up. "What the fuck? You're just going to leave them there to die? That's not right."

"I don't like it any more than you do, trust me, but my hands are tied."

"Yours might be, but mine aren't."

Thomas terminated the call and tossed his phone back on the nightstand in disgust.

"Goddammit!" he exclaimed.

Laura got out of bed. "I know that tone. What are you thinking?"

"Shit, it's up to me now. They're dead if we don't do something."

"Are you seriously contemplating going back in there after what happened last time?"

"No, I'm not contemplating it, I'm doing it." He broke away from Laura and headed out of the bedroom to his son's room and opened the door. "Gavin?"

Gavin and Emily sat up in bed when their father turned on the light. Laura appeared in the doorway and notice her two kids were fully dressed and wide awake.

"What's going on here?" Thomas said with some surprise in his voice.

Emily answered the question. "Gav and I have been talking. We knew it'd only be a matter of time before you came to the same conclusion we did. You know this is the only option."

Thomas raised his hand to his mouth and covered it as Laura sat down by her children.

"We're a family," Gavin told them. "And as a family we have to look out for each other." Gavin looked at his mother and then over at his father. "I don't want Uncle Sam and Uncle Bill to die, and neither do you, which is why you came to wake me up in the middle of the night."

"So you're willing to take that risk?" Thomas asked.

"Yes," his son replied.

"Are you absolutely sure?"

Gavin cocked his head to the side. "Uncle Sam and Uncle Bill always do whatever it takes, in spite of the danger." He turned to his mother. "I'm sorry, but I have to do this."

Laura nodded and pulled her son close. "I know. Just promise me that you'll be careful."

"Promise." Gavin looked over at his father. "It's time to gear up."

Thomas smiled. "That's my boy."

* * *

Before they left for the underground facility Thomas raided the house's downstairs armory. He armed himself with an MP5, Glock 17, a knife and a few flashbangs. Under his tactical chest rig, topped with extra magazines, he wore a Kevlar vest. He also fitted Gavin out with his own Kevlar vest as well. As he left he turned around and placed four more Glocks, with additional magazines, in a backpack.

The four of them left for the underground facility in the middle of the night. Once they arrived they headed to the Tech wing where they found Hobbes, who had never left. He was startled as they entered the room.

"Listen Thomas. Laura. I just wanted to say that I'm so sorry that…"

Thomas held up his hand and interrupted Hobbes. "The Director says his hands are tied so now it's up to us."

"I…I know I'm tired as hell but did you just imply you're planning on rescuing them?"

"Do you think I got all dressed up for nothing? Now, show Gavin and I where they're being held."

It took a few seconds for Hobbes to let it all sink in, but when it did he grinned and began to show them both the village and the building the team were being held in.

"So you're just going to take this upon yourselves?" boomed a familiar voice.

They turned and watched as Robert Duncan, the DCI himself, walked into the room.

"Don't try and stop us," Thomas challenged.

"I wouldn't dream of it, but what you're planning to do is both heroic and reckless."

"Why are you here?"

"I'm here to support you, plain and simple. So tell me, what can I do to help?"

Laura nodded and Thomas took charge. "A medical team on hand when we get back."

"That's it? I can send trained men with you."

"No," Thomas and Gavin said at the same time.

"You're worried about the creatures, right?" the DCI asked.

"Yes, it's too dangerous. The trip back is going to draw them to us for sure. I can't risk it."

The Director nodded. "I'll make the call right now and get a medical team over here."

"Are you sure about this?" Laura asked as the DCI placed his cell phone to his ear.

"You're asking if I'm scared?" Thomas tested.

She nodded.

He leaned in, kissed her and then whispered in her ear. "I'm terrified, but this has to be done. They'd do the same for me in a heartbeat. Don't worry, I'll protect Gavin with my life."

"I know. You're a good man. Just bring everyone home safe, especially you two."

"I will."

"You're lying."

He smiled. "I meant I hope I will."

"Fair enough," she replied.

Thomas bent down and gave Emily a hug. "I'll be back before you know it."

Thomas wasn't prepared for what his daughter said next. "Things are pretty messed up, aren't they?"

"Yes, they are, and we need to find a way to fix them."

Emily hugged him. "Be careful."

"I will."

Thomas stood up and walked over to where Hobbes and Gavin were. In front of them was a monitor that contained an overhead view of the village as well as a larger view of the entire Panjshir Valley.

"You sure you know where you're going Gav?" Hobbes asked for the third time.

Gavin nodded. "I told you, I've got it."

"We ready?" Thomas asked.

"Hold on a second," Hobbes said as he pulled open a drawer and extracted a box. He placed it on the table, opened it and inside was a large, black watch. He pulled it out and handed it over. "Put that on your wrist."

"What's it do?"

"It's a GPS tracker so when you get there I can instantly locate you. I've already activated it."

"Good thinking," Thomas said as he strapped it to his wrist. "Thanks."

"No problem. Also, take this headset so we can communicate."

Thomas put the headset on and then squatted down to address his son. "How long do you think we'll be in there?"

"When we went to California Gabbi said the boat ride took us something like thirty-three seconds."

Thomas breathed in and then exhaled. "And for this run?"

"Right around a minute, I think."

Thomas tightly squeezed the grip of his MP5 without even realizing it. *Shit. That's too long.* "Okay. You ready to go?"

Gavin nodded and the two turned and hugged Laura and Emily.

"We'll be here when you get back," Laura told them.

Thomas pulled the charging handle on this weapon and released it. *Lock and load. Let's do this.*

"Do it."

The portal formed and, with one final look back, the two stepped forward and disappeared.

In the shadowy corner of the room Raven smiled and vanished.

* * *

"They're here," Raven told the group. "It's time to move into position. Victor?"

"Follow me," Victor Bannon instructed as he took flight into the air.

Behind him Yuri, Raven, Anna, Nikolay and Alexei followed closely behind. The Dark District grew smaller as Victor led them towards Gavin's private island; the same location where he took his final breath.

* * *

"Have they made it?" Laura asked Hobbes as she and Emily watched over his shoulder.

"The GPS isn't in range. They must still be in travel."

"But it's already been a minute."

"I don't think traveling to another dimension, or whatever it is, is an exact scien..."

Hobbes stopped talking when a circle suddenly appeared on his monitor four buildings over from where the team was being held hostage. Laura breathed a sigh of relief as Hobbes checked in with Thomas.

"Marasta! Shaythaan!"

"Thomas?"

"Yeah, we're here," he whispered back a few seconds later, "and in one piece. One target down. Where are we?"

"You're four buildings west of their known location. Be careful."

"Tell me about it."

* * *

Thomas squinted as he stepped through to Gavin's island. The sun bore down on him and it was a quick reminder about the extra weight he now carried. He took his time and looked in all directions, but didn't see anything.

I'm not a soldier, and I know I'm over my head, but I'll be damned if I'm going to let some terrorist kill my friends while I sit idly by.

Gavin walked by his father and summoned the boat.

"You okay Gav?" he asked as they stepped inside.

"Yeah."

"You're not scared?"

"A little. What about you?"

"Me too. A little."

"We'll be okay," his son assured him as he lifted the boat out of the water and propelled it over the vast ocean.

"How do you know that?"

"Because of our training, and because Uncle Sam and Uncle Bill are counting on us, that's why."

Thomas smiled as he looked around and once again took in the surreal nature of the activity they were currently engaged in. They were gliding over an ocean in a completely different world, to mount a rescue, and was doing it with his son.

This is unbelievable and just spectacular. But these powers we possess; are they worth it? Could we be the next step in human evolution or are we just amateurs in a game we have no business playing in?

"Get ready. The beach is coming up."

"I want you to stay behind me once we go through, okay?"

Gavin nodded. "I've got your back."

Thomas chuckled. "You're pretty amazing, you know that, right? I love you."

"So are you dad, and I love you too."

Thomas did a final sweep of the sky but it was still clear. The island, that Gavin was taking them to, rapidly approached. The boat slowed and came to a stop fifty feet away. Thomas groaned, rolled into the water and surprisingly found his footing. He put Gavin on his shoulders and, with his MP5 held above the water as well, waded towards shore. Once they were there he put his son down and performed a final equipment check. Satisfied that everything was in working order he gave Gavin the go ahead and the two of them entered the newly created portal that would take them to Afghanistan.

As Thomas and Gavin stepped through they ended up in the main room of a home and startled a man who sat at a table. The man's face turned white. He cried out for help and reached for his AK.

"Marasta!"

Thomas flicked his wrist and the rifle cracked the Taliban in his face, knocking him from his seat and onto the floor.

"Shaythaan!" *Devil!*

The man drew a knife from his waist but Thomas flung the man upwards, slamming him into the ceiling. The knife fell from his unconscious hand. His body dropped and landed with a thud on the floor.

"Thomas?" Hobbes said in his ear.

"Yeah, we're here," he whispered, "and in one piece. One target down. Where are we?"

"You're four buildings west of their known location. Be careful."

"Tell me about it." Thomas brought his MP5 up as he approached the door that led outside. He didn't want to use the weapon if he had to because it's noise would alert the entire village to their presence. "You with me Gav?"

"Right behind you."

"Hobbes?"

"You're clear to cross the alley and hop in the neighbor's backyard."

"Roger that," Thomas replied.

He opened the door, took a quick peek left and right and then the two of them crossed the alley and cautiously made their way behind the adjoining house.

"You're clear for the next two houses," Hobbes told him. "After that the large building, they're being held in, has eight men surrounding it. I don't know how many are inside."

"Understood," Thomas whispered.

Hobbes hesitated and then spoke up again. "Are you sure this is a good idea? I mean, there could be twenty men in there and your wife and daughter are right here watching..."

"Noted. Now shut up and help me."

"Right. Sorry. Keep heading in the same direction."

Thomas and Gavin moved semi-crouched through the next two backyards. They took cover as they came up to the final wall and carefully peeked over. Four guards were visible from their current position, which meant that four more were on the other side of the building along with an unknown number inside with the hostages. Thomas swallowed hard, gripped his weapon even tighter and closed his eyes. The adrenaline coursing through his body staved off how worn out he'd become in the past day.

Just hang in there guys. We're coming for you, but holy shit I'm scared.

"They're not moving," Hobbes said in Thomas' ear.

"I saw that."

"You know, I still have that drone circling overhead. I could use the second Hellfire missile to cause a distraction."

"No. There's no telling how Hamid will react and he could kill them before I even get in there. Just let me figure this out."

Thomas motioned to his son. "I need you to take out the two men on the right, silently, while I do the same on the left, okay?"

Stir appeared next to Gavin a split second later and prepared to engage as Thomas slung his weapon and extracted the edged blade from his tactical vest.

"Ready?"

Gavin nodded.

"Go."

Stir shot over the wall and tore out one of the guard's throats in an instant. Blood sprayed the side of the house in a wide arc.

377

Thomas stood and threw his blade at one of his targets. In midflight he took control of it and moments later it buried itself deep in a guard's back.

Stir wasted no time as he sprung, red eyes blazing, from his first target to the next. The second guard barely had time to register, what had just happened to the man next to him, before his life was silently snuffed out.

As the knife impaled Thomas' first target he forcibly yanked the second guard off his feet. The man lifted a few feet in the air, clutching at his throat. Thomas snapped his neck and then lowered the body back to the ground.

"No indication you were heard," Hobbes informed him.

Fucking go!

Thomas vaulted the wall and ran to the now unguarded door with Gavin on his heels. Stir bounded over and joined them just as Thomas opened the door. When he did five Taliban, including Hamid, turned and stared, open mouthed at Thomas' bold entrance. Thomas instantly ascertained that Sam, Bill, Carl and Eliot were lined up on the left wall, bloody and bruised, but alive. On the opposite side of the room was the video camera that had been used to film the execution the world had witnessed on television.

"Thomas?" Sam barely managed to utter through his cracked and bloodied lips.

The Taliban raised their weapons to shoot the American intruder but before they could their AK's were ripped from their arms and sailed across the room, clattering to the floor in a heap. A few of the men cried out in anguish with broken fingers. One Taliban rushed Thomas and managed to take two steps before his body toppled over. His head rolled and came to a rest at Hamid's feet as Stir stood his ground in the middle of the room next to the

378

man's corpse. Thomas closed the door behind him, without taking his eyes off Hamid, as the other three backed up towards their leader.

"I could cry out and you would be swarmed in a matter of seconds," Hamid boasted from across the room, clearly uncertain of the situation but showing strength in front of his men.

"You could try," Thomas told him, "but you'll end up just like him," he said as he motioned towards the headless guard. "Now Hamid, before I change my mind and decide to kill all of you, secure your men and do it quickly."

Hamid hesitated as his mind tried to wrap itself around what he'd just witnessed. "Who are you?"

"Don't talk. Don't think. Just do it, right now."

Hamid's men, who didn't speak English, looked to their leader for guidance. With a wary eye on the red-eyed creature in the middle of the room Hamid motioned to his three remaining men in the room to get on their knees. Afterwards he proceeded to zip tie both their hands and feet. When he was done he tapped their mouths closed.

"Untie my friends," Thomas commanded.

A yell emanated from outside and Thomas knew they were short on time. Hamid smiled and refused to comply.

"Whoever you are, you're not leaving here alive, and neither are your friends."

"You'll be the first to die, Hamid."

"I've already made my peace with my god. Have you?"

Thomas raised his arm and Hamid flew across the room like a rag doll. He hit the far wall and collapsed, dazed. His men began to struggle against their bonds as Thomas effortlessly pushed their bodies against the two doors, temporarily blocking them from begin opened from outside. Thomas then turned his attention to

379

the hostages turning each one around and stripping their restraints off with just a thought. The men were weak and Thomas knew there was no way they could help him fight back.

"Stir. Guard. Gavin. Portal."

Men from the outside began to pound their fists on the doors and push them open.

Gavin formed his portal and moved over next to his father.

Hamid shook his head to clear it, pushed himself up on his hands and knees, gazed at the shimmering gateway in amazement and began to crawl.

Thomas wasted no time and picked up Sam and literally tossed him through the portal.

One of the doors opened wider.

Bill flew into the portal.

Hamid reached the camera that had fallen over and turned it on.

Stir rushed the opening door and disappeared outside. Screams and bursts of automatic gunfire followed.

Carl disappeared as Hamid recorded what was happening in the room.

Stir reappeared inside, blood dripping from his jowls, and Hamid turned and recorded that as well.

The second door opened and a swarm of AK wielding men pushed through.

Thomas pulled a flashbang from his vest and tossed it in their general direction just as he pushed Eliot into the portal.

One of the Taliban fired his AK at Thomas and missed.

Thomas picked up his son, protecting him from the gunfire, and rushed the portal.

"Stir!" Gavin yelled.

The flashbang exploded just as the Taliban readjusted his aim and fired a second time. He got off three rounds before his senses were crushed by the deafening and blinding explosion.

Thomas was propelled through the gateway and landed in the soft sand as the portal vanished behind them.

Thomas managed to get off his son and cried out in agony.

Sam and Bill were out of it, along with Carl and Eliot. Gavin jumped to his feet looked down at his father as Stir shook the blood out of his jowls.

"Dad, what is it? What's wrong?"

Thomas couldn't answer through the intense pain and barely managed to roll over. Gavin stripped off his father's backpack and immediately saw the three bullets that protruded out of his father's back. The Kevlar vest had absorbed most of the kinetic energy from all three rounds, but not all of it. With his father's help he carefully removed the tactical and Kevlar vests between Thomas' screams of pain. After that Gavin wasted no time and pressed his hands down on his father's back. Within seconds the three bullets were expunged from his flesh and his father's pained expression lessoned more and more with each passing moment. Thomas was left with three large bruises when he made his son stop.

"Thank you. I'm…I'm okay now. Check on them."

Gavin went and hastily used his healing powers on each man. A minute later all four men on the island were feeling much better.

"Where the hell are we?" Carl asked.

"What just happened?" Eliot added.

Sam and Bill gave Thomas a huge bear hug but Eliot and Carl didn't know how to react. The two looked around, wide-eyed and wary, especially at the skeleton that lay in the sand and the small creature that remained next to the boy.

"I'm glad to see you bro but what the fuck did you just do?"
Bill scolded Thomas. "That was totally reckless. Are you
insane?"

"We can't stay here," Gavin interjected. "They're coming."

"Why?" Bill pressed.

A boat materialized and it startled the four men, including Sam
and Bill.

"Save it for another time," Thomas told them, "and get in the
fucking boat, right now!"

The tone in Thomas' voice sliced through whatever resistance
was left because on the horizon loomed a dark cloud.

* * *

"Why aren't they here yet?" Laura anxiously fretted.

On Hobbes' monitor the GPS signal had vanished from the
Taliban village over a minute ago. The DCI, Laura, Hobbes and
Emily had overheard the entire encounter and were relieved as
soon as the tracker disappeared. But when they hadn't shown up
two minutes later they had become worried

"Maybe their injuries slowed them down," the DCI said.

"I hope that's it," Laura replied. "I really do. I mean, the way
they described what came after them the last time…"

Emily wrapped her arms around her mother and looked up.
"They're going to make it."

Just then, in the middle of the room, the portal formed.

* * *

"What the hell is that!?" Sam cried out as the boat sped above
the ocean.

382

"Whatever it is it's gaining on us!" Bill yelled. "Do you have any weapons!?"

Thomas instinctively touched his chest thinking he had his vest still on. "No! Everything was left on the beach."

"Make this thing, whatever it is, go faster!" Eliot yelled with obvious fear in his voice.

"Can't we divert to another island?" Thomas asked his son.

Gavin shook his head. "We'll only pop out in the Atlantic and drown."

Thomas looked at his son's face and then back at the incoming dark cloud. It was then that he knew they weren't going to make it.

* * *

"There they go!" Raven yelled. "Don't let them escape!"

Far up in the sky the evil six led the way ahead of the massive contingent of dark forces.

"There are six of them!" Anna cried out in delight. "That's one for each of us! I call dibs on the boy!"

"Sam's mine," Nikolay raged.

"I have you in my sights Thomas," Victor said with a smile on his face. "You're mine."

* * *

The island appeared in the distance and were seconds away.

"They're right behind us!" Carl shouted. "What do we do!?"

"Prepare to jump out!" Thomas yelled at everyone. "Get to the island as fast as you can and then wait for the portal! Once it appears don't hesitate, just go through it!"

383

Thomas caught Sam and Bill's eyes.

"This is bad, isn't it?" Sam verified.

Thomas nodded. "The kind nightmares are made of. Get ready."

Fifty feet out the boat stopped. Everyone jumped or dove into the water as quickly as possible and began to make their way to the shore. Thomas helped Gavin and as soon as he could put his feet down he picked his son up and trudged through the water towards the sand, along with everyone else. Eliot and Carl reached the beach first. They turned around and pointed up just as two shapes sped out of the sky and tackled them. They began to struggle on the sand.

"What the fuck!" Bill cried out as he rushed forward to help.

Sam was on his heels as Thomas, Gavin and Stir finally emerged from the water.

Bill was then knocked over from his right, and before Sam could react he was catapulted off his feet from the left.

A battle broke out on the beach as each man wrestled for his life.

Thomas looked over his shoulder and two feet collided with his body, spinning him around and down to the ground. Gavin cried out as Thomas watched as Anna Garland wrapped her arm securely around his son's neck. Stir immediately attacked Anna but he passed right through her which made her laugh.

What? What the hell is going on?

"Hello Thomas. I've missed you."

Thomas knew that voice all too well and whipped his head around. He came face to face with Victor Bannon.

"Victor. What are you doing here?"

"Payback."

Thomas was confused and looked over at Anna and his son again. "Let him go!" he screamed at her.

"Awww Gavin," Anna taunted. "Is daddy afraid of what I'll do to you?"

"Look at me Thomas," Victor ordered.

"What do you want?" Thomas heard the fighting rage on behind him. The dark cloud of hatred was no more than ten seconds away. "What do you want?"

"We're taking your lives, it's that simple."

Then, out of nowhere, new shapes ripped the evil off Sam, Bill, Carl and Eliot. A fifth smashed Anna directly in the face and sent her sprawling. A confused look appeared on Victor' face.

Nine.

Thomas didn't know what had happened but wasted no time to push Victor off balance and grab Gavin.

Eight.

Sam and the others recovered and got their feet under them.

"DON'T LET ANY OF THEM ESCAPE!" Raven screamed.

Seven.

"THOMAS!" Victor screamed behind him.

Thomas knew there wouldn't be a second opportunity. "Gavin! Portal!"

Six.

The portal formed. Thomas flung his son through it and Stir bounded in behind.

Five.

"GO! GO! GO!" Thomas hollered.

Four.

Sam, Bill, Carl and Eliot raced towards the gateway.

Three.

It was then that Thomas recognized who helped him fight against the evil forces of Yuri, Raven, Nikolay and Alexei. It was his parents, Michael and Betsy; and his grandparents, Ed and Claire. *Dad? Mom?* Nikolay broke free and barreled towards him like a runaway train.

Two.

Sam and Bill plunged through the portal and disappeared. Carl and Eliot were right behind them. Thomas looked back and saw Victor walk out of the water just as Rebecca punched Anna in the face.

"THOMAS!" Victor yelled again.

One.

Thomas caught Rebecca's smile as he turned back to leave the island.

Zero.

The dark wave of hatred crushed Thomas and sent him tumbling through the portal.

* * *

Emily wrapped her arms around her mother and looked up. "They're going to make it."

Just then, in the middle of the room, the portal formed and Gavin came shooting out of it. He skidded along the cement floor and rolled over a few times just as Stir appeared.

"Gavin!" Laura yelled and rushed to his side with Emily.

The portal crackled with energy and Stir turned to growl at it.

"Are you alright?" his mother asked as she reached her son's side.

Gavin didn't hear her question. "Where's dad!?"

Sam and Bill emerged at that moment and immediately put themselves between the portal and Thomas' family; their eyes and faces filled with fear.

"What's happening!?" Laura screamed.

"Some bad fucking shit!" Bill yelled.

"Where's Thomas!?" she pleaded. "Where's Thomas!?"

"He was right behind us!"

The portal surged and an immense black fog spewed forth from its depths.

"What th…"

Carl, Eliot and Thomas flew out of the gateway like rag dolls, through the black fog and landed hard on the cement floor. Before anyone could do anything hundreds of gruesome and deformed faces appeared out of the dense, black fog. Fingers, long and sharp, reached out to grab anyone with deadly intent. Laura, Emily and Gavin retreated away from the hands and it was then that Alexei Vorobyrov, Nikolay's hitman, took shape right in front of Sam. Alexei's smile sent chills down their spines.

"PORTAL!" Sam roared.

As the portal vanished the dark cloud's tie to the Other Place was severed. Alexei's smile changed to panic as he began to quickly dissipate; turning back to dark fog. The clawed fingers retreated as well and in front of their eyes the dark fog collapsed in on itself and ceased to exist.

For a few moments no one moved, unsure if the danger was over. Laura broke through her fear and scrambled on all fours over to Thomas, who lay unmoving on the floor.

"Thomas! Thomas!"

Sam and Bill went to Carl and Eliot's side to check on their condition. The two were unconscious, and banged up, but seemed fine other than that.

"Thomas! Wake up!"

Gavin and Emily joined their mother by their father's side just as he stirred.

"Thomas?"

"Ouch," he said as he put a hand to his head. "Are we there yet?"

Laura hugged him tight as tears of relief flowed freely down her face. "Dammit. I thought I'd lost you."

He sat up and groaned when he did. "Gav? Where's Gav?"

"I'm right here dad."

Thomas turned and pulled his son close. "I'm so glad you're safe. Sorry about throwing you. Are you okay?"

Gavin nodded and Thomas was relieved.

"The medical team is five minutes out," the DCI told everyone.

Carl and Eliot mumbled and began to wake up as well so Sam and Bill helped them sit up.

"Take it easy," Sam said. "We got'cha."

Bill looked back over at Thomas. "Thanks brother."

"You're welcome."

"And now that I've said that, are you ready for your scolding you said could wait till later?"

54

Saturday Nov 3, 2001

The medical team arrived and was immediately escorted down to the Tech wing where they examined Eliot and Carl, who were experiencing some noticeable memory issues. When Sam and Bill had helped their two teammates sit up they noticed right away that something wasn't right. They figured that maybe they'd been injured when they had been propelled through the portal by the dark cloud.

"What's your name?" one of the two med techs asked Eliot.

"I…I don't know," he replied.

The tech turned to Carl. "And your name?"

Carl only stared back at the man trying to help him, a confused look on his face.

"It's okay," Bill told them. "I'm sure you're just dazed from the encounter."

The techs spent the next fifteen minutes patching everyone up and then were escorted out of the facility as Carl and Eliot continued to sit on the floor. The DCI, Sam, Bill, Thomas, Laura, Emily, Hobbes and Gavin began to debrief each other, exhausted, even though it was three in the morning.

"Sam," Hobbes started, "I'm sorry. I should have…"

"Stop right there," Sam said as he put his hand up. "There was no way you could have known we were walking into an ambush. Hamid knew we were coming; it's as simple as that. I overestimated our ability to successfully carry out the mission and two of my men are now dead because of me and my ego."

Bill put a hand on Sam's shoulder. "Our ego. This isn't all on you brother."

The DCI spoke up. "Well, I for one am extremely happy that you're back in one piece."

"You need to thank Thomas and Gavin for that," Bill stated. "Without their Mission Impossible stunt they pulled, which for the record was absolutely foolish, we would've been executed."

"Foolish?" Laura questioned as she stepped up and got in Bill's face. "Foolish?"

"Laura, hey, I'm just messing around."

She shook her head. "No you're not. You think you can lie to my face?"

"Well, I…"

"My husband and son risked their lives, their LIVES, to save you. And you know why? I'll tell you why. Because Thomas said you would do the same for him without a second's thought. So yes, I may agree with you that it might have been foolish, but they were better equipped to handle the situation than the two of you ever could."

"Honey, please," Thomas implored.

"No, they need to hear this." She turned back to Bill. "Thomas loves you. We all do. And when we saw you on your knees, with hoods over your heads, Thomas and Gavin knew they weren't going to let you die."

"I…"

"I'm not finished. The part of this you're not getting is that they knew the journey through the other side was going to be dangerous, but they went anyway." She stepped back and stood by Thomas' side. "Okay, now I'm done."

The room became quiet.

"You're right," Bill admitted. "Sam and I would do anything for Thomas and shame on me for belittling him for doing the same. I apologize."

"There's no need," Thomas told him.

"Sure there is. I mean, shit, look at us right here, right now. Would I have ever thought my best friend, a children's book writer who lived a hermit's life in the mountains, would one day be rescuing me with a small creature, telekinetic powers and a portal to another world? I mean, that's just ridiculous. If anything I'm jealous. But it happened and I'm very thankful it happened. However, will all that being said, don't make me take that portal again. Holy shit that was frightening. I'm going to have nightmares for weeks."

"I can substantiate that," Sam added. "Do I dare ask what the hell that was?"

"I read Gabbi's report of the encounter that happened earlier this week and why you had to fly home from California," the DCI said, "and her recollection was graphically chilling. What we experienced on this end is something I don't ever want to see again. With that said, what happened on the other side?"

Stir rubbed against Gavin's leg so he bent down to pet him. Emily joined in.

"Gavin and I knew the dark cloud was going to overtake us," Thomas told them. "We had used too much time to recover after we escaped."

"What do you mean 'recovering'?" Laura probed.

"Well..."

"Dad got shot three times in the back," said Gavin.

"What!?" Laura exclaimed as she ran her hands up and down his back. "Are you okay?"

"I healed him. And then I healed Uncle Sam, Uncle Bill and the others."

"And when were you going to tell me about this?" badgered Laura.

"Obviously later," Thomas replied. "That's not as important right now as who we ran into, or rather, who ran into us."

"What do you mean?"

Thomas continued. "We were off the boat and practically on the beach when we were assaulted."

"That's one way of putting it," Sam said. "Driven into the sand out of nowhere is more like it."

"Agreed," Bill said as he nodded. "Out of nowhere."

Laura, Hobbes, Emily and Robert were confused.

"Who?" Laura asked. "What?"

"Ghosts from Christmas past," said Bill.

"Yeah," Thomas declared. "Ghosts. Suddenly we were faced with six enemies; enemies that are dead."

"Dead enemies?" the DCI inquired. "Like who?"

"Well, I was personally body slammed by Victor Bannon. We all remember him, don't we, because I certainly do."

"Seriously?" responded the DCI.

"Yeah," Thomas nodded. "And it doesn't stop there. Anna Garland had her arm around Gavin's throat. You should have seen the look of malevolence on her face. I wanted to kill her."

"Anna Garland. The hit-woman that Robert Aleman, Raven, utilized?"

"The one and the same."

"And she and Victor weren't the only ones," Sam said. "Yuri, Nikolay Dmitriev, Alexei and Raven were all involved in the attack."

"Why? For what purpose?" the DCI asked.

"Victor," Thomas replied, "said that he wanted to take my life."

"What happened? How did you get away from them?" Laura interjected.

"It was Rebecca," Gavin informed them from the floor. "She saved me."

"I'm confused. Rebecca was there?"

Thomas nodded again. "Crazy, right? She, along with my parents and grandparents, came to our rescue."

"But…but how did they…"

"Know?" Thomas said as he finished her sentence. "No idea. But if they hadn't shown up we'd all be dead."

"But you haven't been able to see or speak to your parents for the past four years," Laura replied. "Ever since the…"

"Ever since they rescued Emily and I from Dr. Matsushita's grips. Yeah, I remember. I'm overjoyed they were still looking out for us."

"Okay, so back to the dark cloud and the fight."

"Right," Thomas said as he got back on track. "Rebecca knocked Anna off Gavin and that allowed him to make his portal. I punched Victor in the face, picked Gav up and tossed him through to safety. Again, sorry about that Gav."

"No problem," his son said as he and Emily continued to pet Stir.

"There were only seconds left before the swarm was on us. Sam and Bill ran through next with Carl and Eliot right behind them. It was then that I recognized Rebecca, my parents and my grandparents. It was my hesitation that cost me, and before I knew it the swarm hit me hard and propelled me into the portal. The next thing I remember is coming to and looking up at you."

"You had me worried beyond belief."

"So what happened on this side? Director, you said that the dark cloud came through?"

The DCI shuddered. "It was stuff made up of nightmares. Horrible images. Faces. Claws."

"And Alexei formed out of the cloud as well," Bill added. "His face, it was smiling. But then Sam yelled at Gavin to close the portal and as it disappeared I saw Alexei panic. The cloud rapidly dissipated along with all those creatures that inhabited it."

A low growl emanated from Stir as Carl and Eliot stood up on their own. The group turned towards them.

"Easy Stir," Gavin said as he continued to pet him.

"Where am I?" Carl asked, still somewhat out of it.

"You're safe," the DCI said as he walked over to them. "You're going to be okay. How do you feel?"

"A little out of it," Eliot replied.

"Yeah, me too," Carl added.

"What's the last thing either of you remember?"

"A beach," Carl told him. "Darkness."

"What the hell happened to us, sir?" Eliot pressed.

"For the time being the two of you are confined to this facility. Is that clear?"

"Yes, sir," they both replied.

"Good. I want you to get some sleep and we'll debrief later on today." The DCI turned back to the group. "I'll take them over to the bunks and then I'm heading out. How does meeting back here at two this afternoon work?"

They nodded.

"Good. I'll see you then. Come on you two."

Carl and Eliot left with the DCI and vanished from sight.

"I think Bill and I should head out too," said Sam.

"Umm." Laura's face distorted when she realized that Sam and Bill were still very much in the dark about the school fire. She glanced over at Thomas and gave him a look.

"Oh shit," he said out loud.

"What's going on?" Bill asked.

"What's wrong?" Sam demanded.

"There was a fire at your children's boarding school," Laura tried to explain.

Worry instantly flashed over Sam and Bill's faces. "Tell me they're alright." beseeched Sam.

Laura shook her head. "I can't. They're still missing."

"Missing? What the hell does that mean!?" Bill blasted.

"There were seven casualties and those bodies haven't been identified yet. I'm sorry."

Sam and Bill felt like they'd been punched in the gut as Bill wandered away. "No no no."

"Where are Julie and Kim right now?" Sam asked. "Are they at the house?"

Laura nodded. Sam grabbed Bill and they started to leave.

"There's something else," Laura called out.

Sam turned back. "What the fuck could be worse than telling us our kids could be dead?"

Thomas spoke up. "Take it easy brother. I think what Laura was about to say was that Julie and Kim need you now more than ever."

"No shit. Where do you think we were going before you stopped us?" Sam turned around and kept walking, pushing Bill ahead of him.

"They saw the execution," Thomas shouted. "They saw Darius take one in the head and they watched as Hamid put that same gun to your head Sam."

Sam and Bill veered around the corner and were gone. Laura put her arms around Thomas and hugged him tight. He immediately did the same.

"I'm so happy you're both okay. What Em and I heard over the...well, it was downright upsetting."

"We're here. We're safe now."

"I know. I just can't stop thinking about how long that safety's really going to last, especially now."

Thomas pulled back and gently caressed the side of her face. "I know. But I'm going to do whatever it takes to keep our family protected."

"And I will too," Emily said.

"Me too," Gavin added.

Stir barked and wagged his tail.

Laura smiled. "Well don't think I'm going to be left out of all this. I'm in. Whatever it takes."

"I'll help," Hobbes announced from his desk he'd never left throughout the entire ordeal.

The Clark's turned towards him. "You're family too," Thomas told him, "whether you like it or not. Get over here."

Hobbes smiled, walked over and all five of them managed a huge group hug.

"Thanks," he said.

"No Hobbes, thank you for all your help. Now go home and get some sleep."

"That's exactly what I'm going to do. Well, at least I'll try to after what I saw come through that portal. But I'm sure I'll doze off as soon as my head hits the pillow. I feel like I've been up for days."

"Get out of here," Thomas told him.

"What about you guys?"

"We're going home as well," Laura said.

"Goodnight then."

"Oh, where do you want this GPS watch?"

"Just put it on my desk. Thanks." Hobbes left them alone as he headed out.

Thomas took off the watch and placed it on the desk. "It's really late. Ready to go?"

"I'm thirsty," Emily said.

Gavin nodded. "So am I."

"Alright. Let's hit the break room on the way out."

The four of them, with Stir by Gavin's side, shambled down the corridor, made their way around the circular corridor and entered the break room. Inside Laura opened up the refrigerator.

"What do you want? Juice. Chocolate milk?"

Before either one the kids could answer Stir began to growl again. Thomas and Laura looked over and saw that Stir had faced the adjoining room where the bunk beds were located.

"What's going on Stir?" Thomas asked knowing he wasn't going to get a response. "Something in there you don't like?"

Eliot appeared in the doorway and startled them. "Sorry. I didn't mean to alarm you."

Eliot walked forward, past Stir and towards the break room exit. Thomas and Laura stared at him the entire way. Stir didn't flinch as Eliot passed by and kept his low, guttural grown fixated towards the beds in the next room. Eliot stopped at the doorway.

"May I talk with you?" he asked.

"Ahh, sure, I guess," Thomas replied. He and Laura shared a shrug. "Give us a second, okay?"

"Sure. I'll wait for you by the Lab."

Thomas scrunched up his face.

How would he know about the Lab? He's never even been to this facility.

Laura retrieved two juice boxes, closed the refrigerator and handed them to Emily and Gavin.

"Something's not right," Thomas whispered as they left the break room.

"I caught the Lab remark as well," Laura softly replied. "What do you want to do?"

"Let's see what he has to say at least. There's nothing he can do to hurt us if he tries something."

With the kids enjoying their refreshing drinks the family walked down the corridor to the Lab. As they did they saw Eliot leaning against the hallway wall. Stir uncharacteristically ran towards Eliot, but what stopped the family in their tracks was when Eliot bent down and began to pet Stir, a smile of happiness on his face. Stir then rolled over and let him rub and scratch his belly.

"I can tell from the looks on your faces that you have a few questions," Eliot told them.

"You might say that," Thomas hesitantly replied.

"It's okay. I wanted to talk to you in private because there's something you need to be aware of."

"And what's that?'

"That I'm not who you think I am. I'm not Eliot Marlow. I have his memories but they're not who I am."

"Then who or what are you?" Laura demanded.

"I don't think you'll believe me even when I tell you."

"Cut the shit," Thomas told him. "If you try to hurt my family I'll…"

"I know Thomas," Eliot said. "You'd kill me. But I've been dead before." Eliot took his time and traced the right side of his face. "It's not there and that's going to take some getting used to."

"What's not where? What are you talking about?"

Eliot stood up as Stir wound around his legs, happy as could be. "My scar. My scar's not there. This body…it isn't mine. I don't know how this happened but I do know I'm not the only person it happened to."

Gavin stepped forward and Eliot bent down to the boy's level. "Hey little man. How's Stickers doing?"

"Becca?"

Thomas and Laura flinched.

"Impossible," Thomas stated. "You can't be her."

"It's me Gav. I know I don't look like myself bit I swear it's me. It's Rebecca. Even Stir knows me."

"Bullshit. He's not lying," Laura said.

"Prove it," Thomas ordered. "Prove that you're Rebecca."

"Okay. I first looked out for you and your family in Hawaii. After the attack, once I got out of the hospital, I learned that Laura, Julie and Kim had fled the island. You and Emily, as I found out later, had been taken hostage by Victor Bannon. The next time I saw you was at that elevator and you told me the place was on fire."

Thomas wasn't fully convinced. "So if you're really Rebecca then tell us how you died."

"Anna Garland pulled my life support before you arrived. I know Gavin would have used his ability to heal me, just as he did at the hospital in Hawaii. That's where I got my scar and that's why I kept it, as a constant reminder. You are my family and ever since I died I've been looking over your shoulder."

"He's….well, she's telling the truth," Laura said.

"Becca!" both Gavin and Emily cried out as they ran to the strange man's open arms.

"I've missed you both so much."

"Fucking hell," Thomas breathed out. "I didn't think this day could get any more bizarre."

Laura and Thomas both walked over and hugged Rebecca warmly.

"You know this is completely weird, right?"

399

"You're telling me," Rebecca replied. "Before you walked in the break room I went to the bathroom and discovered a penis where there's never been one. Trust me, that was quite a shock."

Laura and Rebecca laughed. "I'll bet. But look at you. How do you think this happened?"

"This was their plan all along."

"What do you mean?" Thomas asked.

The six that attacked you on the beach. I overheard their plan to take over your bodies. They thought, and apparently thought correctly, that Gavin's portal would bypass the restrictions placed on them."

"Restrictions?"

"Right, this is all new to you. I'll try to summarize. The Caretaker…"

"The Caretaker?"

"One thing at a time. Anyway, when I died or passed on, the Caretaker visited me. He or It is the one that controls what is called the Other Place. This Caretaker placed Membranes…"

"Membranes?"

Rebecca nodded. "Yes, Membranes, around the six. Now, it's my understanding that Membranes prevent an individual from returning to Earth in a corporeal form, and from moving on."

"Like my parents did."

"Yes and no. When they broke the rules the Caretaker placed Membranes around them. That's why Emily hasn't been able to summon them for the past four years."

"But, if that's true, why then? They've visited before without repercussions."

"Well, rumor has it that Emily and Gavin's powers have significantly upset the balance of the afterlife. Once your parents intervened, and helped you escape the underground lab, the

400

Caretaker was left with little choice but to punish them. They can no longer leave the Other Place and are stuck there for eternity."

"And they knew this before they helped me?"

Rebecca nodded again. "Absolutely."

Thomas was suddenly overcome with emotion. "They sacrificed everything so Emily and I could escape."

Laura put her arms around him.

"And they'd do it again," Rebecca continued, "if they could. And that leads me to the beach. I met your parents at my funeral."

"They were there?" Laura asked.

"Yes. We became good friends right away and they've been looking out for you longer than I have, so they knew all about me. Long story short, they listened to me after I overheard what the six were planning."

Thomas wiped his nose. "When they attacked us Victor said he was going to take my life, but I get it now. He meant that figuratively, not literally."

"Exactly. Gavin's portal was the only way they could resurrect themselves. Their only issue was that you would attract the other dark forces. Those forces, combined with our counterattack, prevented their strategy from actually succeeding. Well, for the most part, which leads me to something you need to be aware of."

Thomas' eyes opened wide. "That's right. If you got through then one of them could have as well. Have Sam or Bill been affected?"

Rebecca shook her head. "No, Laura would have picked up on that right away, and they weren't traumatized like Carl and Eliot were. Although that's weird calling myself Eliot, now that his body is, well, me."

"It's a lot to take it," Laura said. "And you're right, I didn't get any weird vibes off of Sam or Bill. That just leaves…"

"Carl," Thomas stated. "I need to go back to the break room right now."

"You're not going alone," Laura told him. "We all stay together, we're stronger that way."

The five of them, with Stir alongside, ran back to the break room and flipped on the light. The beds were empty and Carl was gone.

* * *

Carl Abney pulled the stolen car out of the underground garage and waited as it lifted to the surface. The two guards he had killed, as he escaped the facility, were minor obstacles and he thought of them no more. The barn doors opened and Carl gunned the engine. The car shot out of the barn, down the long driveway and disappeared into the night.

I haven't felt this good in decades. Strong. Vibrate. Young.

Carl looked in the mirror and it took a few moments for him to realize that the face that stared back at him wasn't his own.

I'll get used to it.

Carl gunned the engine and drove as fast as he could.

It's a whole new world for me now. I've got to hand it to Raven; he really knew what he was talking about. But I think I'm the only one that made it through. Eliot wasn't one of us, which means he's something or someone else. I'm alone but that doesn't matter. I went along with the plan only to have a chance at revenge, and there's no better time to start that than right now.

Carl pulled off the highway and found a 7-11. He parked in back and took a quarter out of the console tray. He got out, walked up to a payphone, deposited the money and dialed one of the numbers he'd committed to memory decades before. The phone rang four times before it was picked up.

"It's the middle of the night," an elderly man said. "Who is this?"

"I hear that you enjoy American vodka more than the brand you grew up with in Russia."

A long pause. "Who is this?"

"Come now comrade. I doubt I can convince you of my identity over this public phone. What I will tell you is that I expect your full cooperation from one of the first agents I placed in this country."

"You are Khrebtov Damir Olegovich, or at least you were known by that name before I inserted you into the United States as a sleeper agent a long, long time ago."

"Impossible. It…it can't be you. You're dead."

"I used to be, but that's something that I've recently rectified. It's me Khrebtov, it's Nikolay Dmitriev and I'm back from the dead."

55

Saturday Nov 3, 2001

The faintest tendrils of dawn attempted to creep over the horizon as Sam and Bill parked outside their house. Their minds were on overdrive and they hadn't said a word since they'd left the facility. They let themselves inside, headed upstairs and parted ways as they headed to their own bedrooms.

* * *

"Sweetie," Bill said as he softly stroked Kim's back. "It's me. Wake up."

Kim rolled over towards him and opened her eyes.

"Hey."

She instantly sat up, pulled him close and began to cry uncontrollably on his shoulder.

"The...the kids."

"I know," he said as he held her tight. "I'm here now and I'm not leaving you ever again."

* * *

Julie opened her eyes and nearly screamed at the bloodied man who stood before her, but then stopped herself when she realized it was Sam.

"Are you alright?" he asked as he walked to the side of their bed and knelt down.

"You're really here, aren't you? This isn't a dream?"

He touched her arm and that's all it took. She shrugged off the blankets, embraced him for dear life and let her emotions run raw.

Eventually the torrent subsided enough to where she could speak again.

"How…I mean…you were…"

"It was Thomas. Thomas came for us."

Julie was briefly relieved before she was overcome again. "I just don't know what to do anymore. It's too much Sam…it's all too much."

"Whatever happens, we're going to get through this."

"You don't know that," she sobbed. "You're always doing what you think is right and I have to deal with the leftovers. It's not fair to me and it's not acceptable for our family."

Sam rocked her back and forth while her frustrations and fears bubbled to the surface.

"We'll figure it out," he said softly in her ear.

"I feel alone Sam. I feel so alone."

"I'm here. I'm here right now."

"But for how long?" She pulled back from him. "You made me a promise a long time ago and you keep breaking it."

"I'm doing what I have to do for our family."

She shook her head. "No. No, you like what you do and you always have. But I just can't do it anymore Sam. I'm tired of the arguments and I'm tired of not knowing if you'll ever come home to me and the kids…"

Julie's eyes widened as memories of the school fire filled her head.

"Tell me what happened?" Sam pleaded. "What happened to Amanda and Craig?"

"I…I don't know. They're missing; maybe…maybe dead…" Her eyes filled and spilled down her cheeks as she looked at her husband in pure desperation. "I want them back. I want our children back."

He pulled her back close and didn't let go.

* * *

Before dawn, just after Robert Duncan had gotten home, he'd received a phone call from Thomas Clark but had missed it because he'd been in the shower. Refreshed but tired, the DCI fell into bed next to his wife Emma and hadn't woken up until eleven. Around noon the DCI left his house and noticed that Thomas had called a few more times. He immediately dialed Thomas and after a few rings it was picked up.

"Yes?"

"Thomas. It's Robert. Apparently I missed your calls last ni…"

He cut the Director off with some urgency in his voice. "Sir, where are you right now?"

"On my way back to the facility. Why, what's goi…"

"There's been another breech. The facility has been compromised. Two guards are dead. My family and I aren't going back there."

The DCI immediately became concerned. "What the hell are you talking about?"

"I don't think I should say anything over the phone."

Shit. "At least tell me something."

"Carl and Eliot aren't who they used to be."

"What? What does that mean?"

"I can't over the phone," Thomas pressed.

"Fine. Where can I meet you, at your house?"

"Yes."

"Good, I'm on my w…"

407

A car shot through the intersection and plowed into the right rear side of the DCI's vehicle, sending it into a spin. The phone leapt out of his hand and the DCI's head snapped to the right on impact. On the other end of the line all Thomas heard was a terrible crunching and the sound of twisted metal.

"Sir?"

The DCI's car came to a halt and an unmarked van pulled up alongside the driver's side a few seconds later. Blood was awash on the inside of the driver side window, which had cracked when his head smacked against it, knocking him unconscious. Three men exited the van, pulled open the driver's door and methodically transferred the DCI to the van. It then pulled away from the scene before any onlookers could react.

"Sir?"

* * *

Thomas, Laura, Rebecca, Sam, Julie, Bill and Kim had all gathered and sat around the kitchen table. They were in the middle of discussing the events that had recently affected each of them, including the school fire, the rescue and the undeniable fact that Rebecca was now in a man's body when Thomas' phone rang. He got up, walked away and answered it. Laura noticed a confused look appear on her husband's face as he walked back over to all of them.

"What happened?" Laura asked as he thumbed the end button.

"I don't know, but it sounded like the DCI was involved in some sort of accident. He was on his way here."

"So he knows about me?" Rebecca asked.

Thomas shook his head. "I didn't want to say a damn thing over the phone."

"Probably better that you didn't," Laura stated, "especially since we don't know who we can trust now."

Thomas sat back down. "Listen everyone. I know we're all in this predicament because of me."

"That's not true," Sam said.

"Come on bro," Bill added, "what are you talking about?"

Thomas held up his hand before anyone else could voice their opinion. "This road we've been on began with me back in third grade. It started with Nigel and continued with his brother Albert years later. From the moment Laura and I realized the Emily and Gavin were special our lives, collectively, have been significantly altered and that's the truth whether you want to acknowledge it or not."

The table remained quiet.

"What are you trying to say?" Laura prodded.

Thomas looked around at all of them, aside from Hobbes and his children that were still asleep. "All of you are my family, and I want to keep you safe, but we're facing some deep shit now. By thinking I could make things better by getting into bed with the CIA. Whether it was the right decision or not weighs heavily on my heart. I vow to make this right and do whatever it takes to make it right with each of you."

The house phone rang and Sam got up to answer it.

"Hello? Yes, this is he." Relief washed over Sam's face. "Are you sure? Okay, so where are they then? I understand you don't know but they're my kids and I want them found!"

All eyes at the table focused on Sam.

"Yes sir, I'll leave you to your job. I appreciate your call."

Sam slowly hung up the phone as Julie stood up, tears in her eyes.

"Tell me," she pleaded.

Bill and Kim's lives hung on Sam's next words.

"They're not dead."

Julie rushed to his side and held each other. Bill put his arms around Kim as well.

"What else was said?" Laura asked.

Sam continued. "All of the bodies from the school have been identified, but of the five children that are unaccounted for, four of them are ours."

"What do you mean they're missing?" Kim pressed, her anxiety rising. "What does that mean?"

Sam shook his head. "It means they're missing."

"Well, where are they then? I mean, if they had run off into the woods why haven't they come back?"

Laura got up and moved over to Kim to console her as Julie shook in Sam's arms, emotionally distraught.

"I don't understand. WHERE ARE MY CHILDREN!?" Kim screamed.

* * *

Robert Duncan came to and winced.

Ouch, my head.

He tried to touch his head but realized his hands were restrained.

Why can't I move?

He blinked a few times, clearing the haze from his eyes and focused on the man who stood in front of the chair he was secured to. Confusion swept through him.

"Carl?" the DCI managed to say. "What the hell's going on?" He looked down and tried to move his arms and legs again to no avail. "Why do you have me strapped down?"

Carl smiled.

"Release me right now," Robert demanded.

"I don't think so," Carl replied. "I went to great lengths to setup your abduction within a matter of hours, so why would I just let you go?"

Robert continued to struggle. "What's this all about?"

"You might as well save your energy, Director; you're going to need it. Besides, we have much to discuss."

"Like what? Have you forgotten that you're a member of the Special Activities Division? You answer to me!"

Carl chuckled, walked over and put his face right in front of the DCI's. "Not anymore." He stood up and made his way behind Robert. "I have an array of instruments back here I wish you could see, but no matter."

"What do you want!?"

"Information of course."

"Go to hell Carl," the Director spat out. "You're fucking with the wrong person."

"It's funny. You keep calling me Carl, but Carl isn't here."

Robert suddenly remembered what Thomas had told him. *Carl and Eliot aren't who they used to be.*

"I think you know me by another name."

Carl came around, stared the DCI in the face and sneered.

"I'm Nikolay Dmitriev, and trust me when I say we have all the time in the world to get acquainted."

56
Saturday Nov 3, 2001

Dr. Matsushita wandered out of laboratory, a needle in his left hand and a broad smile on his face. He made his way to the door, the same door that led to his holding room he kept the homeless people he'd abducted. He paused, taking in the moment and entered the room.

"And how are my guinea pigs today?" he asked.

There was no reply, nor could there be. In each of the five beds lay a child; three boys and two girls, of varying ages. They were strapped down with IV needles stuck in the backs of their hands. The drugs in each of their systems kept them extremely docile.

"So who wants to be the first to test out my new medicine?"

Again, no reply.

"Aww, come on now, no one?"

Dr. Matsushita genuinely appeared disappointed.

"Alright then, you leave me no choice." He began to count each child with his right hand. "Eeny, meeny, miny, moe. Catch a tiger by the toe. If he hollers, let him go. Eeny, meeny, miny, moe."

He plunged the needle into the boy's arm, depressed the syringe and extracted it when it was empty. He was very pleased with himself.

"I'm sure your parents are very worried about you, but I assure you they shouldn't be. Any why's that you ask? Because you're my children now and I'm going to take good care of you. All of you are part of this planet's future and together we will cleanse this world. Now, which one of you wants the next injection?"

413

Dr. Matsushita smiled as he looked at the frightened eyes of the five children he'd taken. Setting the bombs as a diversion had been child's play, just as commanding these five students to get in his van had been as well.

"Okay then. I guess I'll choose one of you when I get back."

Dr. Matsushita left Tad, Amanda, Craig, Sarah and Edward alone as he headed back to his lab. His plan was progressing nicely and he couldn't keep the grin off his face.

Oh Thomas, thank you for your vials of blood. They were fresh and exactly what I needed.

He paused.

Strange, but when I think about it I have to admit that you deserve credit for what the world is about to experience. I mean, you definitely deserve some of the credit, even though I'm doing all the work.

His grin turned evil.

Yes Thomas, a new future is coming, and its tidal wave of change will extinguish all who stand in the way.

Visit my website at

http://www.dwneuman.com

If you enjoyed this novel please consider taking a moment and writing a quick review about it (on Amazon). It helps me out more than you know and fuels my motivation! Of course, word of mouth works wonders too! ;)

Thank you!

And you can look forward to book nine, **Shadows of the Children**, sometime in the future.

www.ingramcontent.com/pod-product-compliance
Lightning Source LLC
Chambersburg PA
CBHW072337020726
47506CB00004B/906